LUTON LIBRARIES

BOOKS SHOULD BE RETURNED BY THE LAST DATE STAMPED

ALSO AVAILABLE FROM WESTON OCHSE AND TITAN BOOKS

SEAL Team 666

WESTON OCHSE

SEAL TEAM 666

AGE OF BLOOD

TITAN BOOKS

SEAL TEAM 666: AGE OF BLOOD
Print edition ISBN: 9781781168400
E-book edition ISBN: 9781781168417

Published by Titan Books
A division of Titan Publishing Group Ltd
144 Southwark Street, London SE1 0UP

First edition: October 2013
1 3 5 7 9 10 8 6 4 2

This is a work of fiction. Names, characters, places, and incidents either are the product of the author's imagination or are used fictitiously, and any resemblance to actual persons, living or dead, business establishments, events, or locales is entirely coincidental. The publisher does not have any control over and does not assume any responsibility for author or third-party websites or their content.

This edition published by arrangement with Thomas Dunne Books, an imprint of St. Martin's Press.

"The Bram Stoker Award" is a registered trademark of the Horror Writers Association.

A CIP catalogue record for this title is available from the British Library.

Printed and bound by CPI Group (UK) Ltd, Croydon, CR 4YY

DID YOU ENJOY THIS BOOK?
We love to hear from our readers. Please email us at:
readerfeedback@titanemail.com or write to us at Reader Feedback at the
above address.

To receive advance information, news, competitions, and exclusive offers online, please sign up for the Titan newsletter on our website.

www.titanbooks.com

**FOR MY FATHER,
ROGER OCHSE**

PROLOGUE

CABO SAN LUCAS, MEXICO. AFTER MIDNIGHT.

Emily Withers had been partying a little too hard the last few days. In fact, she could honestly say she'd drunk more tequila than water, which was why she was determined to stay sober for at least the next few hours. Four days in Cabo San Lucas, living the *vida loca* like the end of the world was around the corner, wasn't enough for her to forget that she was the daughter of a serving United States senator; there were people who were just dying to get a picture of her they could use to embarrass her father.

It had happened only once before, during her freshman year in college. Her sorority sisters had dropped her and the other pledges on the other side of campus, with the command to run back to the sorority house. Running fast wasn't a problem. That she and the other pledges had been naked was. As it turned out, there'd been only a blurred image of her naked backside as she rounded the corner of the math and science building. But the papers ran the picture alongside one of her father's speeches on funding public education. The late-night talk show hosts had a field day. Her father was less than impressed and spoke to her at length about the need to pay attention and how she wasn't like other girls. She could have ignored it, but she loved and respected her father. She was serious when she told him it would never happen again.

Which was why for at least the next twelve hours she was going to behave like a nun assigned to the Vatican. No booze. No sex. No cavorting. Just clean living.

She'd been sitting on the balcony all night, staring at the deep blue water of the Sea of Cortez. Everyone else was passed out. She'd stopped drinking around ten and instead had spent the evening listening to those around her, watching the lights of the passing ships, and feeling oddly self-aware.

Now, with the vacation resort asleep behind her, she approached the water. She'd left her shoes and shorts in a pile, along with her cell phone and room key, and wore only the two-piece bikini she'd bought especially for this trip. She dipped a toe in the gently lapping water. It was warmer than she'd expected. She'd thought it might be bracing, but protected from the Pacific by the Baja Peninsula and fueled by the Mexican sun, the water was bathtub warm.

She decided to go for a swim and clear her head. She backed up a few feet, then ran into the water, hopping over and through the waves until she was deep enough that she couldn't feel the bottom. Then she began to swim, her lurching stroke anything but graceful. She carved through the water for a full minute, then stopped, out of breath. She turned as she bobbed up and down in the sea and stared at the many pinpoints of brightness that were Cabo San Lucas. The glittering lights of the Pueblo Bonito Resort and Club Cascadas de Baja across the water became storybook in her tired vision. They looked nothing like the bacchanal palaces they really were. From here they could have made up a princess's castle. They could have been *her* castle.

She bobbed gently for a moment.

Who was she kidding? She was too old to be a princess. Hell, she was too old to be trying to relive spring break. She was twenty-seven, had an MBA from Vanderbilt, and was acting like a girl straight off the farm. Somewhere between her fifth shot of the night and the game of beer pong, she'd looked up and realized that she wasn't having any fun.

A wave beneath her made her rise gently, then fall back.

She was suddenly aware how far out she was. Were there sharks in the Sea of Cortez? After seeing *Jaws*, she used to think there were sharks everywhere.

Another wave. This time she rose higher.

She began to paddle madly back to shore. She felt the adrenaline rush as fear shot through her muscles. She could see the white line of surf where it met the beach, and farther up, her pile of clothes.

Something touched her foot.

She shrieked and sucked water into her lungs. She couldn't continue. She hacked and coughed.

Something touched her other foot and caught it, jerking her down. She disappeared below the water for a second, then popped back up, gasping.

She reared her head back to scream, but was suddenly jerked beneath the water again. She felt a tremendous pressure against her legs. She began moving forward at high speed, her mouth open as she swallowed the entire ocean. For one brief moment she was lifted out of the water, the lights of the resort like a beacon of hope. She glanced down to see the scales of a creature reflecting those lights. Then she was down, into the water, deeper, deeper, until she couldn't see anything, couldn't feel anything at all.

1

NEW ORLEANS CEMETERY. NIGHT.

THAT'LL LEAVE A MARK was spray-painted in garish Day-Glo pink across the front of a seventeenth-century headstone. The out-of-the-way and run-down cemetery was the perfect setting for a horror movie. The ambience was complete with Spanish-moss-hung ancient trees, low ground fog, above-ground crypts crouching like intruders, anomalous statues that could be shrines to the elder gods, and the total absence of sound, except for a tinkling of zydeco on the extreme edge of hearing. And the characters, the complement of characters, inclusive of the astonishingly believable voodoo queen, were as terrifying as they were fantastic. So Petty Officer First Class Jack Walker was pretty pleased with himself that he made this observation while perched high in a tree far away from the action and armed with a sniper rifle.

Only this wasn't a movie. Through his scope, Walker watched as Voodoo Queen Madame Laboy stood imperiously on the raised sarcophagus behind a wall of bulletproof glass, her arms outstretched as if she were the puppeteer for the vast array of undead which were pulling themselves upright from where they lay on the ground. More than a dozen naked zombies clawed their way to their feet, their jerky movements as they tried to operate their dead limbs increasing the creep factor tenfold. Some of them still had Y-incisions from medical-school students' inexpert autopsies. Others were fresher, their mortal wounds still weeping fluid, their expressions full of surprise as if they'd just figured out they were no longer alive.

Walker swung the long barrel of the Stoner SR-25 sniper rifle back and forth as he continued observing the scene through the Leupold Mark 4 scope. The other four members of SEAL Team 666 huddled in the middle of the cemetery. Holmes, Laws, YaYa, and the new guy, Yank, stood roughly back-to-back. They wore body armor, including Kevlar forearm pads, Kevlar gloves, and Kevlar shin guards. They each held a slender two-foot metal baton in one hand and a Marine Ka-Bar in the other. Their heads were completely covered with metal helmets, depriving them of sight, sound, and smell. If they were to survive, it would be by touch alone.

The zombies were pretty much as Walker expected—shamblers. Like sailors after a forty-eight-hour drinking jag in Balibago, Philippines. Several bumped into crypts and were redirected.

Walker's gaze was drawn back to Madame Laboy as she started to sing something in low, guttural French. A mishmash of red and purple satin covered her matronly figure. Her graying hair was piled high and infused with copper coils. Enough of her beauty remained that she could still command a room's attention, not to mention a pantheon of the undead in a Southern gothic cemetery.

At the sound of her song, the zombies snapped their bodies straight and cocked their heads as if they were listening—which after this reaction, Walker had no doubt they were. Within moments of hearing her, they were all staring with dead eyes at the four SEALs. Then, as one, the zombies moved toward them.

Walker wished he could put a round through the Voodoo Queen's head. It wouldn't even be hard. Everything seemed a little easier after he took out the Somali pirates on heavy seas last year at over three thousand meters. Except that the rounds in his rifle stood no chance against the specially designed glass. Still, he could figure out a way to put his rifle to good use. He sighted in, took a moment, and fired. Dust exploded from the ground between Holmes's feet. The SEAL straightened, tapped the man next to him, who did the same to the next, until they were all alerted to the approaching zombies.

Dragging and tripping, the undead moved faster than expected. With their arms out, fingers curled, teeth gnashing, the first wave attacked.

At first touch, each SEAL used his baton to isolate an arm and spin his attacker. Then the knife blade slid along the back until it found the neck. A hard saw with the serrated edge and the head fell free to hang by gristle and skin as the zombie dropped, lifeless once more.

A male voice spoke through Walker's Multiband Intra/Inter Team Radio (MBITR) headset. "Increasing volume to five decibels. SEALs, move apart."

The four SEALs did as commanded. Each one set one foot forward like a fencer, their helmeted faces pointing toward the ground, as they concentrated on what little hearing they were allowed as their only sense.

Holmes encountered a raised crypt and quickly pulled himself atop it. Yank, YaYa, and Laws remained on the ground. They moved their batons and knives in a slow dance, waiting.

They didn't have long. Thirty more zombies rose from places along the ground where they'd been placed earlier. The problem with cemeteries in New Orleans is that the water table is too high to bury someone in the ground. Instead, people must be buried in above-ground crypts, which can run from the utilitarian to the elaborate. Since the SEALs didn't want to raise the dead of unknown families, the crypts themselves were kept shut. Instead, Naval Special Warfare Command had requisitioned a number of cadavers, which had been strategically placed along the ground by a cohort of confused Navy seamen, who knew better than to question the details of their classified mission to relocate the recent dead.

Holmes spun as he felt a zombie brush his lower leg. Walker watched through his scope when she turned to face Holmes. She'd been a beautiful girl before something had smashed in the side of her face. She grabbed the SEAL's leg and tried to pull him to her, but she lacked the strength, instead creating a stationary target for Holmes's weapons. He slammed the tip of the knife into the center of her skull. Her body ceased all function. He pulled the knife free as she fell.

But Holmes had no time to waste. Two more zombies moved toward him. An African American zombie who was tall and muscled enough to have played professional basketball grabbed one of Holmes's arms. An overweight, balding white guy grabbed one of Holmes's legs. Holmes kicked out to rid himself of the zombie on his leg, but as he did, he was jerked off balance by the taller one.

Walker quickly scanned the other three SEALs and saw that while each was engaged, they were holding their own, except for possibly Yank, who had lowered his head and was ramming himself into a clot of three zombies. Still, they were on their feet and fighting, not at all like the SEAL team leader, who was now on the ground and straddled by a freakishly tall zombie. Even while Holmes fought desperately to rid himself of the creature on his chest, the overweight zombie was trying to chew on his leg. Try as the zombie might, he couldn't bite through the Kevlar, nor could he find a way around it with the booted foot of Holmes's other leg continually slamming into his face.

Walker prepared to fire. The objective of the training was to help better prepare the SEALs for situations where they had limited use of their senses. No one was supposed to die. In fact, it was Walker's job to make sure that no one did. Still, he hesitated, watching through the scope as Holmes fought for his life. Walker could afford his boss a few more seconds. After all, nothing was faster than a sniper round.

The zombie kept trying to grab the side of Holmes's head as if it were a basketball. The fact that Holmes had a metal helmet on didn't seem to deter the zombie, and Holmes himself kept acting as if the helmet weren't there. Why not let the zombie try and bite through the composite metal?

It was as if Holmes realized this at the same time Walker thought it. Holmes relaxed and the zombie immediately grabbed his head. He brought it to his face to get a better hold and snapped his jaw shut, breaking several teeth on the metal.

Not being able to see, Holmes had no idea this had occurred, but in one smooth move he slammed the knife into the side of the zombie's head. He continued pushing until the creature tumbled off him. Without hesitation, Holmes scissored his legs and wrapped them around the other zombie's head. Holmes rolled, causing the overweight zombie to tumble headfirst after him until Holmes straddled the zombie. The SEAL team leader no longer had a knife but he still held the baton. He placed one end of it on the bottom of the zombie's jaw and shoved until it disappeared into the creature's brain.

Walker couldn't help but shake his head and smile. "Not bad, Chief. Not bad at all."

Holmes dispatched three more, using the baton in the same manner.

Yank got to his feet from where he looked like he'd been rolling in a pile of dead zombies. Walker made a note to talk to the new SEAL. No matter how much Kevlar he wore, his zeal for battle wouldn't stop a zombie from possibly finding a chink in his armor. Even after this, the metaphor should be lived.

YaYa and Laws each stood in the center of a pile of his own dead zombies. Other than Madame Laboy, the SEALs were the only ones left in the cemetery.

A series of beeps piped through his MBITR, followed by "Control to Triple Six. Training complete. You may remove your sensory-deprivation helmets."

The four SEALs below Walker did as they were told and their faces were revealed.

Lieutenant Commander Sam Holmes, blond-haired, square-jawed paradigm of a SEAL, life dedicated to the cause of freedom.

Senior Chief Petty Officer Tim Laws, blond-haired, lanky, a smile already creasing a long, thoughtful face that hid an intelligence unmatched by the others.

Chief Petty Officer Ali Jabouri, or YaYa, Arab American, dark-skinned, dark hair, built like a runner, trying to prove that he was as apple-pie American as everyone else.

Petty Officer Second Class Shonn Yankowski, African American, shaved head, tattoos, burns along the left side of his face from a house fire back home in Compton.

Just as the SEALs began to high-five and celebrate, each examining the zombies he'd killed without the ability to see, they were interrupted by a terrible scraping sound. All eyes went to one of the raised crypts, this one more elaborate and twice the size of most others.

The four-inch-thick metal cover was moving aside. An immense hand reached from underneath and grabbed the lip of the crypt's lid, a talon the size of a dinner knife jutting from each finger.

The hairs on the back of Walker's neck began to buzz. He'd felt something electric the entire time, but he'd written it off as the zombies or Madame Laboy. But now with the metal cover free, his skin began to tingle. Whatever this was, it was much more than they'd expected, setting off his supernatural warning system like no horde of zombies ever could.

Madame Laboy's voice rose. She screamed a series of words that weren't part of any language Walker had ever heard. Her hands punched at the air in a complex pattern. What she was doing was many levels of mastery beyond the raising of the dead.

Walker watched as the monstrous hand lost its grip on the crypt cover, and let it drop back in place, disappearing beneath it.

Madame Laboy ran around the bulletproof shield and sped toward the crypt. With the help of Yank, she climbed on top of the lid, where she began to spit, and curse, and cast more spells.

"What was that?" Holmes asked.

She ignored him for a moment, then said, "Something I'd

almost forgotten about. Something I'd misplaced."

"Pretty fucking big to misplace," Laws said, casting a worried eye at the crypt.

"You live as long as me and you'll forget a lot of things, *mon petit guerrier*." She stared at him, as if daring him to ask her age.

Laws snorted. He knew better than to upset a voodoo queen.

2

NAVAL SPECIAL WARFARE TRAINING CENTER, NEW ORLEANS.

Triple Six sprawled in the briefing room chairs as they watched the training event unfold over and over and over on the flatscreen television. At first everyone laughed, pointing to where Yank had stepped into the guts of a zombie and almost fallen, or where Laws had missed the same old woman over and over, only to accidentally skewer her when he tripped. But by the fifth time through, no one was laughing. Sure, they'd survived the event, but they all knew they wouldn't have if they hadn't been wearing so much Kevlar body armor to protect them. They could also feel their collective breath cease when the thing in the crypt tried to get out.

"Do we know what that was?" Walker asked.

Laws, who was on his second Big Gulp, paused in chewing on the straw long enough to answer, "Don't remember anything like that in the mission logs."

The logs went back to the Revolutionary War. Triple Six had existed in one form or another since its creation by the First Continental Congress. Their first existence was as the Light-Horsemen, a Continental Army special-mission unit under the command of Lieutenant Colonel Henry Lee, the grandfather of Robert E. Lee. A special unit of Lee's Legion, the Light-Horsemen worked behind the scenes to hasten Cornwallis's surrender, most notably at Pyle's Massacre, the first evidence of the British use of lycanthropes against the colony. Henry Lee's son would command the Red Dragoons during the Mexican-American War, their greatest service coming during the bloody assault at Molino del Rey.

Triple Six had also been known as the Roanoke Irregulars, Jefferson's Order of the Mount, Roosevelt's Special Brigade, and Wilson's Warders. The names changed, but the missions remained the same—a dedicated group of men and a dog assigned a mission no one else knew about to recover, kill, disable, or remove something so far beyond the norm that the average citizen should never know of its existence.

Walker was just beginning to read the mission logs, choosing missions at random, just to become familiar with some of the things the team had encountered before. Covering seventy-two volumes, the handwritten logs were lengthy accounts of the missions, sometimes grinding into excruciating detail about the men, the equipment, and the methods used to take down one supernatural foe or another. It was beyond interesting, and he'd have loved to make the reading of those who'd come before him a priority, but he had his fiancée, Jen, to consider, and he was eager to spend more time with her.

"I do remember Madame Laboy, though," Laws added, looking over at Holmes to see if the leader had anything to add. When he didn't, Laws continued, "She's mentioned several times. Hurricane Katrina and the Battle of New Orleans, for instance."

"The Battle of..." Yank gave Laws a look like he thought the other SEAL was joking. "Maybe it was a relative."

"Maybe so." Laws sipped his Big Gulp, with a slight smile on his face.

"But don't count on it," Walker added.

"You really need to read the logs," YaYa said, his voice barely above a whisper.

Walker noticed that he was still sick. YaYa had been enduring a seemingly unshakable flu. With his jacket zipped up and his hands shoved into his pockets he looked positively miserable.

"If I had more than eight seconds, I'd look at the damn logs," Yank said, still unused to the pace and closeness of Triple Six. At times he seemed to get visibly angry, reacting as if they weren't a close-knit bunch of brothers. "But that helmet shit fucking sucked. When are we ever going to be forced to wear those?"

"Easy, Yank," Laws said, trying to win the FNG over with a smile.

But Yank clearly had something to get off his chest. He leaned forward and came just short of pounding the table. "What sort of team is this to put us with a bunch of fucking zombies? I mean, when you said it, I thought you were kidding. Fuck." He gave the TV, which had been paused on the battle, an angry glare. "If I'd known, I might not have joined."

Everyone turned quietly toward Holmes. "Do you want out?" Holmes asked, his voice low but sharp as a razor.

"No, I just want—"

Holmes cut him off by sitting forward quickly, "I asked if you wanted out. I didn't ask you for your opinion or for your favorite color. A one-word answer will suffice."

Yank breathed through his nose and his nostrils flared. His fists remained on the table, but they seemed to strain to stay there.

Laws set his Big Gulp down and leaned forward. "I think you'd better answer the question," he said softly.

Walker didn't know what everyone else thought as they stared at Yank, but no matter how mad and how mean he looked, Yank seemed more scared than anything else. Walker recognized it because he'd felt it himself. His first day at the orphanage, his first day at BUD/S (basic underwater demolition/SEAL) training, his first day with Triple Six. Walker's life seemed to be filled with first days. Maybe that was the problem. Yank didn't have many first days. And this was his first day embracing the reality of the Triple Six mission.

Finally Yank shook his head. "No."

Holmes nodded and sat back. "Fine. Then stop telling us what you think and start telling us what you'll do. I brought you on because you're a weapons specialist and an expert on hand-to-hand." He pressed the remote and the action continued. "See there," he pointed. "Laws was using the same technique over and over. Although it worked, anything else but a zombie might have figured that out."

"Ouch. Damned with faint praise," Laws murmured.

"What we need," Holmes continued, "are some moves we can transition to when we're concentrating on not using any of our senses."

"Sounds like something out of *Kwai Chang Caine*," Walker said. He'd been folding a piece of paper into an airplane and was finishing the creasing of the wings.

Laws shook his head. "Nuh-uh. You mean *Kung Fu*."

Yank turned to observe the pair as they argued.

"Wasn't that the TV show?" Walker asked.

Laws nodded. "Caine was played by David Carradine. Took the place of Bruce Lee, who originally came up with the idea for the show."

Walker nodded, dropping the paper airplane on the table as he leaned back in his chair. He remembered catching episodes of the show dubbed in Filipino when he was at the orphanage. "Yeah. For sure Bruce Lee was badass, but Carradine was cool. Guess they wanted cool."

Laws laughed. "Actually, they wanted white."

YaYa snatched the airplane from the table, lit the tail of it with a match, and soared it across the room. "Actually," he said, mimicking Laws's tone, "that white man died in a backroom brothel in Bangkok with a noose around his neck and his Johnson in his hand." When the plane crashed into the wall, YaYa added, "Kaboom!"

Everyone stared at the burning airplane for a moment; then Yank went over and stomped it out. YaYa's face held a small smile as he watched the flames disappear, but nothing he had said had been particularly funny.

Holmes snapped everyone back to the topic at hand. "Okay, enough about David Carradine. Let's get back to it. So what do you think, Yank? Can you work something up?"

As Yank studied the film, his fists relaxed. "Sure. Probably something Filipino or Chinese. Either silat or wing chun. I can work up some flowing-hands movement that will allow us to counter anything we need to." He nodded as he thought it through. "Wing chun for sure."

"Good." Holmes turned to YaYa and was about to say something when the door opened and Alexis Billings, administrator for the Senate Select Committee on Intelligence's (the Sissy's) special projects division, of which Triple Six was a part, strode in. She wore a gray dress suit with black high heels. She was about thirty, slender, with red hair pulled back into a professional bun.

Walker recognized the look in her eyes. He'd seen it the day she'd jerked him out of SEAL training, marching right up to his drill instructors on the beach, handing over a letter from their commander, and marching away with him in her back pocket. There was a mission to be completed and she was delivering it.

Holmes started to stand and take her into another room, but she surprised everyone and waved him back into his seat. "No time. We have a problem." She handed a thumb drive to YaYa. "Plug this in."

While YaYa did as he was told, she addressed the team. "Emily Withers, daughter of Senator Christopher Withers, ranking member of the Senate Select Committee on Intelligence—my boss and the approval authority for the Top Secret funding line your unit has appreciated these last few years—has gone missing."

She let the words hang for a moment, then added, "Perhaps 'missing' is not the right word. Chief Jabouri, are we ready?"

He selected a file and the zombie training scene was replaced with the black and white image of a beach somewhere. The perspective was from above, but not directly.

"Emily Withers was in Cabo San Lucas on holiday. That's her…" She pointed at the screen and a young woman walked into the picture. The woman removed her shorts and made a pile of her things on the sand before running into the water. The room remained silent as they watched her swim to the upper edge of the frame. That the camera didn't move with her indicated that it was probably a static security camera. She floated on her back for a few moments, then apparently felt something beneath her. She turned and looked around; then it happened again and she began to swim. Then suddenly she went beneath the water. Everyone sat forward. Yank audibly gasped when she shot back to the surface like a bobber.

"What the hell was that?" Yank asked.

"Wait for it," Billings said, her arms crossed, a frown burying her face.

The girl began to swim again, but was dragged down. Then their voices erupted as she rose from the water in the mouth of a creature that went on and on and on, nearly fifty feet in length, coiling and uncoiling across the waves until both she and the creature disappeared into the water.

"And there you have it," Alexis said, flipping the back of her hand at the screen before turning and giving Holmes a hard look.

"Was that what I think it was?" Walker said.

"If you mean a sea monster, it sure the hell looked like it," Laws said.

"We're not sure what it is," Billings said. "All we know is that it took the senator's daughter."

"Then this is a body recovery," YaYa said.

"Not necessarily," Billings responded.

YaYa pointed at the screen, a look of disbelief on his face. "We all saw what happened. She was floating in the water, along came a sea monster, and she became a snack." Realizing his own words, he gulped and looked down. "I mean... she was taken."

Billings had kept her eyes on Holmes the entire time. "What do you think?"

Holmes sighed. "Although I tend to agree with YaYa, there's a window of possibility."

Yank looked from Holmes to YaYa with visible incredulity. "Really? Please tell us, because I don't see it. I'm with YaYa. I saw her taken. You saw her taken. Hell, we all saw her taken."

Holmes looked at Laws. "Do you want to explain it to them?"

Laws nodded. "Sure." He stood and walked to the screen. It had been rewound to where the creature was first revealed and zoomed in until it was almost completely pixellated. "What are the odds that in the whole wide universe, a single sea monster or whatever the fuck this is, just happened to be cruising the beaches of Cabo San Lucas, and just happened to find the daughter of one of the top five highest-ranking politicians in America?" He turned. "Walker, what do you think?"

"Pretty long odds, sir."

"Pretty long, indeed."

"And you, Laws?"

"What Walker said."

"Could just be coincidence," Yank surmised.

This answer engendered a broad smile from Laws. "Out of the mouths of babes. Coincidence, you say? That word is the reason Triple Six exists. We don't believe in it. When someone else says it, we know it's time to investigate."

"So you think someone could be behind this? Someone arranged to snatch her?" Walker asked.

"Either that," Laws's smile faded and was replaced by complete seriousness, "or it's mere coincidence."

"Doesn't matter what it is. We're on mission. Everyone get ready. We leave in an hour." Billings stepped forward. "One more thing. On an unrelated matter, a shipment from the Salton Sea warehouse was hijacked. We need to track the load."

"You got GPS on it, right? Radio-frequency IDs?" Holmes asked.

"We do, but this is pretty sensitive. Several crates of chupacabra bones. We don't want some local cop shop involved. We want to keep this in the family."

Holmes thought about it and nodded. "YaYa, I'm sending

you. Stop by Balboa after and get rid of whatever bug you have, then Charlie Mike and link up." He turned back to Billings. "Anything else?"

"No, except I don't have to reinforce how—"

"No, you don't. If she's alive, we'll track her down. If she's deceased, we'll find her body."

"Thanks, Commander."

"Don't thank me. It's what we do. Come on, SEALs. Get your asses in gear."

3

NSW TRAINING CENTER. LATER.

Everyone cleared the briefing room and headed to their bunks in the dorm. They'd been at the New Orleans NSW Training Center for nearly a week and had expected to stay a week longer, so no one was ready to go. Still, the nature of being in the military had taught the SEALs of Triple Six the ability to pack and move with little or no preparation. They had their go bags already packed and would most likely travel straight to the mission, which meant their personal items would be shipped back to their building on Coronado Island.

Yank hurried after Laws. "What did that mean? What you said back there."

"What did I mean with what?"

"When you damned the faint praise."

"Ah. That. 'Damn with faint praise, assent with civil leer, and without sneering teach the rest to sneer; willing to wound, and yet afraid to strike, just hint a fault, and hesitate dislike.'"

"Sounds like Shakespeare."

"More than a hundred years too late for that. Alexander Pope said it."

"It talks about fear."

"Not like you think." Laws cracked a quick smile. "It talks

26

about one's inability to criticize because of a fear of what someone else might think."

"Were you saying that about me?"

"Easy, Yank. If you're going to work in this team, you have to take it when we give it, and give it when we deserve it. Our trust and camaraderie are what makes us special. Our ability to turn that into the fuel to run an operation against supernatural forces is what makes us Triple Six."

"I hear you. It's just hard. I've been fighting my whole life and this isn't like any other team."

"The sooner you realize that we're not the enemy, the sooner you'll enjoy being a part of Triple Six."

"It's been a long time since I trusted people enough to do what you're saying."

"It better not be too much longer." Laws reached out and shook Yank's hand and held it. "Holmes is right. We don't need any dissent or discontent. You want to leave, then go. You want to stay, then change." He let go of the other man's hand. "Period."

Yank watched Laws go. He knew the deputy commander was right. Yank had to rein in his reactions. They might have kept him alive on the streets of Compton, but there it was every man for himself. His existence as part of the team meant that he had to offer and accept a certain amount of trust.

He went to his bunk and grabbed the kit bag labeled PETTY OFFICER SECOND CLASS SHONN YANKOWSKI. That name really said his entire story. He could have chosen the name of his father, who'd ended up doing life in Chino. Yank had never met the man, but knew he'd been a thug for the Twenty-second Street Hustlers and part of the Bloods. His last name had been Johnson, but Yank had refused to take the name of a man he'd never met. He could have kept the name of his mother, who after spending his first six years clean and sober, had broken down into the sorry caricature of an L.A. drunk. Named Rennie Sabathia, his mother had called him Shonny, which went well with her last name. And he'd owned that name, right up until the day she'd died in the fire and he'd earned the burns on the side of his face. At thirteen, he'd met Joseph Yankowski, recently transferred from Chicago to Los Angeles as part of the longshoremen's union. Uncle Joe, as Shonn learned to call him, ran a foster home in San Pedro, and Shonn soon found the first stable and safe place he'd ever known. Fostering turned to adoption and by the time Shonn turned eighteen and made his desire known that he wanted to join the U.S. Navy, he also changed his name to Yankowski, out of respect and love for Uncle Joe—not really an uncle, not even a relative, but more of a father than he'd ever imagined.

"You daydreaming?" Walker asked as he passed, carrying his own bag. "Come on, let's see the weapons sergeant and see if NSW has anything we can use."

Yank shook away the reverie and hurried after the team's sniper.

4

CORONADO ISLAND. MORNING.

Holmes stared at the table with the empty chairs. His SEALs were getting ready for mission. He should be too, but he couldn't help contemplating the empty chairs. Not only did they represent the current members of Triple Six, but those he'd lost as well. The deaths of Ruiz and Fratolilio were fresh in his mind. Ruiz had died at the hands of the demon Chi Long and Fratty had been almost beheaded by a chimera in the hold of a cargo ship in the port of Macau. Not only had they been incredible SEALs, but they'd been incredible men, too. Then, of course, there was Chong, the sniper whom Walker replaced. He'd spent a year with the team without so much as a scratch.

Then came the mission against Geronimo. They still didn't know who or what had killed Chong, but they'd taken the body, along with the body of HVT1, out of Pakistan. Leave no man behind. They'd brought Fratty back as well, but Ruiz hadn't been so lucky. That he'd evaporated in the explosions of a dozen MOABs (massive ordnance air blast bombs) made Holmes confident that the enemy didn't have him. Still, he wished he'd been able to return the SEAL's body to Coronado.

And there were the others: Ling, Evans, Close, Smith, Forsythe, Unger, and Jensen. Each had gone down in the service of a nation who knew nothing of their sacrifice. Classified Code Word, the missions of Triple Six would remain unknown to the public probably long after America ceased to be a nation. Only a few select members of Congress and those who passed through the revolving door of the White House ever knew what a team of five dedicated, unheralded men were doing for their country.

Which was as it should be.

"Everything okay, boss?" Laws asked, poking his head into the room.

Holmes gestured for Laws to join him. As the other sat, Holmes silently acknowledged how lucky he was to have someone like Tim. Not only was his eidetic memory of incalculable worth to the team, but he was a true polymath. Like Leon Battista Alberti, the fourteenth-century Renaissance man who was at once an architect, an artist, an historian, an astronomer, and an athlete capable of jumping over a man's head from a standing position, Laws had a sum of parts which seemed so much greater than his whole.

"What's shaking, Kevin Bacon?" Laws asked, slipping his feet onto the table and leaning back. He wore a smile that he should have trademarked.

"Remind me how long I've been doing this?"

Laws leaned forward. "Uh-oh. It's one of those conversations."

"Just remind me."

"Five years, three months, seventeen days, six hours, and about eleven minutes."

"How many missions?"

"Forty-seven."

"And how many SEALs have we lost?"

"Ten."

Holmes was silent for a good minute, digesting the figures. He knew they didn't really mean anything. Can one measure patriotism with math? Can numbers really represent the value of the well-being and peace of Americans? Still, he hoped for an algorithm, or maybe an equation that he could populate with these numbers to determine if it was all worth it.

"It won't add up, Sam," Laws said. "Stop trying to make it work out. We've done our best. And I wouldn't have anyone else lead the team but you."

Holmes waved away the compliment as he stared into the past. "I get that. No need to blow smoke up my ass. It just gets old sometimes." He glanced up at Laws. "This isn't the first time I've thought about moving on, you know."

Laws nodded thoughtfully. "This isn't the first time we've had this conversation. I'm not going to remind you what we told Yank today."

Holmes sighed and leaned back. "Another new guy. Another Type A personality I have to mold and forge."

"It's in your blood. You love it."

"Do I? I mean, do I really?"

Laws steepled his hands. "What would you do if you weren't doing this? Do you really think you could go back to the teams?"

Holmes looked pained, as if the decision were too much to even contemplate. What he was experiencing wasn't self-doubt, it was more the result of being in one place for too long. How many times was he willing to roll the same patriotic wheel through the mud just to get the same result?

"I do love it. With two failed marriages behind me, the only successful relationship I've ever had is with the SEALs. Billings told me that if I ever want to move on, I'd have a position on her staff."

"Would you take it? Would you work for her?"

"She's sharp and she's smart. I just might."

"So this is it? You've made a decision?" Laws's patented smile returned. "You're ready to go out to pasture?"

Now it was Holmes's turn to smile, only where Laws's grin always held the idea of a punchline, Holmes's held the promise of pain. "Maybe not just yet. Let's see about the senator's daughter first, then I'll make a decision."

Laws stood. "Just let me know. We'll need some time to pool enough money for a hearing aid and walker."

"Very funny."

Laws grinned from ear to ear. "I thought so." He pushed out of the chair and left.

Holmes remained sitting for a time. He wasn't ready to quit. Not just yet. Hell, maybe not ever. He just needed to hear the words out loud. Sometimes hearing what he was thinking helped put it all into context.

5

LOS ANGELES. DAY.

YaYa felt like shit. On top of that he was traveling like a tourist. They'd hurried him to the airport and he'd suffered through a TSA screening and the subsequent pat-down after the shrapnel near his spine sent the machine off. Then he'd missed his connection in Denver. He'd had to wait in the terminal while a group of about a hundred professional zombie walkers, still dressed in their costumes and made up from their gig in Kansas City, practiced their zombie walks, both terrifying and exciting the other bored tourists. All YaYa wanted to do was shoot them.

When he boarded his flight to L.A., he got bumped up to first class. He'd usually enjoyed the unasked-for treat. Free beer, free food, and premier attention by a hopefully foxy stewardess, but this time all he wanted to do was sleep.

When the plane finally took off, he found himself returned to the primordial forest in Myanmar, where he'd killed a supernatural creature known as a *qilin*. He'd been with Walker on the mission to rescue the other members of Triple Six, who'd come under the control of an ancient Chinese demon. They'd crashed a motorcycle and one of the chimera monsters had dragged him into the woods. He'd been able to kill it with one of its own spikes, but it still left him ass-deep and otherwise weaponless in the middle of nowhere.

He'd been wounded too. He still had scars from where it had grabbed him on his lower leg. He'd taken a week of comp time after the hospital had released him. His sister had asked what had caused the injury and had noted that it looked like something had bit him. He'd had to make up a story of a rabid Great Dane, because to tell the truth would have been to break the classification, regardless of whether anyone would believe him or not.

He'd also hurt his left arm. At first he'd thought it was only a bite, or maybe a cut. His other wounds had healed, but this one was proving to be stubborn. What had been a very small wound had festered and grown until it had spread over the whole of his forearm, a mosaic of greens and purples. If he brought it to his nose he could detect a distinctly unpleasant aroma. So he didn't do that. In fact, he tried to ignore it. He kept it wrapped and spent much of the time trying to forget about it.

There'd been something about the forest. It wasn't just that it was filled with exotic flora, it was something else. He'd thought about it every day since the mission. He'd replayed the event over and over until he wasn't sure if it was something he'd invented or if it was reality as it had existed. Bottom line was that there'd been something wrong with the place. In his memories, there'd been almost no sound at all, except for the sounds from the monster that he'd fought and killed. The insects, animals, and birds could have been silent because of the *qilin*. Certainly, if there was an alternative, he didn't know what it was.

But he did remember the feeling of being watched. At first it had been an anomalous idea of something tracking him. But when he'd stop and look, instead of it going away, it stayed with him. Then it evolved into a certain curiosity. He'd felt that it—whatever it was—wanted to understand him. Just as he might watch an insect pick a path from one tree to another along the forest floor, so did this thing watch him.

At one point the idea of twelve came to YaYa. It began with just the idea of the number. *Twelve. Twelve. Twelve.* But then it became more, once he exhibited a curiosity about the number. His unasked question was responded to in like manner as he had the idea of *twelve eyes*. *Twelve eyes* watching him. At the moment of that thought, he remembered vividly halting in the middle of a copse of giant Myanmar trees. He spun in the silent forest until he spied six birds sitting on a branch of a tree. The birds' bodies faced the same way, their heads were turned the same way, and they were all watching him from pairs of inscrutable black eyes. He moved away from the birds and felt the weight of their stares. He moved left, then right, and each time the birds moved their heads in unison, tracking him as if they were mere appendages to one larger will.

As he expressed his curiosity about *it*, he felt it in turn expressed an uncertainty to him. He wanted to know more about it. He wanted to understand what it was he felt, and how he was able to detect something he didn't see.

Then he'd lost time. He'd never know how much time had passed, but he knew it had. When he became aware again, his body ached. The light was different. The entire feel of the forest had changed. He heard insects, the scrabble of creatures in the canopy, and the calls of beleaguered monkeys from higher in the trees. The birds were still there, only now they weren't looking at him. They were no longer in identical positions. They now moved and pecked along the branch as any bird would do. This time when he moved, they took to the air in an explosion of flapping wings.

After his flight landed at LAX, YaYa left the terminal and found Special Agent Alice Surrey waiting for him at the curb. She had the same ability enjoyed by the actress Kathy Bates, to be able to look at once matronly and unassuming as well as professional. She wore black pants, black shoes, a white shirt under a dark blue jacket with the letters NCIS on the back.

"You look like shit," she said.

Instead of answering, he leaned his head against the window.

"I'm serious."

"About what."

"You look like shit. Are you sure you're up for this?"

He nodded. "Just have this cold I can't shake. It's nothing."

"Suit yourself. We've tracked the shipment to a warehouse in the City of Industry. Local PD has it under surveillance and is stopping anyone leaving the premises."

"Do we know how many are inside?"

"No idea. But there are less than a dozen cars in the parking lot, if that helps."

"Do you have an issue for me?"

"In the trunk. MP5, just as requested."

"And backup?"

"SIG 226. I also have a set of body armor."

"Nice. Eager to get this finished and get back with the team."

YaYa leaned his head against the window and watched the traffic. Beneath the sound of the wheels on the road, he heard a voice calling to him. He strained to understand it, but try as he might, he could barely discern it. All he knew was that he was meant to listen to this and it was only for him.

"What?" he asked, becoming aware that Alice had asked him a question.

"Are you okay? I was talking to you and you didn't respond."

How long had he been out? What the hell was going on? He pulled down the visor and flipped open the mirror. He had puffy bags under bloodshot eyes. His skin held a gray tinge. He did look like shit.

"What'd you say?" he finally asked, putting the visor back in its place.

"I asked how the mission with the tattoo suits went. Did everyone make it?"

He stared at her for a moment. He'd forgotten about her help at the Chinese restaurant. They'd had to clear the basement and the subbasement of Snakeheads—Chinese mafia—as well as a healthy number of homunculi. An OSI and an FBI agent had died during the attack.

"Yeah. We all made it," he said, lying because the loss of Ruiz wasn't any of her business. "Touch and go, but mission accomplished." His forearm began to pulse. He rubbed it.

"And the suits?"

"All but one. We don't know where that is, but I imagine it'll turn up sooner or later."

She laughed. "You know you're not the same as you were when I first met you."

"I was new to the team then," he said. Flashbacks of the last mission snapped across his mind, including the demon that had almost killed them all. "I've seen things."

"I can tell," she said.

They drove in silence for another thirty minutes, then turned off the highway. After navigating side streets for ten minutes, she pulled into the parking lot of a generic warehouse in a row of similar warehouses. YaYa didn't know what the City of Industry built, but if he was told warehouses, he'd certainly believe it.

Under the gawking eyes of the local PD he removed his hoodie, slid into the body armor, then slipped back into the hoodie. He used a shoulder holster for the SIG and cinched it tight to eliminate the folds in the material. He checked the pistol's slide, then the ammo. Satisfied, he grabbed two extra clips, and slid the pistol into the holster, all while being scrutinized by half a dozen officers who wanted desperately to know who this sickly Arab dressed like a bum was and why he was here. After inspecting the MP5 and running it through a series of dry fires, he nodded, grabbed five magazines, and declared himself ready.

He and Surrey moved to a side door.

"The PD will breach from the front and the back," she said. "We'll give them ten seconds, then enter."

YaYa didn't like the plan. "What's to keep us from crossing fire?"

"PD isn't going to enter farther than a few feet, enough to establish an inner perimeter. The only people in the middle of the room will be beegees. Did I say it right?"

She'd used Holmes's term for bad guys, *beegees*. "Yeah, you said it right."

"Should I give the go-ahead?"

"Everyone waiting for me?"

"Of course. What would a party be without a U.S. Navy SEAL?"

6

SOMEWHERE OVER THE GULF OF MEXICO. DUSK.

Walker sat with Yank in the middle of the C-140 Starlifter, remembering when he'd been the new guy, or FNG as they so fondly called it. He'd been the butt of all jokes until YaYa had arrived, a replacement for Fratolilio, who'd perished during the battle with the first Chinese chimera they'd discovered in the hold of a cargo ship in Macau. Now Yank was the FNG, although no one was really giving any good gibes to the SEAL.

Part of it was probably because he could kick any of their asses. An expert in the Hawaiian martial art of Kapu Luailua, he also held varying ranks in Krav Maga, Gracie jujitsu, savate, pencak silat, wing chun, Muay Thai, Kali, and Jeet Kune Do. The latter was taught by Ron Balicki in Los Angeles, who'd had a significant impact on Yank's journey to becoming a warrior. Not only had Balicki created his own MARS system, but by working with him, Yank had had the benefit of also working with his wife, Diana Lee Inosanto, and her father, Dan Inosanto, Filipino fighting master, escrimadora, and best friend to the late great Bruce Lee.

Yeah, the team was a little in fear of Yank. But Walker couldn't let that stick. Growing up in an orphanage, he knew what buttons to push. He knew the FNGs of the world had to prove themselves.

Yank had to earn his way a little bit more. He had some FNG work to do.

They were breaking down four HK416s that were still in the packing grease from the factory. The first thing Yank had done when assuming the job as the Triple Six weapons sergeant was to get rid of the MP5s. "Too much like a bunch of Crips driving by a bus stop, or Colombians crashing into a hotel room. This isn't some South American drug deal, this is a military mission." Although it was Holmes who'd kept the tradition of using MP5s, he hadn't said a word and had let Yank have latitude to modernize their equipment. "These barrels weren't meant to sustain the rate of fire we do," Yank had said, referring to the MP5s. "The manufacturing processes used on these are twenty years old. That they haven't jammed is a miracle. We're switching before they have a chance to, boss."

And with that, every member of Triple Six had been forced to learn the HK416. Not that it was an issue. Everyone, with the exception of Walker, had worked with the weapon in the past. Similar to the M4, it was an easy transition. Walker hadn't, because he hadn't ever worked as a SEAL outside Triple Six. In fact, he hadn't finished training until recently. Probably the only SEAL ever to be awarded a BUD/S device and go on mission before he'd actually graduated. Adjusting to the 416 wasn't such an issue, however. Their models had OTB (over the beach) capability, meaning they could fire coming straight from the water. YaYa, who carried a Super 90, was going to be allowed to continue carrying the shotgun. Yank wanted the team to have the extra firepower if needed. But YaYa's knowledge and ability with the 416 still had to be the same as the others. Just like Walker, whose primary weapon was the SR-25 sniper rifle.

Produced by a collaboration with United States Delta Force and the German arms maker Heckler & Koch, the 416 used a proprietary gas piston system allowing for reduced time between firing and less cleaning by the operator. With the 10.4-inch barrel, it was as agile as the MP5, but had a greater round throughput and a higher cyclic rate of fire. The rifle used standard NATO 5.56mm ammunition, which had greater stopping power than a 9mm. The rifles were augmented with Tango Down front grips, Gen II 30-round magazines contoured to reduce the wobble, holographic diffraction sight, and an AN/PEQ-2 laser indicator with visible-spectrum, infrared, and IR-spectrum illuminator.

Walker and Yank set about getting the weapons ready for action. Yank was deep in concentration, wiping each piece and setting it aside for re-oiling.

"I heard you don't like jumping out of planes," Walker said. He glanced at Laws, who rolled his eyes. Walker had heard of Yank's predilection for landing inside a plane rather than jumping out of one. Word gets around and such things are ammunition for the verbal sport of FNG baiting.

"Where'd you hear that?" Yank asked, cool and easy. Too easy.

Walker made a show of trying to remember, staring at the ceiling and wrinkling his brow. "You know, I can't recall. Heard it from a lot of people though." When he noticed Yank looking at him, he added, "Saw it online, too. And I think the bathroom wall of a club in Patpong." He turned to Laws. "Was it Patpong?"

Laws shook his head. "I saw it spray-painted on the ceiling of a brothel in Tijuana."

"Funny thing," Walker added. "But I also saw it in the bathroom at the Hobbit House," meaning the all-midget-staffed restaurant and bar in Manila, Philippines.

"That where you met your girlfriend?" Laws asked.

"No," Walker said, making a play at looking really sad. "But your mother was lap dancing as they held her like a beach ball."

This had Yank laughing... until Walker redirected the conversation back to him again.

"Good thing there's an airport in Cabo San Lucas. Listen, Yank," Walker said, leaning in conspiratorially, well aware it was like leaning into a lion's mouth. "We'll jump into the Sea of Cortez and wait for you. After you land and hail a taxi, then find a small boat, then engine out to us, we'll begin the op. I know it's a lot of moving parts, and I know you'll be tired and stuff, but you think you can manage to stop on the way and get us some Happy Meals? After treading water in the ocean for all that time we're going to be hungry. I'd also like—"

Yank leaped atop him. Walker fought off the choke hold for a brief moment, then lost his grip on Yank's wrist. Yank sank his forearm into Walker's throat, but held off squeezing. Instead he said, "I do *not* get Happy Meals. I won't stop and bring them to you. Understand?"

Walker breathed through his teeth a moment before he answered. "How about a burrito then? Maybe some of those delicious churr—ow!"

Yank shifted positions and isolated Walker's right arm before Walker knew what was happening. Throwing over both of his legs, Yank pulled on the arm and arched his back.

Walker gave in. "Okay—okay!"

Yank let go and rolled to a sitting position.

Walker was slower getting to his feet. He alternated between rubbing his neck and his shoulder.

"Do we understand each other?" Yank asked. Walker nodded. "Sure. No Happy Meals. No burritos. But look on the good side."

"What good side?" Yank's eyes narrowed.

"You didn't say anything about a personal pan pizza."

Yank was about to launch himself when Holmes commanded they stop.

Yank sat with fight still lingering in his eyes.

Laws walked over to Yank. "Will you hold the pepperoni?" He placed a hand on his stomach. "Gives me gas."

Yank gave him a look, then finally broke into a grin.

Laws laughed, which at last made Yank laugh, too.

Holmes stood and helped Walker to his feet, making a show of dusting him off. "If you girls are done playing naked Twister, we got a mission brief in five mikes, then I want everyone to suit up and JMPI each other. I don't want this to be a cock-up." Holmes turned to Yank and gave him a stern look. "And do as Laws says, hold the pepperoni. It gives him gas."

"But I'm going to jump with you," Yank said, his brows coming together as he looked at the others.

"Is it okay?" Holmes asked. "Are you sure? I mean jumping out of airplanes is real scary."

Yank nodded vigorously; then he shook his head, desperate to both please and communicate. "I want to jump. It's no problem, sir."

"Then you'll be second in the stick. I think I have an old chute somewhere here that was packed for a jump into Vietnam." He left Yank staring.

Laws stared as well, his mouth half open. He looked from Yank to Walker. "Was that a joke? Did the boss joke? Christ and a BB gun, but I just heard the boss crack a joke."

"Don't know what you're talking about," Holmes said, sitting back down, a private little smile alive beneath his blue eyes.

"Right, boss." Laws smiled and leaned back. "Right."

7

CITY OF INDUSTRY. AFTERNOON.

The door whispered to him. He closed his eyes to better hear, but it was as if someone was on the other side, trying desperately to communicate. Try as YaYa might, he couldn't figure out what the other person was trying to impart. He leaned his head against the cool metal of the door and allowed his hand to drift toward the doorknob. When he touched it, the voice grew louder, but so did another voice.

"Hey!" He felt a hand on his shoulder as Alice whispered harshly. "What are you doing? We haven't been given the signal."

YaYa glanced around. He removed his ballistic glasses and wiped the sweat away from his eyes. Good question. What *was* he doing? He gritted his teeth and grinned. He replaced the glasses and reset his grip on his 9mm pistol.

During the premission briefing, he'd been introduced to all the other Naval Criminal Investigation Service agents, but there were just too many names to remember, except the one assigned to him and Alice—Rio Youers. The plan was for three police tactical unit teams with full body armor, ballistic shields, and M4 rifles to hit the front and side doors and loading dock. Each team was backed up by a pair of NCIS agents carrying pistols and wearing chest protection. YaYa waited with Alice and Special Agent Youers.

The young agent seemed too eager. Too bright-eyed and bushy-tailed. He was even smiling.

Luckily, they didn't have long to wait.

The tactical radios buzzed with action, and then YaYa heard a pop, then a bang, then the sound of M4 rounds firing into a big space. After fifteen seconds, Alice motioned for Youers to open the door. When he did, she braced against the doorjamb, peered into the interior, then began to move to the nearest barrier. Youers moved behind her and YaYa followed next.

Inside were hundreds of reclaimed refrigerators. Some were stacked five high and banded together to keep from falling, but most rested on the ground. A skylight that ran the length of the center of the ceiling let in daylight. A giant metal shelving unit against the far wall held several hundred more refrigerators with their doors removed. YaYa had no idea what all these various refrigerators were doing here. It could have been a madman's collection or it could have been something more determined.

A scream suddenly split the temporary peace inside the structure. Gunfire followed, at first intermittent, the tactical unit's concentrated fire. YaYa watched as a shadow moved almost faster than he could see, running toward the far wall. Bullets bit into the concrete and the refrigerators in a terrible hail of violence. What had been moving superhumanly fast stopped, twisted, and fell. It was a man. But how had he moved so fast?

YaYa moved toward the body in a crouch. Youers and Alice came behind. He knelt by the man and examined him. Mid-twenties, Hispanic. Several tattoos, which could probably be traced to one Mexican mafia organization or another. But no amulet or ring or item that YaYa could see that would provide the reason for the superhuman speed. Just a dozen bullet holes, including one through the jaw that had shattered teeth and bone.

Alice tapped him on the shoulder. "I think you need to come and see this."

"Are we clear?"

"All clear. We're bringing in dogs to make sure, but it looks like this guy was the only one."

"Okay. But what was he doing?"

"I think you'll find the answer over there," she said, pointing to a place in the center of the room blocked by a line of refrigerators.

YaYa stood. He must have moved too quickly because he felt nauseous and began to tip. Alice caught him.

"Are you sure you're okay?"

"Let's just get this done," he said. He pulled his arm roughly from her grasp. "Lead the way."

She frowned but held her tongue and motioned for him to follow her. YaYa knew he shouldn't have acted that way but he couldn't help it. What did he care anyway? She'd get over it. He realized he was acting strangely, as if he were an observer outside his body. And like that observer, he had no power to correct it.

Youers passed him and gave him a dirty look.

YaYa followed. The sight that greeted him in the center of the room made his steps slow. Several tables were strewn with what had been a carefully constructed chemistry lab. Gunfire had destroyed part of it, but that's not what drew his attention. Three monkey-like creatures hung eviscerated from a metal rod over one of the tables. With orange skin, wicked fangs, and impossibly long arms, they looked like a crazed melding of a Chucky doll and Stretch Armstrong. Only they weren't. YaYa knew exactly what they were—homunculi. Golem-like creatures created through alchemical magic to serve the will of their creator. The last ones he'd seen belonged to the Chinese mafia known as the Snakeheads. He'd never heard of any of the Mexican mafias using them, but there was probably no reason they couldn't. Another thought came to him. The Snakeheads could be working with the people who'd created this lab, but for what purposes he had no idea.

"Do you recognize them?" Alice asked, nudging one of the homunculi with the barrel of her gun.

YaYa nodded. "We need to make sure everyone in the room is properly debriefed."

"I figured as much."

Youers came up beside her. "So this is what you were talking about. Damn things look evil."

Alice offered YaYa a weak smile.

He just looked at her and shook his head. "Wonder what they were doing with them."

He spied the boxes that had been hijacked. One had been opened, but the others seemed to be untouched. The bones were gone from the open box, but off to the side were a large mortar and pestle, and inside the mortar was a fine white dust. He spied a basket of unfilled vials, the kind someone would wear around the neck. What quality would a chupacabra bone have? He examined the array of broken and unbroken glassware, but couldn't figure out what they would do with them. And what did this have to do with the homunculi?

YaYa shrugged the questions away as exhaustion swept through him. They'd have to figure that out later. For now, he needed to get this packed up and shipped back to the Salton Sea facility. He'd just begun to organize the removal when a nasty, guttural voice in his head whispered harshly, "Look up!"

Without thinking, YaYa complied, and saw a shadowy figure moving swiftly across the top of the highest level of refrigerators. He pointed his pistol in a two-fisted grip and fired. The shot missed, but the sound of it caused everyone to jump, then follow the aiming point of his pistol.

A man moved along the top of the row, then disappeared on the far side. YaYa and Youers were closest and ran to intercept, thinking he might climb down. YaYa's exhaustion made him slower than Youers. That YaYa had been a near-Olympic-class runner just weeks ago was testament to what was happening in his body, he thought.

He heard Youers shouting for the guy to halt, then gunshots. YaYa got close enough to see a man sliding a twelve-inch stiletto beneath Youers's rib cage. Youers went stiff and straight, his face losing all expression. The man held the agent's gun hand and gently laid him to the ground. Removing the blade, the man paused and for a moment stared into Youers's eyes.

Then he moved. Impossibly fast, knife held forward like a lance. YaYa didn't have the time to move out of the way, but felt his body picked up and slung against a nearby refrigerator, hard enough to knock it over. He lay stunned, unable to move. When he finally got to his feet, Alice was kneeling next to Youers, pleading with him to not die. YaYa stumbled over to Alice just as life left the young man's eyes; as for the killer, he was nowhere in sight.

An hour later, with dead homunculi, the glassware, and the remaining chupacabra bones stowed into the back of a CIA SPG van and headed once more for the Salton Sea facility, YaYa stood in the aisle of a pharmacy, staring at the myriad medicines they had to cure bloating, dehydration, acne, diarrhea, and headaches. There were salves to relieve itching and burning and dry skin. There were bandages and splints and crutches and slings. What they didn't have was what he wanted most. After searching the aisles, knowing they couldn't possibly have what he needed, he was nevertheless disappointed that he couldn't find a salve, cure, pill, capsule, or bandage that would deliver him from being possessed. He rolled up his arm and saw that the greens and purples from the wound had spread from his elbow to his wrist.

He knew that he'd have to tell someone. He'd rather do it in person than have the others learn of it without him there. He choked back a sob, then reached up and grabbed a bottle of milk of magnesia. He walked toward the cashier, but at the last minute turned to the door, shoving the bottle in his pocket like a lowlife thief.

So he wasn't surprised when he set off the alarm and the glass door slid shut in front of him. And he also wasn't surprised when he pulled out his pistol and shot the glass out. What did surprise him was Alice on the other side of the glass, her own pistol out and aiming straight at YaYa's head.

"What the hell are you doing?"

YaYa glanced down at the gun in one hand and the milk of magnesia in the other.

"Drop the gun, SEAL," she commanded.

He stared at her, ready to kill her, his face feral, his lips peeled back, his free hand wanting to rend and tear and break. Then he did what any self-respecting possessed U.S. Navy SEAL would do.

He cried.

8

FIVE THOUSAND FEET OVER THE SEA OF CORTEZ.

They were given the ten-minute warning. They were jumping in and didn't know when they'd be back, so they wore their wet gear and carried their dry gear in waterproof bags, which contained their weapons as well. Emily Withers had gone missing almost exactly twenty-four hours ago. If they found anything it would be a body. Still, after replaying the recording of the giant creature taking her, they concluded that they might need to be prepared for additional threats, so they also carried knifes sheathed to their legs, as well as gas-operated spear guns.

Laws wondered if they'd really encounter the giant fish. Their mission brief had included the history of the oarfish. It could grow upward of fifty, sometimes sixty feet in length. It was long held that the oarfish was perhaps the start of the mythology of the sea monster, sailors spying the great long bodies, either alive and beneath the waves, or washed up on the shore. The species held a fondness for the protected warm waters and rather shallow bottom of the Sea of Cortez.

But these great eel-like fish were not alone in these waters. The giant Humboldt squid also called the Sea of Cortez home. Some thought it might have been the inspiration for Jules Verne's sea monster that attacked the *Nautilus* in *20,000 Leagues Under the*

Sea. Whatever the truth was, the millions of tourists that came to swim in the lusciously warm waters had no idea of the sheer size of the squid that swam beneath them.

Never having seen a sea monster in person, Laws found that part of him actually wanted to. Growing up on the back lots of Hollywood studios, he'd seen his share of movie props. The head and teeth they'd used in the final scene of *Jaws* had terrified him for months when he'd first seen them after watching the movie.

But another part of him didn't want anything to do with sea monsters. They'd grown from small eggs to become as large as they were. Each and every one of them, in its own way, had become the ultimate predator, needing to feed on everything else, anything else, just to survive. Was that what had happened to the senator's daughter?

The ramp opened and air rushed in. He set his goggles and checked the valves of the man in front, just as his were being checked by the man behind. He heard the countdown in his intrateam underwater radio system and prepared to step off. Then came the moment, and he let the wind take him.

They jumped at five thousand feet, so it wasn't going to be a very long trip. Still, he saw the twinkle of Cabo to his right and the lights of mainland Mexico farther off to his left. Beneath him, as he rushed seaward through the wind, he spied lights of varying brightness from each of these boats, both commercial and private.

When he hit a thousand feet, he lowered his dry bag on a line. He watched the altimeter and GPS on his wrist and began flaring, using the risers to bring him on target and slow his descent. When he was ten meters, he released his dry bag, and when he was five meters he released the chute. He had time to press a hand to his goggles; then he was slicing into the warm water of the Sea of Cortez. As warm as it was, it was a shock, and he felt his chest tighten as he held his breath. He allowed himself to sink, pressed his regulator into his mouth, and cleared the air. Once he was certain his breathing apparatus was functioning, he freed his fins from where they were attached to his side and pulled them over his feet. Then he turned to regroup with the others.

They swam to the tactical underwater vehicle that Holmes had lowered on his own line. Laws powered it up and cycled it through its checks until he was sure it was ready to go. While he cycled through the setup and sonar, Holmes established coms. The mission plan was to move outward in a concentric circle while Yank and Walker held on to either side, ready to defend or attack if necessary. Holmes was a free floater and would move diagonally behind the Big Wheel-sized underwater craft and ensure that nothing came up behind them.

The light of the TUV gave them nearly five meters' visibility. But their true vision came from the sonar, which could read seventy meters and showed depth, direction, and relevant size on a five-inch circular green display.

They'd landed fifty meters due east from where Emily Withers was taken. They began their concentric circles moving outward at a patient clip. Single fish appeared as yellow dots. Small groups of fish appeared as orange clumps. Large fish were shown in red. Here and there an occasional orange clump flashed to red, demonstrating a merging of fish schools. One came right toward them. Laws communicated this to the team just as the school of fish approached, then split, swimming madly away. To Laws they appeared to be nothing more than a thousand or so ten-inch blacklip dragonets, orange with black dorsal fins.

Then came a fish that was chasing them, a smooth hammerhead shark, eager to continue its mobile buffet. But when it saw Triple Six, its eyes on the end of the hammers grew wide, and it spun around, disappearing first from sight, then the sonar screen. The hammerhead was about four feet, hardly a danger to the team. If it had been in a hunting party with a dozen or so, they might have become aggressive enough to attack.

The water suddenly cooled. Laws checked the depth and saw that they'd found a drop-off of more than thirty meters. Half a minute later a single orange and red dot began to move toward them from west and down. Laws communicated this to the others, noting that it was now solidly red. He stopped the TUV, pointing it toward the oncoming sea creature. About the time he noticed that there were no other fish around, not even small ones on the screen, it began to come into focus.

Swimming as if it owned the ocean, an oarfish appeared whose body seemed to flap like a riffle of fabric. It saw them, acknowledged them, then swam around them. It became obvious that this fish, easily ten meters long, couldn't grab a person. Even though it was as long as two Cadillacs end-to-end, its mouth was barely large enough for a human hand. Doing mental math, Laws suspected one would have to be five times the size of this one for it to have a mouth and jaw long enough to grab a person. And he doubted one that size existed.

Although...

The fish turned and went back the way it came.

Laws moved the TUV after it, if only to see if it might lead them to more oarfish, perhaps even larger ones.

They'd traveled about two minutes when a red blob invaded the right edge of the sonar. It moved quickly toward them. Laws had to stop and turn to face it. When he did, the spotlight captured a giant bullet-shaped head, easily the size of a Fiat 500, hurtling through the water toward the smaller oarfish. Long tentacles trailed behind the giant Humboldt squid, as did two clublike appendages.

It was clear the oarfish couldn't match it with speed, and it had no way to defend itself; even so, it turned toward the squid. For a moment, the oarfish was straight as an arrow and it appeared that the squid would impale itself on the creature. But at the last second, the squid's bullet-shaped body rose, exposing the two clublike appendages, which shot out and grabbed the oarfish, drawing it to the nest of tentacles. The squid's giant parrot-like beak descended from the body and began to rip free great pieces of meat from the length of its prey.

The water was suddenly filled with blood and pieces of floating fish meat. Remembering the shark, Laws reversed the engine of the TUV and backed away. He was perhaps ten meters back when the first of many orange dots crept on to the screen and began moving toward the red blob that was the feasting squid. The only thing worse than being in the middle of a pack of hyenas feasting on the Serengeti Plain would be to be in the middle of an ocean with blood in the water and a hundred sharks eager to feed.

"Chief—we've got to go!" he shouted into his mask.

He punched the power on the TUV to full, and swung around. Soon they were moving at max speed, still pathetically slow compared with how fast a shark could move. Walker, Yank, and Holmes were kicking madly with their fins, giving the TUV an extra couple of knots. Still, the inevitable happened as a cluster of sharks spotted them and gave chase.

Laws elbowed Walker and pointed behind them. Walker kept kicking, but turned, brought his spear gun to bear, and fired.

Laws spared a glance. The shot had missed.

While Walker reloaded, Yank turned and fired.

This one got the lead shark through the head.

Holmes fired and skewered another shark.

Soon, there was more blood in the water and no matter how intent the sharks had been to chase down Triple Six, they couldn't fight a million years of evolution screaming at them to eat the weak.

As Triple Six disappeared into the dark water of the Sea of Cortez, the hammerheads fed on their own.

9

ABOARD HMS *RESOLUTION II*. NIGHT.

A fifty-four-foot fishing yacht waited for them when they bobbed to the surface. They boarded, dragged the TUV with them, then began removing their scuba gear. The stern deck was lit by a pair of lights from the cockpit, which could be reached by ladder over a bunkroom with two long benches and a bar at the back. Meanwhile, a tall African American with a close-cropped, dyed-yellow Afro brought out a six-pack of Corona. He wore UDT shorts, flip-flops, and a shirt that said *I'd Rather Be Fishing*. He had a soul patch beneath his lower lip in the shape of a diamond.

When he passed the beers out, Holmes said, "Thanks, J.J."

"No problem at all. Glad you had the time to come down and do some fishing."

"Except it's not your kind of fishing," Walker said, standing with his wetsuit peeled down to his waist. He drank deeply from his bottle.

"You don't know what kind of fishing I do down here," J.J. said. "I could be doing anything."

"Knowing you, I bet you spend most of your time fishing for mermaids," Laws said good-naturedly.

"I do spend a considerable time in search of Mrs. Jones number five. I keep doing interviews, but still not hiring."

"Interviews." Laws snorted. "Good one. Here, let me introduce someone to you. Petty Officer First Class Jack Walker and Petty Officer Second Class Shonn Yankowski, meet Lieutenant Commander Jingo Jones, BUD/S Class 231."

"Retired," J.J. added. "You can call me J.J., just don't call me Jingo."

"J-I-N-G-O and Jingo was his name-o," Laws said, as if on cue.

"Need I say more?" J.J. looked pained as he took a sip of his own beer.

Walker stuck out his hand. "Call me Jack."

"You can call me Yank, then," the newest SEAL added.

Triple Six finished unsuiting, then climbed into shorts and T-shirts from their dry bags, which J.J. had retrieved for them. When the scuba gear was stored and Holmes had reported in to Billings, they sat around relieving the stress from the mission.

"So, what brings your spooky selves down here?" J.J. asked.

Walker and Yank glanced at each other.

Laws stared at Holmes, deferring to him.

Holmes leaned forward, elbows on his knees, staring into the beer bottle. "How much do you know about my team?"

Not *our* team and not *the* team, but *my* team. Walker liked the sound and feel of it. It gave him a strong sense of belonging.

"Other than the rumors, not much. I know you guys had a serious op in Southeast Asia. I know you did something in West Africa last year. I know that right about the time I was getting ready to retire there were rumors of you guys somewhere north of Point Barrow, Alaska, doing something in the snow." J.J. looked at the others. "SEALs don't do snow."

"We do if there's an abominable snowman taking out scientists studying the ever-expanding hole in the ozone," Holmes said matter-of-factly.

Everyone was quiet for a moment as J.J. stared at him, wide-eyed. Then he said, "Just like that. You're going to tell me just like that."

"This isn't an interrogation. You wanted to know, now you know."

"Is this a read-on?"

Holmes nodded.

J.J. stood and hammered the air with his fist. He glared at Holmes, shaking his head. "Fuck. Why'd you do that?"

"We need your help."

"I would have helped, Sam. You didn't have to lure me in."

"What just happened?" Yank asked.

Laws grinned conspiratorially. "See, J.J. wanted to remain aloof and too cool for school. As long as he wasn't read on to our mission, he had zero responsibility toward us, other than past friendship. But the commander headed him off at the pass and gave him classified information. Now either our boss is off reservation and illegally divulging classified information, or he spoke with Billings, who gave permission, knowing that once J.J. knew the mission, he'd be forced to assist us."

J.J. nodded. "What he said."

"You left off one thing," Holmes said.

"And what's that?" Laws asked, and then he grinned from ear to ear. "Don't tell me she authorized that."

Holmes nodded. "She did." He turned to J.J. and stood. "Lieutenant Commander Jingo Jones," he began. "You—"

"Oh, hell no," J.J. said, as if he knew what was coming.

"—are hereby RTD—returned to duty for a period not to exceed one week, during which time you incur all the benefits of an active duty Navy seaman, and must adhere to the regulations thereof."

"Fuck me." J.J. took a deep swig of his beer. When he was done, he added, "Don't expect me to cut my hair."

"You can keep the hair." He placed a hand on J.J.'s shoulder. "Listen, man, this was the only way I could do this. We seriously need your help and time is of the essence."

J.J. shook his head, then went and brought back six more beers. He was about to pass them out when Holmes shook his head. "No more. We're on mission."

J.J. pointed at Yank. "And that, my little brother, is why I quit the fucking navy. Too many rules." He took the beer back inside, this time returning with water bottles. He passed them out, sat down, and looked expectantly at Holmes. "Okay motherfucker. Dish."

Holmes smiled tightly. He gave J.J. the Cliffs Notes version, while Laws brought a tablet computer from his dry bag and showed the footage. When they were done, J.J. sat back and stared at the members of Triple Six. Walker couldn't tell if he was astounded or if he couldn't believe what he was being told. But then he did something Walker never would have anticipated. He broke out laughing. The laughter continued, while the members of Triple Six became increasingly uncomfortable.

Finally Holmes couldn't take it anymore. J.J.'s laugh had gone from humor to ridicule. "Do you want to share?"

J.J. choked and finally stopped. "And you're serious about all that sea monster shit?"

"Yes."

"And about the senator's daughter?"

"Yes."

"Who told you that it was an oarfish that took her?"

"SPG. Special Projects Group. Analysts and specialists from the agency providing direct support to our ops."

"They must be on a Jules Verne kick, because there aren't any oarfish big enough on the planet to carry off a person like I saw there."

Walker jumped in. "How can you be so sure?"

"I know these waters better than the honeyed thighs of the lady who does my hair, and let me tell you, I know those thighs. If there was an oarfish that size, then you're talking an apex predator. I'd know about it before I ever saw it. Schools of fish would go missing. Sport fishing would be disrupted. A hundred different things would be affected. No, ain't no oarfish that big."

"What about a Humboldt squid?" Walker asked.

"Sure. They get that big, but they don't look anything like what took this girl."

"Then what is it?" Yank asked, looking from one team member to another. "If you're so sure what it isn't, then tell us what it is."

J.J. stared at the frozen image on the tablet. "It has the length of a mature oarfish. I see that. I also see something like dorsal and pelvic fins." He shook his head. "This is definitely not an oarfish. If I was to bet, which I won't, but if I was, I'd say it was an axolotl. But that can't be, because the largest one I ever saw was about this big." He held his hands about a foot and a half apart.

"What's an *axolotl?*" Holmes asked. "Maybe it's a giant one."

"Still hard to believe. An axolotl is actually a salamander and not technically a fish. Locals call the small versions *ajolete*, but it's really old Aztec, mainly found in Lake Xochimilco beneath Mexico City."

"Wait—there's a lake beneath Mexico City?" Walker asked. "Do the Mexicans know this?"

"More than that. There's a whole other city down there. The Spanish built right on top of where the Aztecs used to live. And now the *ajolete* are near extinction. Can't be more than a few thousand left. What makes them interesting, which is why I actually know something about them, is that during their larval stage they don't metamorphose, which means they retain their ability to breathe underwater as well as breathe air. In fact, they can actually walk."

"You're talking like an expert," Holmes said. "Didn't know you had a degree in marine biology."

"Hardly." J.J. shook his head. "During the long hours between fish strikes there's little to talk about other than the sea. I had a foursome hire me out for a week. Archeologists, I think. Some of it must have rubbed off on me."

"Here," interrupted Laws. "I did a search and found some references. Look at the picture."

Everyone crowded around Laws and his tablet, which showed a small salamander with wavy appendages around its body, similar to an oarfish's.

"How could one get that big?" Yank asked.

"Radiation?"

Laws shrugged. "Go ask Godzilla. I don't know."

"And you're sure this picture isn't doctored?" J.J. asked.

Holmes and Laws looked at each other.

J.J. persisted. "You did have someone check, right?"

Laws spoke first. "This came from a security camera on a hotel."

"Which just happened to be pointing down at the area the senator's daughter was taken from. Right?"

"But why would someone want—"

Laws turned to Holmes. "She might still be alive."

Holmes nodded thoughtfully. "Got to make a call."

"Now we're talking." J.J. sat down on one of the benches and crossed his legs. "Jingo Jones to the rescue once more. What else you bad new SEALs need from this old-timer?"

10

MANHATTAN BEACH. DUSK.

The setting sun transformed the offshore marine layer into a Jackson Pollock canvas of reds, blues, and pinks. A thin band of brown showed the demarcation between sea and sky. It was a view someone could stare at for a lifetime, which was probably why Southern California beachfront property cost more per year than most people could make in a lifetime. Too bad the sight only lasted for a few moments, tucked at the end of a bustling day and before the fullness of night descended.

But YaYa was thinking of none of this as he stared at the horizon. Instead, he was listening to voices in languages he shouldn't be able to understand. Earlier, when he'd been in the pharmacy, he'd become vaguely aware that every now and then he could catch the reflection of something that couldn't be there—a broken and twisted figure, legs like a grasshopper's attached to his forearm; it had a triangular-shaped face with vaguely human features and stared back at him with glowing eyes above a drooling, misshapen mouth that was always moving. If he listened closely enough, YaYa could hear what it said. If he listened even closer, he could understand it.

After the sun set, YaYa returned to the SUV and rode slowly down Manhattan Beach. Three-story homes and a sidewalk were on his left. Parking spaces, a wide strip of beach, and the Pacific Ocean were on his right. Surfers were enjoying the last few sets and would be returning to their cars. They'd probably stop for a burger at Fatburger over on Artesia, or for a pizza at California Pizza Kitchen over on Sepulveda on their way home. They might even stay and build a bonfire. The life of a Southern California surfer was a special one, and it was something he counted on.

And there it was.

YaYa pulled the SUV into a slot beside an old 1973 Chevy Impala. Far from showroom shape, this car had been beaten and crashed so many times that the sky-blue sides appeared as if they were made of Bondo and undulated like the sea. He got out of the SUV and looked toward the Impala's front tire. Sure enough, what he'd thought he'd seen was there. A set of keys. After all, no self-respecting car thief would steal this beater. He examined the pod of surfers out in the water waiting for waves and saw that the beach was clear. All he had to do was be fast enough.

He grabbed the keys and opened the trunk. Inside was a spare tire and a case of beer. He removed the tire and beer and placed these behind the SUV. Then he opened the back of the SUV and grabbed Alice, who was just now coming to. He dropped her into the trunk and checked the tightness of her cuffs. He pulled several plastic cable ties from his pocket and cinched her ankles together, then attached the cuffs to the ties on her ankles. As he was adjusting her gag, she opened her eyes. He punched her three times, quick, then slammed the trunk.

He spied several surfers angling for a wave. Another was staring right at him and shouting something. YaYa gave the man a quick salute, got into the Impala, and started it. "Paint It Black" blasted from the speakers as he backed out of the space. He had half a tank. In a boat like this, it might get him halfway to San Diego.

Part of him wondered if Alice would be okay. Part of him didn't care. He drove away, careful to stay within the law. As he passed the SUV, he engaged its lock using the fob. A block later, he tossed the fob into the bushes.

"What'd you say?" He angled his head and began to listen to the voices as they told him what they wanted him to do.

11

CABO SAN LUCAS. MORNING.

They waited until morning to pull into port. Holmes had called and asked Billings if the video had been evaluated. Then at three in the morning she'd called him back. Much chastised, the SPG credited whoever made the video with superior talent. They'd done a cursory pixel check when they'd received it, but didn't determine any pixel shift and believed it to be genuine. Additionally, the fact that it had come from a remote security camera added to their sense that the video was real. They had no protocol for deciding which videos should be evaluated or not, and had instead counted on the tasking element to ask them for evaluations. In this case, it should have come from Triple Six. Because one wasn't asked for, one wasn't conducted.

As it turned out, the video was a fake. Color filter array correlations in the area where Emily was supposed to have been taken by the creature were disrupted and showed significant lack of color spectrum pixellation. Bottom line was that although SPG was unable to as yet break through the concealment algorithm, no one could accurately state what had happened to Emily. But what they could say with a high degree of certainty was that she was not taken by a giant sea monster. Which left several questions. Why choose a sea monster? Why manipulate the video in the first place?

And why choose as a sea monster an impossibly giant axolotl?

Even without the answers, Billings was able to garner full support from the CIA. Through SPG, she coordinated ground support through the U.S. Embassy in Mexico City. One of their assets would be in contact—ex-Zetas cartel hit man turned U.S. counter-narcoterrorism operative. He was due to meet with them sometime later that morning. Holmes had arranged for them to stay at a hotel downtown, one used by Mexicans rather than moneyed tourists.

Holmes was now certain, as was the rest of the team, including J.J., that Emily was alive. After all, why take so much effort to hide an abduction unless care was going to be made to keep the person alive. That there had been no ransom was worrisome. That someone tried to hide the fact she was even kidnapped was even more worrisome. Triple Six had to get to the bottom of this. Without any solid leads, their only option was to grab as many local bad guys as possible and interrogate them. Someone had to know something. Mexico's subculture thrived on graft. Money had to pass from one hand to another for someone to have been able to get away with kidnapping in the area and it was Triple Six's job to discover who it was.

Hotel Boutique Casa Poblito on Hidalgo Avenue was their accommodation of choice. It was a square one-story hotel with a single entry and exit point with a gate that could be locked. Each room had a window air-conditioning unit. The center courtyard had a pool and a large cabana. It had twenty-four rooms, eighteen of which were rented until this morning. By noon, everyone would be out and Triple Six would have the place to themselves.

Holmes also coordinated with an old friend, Major Navarre of the Grupo Aeromóvil de Fuerzas Especiales, or GAFE, which was the Mexican Special Forces. He didn't require GAFE's assistance, but he wanted his friend to know that they were in country and that they were conducting a covert operation, in the event local police or even federal police became involved. Navarre would create documentation that they were conducting a joint special-operations exercise, so if needed, the paperwork could be immediately produced. If it turned out they didn't need the backup, then the documents would be destroyed. Plus it was just good planning to have a team of Mexican Special Forces on standby, even if you were SEAL Team 666.

J.J. took them to a late breakfast, loudly announcing that his companions had been charter fishing with him and had caught their weight in dorado and crevalle. They ate *chilaquiles* and eggs, which were nothing more than eggs served over tortilla chips, in this case with chorizo, *queso fresco*, and black beans.

After confirming that the hotel was available, they bag-dragged eight blocks and entered through the central door. Holmes passed a stack of money into the hands of the owner, and with one last glance, the owner hurried into the street. They had the hotel for three days, at which time they could extend their residency if needed. And the owner didn't mind. After all, he'd been paid three times the rate on every room. A dump like this probably hadn't been full in years, much less drawing the kind of customers who paid regularly.

"Walker and Yank, clear the rooms," Holmes commanded. Turning to Laws, he said, "Establish coms and check out the electronics." To J.J. he handed a placard that read QUARANTINE in Spanish, and a padlock. "Seal the front, then check the businesses around here and find out who the cops are who patrol this area. We want to make friendly with them." He passed over a smaller stack of Benjamins. "Let me know if you need more."

It didn't take long to place the sign on the door, get a worried look from a bum nearby, and lock the gate. Then J.J. was bopping down the street, pretending to own the universe.

Walker and Yank drew their SIG Sauer P229s and began room clearing per SOP. Entering simultaneously through each door, one low, one high, each of them covered a sector of the room to allow for greatest coverage of fire. They'd cleared two rooms when Walker was surprised to hear Holmes's voice speaking to someone else outside.

"You don't have a last name?" Holmes demanded.

Walker tapped Yank on the shoulder and both of them slid from the room. Holmes stood with his hands at his sides. To anyone else he might have appeared relaxed, but Walker recognized the tension in his boss. Holmes was addressing someone in the shade of the cabana near the pool in the central courtyard.

"I have had many last names. Since one is as good as the other, if you wish me to have a last name, then choose for me."

"Or I just call you Ramon?"

"This is good, too."

Walker peered around the corner. He saw a man seated in a chair beneath the cabana. He wore linen slacks and a linen jacket over a white shirt. The shoes on his feet were perforated to let air in. Gold dangled from his wrists and a large necklace hung around his neck. He appeared to be about fifty, had a solid head of hair, and was handsome in the way older Mexican men often seemed to be.

But there was something else, too. Something different about this man that made Walker's skin buzz. The other SEALs called it his supernatural early-warning radar. He'd called it a pain in the ass until he learned to control it. He still remembered the first time on his first mission, falling to the ground and doing the kicking chicken as a seizure completely took him over. It was one reason he'd been selected: his past history of being possessed by a Malaysian grave demon was reason to elevate him above all the other candidates. He'd since come to terms with his sensitivity and used it for the team's benefit. So now that he felt the buzz, he had to wonder who—or *what*—was speaking to Holmes.

He moved out in a combat crouch, training his pistol on the man. "Chief, step back."

Holmes did as he was told, taking several quick steps backward as he drew his own pistol. "What's going on, Walker? You feel something?"

"Yes, sir. Closer I get. Yank, to me," Walker yelled.

Yank appeared on the other side of the cabana, his pistol in a two-handed grip, his face a mask of serenity.

Ramon hadn't moved. He sat, acting as if three SEALs weren't pointing their weapons at him. He turned to look at Walker.

"So... you've been involved with such things before."

"Yeah, I've been around. So what is it? Are you demon or a man?"

Ramon laughed. "I've been called both quite frequently of late. One man's man is another man's demon."

"I think you better explain yourself," Holmes said, tightening his grip on his pistol. "Tell us what's going on."

The former Zeta hit man smiled sadly, much as he probably did with his targets right before he murdered them, thought Walker.

"Doesn't a man have his privacy?"

"We operate as a team. We have no privacy. We're brothers."

"And if I tell you, then I'll instantly be a brother," Ramon said, snapping his fingers.

"Well." Holmes seemed to consider it. "Maybe a stepbrother."

"Once removed," Laws added, coming up behind them.

"But you need me. The embassy sent me."

Walker detected a strange tone in the man's speech, as if he was really upset about not being brought into the fold but hiding it well.

"You'd probably help us, but we'll move on without you," Holmes said.

"And what happens to me then?" Ramon shifted his eyes toward where Yank had him covered.

Holmes shrugged. "I guess that's up to you."

It was a real Mexican standoff for almost a full minute. The silence in the courtyard was disrupted only by the sound of the pool filter, Walker shifting his feet to get a better line, and cars rumbling past outside. Finally the man in white held his hands out to his sides and slowly got to his feet.

"I was a hit man for the Zetas cartel and could get at any target, regardless of where they were," he began, making eye contact with each and every member of Triple Six. "No one could figure it out. They'd watch for me. They'd plan for me. On occasion I'd have the audacity to tell them I was coming. Once I even gave them the time." He shook his head sharply. "Didn't matter. Was nothing they could do. If the Zetas wanted you dead and they called me in, it was a done deal."

"I thought you said the embassy sent you," Laws noted.

"Alas, I did my job too well. My former employers tried to get rid of me. I had to—how do you say it—change teams."

"How'd you do it?" Holmes asked. "I mean, you told that story for a reason. How'd you get away with killing so many people?"

"Let me show you." He held up his right hand. His lips peeled back slightly as he concentrated on it. The fingers grew long, talons sprung from the nails, and sand-colored hair shot forth from the skin.

"Skinwalker," Laws said.

Ramon smiled.

"Now I see why the cartel wanted you dead," Holmes said.

Ramon flexed his hand and it returned to human form. "Yes. A sad thing when you can't trust those you work for."

"You said it before. The problem with being the best is who's out there who can stop you?"

"I would think you know that problem very well, Lieutenant Commander Holmes." Ramon sat back down. "Can we begin now or is your man going to have another feeling?"

For a second it looked like Holmes was going to carry the situation to the next step; then he dropped his weapon and shoved it into the waistband behind his back. "Nah. I think we're ready to get to work."

The other SEALs followed Holmes's lead. Walker felt a little relief, but not too much. He was still in the presence of a skinwalker, or what legends generally referred to as a werewolf.

12

HOTEL BOUTIQUE CASA POBLITO. AFTERNOON.

As it turned out, Ramon was a gold mine of information. He'd been a one-man killing machine for the Zetas, responsible for more deaths than a Salvadoran hit squad. Working against the other cartels, the Zetas had tried to poise themselves on top of the power pyramid. Instead of fighting for territory, they fought for smuggling routes and constantly worked against other cartels.

Ramon explained the structure. There were eight major cartels. The Gulf Cartel, the Beltrán Leyva Cartel, La Familia, the Sinaloa Cartel, the Juárez Cartel, the Tijuana Cartel, the Knights Templar, and Los Zetas.

The Gulf Cartel, which controlled the Baja Peninsula, was one of the strongest in men, arms, and influence, until they began to fight among themselves. It was now broken into two factions, Los Metros and Los Rojos, each struggling to claim the territory it once had. In 1999, the Gulf Cartel was responsible for the formation of Los Zetas, hiring thirty-one GAFE soldiers as assassins; these soldiers turned several border towns into ghost towns, their violence and cruelty unmatched and unchecked. When the leader of the Gulf Cartel was captured in 2008, Los Zetas seized the opportunity to swell their ranks to more than three hundred former special operations soldiers, and thus became the dominant force in human and narcotics trafficking.

La Familia was formed by members of the Gulf Cartel who splintered off to create an organization similar to the Zetas, in order to attack the Zetas and keep them away from the Gulf Cartel. What had initially appeared to be a parting of ways turned into a savvy reorganization. But in mid-2011 the Gulf Cartel was overcome by its own infighting, resulting in the Knights Templar, which had since flourished in the absence of La Familia. Knights Templar aligned itself with the Sinaloa Federation in an attempt to root out any surviving members of La Familia and prevent Los Zetas from expanding into the territory.

The Sinaloan cartel was perhaps the largest of the big cartels. Because they had infiltrated the Mexican military and judiciary, many of their operations had been unopposed, especially in the valuable Texas money corridor. Additionally, instead of fighting the Zetas they formed alliances with them and jointly destroyed the Sonoran, Colima, and Milenio cartels.

Both the Tijuana and Juárez cartels held only a fraction of the power they had enjoyed a decade earlier. While both still controlled the flow of drugs and humans through their cities, they were ignored by the other cartels, much as a person from the city would ignore someone from the country.

The Beltrán Leyva Cartel was believed to have disbanded. But as late as 2005, the cartel had its tentacles into Mexico's police, political, and judicial offices. They were even able to place operatives in Interpol offices, in a program to redirect the country's counternarcotics efforts away from their cartel, and place the crosshairs firmly on the Gulf Cartel. The last of the four brothers who once ran the cartel, Héctor Beltrán Leyva, went into hiding. Both the U.S. and Mexico had a multimillion-dollar bounty for the man's capture and arrest. But no one would ever be able to claim it, Ramon told them, since the disappearance was actually the result of him infiltrating Leyva's Badiraguato compound and disposing of the drug lord in a method that was untraceable. Over the period of a week, Ramon ate him, leaving the bones, hair, and nails to bleach beneath the hard, unforgiving sun on the slopes of Cerro Algodones.

After the information dump, Holmes ordered Laws, who'd reported that the hotel office had a serviceable computer with an average wireless connection, to contact SPG and have them form link analysis chains. They'd search for links in financial transactions, vehicle movements, personnel movements, as well as telephone and IP addresses. These methods had been used for decades, and resulted in uncovering culprits of seemingly unsolvable crimes, such as the Khobar Towers bombing.

Holmes wanted SPG to follow whatever linkage they could from the hotel security camera back to the nearest cartel. Once they determined the linkage, they could, with information from the Mexican federal judiciary, determine which members of that cartel were in the area. Holmes also wanted more information on Ramon, and asked that SPG do a deep dive to provide a comprehensive report. Finally, Holmes asked that Laws get a list of all current issues before the Sissy, including those brought forward from previous sessions.

Holmes approached the newest SEAL and placed a hand on his shoulder. "Yank, I want you to patrol. Keep the integrity of this building together. I don't want a bunch of beegees sneaking up on us."

Just then J.J. returned. When he saw Ramon, he asked, "This the guy?"

"Yeah, this is the guy." Holmes turned to Ramon. "Who controls this area?"

"If you mean southern Baja, then the answer is no one. The answer is also everyone. The area has been in dispute. Just when someone establishes a foothold, the other cartels and the judicial system gang up on them."

"Are there any Zetas around?"

"I'm sure there are."

"What about Gulf Cartel or Knights Templar?"

"Probably some of them, too."

"I assume they'd all be tied into the local politics and businesses."

Ramon nodded. "I'd assume the same."

"Okay, here's what I want: Ramon, I'd like you to find the local Zeta facilitator and bring him in. Yank and I will go after the Gulf Cartel operative, and J.J. and Walker will go after the Knights Templar."

"Uh, boss," Walker said, "one problem."

"What's that?"

"We don't know where they are."

Holmes smiled broadly. "We don't have to." He pointed at J.J. and Ramon with both hands. "They can tell us."

J.J. smiled awkwardly. "Wait a minute. What are you saying, Sam?"

"Don't try and tell me you've been operating a charter without having paid, promised, or worked for one or all of the cartels."

"But that would be cooperating with a criminal organization. I'd lose my clearance if I'd done such a thing."

"Stow it," Holmes said. "Save it for the polygraphers. I know what you have to do to survive. It's one of the reasons we're using you. Do you think we need an overweight, out-of-shape former SEAL to back us up, or do you maybe think we need your boat and your knowledge of the area?"

J.J. looked hurt. "I'm not overweight."

Holmes gave him a disbelieving eye. "So?"

"I know the Zetas here," Ramon said. "Juan Carlos is the man you're looking for."

Holmes turned to Ramon. "Does he know you?"

"By reputation."

"Good, then when you go to bring him in he won't say much."

Ramon smiled. "He won't say nothing at all. I assure you."

"Not so fast. We want him to talk when he gets here, so let's not do anything irreversible."

Ramon nodded.

Holmes turned to J.J. "So? Memory any better?"

"I know a guy who belongs to the Gulf Cartel. He claims to be connected to everyone."

"Excellent. Then you and Walker go bring him in. And if he knows the location of a Templar, bring the Templar along as well."

"Alive?"

"Please." Holmes turned to Walker. "And Jack," he said, with a rare use of his first name.

"Sir?"

"You're in charge. Make sure you guys don't get into any situation you shouldn't. Know what I mean?"

Jack knew exactly what his boss meant. He'd almost gotten the team killed several times because of his inability to restrain his curiosity and remain in position. Curiosity might have killed the cat, but it could never be the death of a SEAL.

13

CABO SAN LUCAS. AFTERNOON.

They needed a car. While they could walk or take a taxi to Hotel Finisterra, bringing back a hostage in the same taxi might prove to be a little distracting, if not straight-up problematic. So J.J. made a call. Soon a thirty-year-old woman with flaming red hair, enough blue eyeshadow for three people, and a muffin top that threatened the fabric of her pants dropped off a four-door gray and brown beater that had been a Toyota Corolla about a thousand years ago. J.J. kissed her and promised her something in Spanish that made her blush. She watched them leave with heavy lids, probably already imagining the benefits she would reap for her help.

J.J. spent the next thirty minutes doing surveillance detection. Hotel Finisterra was a mere 2.4 kilometers down Cabo San Lucas Street. They could have been there in two minutes, but then they wouldn't have known if they were dragging any surveillance with them. It was bad enough that they were alone; they didn't need to announce the place from which they were operating.

Cabo San Lucas had two faces. There was a tourist side that was glitz, brass, and crass, then there was the Mexican side that was tired, dirty, and hidden outside the exclusive resorts that desperately didn't want anyone to leave them. And for the most part no one did. There were occasions where tourists, eager to see the *real* Mexico, would travel outside the guarded gates of the resorts to the stalls and shops that rimmed the outside perimeter of the seaside resorts. They'd buy shot glasses decorated with pictures of Pancho Villa, T-shirts with images of sharks wearing sombreros, knockoff purses, glued-together wooden dinosaurs, and worked-metal lizards, believing all the while that this was the real Mexico.

Having grown up in Subic Bay, Philippines, Walker couldn't help but see the similarities. So many sailors spent their time on land within two miles of the main gate of the base, believing that all Filipina girls wore miniskirts, seductive smiles, and had long and flowing hair. They had faith in the idea that there was a bar every ten feet, that all food came from street vendors, and that everyone spoke a cute version of broken English.

Which, of course, couldn't be further from the truth.

Mexicans living near tourist areas, like Filipinos living near the same, found themselves trapped in an equatorial snow globe of make-believe, where expectations were met threefold in the hopes that gringos the world over would shower them with Benjamin Franklins. Not at all a version of reality they'd want or accept if they lived anywhere else, but they lived where they lived and adapted as best they could.

As J.J. drove a leisurely surveillance-detection route, Walker saw the evidence of this lifestyle. The acrid smell of tequila from piles of broken bottles was an ever-present odor. The low buzz of flies, hovering like black halos over piles of excrement, was a constant sound beneath everything. Something had been dragged fifty feet down the street, leaving a long red smear. Could have been a stray dog. Could have been a stray cat. Could have been anything, but no one seemed to care. People just walked right through it. They never considered stepping around. It was just something that was there.

From the dirty streets to the white stucco, often stained and badly in need of repair, or the broken cinder blocks that composed the walls of most buildings, the humid air smelled of burning tires and cooking meat, with the slight taint of garbage beneath it all. Here and there a car was parked against a curb. More often than not, it was stripped or missing an important part. Trash piles appeared every two blocks. Instead of bins, locals would get friends with pickups to help them move what had accumulated on the street to a nearby dump. The occasional dog, usually a chimera of something tan, black, and mean, either loped or limped, sniffing at everything that might be edible, including the occasional bum curled up in a doorway. The people were a uniform shade of exhausted, lugging food, stock, lumber, rock, and the detritus of everyday living on their shoulders, in their arms, on their backs, and often affixed to the back of a bicycle. Every so often, Walker would spy a tourist family who'd wandered too far afield, staring in fear at a Mexico they had not been promised in the glossy brochures.

And, of course, there were the police forces. The municipal police handled traffic and the policing of their own citizens for the most part. The Policía Federal Preventiva, or *federales*, were ever-present because of the tourist industry and the transit of both drugs and people. Walker and J.J. passed several blue and white municipal police pickups, the policeman usually standing nearby or leaning against their trucks. They also passed *federales* sitting inside their newer armored SUVs, air-conditioning blowing while they observed all those who passed.

J.J. hadn't shown any nervousness until they passed the first *federales* SUV. When they passed the second and he became even more nervous, Walker had him pull over.

"What is it? Are you in trouble?" he asked.

"Have you heard of the Bite? *La Mordida*?"

"No. What is it?"

"It's the bite the police take out of your wallet to keep them from doing something worse. It's better to be bitten than to be eaten, they say."

"And you haven't been paying?"

J.J. watched behind them in his rearview mirror. He licked his lips, then turned to Walker. "Let's just say that things have been a little slow."

"How does it work? Do they come to you?"

"They used to, but now it's all done online."

"Could be tricky. Leaves a paper trail."

"They have a set of charities I give to. One is legit, the others aren't. Or is it the other way around? Regardless, I got a visit last week. They're hungry for a bite."

"*La Mordida*."

J.J. nodded, then pulled back onto the street. Assured they didn't have a tail, he drove straight to Hotel Finisterra. Once a proud gem in the all-inclusive-resort game, it had been left behind. With its fading paint and out-of-date architecture, it was immediately obvious the hotel was a discount resort. During spring break it probably had girls hanging naked from every balcony, but they weren't the sort to be picky where the food and tequila were always free. Now Walker saw overworked housewives trying to herd their children together and enough over-sixties to make him think he'd landed in the middle of a shuffleboard convention.

They pulled up to the valet and J.J. tossed the young man dressed like an Aztec warrior the keys and a few dollar bills. The young man glared at the car as if it were an insult. He turned to say something to J.J., but J.J. was already inside. Walker merely smiled at the valet, then hurried to catch up to the former SEAL.

Regardless of the exterior state of the resort, when entering through the doors one was met by a scouring wash of cool air. On one side of the lobby was a series of counters with aquariums built into the walls behind them. Hundreds of multicolored fish swam inside like a living painting, while handsome young men and women dressed in burgundy suits with white shirts worked tirelessly to make the tourists feel like the kings and queens of a far-off land where even the lowest of Westerners sat taller than the locals. The lobby's other side was full of low-slung leather couches, chairs, and rugs on tile floors. Instead of a wall of aquariums, there were floor-to-ceiling windows revealing a series of terraced pools, graduating down to the Sea of Cortez.

J.J. moved to a coffee kiosk and ordered an iced coffee. As he stood, tapping his foot impatiently and waiting on the barista, he scanned the people sitting in the chairs. He small-talked with Walker to keep up appearances. Since Walker didn't know who they were looking for, he kept his eyes on the barista, which wasn't an unpleasant experience at all. Just about the time she delivered the coffee with a flutter of her eyes and a shy smile was when J.J. made a slight motion with his head toward one of the couches.

Walker winked at the girl, then shoved his hands in his pockets and moved toward the windows. He angled so he would pass beside the couch in question. Sitting on it was a young man dressed like a *Saturday Night Live* pimp and a bespectacled elderly woman reading a book. The man was about five foot six. His T-shirt and slacks were so tight that if he was concealing a weapon it had to be inside of him. He'd used a thin application of eyeliner to bring out his eyes. He was handsome in a slender Enrique Iglesias sort of way, but when he got up and approached a young woman getting off an elevator, Walker didn't know what to do. Were they going to follow him? Were they going to take him down?

They walked arm in arm out the door.

Walker remembered too late that Holmes had put him in charge and as such he should have established safe and recognition signals with J.J. prior to going inside. They also should have had a backup plan. He was mentally kicking himself when J.J. began moving. But he didn't follow the pair out the door. Instead, he sat down beside the elderly woman. He raised a hand and gestured for Walker to sit down on the other side of her. Reluctantly, Walker nodded and soon found himself ensconced in a cloud of lavender.

"Greetings, Señora," J.J. said as he sipped at his iced coffee.

The woman tightened her mouth, but made no move to reply.

"Let me introduce you to my friend. His name is Bob. Say hi, Bob."

"Hi, Bob," Walker said.

He watched as her mouth loosened slightly into an almost smile, then tightened back. He noticed that the book she was reading was Roberto Bolaño's *Los Detectives Salvajes*. The dead Chilean-turned-Mexican-Trotskyite's books had become immensely popular after his death; even Jen had read them, placing them spine-out beside the likes of Gabriel García Márquez and Pablo Neruda. He'd expected something else of an elderly Mexican matron.

Then he looked a little closer and he noticed the size of the pores on her face. He glanced at J.J. over her shoulder and couldn't help but notice his knowing smile. Walker returned his gaze and took in the pieces of the woman, rather than the whole. He began with the hair. Blond with hints of gray. He'd taken it originally to be professionally coiffed, but now that he was looking at the individual hairs, they just seemed too thick. And the skin. The skin was too soft to be that of an elderly woman. He had to give credit. The application of base had made the skin seem old, but he could tell from where the makeup met the lower neck that the skin was younger than it appeared to be. And then he saw it. The Adam's apple. The idea that only men had them was a fallacy, but it was true that men had larger laryngeal prominences, and this one was anything but subdued.

"And to whom do I have the pleasure?" Walker asked, holding out a hand.

She glanced at it, then glanced at Walker's face before turning to J.J. "You're an ass," she said, in a voice painfully lacking in feminine qualities.

"I might be, but I need to talk to you."

"And who is this, your new lover?"

J.J. glanced quickly at Walker, then grinned. "No. Just a friend."

"So what do you want? I have business."

"We do too. We need you to come with us." Seeing the tightening of the shoulders, J.J. added, "We'll make it worth your while."

"You know who I work for, Jingo."

"I do. And you know who I worked for. Isn't that right, Jaime Gonzalez?"

Her eyes narrowed. "What's going on?"

"Not here," J.J. said. He stood and held out an arm, bowing slightly like an Old World gentleman. "Take my arm."

"And if I won't?"

"Then we'll carry you out."

"I might scream."

"And when Bob here rips off your wig and shows the world who you really are do you think you'll ever be able to come back?"

The tightness of the lips relaxed to reveal a man's teeth, complete with a gold incisor. "You boys going to treat me like a lady?"

"Of course."

Jaime Gonzalez gently closed his book. He stood and smoothed his dress; then he held out his left arm to Walker.

"I count on you to treat me with the respect you would your mother."

Walker hesitated. "My mother's dead and she never crossdressed."

Jaime stared at Walker, then grabbed his arm. "You seem like one of the good ones. Too bad you're hanging with this old fag," he said, glaring at J.J. Then he let Walker lead the three of them from the resort.

14

CABO SAN LUCAS. LATER.

Yank held on to the handlebars for dear life. He hadn't ridden a motorcycle in several years, but the Suzuki dirt bike was necessary if he was going to keep up with the mark.

They'd approached him in the Nefertiti Hotel as planned with Ramon flanking one side and Yank the other. He'd have preferred a smash-and-grab, but Holmes wanted this low-key, so he had to act semicivilized. Juan Carlos was a Zetas cartel facilitator, in place to ensure that mafia members transiting through Cabo San Lucas, or those operating in it, had everything they needed. He wasn't so much a criminal as he was a procuring agent. Whether it was booze, drugs, sex, or extravagant food, Juan Carlos could make it all happen with ease.

He wasn't much to look at. He was about five foot five and balding, and his paunchy stomach and thin legs promised that his days of sports were long gone. So when he leaped up and took off like an Olympic sprinter after he saw Ramon, Yank couldn't have been more surprised. Yank had taken off after him, but had found it impossible to keep up, soon tiring and slowing. But Juan Carlos kept on running. When Yank knocked down a motorcyclist, his first move was to grab the bike and use it to follow the man. And when he sped up, so did Juan Carlos.

Where did he get his speed? Yank wondered.

He cranked the throttle, leaned forward, and held on as the studded tires ate the ground beneath him. Sand and rock spit out the back end, firing indiscriminately into the crowds gathered at the outdoor tourist markets. Every so often, he'd spy the man still running up ahead of him. His arms were pumping, his legs were churning, and all the while he was moving forward as fast as he could.

They were nearing the water. Soon, the quay would be before them. When he saw that Juan Carlos wasn't about to stop, he couldn't help slowing the motorcycle. What was Carlos going to do? Go flying off the end like a stuntman?

As he slowed, he saw Ramon zip past, his legs propelling him as fast as the other man's.

Suddenly Juan Carlos pulled up at the edge of the quay.

Ramon hit him square in the back, a move that took them both flying into the water.

Yank glanced behind him at the trail of upset Mexican peddlers and knew he shouldn't be where he was. A pair of policemen were pushing their way through the crowd. One thing was sure, he couldn't go back. He did what anyone would do in his position. He spun the throttle, shot forward, and flew off the end of the quay. As the bike began to fall first, he let go, letting it smash into the water. He flew another dozen feet, then hit the water as well, but he'd had time to arrange his limbs so that when he hit, it was sideways.

He sank and turned to his right beneath the water. He'd spied a sailboat at the end of the quay. It took all of his breath before he felt the stern rudder. Then, when he was certain he was amidships, with the bulk of the boat between him and the quay, he let himself come up for air. He wanted desperately to shoot to the surface and gasp in great gulps of oxygen, but he fought it. Instead, he rose slowly, letting air through his teeth to alleviate the burn in his chest.

He saw that he'd been right. The boat, which turned out to be a 2008 Beneteau 37, did hide him from view.

"What's your name?"

He looked up and saw, leaning over the boat's side, a head of blond hair backlit by the sun to create an almost blinding halo. He could just make out her face in contrast and tell that she was fond of piercings.

"Yank. What's yours?" He held out his hand.

She shook it. "Mindy. What were you doing chasing that man?"

"He has something we need." He changed the subject. "You sound like you're American."

"San Diego."

"Oh yeah? Where?"

"Do you know San Diego?"

He grinned, enjoying the moment talking to an undoubtedly beautiful San Diego blonde on the tip of the Sea of Cortez after the end of a motorcycle chase to catch a superhuman Zeta facilitator. He knew San Diego like every SEAL knew San Diego. He could tell her about so many places. But telling her he knew San Diego he might as well say to her, *I'm a U.S. Navy SEAL.*

"No. Never been. Is it a nice place?"

She frowned. "It's boring there."

"Not so boring here."

"Oh. It's boring here, too. It's just that sometimes I see things like you flying through the air."

"Oh, really? So this happens often?"

She made a face. "Or something like it." She turned back as someone called her name from on deck. "Listen, I have to go."

"Okay."

She disappeared for a moment, then popped her head back. "We're going for some fuel. If you can hold on, we'll bring you into the marina."

"That sounds good, Mindy," he said.

She tossed a set of boat fenders over the side, one with a trailing line. He submerged except for his face and grabbed the line. Soon, they were putting into the marina on the Beneteau's diesel engine. Once they reached the docks, Yank let go of the line then dove, only coming back to the surface when he saw the lighted slats above him. When he did, he wished he hadn't. Where the water in the lagoon was clear, down here was a collection of dirt and soot and trash, filmed over from lack of a current.

It took him half an hour to make it to the end of the marina. It took him another half hour still to make it back into town. Thankfully the Baja sun dried him quickly. Another twenty minutes found him rapping on the gates of the hotel they'd occupied, where he hoped to link back with Ramon.

Laws came to the gate, chewing on a piece of fruit.

"Wondered what happened to you. Ramon and the other guy were back here an hour ago. We're about to get started."

Back here? Started? What was going on?

Laws let him in, then locked the gate behind them. He patted Yank on the back. "Have fun out there?"

"Er... yeah."

"Good. Excellent. Here, have some mango," he said, handing over a half-eaten piece of fruit.

Yank took it, but didn't want to take a bite. Instead, he held it awkwardly as they entered the pool area. And what he saw there drew him up short.

15

CABO SAN LUCAS. DUSK.

Walker crouched on the roof. He had his SR-25 close by, already mounted on a tripod and the scope calibrated, but he'd also stashed an HK416 at either end of the roof under ventilation hoods. He wanted to be able to move when needed, and when moving, he wanted access to a weapon. He'd also placed motion detectors synced to his MBITR on the rooftops, so that anyone attempting to climb in the dark would be detected by a blistering alarm sent through his earpiece. He was as ready as he ever would be. He just had to wonder if what they had planned below was about to get real loud.

Holmes and Laws had disassembled the wood from the cabana. They ran the center pole so it crossed above the pool and joined the roofs on either side of it. Hanging from the pole in three places were Jaime Gonzales, now out of his dress and in his underwear, Juan Carlos, in his underwear and seventeen shades of pissed off, and Mike Sanchez, member of the Knights Templar, former U.S. Army Special Forces turned banger for the mafia. The ropes were affixed to their ankles. Their hands were tied together behind them, then also tied to their ankles, making their backs arch painfully.

Jaime and Juan Carlos hung like dead fish, while Mike Sanchez was having a fit.

"—you fuckwads think you're doing? I'm an American. You can't treat me like this!" Sanchez had a tanned bald head with a tattoo of the U.S. Army Special Forces symbol on the top. He had tattoos all over his chest and arms, but his back was a clean canvas. He wore UFC board shorts and had silver nipple rings.

"Now, Mike," Laws said, in a style Walker had come to recognize. As their intelligence specialist, Laws often took the lead on interrogations. Walker remembered how he'd interrogated the Chinese mafia member in San Francisco on Walker's very first mission and how he'd gently coerced the guy into talking without ever making an overt threat. Laws was good at what he did. "How do we know you're an American when you're over here representing the concerns of a Mexican narcotrafficking mafia?"

"I am no Mexican narco mafia man."

Laws walked over to a table where he had a bottle of tequila, a bowl of limes, and some ice. He combined these in a blender, pulsed it for a few moments, then poured the contents into two large margarita glasses. He handed one to Holmes, who was sitting in a chair watching the events, then sipped his own.

"Mmm. This is good," Laws said, smacking his lips together. "Wish I had an umbrella, though."

The Templar wormed furiously on the ropes. "Hey, I'm talking to you!"

Laws sipped again, turning to Holmes. "What do you think? More ice next time?"

Holmes sipped regally and nodded.

"I said *hey*!" As the Templar moved on the rope, the cinch around his ankles and hands became tighter. "Ow, fucking hurts." His entire demeanor changed as he asked, "Can you loosen this?"

Laws looked happily at the other two.

Juan Carlos shook his head. "Fucking *cabron* motherfucker won't shut up."

Laws turned to Ramon. "Was he this difficult when you found him?"

"This kind was born difficult. But no, it was an easy thing to do."

Laws shook his head. "So disappointing."

"What?" Mike asked, afraid to move any more than he had to now that he'd discovered what the movement would do.

"Michael James Sanchez, formerly of Seventh Group. Last seen speeding down the All American Expressway out of Fort Bragg and suspected to be carrying five kilos of uncut Colombian. Graduate of the Q Course, 2005, combat diver, military free-fall parachutist course, blah, blah, blah. Graduated as an 18B, Weapons Specialist. Tours to Panama, Bolivia, and Colombia." Laws turned to Holmes. "Now we know how he got the coke. When an Army CID investigation pinned you as the center of a new drug network in Fayetteville, you were gone." Laws sipped at his drink. "And lookie, lookie, we got a cookie. Here you are."

Sanchez's face was beet red. "I don't want to go back."

"Really? Seriously?" Laws appeared confused.

"No. Not at all. Please, don't make me go back."

"Like I said—disappointing. Is this what they taught you at SERE school? To beg for your life?"

"Dude, seriously. Who *are* you guys?"

Now it was Holmes's turn to answer. "Sorry, chum. Need to know."

Sanchez glowered for a moment, then seemed to realize something. "It's the shorts. I should have known. You're fucking SEALs."

Laws turned to Yank, who held his HK416 loose in his arms. "Did you know that you're a fucking SEAL?"

"I'd know it if I was fucking, sir."

"I thought so." Back to Mike. "You I don't like." He snapped his fingers to J.J. "Lower him please."

J.J. let the rope loose until Mike's head was below the water, then pulled him back up so only his hair touched the surface. Sanchez shook his head and gasped.

"You other two. I know you speak English so let's not play

the game where I say something and you pretend you don't understand. Here's the deal. We have three people and only one free pass out of here. We need an answer. The first person to answer correctly gets the pass."

"What happens to the others?" Juan Carlos asked, his eyes narrow.

Laws sighed. "It's like when you go to buy a luxury car. If you have to ask the price, you can't afford it."

"Then what do you want to know?" Juan Carlos asked.

Laws sat down in a chair beside Holmes and sipped his drink. No one said anything for a time. Finally, it was Mike who broke the silence.

"Dude, would you just fucking tell us what you want to know?"

Laws shook his head. "You have to tell me."

Mike made an unintelligible sound. "How can we tell you what you don't know?"

Laws shrugged. "It's going to be pretty fucking sad if you don't know. Here we thought you did. If you truly have no idea why people like us would be stringing up people like you, then I'm afraid you're going to have to pay for our mistake."

Mike bitched and moaned and tried to weasel for the next ten minutes. Jaime and Juan Carlos looked at each other but said nothing. Laws calmly made more virgin margaritas for him and Holmes. J.J., Yank, and Ramon sat back and watched the situation carefully.

16

HOTEL BOUTIQUE CASA POBLITO. LATER.

Walker was the only one doing something. He'd seen them earlier, but had written them off because they didn't seem to be moving in his direction. But while he'd been paying attention to the show below, they'd managed to inch closer and closer until they were half a block away. There were five of them. Gangbangers. In their teens. Each had a piece tucked into their pants, revealed only when they turned, their shirts flaring to show the weapons nestled at their waistbands.

He moved low across the roof to the Stoner, got prone, and examined them through the scope. It was immediately obvious that they were trying not to look directly at the building. Using a series of sidelong glances, they kept their eye on it, though.

Walker decided that they needed to know a little about what they were about to do before they did it. He could just put a round through one or all of them, but would probably lose *good guy status* if he did. So instead, he sighted and slammed a round through the bottle the lead boy was carrying. The sound of the glass breaking in the street was louder than the sound of the suppressed round leaving through the silencer screwed into the end of the SR-25's barrel.

The bangers scattered, three running full-speed back up the

street. The other two, including the one who'd held the bottle, ducked into doorways.

Walker waited a second for one to poke his head out and look. When he did, his large brown eyes went wide as a round tore into the stucco mere inches from his head. He took off after his friends.

"Walker, report," came Holmes's voice.

"Five potentials. Four scattered. One left. They know something's going on here."

Walker listened as Yank was ordered to the roof, and then they were both commanded to secure the perimeter. When Yank arrived, he reported what he'd seen. They each took an end of the roof, switching to infrared when the sun had set, all the while listening to Laws take the mafia men to school.

17

CABO SAN LUCAS. SWIMMING POOL. LATER.

It was Juan Carlos who spoke next. "It's about the girl, isn't it?"

Laws smiled broadly as he sat in his chair, legs crossed, drink in his hand. "Isn't it always about the girl, J.C.?"

The Gulf Cartel man didn't smile, nor did he indicate that he thought the comment was even remotely funny. Instead he shook his head. "This is a mistake, you know."

"A mistake to take the girl, or a mistake to know about it?" Laws leaned forward. "You see, I don't think you took her. None of you. But what I do know is that you're all wired so tight into the day-to-day activities of this town that nothing passes through Cabo without your knowledge."

Juan Carlos's eyes flicked to Ramon. "Did you ask this one?"

Laws glanced at Ramon, whose face remained placid in the creeping shadows of the night. "He's the one who helped us find you."

Juan Carlos sneered. "Of course he did. I wouldn't expect the likes of him to do anything else."

"But you know about the girl. You admitted it." Laws uncrossed his legs and stood. He handed his glass to J.J., who took a sip and made a face, expecting to taste liquor.

"We all know about the girl," Juan Carlos said.

"Then why didn't you say anything?"

Juan Carlos and Jaime closed their eyes.

Laws stepped closer. "Come on, Mike. Talk to me."

"Dude, you know what El Diablo right here is going to do to us once we talk, right? That fucker is going to kill us as sure as I'm hanging here."

"You mean, Ramon?" Holmes glanced at the man. "No, he won't."

"Yes, he will," Jaime said with absolute conviction.

"No, he won't, because he's going to travel with us to wherever the girl is, which will give you time to pack up and get out."

The others opened their eyes and seemed to exchange some unspoken agreement in their gazes. It was Juan Carlos who spoke for them. "*Leprosos.*"

"What?" Laws creased his brow. "You'll have to excuse my Spanish. It's a bit rusty. Did you say *leprosos?*"

Juan Carlos nodded.

Laws turned to Ramon. "Does he mean lepers?"

Ramon stared hard at Juan Carlos. "It's what it means, but I don't understand it."

Laws made a face. "Lepers as in their skin rots and their fingers fall off? Lepers like in the Bible kind of lepers? Those kind of lepers?"

"Are there any other kind?" Holmes asked. "Find out where they took her."

"Where'd they take her?" Laws asked, rounding on Juan Carlos.

"The mainland. They took her by boat."

"Yeah, but where?"

It was Jaime's turn to speak. "They came from Alamos. We tracked them as they left, but didn't think nothing of them."

"What do we know about Alamos?" Laws asked Ramon and J.J.

J.J. shrugged. "Old city. Colonial."

Ramon nodded in agreement. "About six hundred klicks."

"And the giant fucking fish?" J.J. asked. "Ask him about the giant fucking fish that doesn't exist."

Jaime tilted his head. "Lots of strange fish in the Sea of Cortez. Could be anything."

They were interrupted by a strangled cry from the roof.

Holmes leaped up and ran to the front gate, where he immediately began to open fire with an HK.

J.J. tied off the hostages to keep them from drowning, then ran to help. Laws grabbed his rifle and checked the rooms to make sure no one was breaking in through the barred windows. Ramon stood staring at the three dangling cartel members.

18

CABO SAN LUCAS. ROOFTOP. NIGHT.

Walker saw Yank turn a man into a pretzel, then hurl him to the street below. But he didn't have a moment to admire Yank's graceful martial-arts skills. Instead, Walker ducked a knife to his own face, then brought his hand up and grabbed his attacker's throat, simultaneously pulling and squeezing, until his opponent had no choice but to drop his weapon and try and free himself. Walker kicked out, sending him twisting to the street to join his cohort. He landed with a wet sound and didn't move again.

Walker wasn't sure how the attackers had made it to the roof. Although it was really too much area for two men to cover, they should have noticed. Probably the combination of the activity on the streets and listening to the interrogation near the pool had conspired to create the perfect window for the attackers to pass through. They'd survived this time, but the next time they might not be so lucky.

Walker heard the sound of gunshots from below, which meant they, whoever they were, were trying to breach the front gate. The shots weren't suppressed and sounded like nines.

"Ghost proper, this is Ghost Four, we have beegees on all sides, closing in. Recommend regrouping at point Bravo."

"All Ghost, this is Ghost proper, bug out. I repeat, bug out to point Bravo."

It was now officially every man for himself. That said, Walker had the sniper rifle and a duty to make sure the other men made it. He scanned the streets, counting five, ten, fifteen bodies moving from the north. Another ten were moving from the south. They'd seriously underestimated the effects of capturing these Mexican mafia facilitators. Triple Six had unintentionally disturbed a narcotrafficking anthill.

Yank dispatched one more man; then he was over the side, carrying his own battle into the streets and alleys.

A burst of nonsuppressed automatic fire blasted through the night like a volcano eruption. Triple Six had arranged to pay the police to look the other way, but this was too much to pretend not to notice. The police would be coming most *ricky tick* now that the sounds of the battle were carrying toward the tourist areas.

Walker ran across the roof, aiming for the front of the building. He glanced into the courtyard and saw that the ropes had gone slack. All three men were floating in the pool, dead and drowned. Not supposed to have happened.

When he reached the front, he saw a group preparing to rush the doors. He shouldered the rifle and immediately opened fire, taking most of them down in controlled three-round bursts. Those who remained scattered, as the combined weapons of Holmes, Laws, and J.J. forced them back. Seconds later, the three ran out the door and into the street.

Walker lay prone and followed their transit, only once having to fire during their retreat to stop a pursuer.

The others had escaped. The only problem was that he was alone now. He collected the alarms and shoved them into a pack. He glanced again into the courtyard to see if he'd missed anything. He'd yet to see Ramon, but that guy had a way of moving faster than expected. Except for the three bodies, the courtyard was empty. Strange that they were dead. It wasn't like anyone on the team to kill so indiscriminately. He found his way to the back side of the roof, and after checking, let himself down. He crept to the corner and looked out. A single man stood in the middle of the road preparing to fire at the backs of Holmes and the others. But as Walker watched, a blur ran into the man, slowed to momentarily reveal the figure of Ramon, then sped on. The man stood for a moment, then fell, a knife solidly in his back.

19

CABO SAN LUCAS. EARLY MORNING.

Triple Six met in a warehouse along with J.J. and Ramon. No one was badly wounded, although Laws and Yank had their share of bumps and bruises. They briefed each other on what they'd seen. That all three mafia members had been killed was an issue, but there was no one to firmly blame. Although J.J. was the last one left with the tied-off ropes, Ramon was the last one in the courtyard. It didn't take a genius to speculate the rest. Looked like Mike Sanchez had gotten it right after all.

How they'd been discovered was also of no interest to them. It'd been bound to happen. They could have papered the streets of Cabo with dollar bills and still had someone check them out. The money, combined with the sudden and very public abductions of several prominent cartel members, was enough to get every wannabe-lone-ranger-gunman running to their aid. After all, if they were rescued, how much would their rescuer be rewarded?

But they did have two problems. They'd been forced to leave most of their stuff behind and J.J. had found out that his boat had gone missing, which meant that they had no obvious way to cross the Sea of Cortez.

As far as resupply, they could have weapons, ammunition, and equipment delivered by an NSW support team within eight hours, but they didn't want to stay in place to wait for it. Time was ticking and every hour, every minute, every second might make the difference between the girl's life or death. As it was, they felt like they'd finally made a break and didn't want to lose their lead.

Ramon came up with one possible solution. He knew several smugglers with ships. They could stow away beneath the waterline and make the mainland in twelve hours. Add an additional three-plus hours to travel by road to Alamos, and it was an almost fifteen-hour trip.

Too long.

Too much could happen in fifteen hours.

They had to figure out a way to shorten the distance. Twenty minutes and a few shouted negotiations later, Holmes had the solution. They made it to a quay beyond the resort area and rendezvoused with the Mexican navy. A CB 90 combat boat capable of forty knots waited for them. Once they boarded, it tore away from shore, heading roughly due east, at a steady thirty-seven knots.

The SEALs found spots both on and below deck to sleep. Ramon, on the other hand, found himself incapable and tossed around like a wet cat.

Two hours after the sun rose, the CB 90 slowed. An MH-53 Pave Low helicopter bearing Mexican military idents appeared, flying low over the water. It flared above the rocking vessel and ropes uncurled, with Palmer rigs at each end. Each SEAL slid into a rig, as did Ramon, and the helicopter took off, turning and heading into the sun, the men dangling like hooked fish above the choppy water.

One by one they were hauled in. Once all were inside, Holmes greeted the senior man aboard, Major Carlos Navarre. They'd worked cross-border operations near Arizona less than a year ago and had a grudging respect for each other's work. Navarre had owed Holmes a favor, though, for letting several *federales* go free who were knee-deep in a Zetas cartel plan to use chupacabras to transit drugs across the border. The release of the federal cops hadn't sat well with Holmes, but then the politics of Mexico were different from the politics of America.

The Pave Low was a retired U.S. Special Forces helicopter, capable of carrying thirty-seven soldiers with a top speed of two hundred miles an hour, around the world if air-refueled by C-130s. In this case, they had enough fuel to make their destination. They also probably wouldn't need the firepower, which was too bad. It was always sad to waste the potential violence of three M134 miniguns, each one capable of raining six thousand 7.62mm rounds on a target.

Ramon was the only one not at all happy. His white Cubavera slacks and shirt were covered in blood, soot, and dirt. Not that there was a men's clothing store around. He'd have to stay in them until they reached civilization.

Laws, Yank, J.J., and Walker sat on the floor, alternating one side of the helicopter or the other. Their legs almost reached the other side. Ramon joined them, letting himself down easy on the perforated metal floor.

Walker's comment, "Welcome to the SEALs," was met with a sour grimace and anger-filled eyes.

Each SEAL still had his SIG Sauer P229 and HK416. Navarre provided reloads for these, along with reloads for Walker's SR-25. Vitamin packs and energy drinks were passed around, while Laws checked the unit's MBITR communications equipment.

Holmes, who'd previously called SPG and NSW to coordinate a reissue of equipment at Alamos to replace what they'd had to leave behind, contacted Billings and brought her up to speed. She was on her way to a meeting at Langley to provide them more support and would let him know the results.

In the rear of the Pave Low, far away from the others, Yank got Walker's attention. "Can I have a second?" he asked, speaking low and eyeing the others.

"Don't even have to ask, Yank. What's up?" Walker had his Stoner apart on his lap and was wiping sand from the parts.

"The mission—is it always like this?"

"Like what? Filled with crazy supernatural shit?"

"Yeah. Like that."

Walker reattached the barrel, then the sound suppressor. "If it was a regular mission, then they'd use regular SEALs."

"But we are regular SEALs."

Walker glanced at Yank and smiled. He'd thought the same thing many times and had only recently come to terms with it. "I see it like this, Yank. Do you remember screening and selection?"

Yank nodded, thinking of the three-day battery of questions and exercises each man performed prior to selection to become a U.S. Navy SEAL.

"There were so many questions no one remembers what they asked. But the psychs had a method to their madness. I'm not sure what it was. Maybe they try and figure out which ones of us have the capacity to accept the supernatural. Maybe they're looking for folks who won't freeze, because even a SEAL might freeze if he comes face-to-face with a vampire."

"Have you seen a real vampire?" Yank asked with awe.

"No. I'm just using that as an example. The point is, they decided based on our answers to their questions that we were the best candidates for this special unit." He finished snapping the Stoner back together. "There's another side to that argument."

"What is it?"

"What if we're the ones who answered the questions wrong? What if all the really good SEALs go to the teams and Triple Six gets us. The rejects. Sort of like Kelly's Heroes."

Yank's gaze touched briefly on the other men before turning back to Walker.

"That was something Laws said to me," Walker said. "It makes a certain amount of sense."

Yank nodded but didn't say anything.

"I guess my point is that we'll never know. We just have to Charlie Mike until Holmes says quit."

"Everyone hold on," Holmes yelled. "We have incoming rounds."

Yank and Walker stared at each other for a moment, then scrambled for a handhold.

20

SOMEWHERE DARK AND PUTRID.

The stench was unbelievable. Part roadkill, part earthy loam, the odor had been with her for days. She could neither see what it was nor touch the source. They'd kept her blindfolded, even in the dark. They'd thrown her in the trunk of a car, then moved her onto what felt like a ship. She'd retched uncontrollably for hours, the combination of the rolling darkness and the constant smell sending her into fits of purging. Her own vomit fueled even more retching until she was shaking and dehydrated, too weak to move away from her own mess. She was stable now. Sometime between when she'd been sick and now, she'd passed out. When she'd awoken, she was clean, wearing a full-length, lightweight dress, and lying on a flat, unmoving surface.

But her hands were still tied.

As were her feet.

And even clean, with fresh clothes on, the stench was unbelievable.

She understood what had happened. She'd been kidnapped because of who her father was. She could also make out some of what her captors were saying. Her mother had taught Emily her native Spanish before she'd passed away from breast cancer. Emily had been too keen on trying to be as white as her blond-haired Barbies to pay attention to her mother's instructions. She regretted she hadn't been a better student, not to mention a better daughter.

With little else to occupy her mind, she'd thought about the events of her capture for a long time. A giant sea creature had taken her. What it was, she didn't know, but it hadn't hurt her. It had merely taken her a mile or so down the beach and left her adrift, where a boat had picked her up, disoriented, and crying.

Why hadn't they just taken her from the beach? Why not from her hotel room? It made her wonder if it wasn't a signal for her father.

With little else to do but think, she twisted and wound around the problem, her mind going in a thousand directions.

Anything to keep the smell at bay.

Anything to keep the fear away.

21

SOMEWHERE OVER THE SEA OF CORTEZ. DAWN.

The MH-53 Pave Low bucked like a wild mustang. The SEALs had grabbed on to the netting attached to the sides and locked their legs together, but Ramon wasn't so lucky. He was tossed about before he was able to grip the netting. The Pave Low slewed to the right, then dived down.

Walker shut his eyes to hold off the dizziness.

The copter's M134 miniguns ripped the sky wide open as they made life miserable for someone in the water somewhere below.

"What the hell is going on?" Yank yelled to no one in particular.

Walker wanted to know the same thing.

Holmes listened to his earpiece, then said, "Smuggler boat. They have a fifty-cal."

A fifty-cal wouldn't do much damage to the Pave Low, not unless it got a lucky shot. Although Walker wasn't sure of the altitude, they were probably nose on the target now, the M134s still blazing away.

The whine of the engine changed as the Pave Low turned toward the sky. The miniguns ceased firing and they heard several pops from the belly of the Pave Low.

"Antimissile measures." Holmes's eyes widened. "Hold on—incoming!"

Walker was reminded once more how vulnerable he felt. Flying in a helicopter always seemed like riding in a tin can. At least on the ground or in the water he had some control over his life. But here in the sky, surrounded by metal that someone else was driving, he might as well be rolling downhill in a barrel.

An explosion rocked the Pave Low to one side, almost sending it tumbling. Everyone's legs left the floor. What they didn't hold on to flew into the wall, including their rifles, their pistols, ammunition, and anything else that wasn't tied or nailed down.

Ramon spun in the air, howling.

When the helicopter righted, everything that had been slung into the air came back down. The SEALs growled in pain. Yank especially, as the butt of his rifle came down within an inch of his manhood. This time Ramon was able to grab hold of the netting. His eyes were wild. His face was sea green.

Then the Pave Low spun in a one-eighty so fast it made them dizzy. The miniguns opened fire again, shoving several thousand pieces of lead into something that very quickly exploded.

"Mistral missile just missed," Holmes said. "Launched from a smuggler security ship."

Walker tried to remember which missile was a *Mistral*. It was French. It was man-packable, and could be fired from the back of a boat. It also had high-density explosives with tungsten balls. Pretty awesome little system that could very easily bring down a Pave Low and ruin everyone's day.

More rounds from the miniguns and more explosions. World War III was happening right outside the airship and they didn't even have a window from which they could watch.

Finally the miniguns stopped firing and whined down to nothing as they spun to a stop.

Major Navarre sauntered out of the cockpit, grinning like the king of the world. "*Pendejos* thought they could take us on. Look at them now. Fish food." He laughed and patted several of the SEALs on the shoulders. "I hope we didn't scare you," he added.

Walker exchanged a glance with Yank. The FNG from L.A.

looked terrified. Still, as Walker watched, Yank gulped back his fear, hid it beneath a mask of macho, and laughed with the others.

Yeah, the FNG would fit in quite well. The secret was that it wasn't about whether someone was afraid, it was more about how they dealt with their fear.

Walker joined in with the others, laughing good-naturedly. He'd rather be punching the good major, but instead he laughed. *Ha ha. Funny. Hilarious. Just don't fucking do that again.*

22

NORTH ISLAND NAVAL AIR STATION, CORONADO ISLAND. EARLY MORNING.

YaYa had no earthly idea where he'd left Alice. He was pretty sure he hadn't killed her, but he couldn't be certain. Although there wasn't any proof either way, there were flashes of memory and she was nowhere in them.

Road-raging down the 5.

Flashing a gun at a motorist from Minnesota.

Stuffing his head into a bag of cheese curls in a convenience store south of San Clemente and barking at the clerk.

Parking his car and running back and forth across the highway next to the famous sign of a father, mother, and child running across the highway, just north of the Border Patrol checkpoint near Oceanside.

Snapping at the ocean, kneeling on the sand, his fists in front of him.

Howling at the lights on the Coronado Bay Bridge.

And now here he was, soaked to the bone and dripping water, outside of a building on Coronado Island with a sign out front labeled CORONADO PEST CONTROL. Where was he and how had he gotten here?

His arm pulsed hard enough to bring him to his knees. He looked at it and saw that the infection had not only spread to his entire forearm, it now occupied the fulcrum of his elbow. It was green and blue and purple. Neither color by itself could be good. Together they had to mean that something colossally bad was happening.

He looked up again. Pest control?

Then he remembered. This was his home. It was where he both worked and lived. Inside was what they affectionately called the Mosh Pit. And he was wet because he'd lost his ID somewhere and couldn't get on base the usual way. How far he'd swum or how long he'd swum was a question he couldn't answer. He was a SEAL, so swimming was the least of his problems.

He punched in his code and went inside. An Intelligence Specialist First Class sat slumbering behind the reception desk. He awoke with a start.

"Oh, I didn't know." The guard glanced down at a line of photos. "Chief Jabouri, sir." He stood stiffly.

YaYa waved him back down and staggered through a door into the interior of the Pit. He passed a glass-enclosed bookcase that held the logs of the unit. Across from it and around a corner was a cryptobiologist's dream. Trophies from past missions and pieces of creatures adorned the wall like a supernatural big-game hunter's wall of pride. Horns, heads, even a taloned six-fingered hand jutted from the wall.

He staggered to one of the couches in the room and fell hard into it. He cradled his wounded arm and whimpered. A climbing wall stood behind him. Far above, near the skylights, was netting that they'd used to improve their balance. Dorm rooms were behind and to his right, while on top of these was a workout room and the kitchen.

After staring at the wall for a good ten minutes, he forced himself to his feet, walked over and retrieved the six-inch claw. It had belonged to a *qilin*, one of the chimera creatures they'd encountered on the mission to Myanmar. He grabbed the claw in his right hand and placed it on the swollen tissue of his left arm. He gritted his teeth and sliced the skin open.

The pain drove him to his knees. He cried out.

The door to the Pit opened and the IS1 came running. "You okay, sir?"

YaYa roared, "Get out! Leave!"

The IS1 stared at the bloody scene for a moment, then reluctantly hurried back to where he guarded the entryway.

YaYa gasped as blood and pus seeped out of his arm. It smelled of sickness and death and made him gag. Instead of covering the wound, he squeezed the edges, trying to pump more of the nasty substance out of him. As bad as the arm and the pain made him feel, he felt better now than he had before he'd lanced the wound.

He found his way to his feet and made it to the bathroom in his dorm room. He got in the shower fully clothed and let the warm water cleanse him of his journey. He held the wound to the water and watched as more and more pus slid free.

He felt himself slipping. Something beyond his understanding was going on and he couldn't stop it. And worst of all was that his team needed him. Even now they were probably hurling themselves into harm's way without him. They might be wounded. They might be in need of his electronics expertise. They might just need his firepower. And here he was, standing in a shower back at base and crying over an infection in his arm.

A few moments later he turned off the shower and stepped out. He slipped out of his clothes and stood at the sink, dripping. He grabbed a bottle of aspirin and opened it into the sink. With his right hand, he punched the pills until they were mostly powder. Then he grabbed a handful of the substance and wiped it on the open wound. It had an immediate dulling effect. Then he grabbed a length of gauze from the medicine cabinet and wrapped it tightly, taping the ends and the middle to ensure it wouldn't slide or twist apart.

Finally clean and dry, he changed into mission clothes. He got online and contacted SPG through their secure server to let them know he was mission ready. Then he sent an email to his father. His old man had never wanted him to join the military, much less become a SEAL. His father had wanted him to become a holy man like himself. He wanted him to better learn the teachings of Allah and live a better life.

Allah is in our blood, he'd cried. *You can't fight against blood.* Such was the old argument.

YaYa believed that he could be a better man by being part of society. He also believed that the world needed positive Muslim role models. It seemed as if every time Mr. and Mrs. Caucasian or African American saw a Muslim, the first thing they remembered was the loss of the towers. The tragedy was certainly a horrific cultural mnemonic, but it shouldn't serve to define all Muslims.

So while his father would prefer they become reclusive and live among themselves, YaYa believed that they should open their mosques and reveal themselves as the peace-loving, God-fearing, good and caring people they were.

Although he hadn't actually spoken to his father in over a year, he'd started to write him. Since Myanmar they'd begun to email more. Even if it was mere bits and bytes instead of actual spoken words, it was nevertheless a form of communication. At this point, YaYa would take what he could get.

So he began his email with *Dear Father.* And then he sat there. What was he going to say? How was he going to describe his feelings?

Dear Father, I think I am sick.

Dear Father, I might be possessed.

Dear Father, maybe you were right.

Dear Father, I miss you.

23

LANGLEY, VIRGINIA. CENTRAL INTELLIGENCE AGENCY. MORNING.

Alexis Billings sat in a chair outside the office of the deputy director for operations. Unlike the director, who was a political appointee and a very public member of cabinet, the deputy director of operations held the real power. Deputy Director McKinney was just such a man. A career CIA agent, he'd risen through the ranks as reports officer, desk officer, clandestine support agent, field agent, chief of station at half a dozen embassies. He knew the field. He knew the process. He knew the personnel. And most of all, he knew that someone in the agency had fucked up.

To what degree, Billings didn't know. All she knew was that she'd received a call late last night from the agency representative to the Sissy, asking her to meet with the deputy director regarding some information the agency had in reference to the missing senator's daughter. Her agency counterpart, Sarah Pinborough, also of Bryn Mawr, had ended the call with the words, "They want to explain why they knew about the possibility of a threat but never let anyone know about it."

All Billings had to do was let the senator know that the CIA had advance knowledge and didn't do anything about it and he'd come down on the agency, the director, and their budget like a metric ton of bricks. Everyone knew it. Which was why she was sitting in Deputy Director McKinney's waiting room at 5:45 A.M.

"The deputy director will see you now," said the prim woman at the reception desk.

Billings stood, smiled a thanks, then strode to the executive door. It was opened before she got to it by an assistant, who beckoned her in.

"Ms. Billings," the deputy director said, standing behind an impressive oak desk. The wood was burled like a tiger's eye and glistened in the fluorescent light of the room. "Please come in."

McKinney was unimpressive to look at. Middling height, slightly overweight, balding and with a weak chin, he might have been more at home as the night manager of a grocery store... which is what made him perfect for his job at the agency. Too many people had made assumptions about his appearance and his intellect and found themselves at a severe disadvantage because of it.

His suit was Savile Row, navy blue. He wore a Yale tie. He stepped out from behind his desk and offered a manicured hand. "So happy you could see me at such an early hour."

"So glad to be seen," she said curtly. "It's my understanding you have something you wish to say."

"Ready to get to the point, I see." He gestured to the other man in the room. "May I introduce Mr. Christopher Golden. Mr. Golden directs our many special projects groups, including the one we've provided to directly support your special unit on Coronado."

"Triple Six," she said. "Your SPG has provided good service." She saw no reason not to give credit where it was due.

Golden nodded, but didn't say much. He didn't even step forward to accept her proffered hand. Instead, he had a pained look in his eyes. Where Deputy Director McKinney glistened with refinement, Golden seemed a pale reflection. Although physically the men could have been cousins, Golden wore an old wool suit that had been dry-cleaned so many times the fused wool gleamed through. His nondescript tie was of an uncertain age and the collar of his white shirt had long ago broken down and lost form. The deputy director was a manager. Golden was an intellectual.

Billings pulled her hand back and smiled softly. Golden didn't want at all to be here. She wondered if he wasn't being offered as a sacrificial scapegoat. She'd be ready for it if that was going to be their strategy.

"Please, sit," McKinney said. He waited for Billings to do so, and then he sat himself. "Would you like some coffee? I've taken the liberty of having some made."

As if on cue, the door opened and the prim woman at the front desk came in carrying a silver service. She placed it on a table to the right of the desk that seemed positioned there for just that purpose; then she left.

Billings let McKinney pour a coffee for her and himself, then waited until both of them had a moment to taste their own. She knew the silence was an intimidation device. She was to fill it either with her own chatter, or by looking at the awards and decorations of a man who'd served the agency for more than thirty years. Presidential letters and congressional awards festooned walls among African spears and World War II Nazi memorabilia.

She gave the silence three minutes, then snapped it.

"I understand you have some information about the disappearance of Senator Withers's daughter. I also understand that you've known about the possibility far longer than any of us."

"To the point." McKinney smiled, but it was more of a grimace.

"So tell me the story. Might as well start with 'once upon a time,' because if it doesn't end with 'and they lived happily ever after,' someone is going to lose their job." She glanced at Golden. "Maybe multiple someones."

McKinney steepled his hands and leveled his gaze on her. Although he was the deputy director of operations for the CIA and she was merely a staffer for a senate committee, she held the power of the purse in her hands. Not that she could vote or sit in any of the meetings, but the senator counted on her for advice and had not taken it on only one previous occasion, much to his own chagrin.

"Once upon a time there was a cartel in Mexico who wanted to change the world," McKinney began. "This is the beginning. Golden, please tell Ms. Billings the rest of the story."

Golden, who'd refrained from coffee, began to pace. Billings had to turn in her seat to watch him.

"So here's what we know. Emily Withers has been under surveillance on five occasions by unknown members of Los Zetas. The last three of these occasions were during her previous visits to Cabo San Lucas."

He paused here for Billings to take it in, then continued.

"On four of the occasions, we had agents conducting counter-surveillance and providing overwatch for the senator's daughter."

"And on the fifth?" Billings asked.

"Our agent went missing."

"When?"

"When what?" Golden asked.

"I asked you when you found out the agent went missing," she said in a voice that could cut ice.

Golden exchanged a look with McKinney, who nodded, then stared out his fifth-floor window at the Potomac.

"Before Emily Withers arrived in Mexico."

"And you didn't send anyone else?"

Golden murmured something.

"What was that?" she asked.

"We didn't think it was necessary."

Billings turned toward McKinney and repeated the words. "'We didn't think it was necessary.' I see."

McKinney turned away from the window and back to her. "There's something else."

Billings smiled sweetly. "Isn't there always?"

Golden sighed as he wrung his hands. Finally he spoke. "Through an electronic intercept of Zetas cartel data, then by sifting through millions of conversations and information pulls, we found reference to a program, not unlike that which Hitler pulled, partnering with the Thule Society and searching for powerful supernatural entities and weapons that would help them create their own ideal world order. It appears that the Zetas cartel, in an attempt to pull themselves out of the quagmire of cartel-on-cartel violence, has devised a plan to reinstate old Aztec rule, and with that, a return of the old gods."

He let the words hang in the air for a few moments. To anyone else but the deputy director and the administrator, such an assertion might seem criminally negligent, if not insane. But they'd heard and seen enough to know that the threats posed by the universe toward freedom were not only those made by man.

"One more thing," Golden said, shifting his gaze momentarily toward McKinney.

"Another one still?" Billings remarked.

Golden nodded. "You might remember the tattooed skin suits your men found first in San Francisco and then Imperial Beach. The man in Myanmar used the suits to channel the spirit of a Chinese demon. The nature of the suit, being made from the skin of many, plus the very nature of the tattoos, created a tool with which the man could wield the power of but not be killed by the creature he was trying to channel."

"One of the suits went missing," she said. "We traced it to the Zetas."

"You traced it to the Zetas," Billings repeated in a monotone. She let it sink in for a moment, then asked, "Did you not make the connection between the suit and the Zetas' desire to harness the old gods?"

Golden frowned and seemed put out to have to explain himself. "The two things weren't connected," he said tightly.

"Just like Emily Withers isn't connected."

Golden frowned and shook his head. "We see no connection at all."

Billings glanced at McKinney before she spoke. "And how did you come to that determination? Magic 8-Ball? Rock-paper-scissors? The flip of a coin?"

The older man sputtered and fluttered his hands. He looked to his boss, but Billings had been right. The man was a sacrificial lamb.

"Answer her, Chris."

The director of Special Projects Groups wanted nothing more than to not answer. It was clear that he believed that the whole process was beyond him. Still, he reluctantly answered. "There is no connection."

Billings drilled in. "Are you telling me that no one in any of your special projects groups believed there might be a connection?"

"There were some," he said with exasperation. "But that's just coincidence. We're working on pattern analysis that—"

"What was that you said?" Billings placed the saucer and coffee cup on the edge of the deputy director's expensive desk. She held up a finger. "Did you say coincidence?"

McKinney's expression became pained and he stared into the depths of the paperwork on his desk.

"Did you say coincidence?" she asked again. "Like when a man gets sniper training by the Soviets and then assassinates an American president? That kind of coincidence? Or like the coincidence where several groups of Arab-speaking flight students are learning how to take off but not how to land? That kind of coincidence?"

"Don't you dare!" Golden said, his fists shaking. "That was the FBI—on both occasions."

Billing stood. "Don't *you* dare, Mr. Golden. Don't pretend you didn't have prior information regarding each of those events. Perhaps the FBI is as much a scapegoat as you are. Let me say this one time. When we discuss supernatural objects and the desire for someone to use something to become greater than they have any right to be, we do not use the word *coincidence*. One man's coincidence is a Triple Six mission."

She turned to McKinney and held her hands together in front of her as ladylike as she could. "This is what's going to happen. The CIA is going to render every possible assistance necessary. Everything we need you will provide. Aircraft. Satellites. Assets. Recruited agents. Everything. You will send an SPG for direct support. Wherever the mission is, I want the SPG there on hand, regardless."

Golden sputtered again, but she wasn't looking at him. She was looking at the deputy director.

"Now," she said. "Who will be my point of contact?"

"Chris, assign a POC for Ms. Billings."

Golden's outrage was obvious. After all, she'd stepped into his analytical universe and bitch-slapped him.

"Chris," McKinney repeated himself. "Who is going to be Ms. Billings's POC?"

"Jennifer Costello. Her team will be available to you. We'll let her know she has all the assets at your disposal."

"My team is heading into Alamos, Mexico. Do you have a safe house there? Assets? As in recruited agents?"

"We're getting into some pretty sensitive operational activity, Ms. Billings." McKinney delivered the statement with a smile.

She returned the smile. "I'll let Senator Withers know you've decided not to provide what is necessary to save his daughter."

His smile fell. "I see how this is."

"We also want the freedom to move in Mexico. Please see that this is coordinated. Contact whomever you need to within the Mexican government. Cash in whatever chits you need."

His smile fell even further.

"I have every confidence in you, Deputy Director. As does the senator. When he gets his daughter back safe and sound you'll be one of the ones to whom he will demonstrate his goodwill. If things turn out to be unfortunate, well, then I'm sure he'll make sure you're taken care of as well. Thank you for your time."

The trick to walking out of a room was to never look back, no matter how badly she wanted to see the looks on their faces. The only face she saw was that of the prim secretary, who gave her a look filled with secret approval.

24

MINAS NUEVAS, MEXICO. ABANDONED MINE. MORNING.

The Pave Low landed at an abandoned mine northwest of Alamos. They didn't want to land inside or near the city. The presence of the military helicopter might spook whoever it was who held Emily Withers.

They had three cars waiting for them when they arrived. Each one had been a magnificent piece of Detroit machinery when it was built in the 1970s. But cartel wars, the high Mexican desert, and the complete absence of car washes had transformed the three Cutlass Supremes into studies in Bondo, baling wire, and the inventiveness of the needy.

Triple Six split off and prepared their weapons. Entering the city, they didn't know if they would be going in hot or not. Their MBITRs were working, which wasn't necessarily the norm. The systems were made for intrateam communications, and there were some things the SEALs did that they had trouble surviving. Like a Low Altitude/Low Opening (LALO) night jump into a Myanmar rain forest and the predictable ricocheting off of trees.

All the HK416s and SIGs were in good working order, although Yank wished he had more firing pins in the event he had to make field repairs. Only Yank and Walker had body armor, which wasn't as Holmes would have liked. The good news was that their resupply was on the way. Billings had been given carte blanche, so the expectations were high. She'd also arranged for a safe house and access to agency assets. Holmes wasn't sure what she'd said to get this sort of support, but he wished he'd been in the room.

Major Navarre and one of his men left in one of the cars and headed into Alamos to reconnoiter. They'd get them to the safe house, but would have to pull back after that.

After they left, Holmes brought the men together and asked Ramon and J.J. to join them. They gathered around an abandoned VW Beetle that had been opened like a tin can and used for a fire pit.

"YaYa and Hoover will be joining us soon. Nice to have the team complete," he began. "Not sure how Hoover will deal with Ramon, but we'll have to be prepared."

"Hoover?" Ramon asked.

While the team had been at the Naval Special Warfare Training Center in New Orleans, Hoover had undergone his yearly checkup at the military dog hospital in Bethesda, Maryland. They hadn't seen Hoover in two weeks. Holmes couldn't help but note how getting him back felt right.

"Our dog," Walker said. "A Belgian Malinois."

"You have a dog?"

"We've had a dog on the team for more than two hundred years. It's something we do," Holmes said.

"Glad to see YaYa, too," Laws added. "Boy hasn't been the same since Myanmar."

Holmes nodded. "It was his first mission. Sometimes it takes a while to work things out."

Everyone turned to Yank.

"What's everyone looking at me for?"

Laws and Walker laughed. Each had been the FNG at one time or another and remembered the uncertainty of their first mission. "We've also been given an agency contact and a safe house," Holmes said.

"Now that's something new," Laws said. "Not often the agency will give us the results of their hard work at espionage."

"Who owns the safe house?" J.J. asked.

"Some organization called the Order of the Sacred Knights of the Virgin of Valvanera." Holmes turned to Ramon. "Have you heard of them?"

Ramon laughed out loud. "The Knights? Your agency has them as your safe house?" He shook his head.

"What's wrong with them?" Laws asked.

"Nothing I suppose, if you don't mind their ideas of grandeur. Each of them is like a Don Quixote."

"Can they be trusted?" Holmes asked, showing uncertainty at what he was hearing about the Knights.

"Can a crazy man be trusted?" Ramon shrugged. "I don't know."

"What else do you know about the Knights?" Holmes asked.

"It's a monastic order created to protect the Virgin in Mexico. Much like yourselves, I suppose, except they don't work for a country, but rather an idea."

"When you say the virgin, do you mean the Virgin Mary?" Yank asked.

"Yes and no," Laws answered. "The Virgin in Mexico is a little different. There's an incredible native influence on the belief of the Christian Mary. Take the Virgin de Guadalupe, for instance, or Our Lady of Guadalupe."

"Is that the one they see on walls and in toast?" Walker asked.

Laws nodded. "It's what you call a Marian apparition, which is an appearance of the Virgin Mary. Now this goes all the way back to Cortez, who was a native of Extremadura, Spain, which is the original home of Our Lady of Guadalupe. He had a basilica built on Tepeyac Hill, outside of what is now Mexico City, but what was then Tenochtitlán, the capital of the Aztecs. The importance of the location is that the basilica was built on the Aztec temple worshipping the goddess Tonantzin, which early Spanish priests used to convince the Aztecs that the two were one and the same."

"Another Aztec reference," Walker said. "There seem to be a lot of them."

"You're right," Laws nodded. "The Virgin of Guadalupe as she exists in Mexican culture is a syncretic icon. If you worship one, you're worshipping them both. We're also two days away from the Fiesta de Nuestra Señora de la Balvanera. More than ten thousand worshippers will descend on the city in devotion of the Virgin. Incidentally, *Balvanera* is a colloquialization of Valvanera. For the last seven days there's been a growing procession going back and forth between Aduana and Alamos, carrying an image of the Virgin with them."

"My guess is that the Knights are going to be involved in that," Yank said.

"So amidst the celebration and the extra ten thousand people we're supposed to find the senator's daughter?" J.J. asked. "They sure don't make it easy."

"Might not be as hard to find as you think," Ramon said. "If the Knights are tied into the town, they'll know where *leprosos* could be. It's all a matter of understanding the lay of the land. So yes," he said grudgingly, "maybe having the Knights on our side is a good idea."

"So it's *our* side now," Laws said.

"As long as we don't go back up in any fucking helicopters, yes!"

25

The Knights called a three-hundred-year-old shoe factory home. Although it hadn't manufactured shoes since Pancho Villa rode a horse, it was still structurally sound and had been retrofitted with enough rooms to house the members of the monastic order and their guests, when they had them.

Navarre had returned after his reconnaissance. The town was a madhouse, but since the procession was moving back and forth along a different road, their journey to the safe house would only take twenty minutes, if that. Everyone piled into the three cars and drove into Alamos.

Navarre, Holmes, and one of Navarre's men were in the first car. J.J. and Laws were in the second car, and Walker, Yank, and Ramon were in the third. Walker was behind the wheel, and as he drove into town, he recognized the difference between Cabo San Lucas and Alamos immediately. There was no dichotomy between the haves and the have-nots here. Or if there was, it was undetectable from an outsider's point of view. One of the things he noticed was the lack of foreign tourists. This was a Mexican town for Mexicans, not for tourists. The streets were clean. The buildings were free of graffiti. Many of the buildings were older than America, or at least as old. Two-, three-, and four-story whitewashed colonial buildings lined the streets. Families moved together dressed in colorful clothing on wide sidewalks. They passed numerous open-air markets, vegetables gaudy with their healthy color.

The SEALs circled the Plaza Principal Alamos, which was ringed by towering royal palm trees. A gazebo was set in the middle, much like in an American park, from which a *norteño* band was playing ranchero music. The plaza was framed on one side by the *Iglesia de Alamos,* the great church with a seven-story-tall steeple along one side. Made of hand-cut stone, this was the home of the Virgin of Balanera.

They headed south about six more blocks. Walker saw Navarre's man wave him into an alley. He turned in, drove about ten meters, then turned again into a private lot behind an immense U-shaped building which had to be the old shoe factory. Walker left the keys in the car. He and Ramon exited and moved quickly inside.

They were led to a large room on the first floor that seemed to be both a common area and an area of worship. At one end of the sixty-by-thirty-foot space was a raised dais on which a shrine was built. Walker only glanced at it, but was still able to make out many different paintings of a Virgin inlaid in the wood. Instead of taking the time to examine the shrine, he was more interested in the men arrayed before it.

He counted roughly thirty men of all ages. They were as different as could be, but the one thing they all shared was a fire in their eyes. They didn't wear a uniform, but several wore the same necklace—a stylized cross and sword encircled with what looked from his vantage to be barbed wire.

"Is this all of them?" one asked Holmes. Rail-thin, the speaker had the stature of a military officer. His head was shaved and he had tattoos on his neck descending past his collar, disappearing beneath his shirt. His skin was dark like a mestizo's, or perhaps, thought Walker, an Aztec.

"This is it," Holmes said.

The man turned toward the SEALs, J.J., and Ramon. He gave

Ramon a long hard look, then smiled the sort of smile a man wore who was unused to humor. "Welcome to our, how you say, military camp... no, castle. Yes, welcome to our castle." His English was rough, but understandable. "We are the Cuadrilla de los Caballeros Sagrados de la Virgen de Valvanera."

"Order of the Sacred Knights of the Virgin of Valvanera," Laws translated.

The man nodded. "I am Colonel Inquisidor Juan Francisco de la Vega and these are my caballeros." He turned to point to the men, who in unison slapped their chests with an open hand and saluted in the British style.

The members of SEAL Team 666 snapped to attention and returned the salute in the American way. They held it for as long as the caballeros held theirs; then as one, everyone returned to ease.

"Today *mi casa es su casa*," Vega said. "You'll forgive me if we cannot be of much help. My men have been guarding the Virgin." As he said the word, he and his men crossed themselves. "We have two more days and then we can help you. But for now, please be at home."

Then he turned, said a quick word to Holmes, and left. Most of his men left with him, except for a handful. These came and introduced themselves, but Walker didn't remember their names. They showed the SEALs to their quarters and then left them alone. Holmes gave them about half an hour to wash and relax before he had everyone meet in the common room downstairs.

"Here's where we're at," Holmes told them. "SPG is inbound along with YaYa and Hoover. They should get here within the next three hours. During that time, we're going to try and find the *leprosos*."

"Any news on who they might be?" Walker asked.

Laws and Holmes exchanged glances. Laws answered the question. "Yes. Vega knows of a group operating in Alamos. Since the group doesn't seem to be posing a threat to the Virgin, the Knights have left them alone. Still, they know who the *leprosos* are and why they're here."

"So who are they?" J.J. asked. When everyone looked at him, he spread his hands. "What? Am I the only one who wants to know?"

"They are called Los Desollados. They are neo-pagan Aztec worshippers."

"What does 'Los Desollados' mean?" Yank asked

"It means the Flayed Ones," Ramon interjected. "I should have known." He shook his head. "Those *putas* are bad news. They worship Xipe Totec," he said, making the X sound like an S. "They believe that all the bounty comes from their god and by him giving his skin to them for sustenance, they are then able to live."

"They. Eat. Skin?" Yank asked, pronouncing each devastating word carefully.

Ramon nodded. "And they wear skin, too—but not their own. This is why the facilitators probably thought they were lepers. They were wearing the skin of the dead and much of it was probably falling off."

Walker shook his head in disbelief. He'd seen enough to where this sort of thing shouldn't faze him. But cannibalism, especially the eating of a person's skin... it just seemed so absolutely primitive that he felt himself becoming sick at the notion.

"The idea as I understand it is for the Flayed Ones to wear the flesh for the period between the new moon and the full moon as it rots. During the full moon they step free from the skin, symbolizing rebirth and shifting from the old to the new."

"And these are the ones who have the senator's daughter?" Yank asked.

"We're going on that premise," Laws said. "The good news, if there's any to be had after Ramon's explanation, is that we know where the Flayed Ones are headquartered. They're holed up in an abandoned asylum on the western edge of town."

"Of course they are," J.J. said, frowning. He repeated the words "abandoned asylum" before shaking his head.

"Walker and Yank," Holmes said, pointing at the pair. "You're currently the only ones with a full kit. I want you on site and ready in case the Flayed Ones decide to move before our new gear gets here."

"Clear, sir."

"And the rest of us?" J.J. asked.

"We need to come up with a plan of attack. I have some rough schematics of the building. If Emily Withers is in there, we might only have one chance at getting her out safe. We're not going to turn this into another Waco. We'll get information, then act."

Laws nodded as he made eye contact with each and every member of the team. "Getting her out dead is the same as not getting her out at all."

26

After they'd made their plan of attack, J.J. went to scrounge some space for the incoming personnel and Ramon took off on his own accord. He was going to see if his contacts were still around, he said.

Holmes and Laws were the last to leave. Laws could tell that Holmes was worried about something. "What is it?"

"Couple of things," Holmes said. "First is the SPG coming. I don't like the fact that I'll have a group of analysts I'll need to take care of. That's bad enough, but to also have—"

"Walker's girlfriend," Laws said, finishing the sentence. Although Walker had tried to keep it low-key, the team knew about his relationship with the young CIA gal in charge of the SPG. "Yeah, I've been thinking about that too. Not that there's anything we can do about it."

"I agree. Billings probably thought it was going to help to have them on-site, but this isn't the other side of the world. This is Mexico. We have contacts here and could reach out in real time to get whatever support we need."

"She meant well, I suppose."

"The road to hell is paved with meant-wells."

Laws wiped his face, as if he could wipe away his fatigue. "We

127

just have to count on them to keep it professional. Do you want me to talk to them about it?"

Holmes shook his head. "If they don't know how to be professional now, no amount of words is going to make them grow up."

"I think we'll be all right, boss. What was the second thing?"

Holmes glanced around to make sure they were alone. "Do you feel like we might be getting led by the nose?"

"Glad I'm not the only one."

"So you felt the same way." Laws nodded. "In some ways, this is like the Myanmar mission. We could just never get ahead of it. Just as soon as we'd get more information, that would spur us on to another part of the mission. This is starting to feel the same."

"Not at all what we're used to. Remember the 'cabras on the border?"

"Simple mission. We knew there were chupacabras around. We used intelligence to project where they might be. We put men on target, found the 'cabras, then took the beegees down."

"Right." Holmes tapped the wooden table. "Where's our projection? Where's our intelligence? We have Ramon giving us information that we should already have."

"Ramon is another issue."

"He sure is. But with regards to the intelligence, if the SPG is going to be with us then we're going to keep them busy. I want multiple projections regarding the possible plight of Senator Withers's daughter. Enough of this reacting. I want to do some proacting. We'll have them input all the raw data we have, then have each of them use their thirty-pound brains to figure it all out."

Laws couldn't agree more. If they could get ahead of the mission then maybe they could get to the girl while she was still alive. Still, there was the issue of Ramon. Neither Laws nor Holmes trusted him. Not only because he'd been a hit man, who by necessity was morally bankrupt, but also because they couldn't be sure of his loyalty. As far as they knew, he worshipped at the Church of Ramon and anything else was secondary. That wasn't the way the

SEALs operated. They placed themselves second to the mission.

Holmes stood to go, then stopped and snapped his fingers. "One more odd thing."

"Odd?" Laws chuckled. "What isn't odd about anything we do?"

"Nevertheless, this is odd. I got a sitrep regarding the recovery of the 'cabra bones, which for the most part are on their way to the Salton Sea facility. Looks like it went off without a hitch. YaYa secured the items, then left with Agent Alice Surrey. Remember her?"

"Yeah, I remember. So what's so odd about that?"

"She's missing."

"Missing?"

"Yeah."

"You're right. That *is* odd. What did Jabouri say?"

"He said that she dropped him off at LAX after the mission."

"Do we know if that's true?" Laws asked.

"No reason to doubt YaYa, so no, I haven't checked. But they found her SUV on Manhattan Beach... empty."

"They found her SUV on the beach? What was she doing there?"

"Like I said, it's odd. And it probably has nothing to do with us, either. Alice is a successful NCIS agent. I'm sure she's made a lot of enemies."

Laws was getting a feeling that worried him. "I'm sure that's it. Still, I might have a word or two with Jabouri. Perhaps he can shed some light on this *odd* situation."

While Holmes went to check on J.J.'s progress, Laws remained sitting, thinking about the need for better intelligence, Ramon's loyalty, and the odd circumstance of the missing NCIS agent. He had a policy about odd circumstances and coincidences, and he was hardly ever wrong.

27

ABANDONED ASYLUM. AFTERNOON.

After dressing in the local style of cotton shirts and slacks loose enough to hide their body armor, Walker and Yank made a circuitous route, traveling on the back alleys and side streets, to their final destination, the abandoned asylum believed to house the cult that wore other people's skin.

They hadn't received too many looks, probably a benefit of the pending religious holiday. Any other time, a blond-haired gringo and a young black man might have received a modicum of attention, but the locals were too busy celebrating or trying to make money at their open-air markets to care.

Each of them carried packs. Walker's held a broken-down SR-25 and Yank's held a broken-down HK416. When they finally found the asylum, it was a two-story building at the end of a street called La Esperanza on the very edge of town. The nearest buildings were two homes, a farmhouse, and a tractor garage. These were to the west of the asylum and none of them offered a decent prospect for surveillance. Forest grew to the north, east, and south edges of the asylum, making those directions even more difficult to surveille from. Their only hope was to move back to a higher location.

A five-story building sat at the corner of Quinta del Rey and

La Unidad. The first floor was a *farmacia,* but it was closed for the holiday. They didn't hear anything from the other floors and had to assume they housed some sort of businesses as well. They waited for the right moment, then scurried up the fire escape, pulling it up with them as they made their way to the top. Once on top of the building, Walker checked for possible avenues of countersurveillance, but didn't find any place high enough to observe them as they were watching the asylum. They established an observation post with Yank providing security.

Once that was done and they'd checked in with Laws, they settled in for a long wait. The target building was L-shaped, with the leg of the letter pointing toward the west. This created an entryway that had an overhang. The front doors were chained shut, meaning there must be a different avenue of ingress and egress, probably from behind. Half the windows had been busted out. A third of the ones left had been boarded up. Walker began the task of dialing in the windows at full magnification to see if he could detect any movement from within.

"Know what's been bothering me?" Yank said, breaking the silence.

"What's that, noob?" Walker had the bipod in place to support the barrel. At these distances, even the smallest shake would throw his vision off by meters.

"Ramon and that Juan Carlos guy. I forgot to tell Holmes or Laws, but they were fast."

"You shouldn't forget those things. Still, Ramon is a lycanthrope. Maybe that makes him faster than normal."

"What about Juan Carlos? He wasn't a lycanthrope."

"How do you know?"

"If he could change into something, then why'd he let himself get caught? Why'd he let himself get killed?" Yank asked.

"Yeah. And him getting killed bothered me, too," Walker said. And it had. The idea of killing the informants went perpendicular to his idea of right and wrong. "Either Ramon or J.J. killed those men. If I was to bet, it had to be Ramon."

"Well," Yank said, drawing out the word. "We don't know a lot about J.J. either, but I'm with you. I'd trust a former SEAL before I would a mafia-hit-man werewolf any day."

Walker thought he saw movement in a window. He zeroed in and stayed there a moment. Yeah, there it was again. Nothing specific, just something moving across the interior. He held the scope in place to see if he'd be able to get a better picture.

"When you say fast, how fast are we talking?"

"Comic-book fast."

"What do you know about comic books?" Walker asked.

"What? Can't a black kid from Compton collect comics?"

"I have to admit, I find it hard to believe. There is a stereotype, you know."

"Yeah, no shit. The way LAPD profiles, I know all about stereotyping. Just the same, I did read my share."

Walker laughed. "Where? In juvie?" But he noticed that Yank wasn't laughing. He took his eye off the scope long enough to glance at the other SEAL. Yank had the look of a killer. "Whoa. I didn't mean... were you really in juvie?"

"Three weeks."

"What for?"

"Part of the Scared Straight program. My parent, the one who gave me my name, decided I should go to jail for a little while so I could see how bad it really is. He arranged this before I'd even lived with him for a day."

"Seems like it worked out."

"Oh, it worked out all right. Scared the shit out of me. The way the program worked was that I'd only be in general population during meals. The rest of the time I was in my cell. It just so happened that the only thing they had I could read were comics. Not the cool Marvel comics, with the X-Men and all their shit, but some old DC comics. Not even good ones like *Batman* and *Superman*."

"Don't get me started on *Superman*," Walker said. "You talking *Wonder Woman, The Flash, Rubberband Man*... those?"

He turned back to his scope and found his sight picture again.

"Yeah. There were a couple of Lobos in there. I liked him. Got to love it when they make a brother an alien and he gets to beat up on Superman."

"Lobo isn't black," Walker said definitively.

"What… because he's blue-skinned you decide he's white and not black?"

"No, idiot. I'm just saying he's not black. He's blue."

Yank shook his head as if the secret of the universe had been laid out in front of Walker and he'd missed it. "You'll never understand. Being a brother is something you get on the inside. Lobo is a brother. Pure and simple."

There it was again.

"They also let me read a *Green Arrow* and about a dozen *Swamp Thing*s."

"Which version?" Walker asked as he tried to will whatever it was to stop by the window so he could pinpoint it.

"Alan Moore version."

"That was early eighties. Good stuff."

"How'd you like *Swamp Thing?*"

"At first I was like, what do I care about some tree with legs that talks and roams about the swamp. It just didn't interest me."

"Yeah. *Swamp Thing* is like that at first. But then it grabs you."

"With both hands. It was the whole idea that there were all these superheroes everywhere, but it was *Swamp Thing* who knew that there was this little girl who was the Antichrist and was going to destroy the world."

"The quintessential underdog."

"Man, he was underneath the underdog."

And finally, there it was. The figure of a man standing by the window. He seemed to be almost looking at Walker. He stepped closer to the window and Walker could make out features. It was a man, but his face was all wrong. It was as if he were… wearing someone else's face and it was a little lopsided.

"Got them. I see one. Radio it in to Laws."

Now it was Walker's chance to see if he could find some more. He wanted to know which rooms they were using. He also wanted to know if there was a concentration of them, or possibly where the girl was being held. He spied another seven figures over the next hour and managed to locate a central area on the third floor that had the most activity. But that was as good as he was going to get from his vantage point.

It was time to get a little closer and see what was on the other side of the building. Plus it was getting dark, which would be to their advantage.

"Ready to play a little Swamp Thing?" he asked Yank, as he stood.

"What? Oh, we going to go peek into windows?"

"Something like that. You game?"

"Definitely."

"Work your way to the south and then behind. We'll be in contact the entire time and I'll make sure your way is clear."

Yank decided to leave his HK topside. He was out of place enough being himself. Carrying a combat rifle would probably raise even more suspicion. He rechecked his coms, made sure his do-rag was covering it, then hurried back across the roof. He was over and gone in less than a minute.

Walker watched as Yank moved across the street and down the lane. When he got to the intersection that led straight into the asylum, he turned right, then ducked behind the tractor garage. Walker scoped the way clear and let Yank know he could move to the tree line.

"Nice and easy. Pretend you're a lost Mormon instead of a U.S. Navy SEAL ready to hurt someone."

"Never seen a black Mormon before," Yank said softly as he strolled toward the tree line.

"Must be two or three," Walker said, intent on ensuring Yank made it unnoticed. "Maybe even four or five."

The foliage wasn't thick. A combination of acacia and some sort of evergreen made for something just thick enough to camouflage a person, if not hide them completely. Someone looking close could see the outline of a human form, but then again no one should be looking that close. If they were, it would finally give Walker a chance.

"Okay. Move slowly. Don't disturb any of the outer branches." Walker doped the scope for a closer look at one of the windows in the asylum. He only had a view of the edge of the side windows and couldn't see inside, but he was almost certain he saw—"Stop!"

Yank halted about six feet into the tree line.

"Step a foot to your right. A little more. Good." Walker swung the scope back to the window. Did he just see what he'd thought he'd seen? He silently begged the person in the window to show himself, but whoever it was had some decent discipline. "Okay. Move carefully now. You might be watched from the window on the second floor. Third from the right."

Yank took a few more steps, careful to always keep a trunk between him and the building. "Someone in the window. Shit— they have a bead on me."

Walker thought quickly. First of all, anything they were about to do would absolutely destroy any element of surprise. But that paled in comparison with getting Yank hurt, or worse. Walker had three choices, four if you counted doing nothing as a choice, which he refused to consider. Yank could either move away slowly, move away quickly, or move closer.

"Talking about the speed again. You said Ramon was running at comic-book speed. Was it like the Flash?"

"What? Yeah, definitely like the Flash. Or in the movies when someone runs so fast that it can't possibly be real? It's like that. Are you sure now's the time to talk about this?"

"Here's what I want you to do. I want you to be the Flash. Not like the Flash, but become the Flash. Zero to sixty in less than a second."

"Which direction?"

"Toward the building." He heard the silence and knew Yank wanted to ask a question but knew better. This was all about trust. "Wait until I say *move,* then don't stop until you're kissing the wall. Roger?"

"Wilco."

Walker sighted in on the window. He let his fingers flit near the bullet drop compensator knob, but decided against it. The range was close enough where the feet per second would make up for any drop before the round reached the target. If only he had a target to shoot. He sighted in, ready to fire.

"Ready. Set. Move."

Yank shot out of the woodline toward the building faster than Walker would have thought possible.

A sound suppressor appeared from the window. As it tracked Yank's movement, more of it showed, until a clear half of the rifle barrel was visible. Problem was that it couldn't keep track of Yank. That is, until Yank stopped moving. As Yank hit the wall, the shooter leaned out to take a shot. That's when Walker sent two rounds into the target's face.

"Catch," he said.

The shooter dropped the weapon, a Soviet-era Dragunov. Yank managed to catch it, then stepped out of the way as the shooter toppled to the ground next to him.

"Pick up the trash and bring it here," Walker said. "Move."

Yank tossed the man over his shoulder and ran back into the woods. With the long rifle in one hand and his other holding the dead shooter in place, there wasn't any way to hide what he was doing. So he made the best decision possible. He buried the rifle beneath some brush, then adjusted his grip on the dead man so it looked as if he was helping home a drunk friend.

As if on cue, a car approached on the road and drove by the pair. Walker watched through his scope, aware that if needed, he could reach out and silence whoever it was who would raise an alarm. But those in the car merely glanced at Yank and the dead man, then kept going. Once they passed, Yank crossed the road with one of the man's arms draped across his shoulder. Never mind that blood from the dead man's chest wounds had soaked Yank's shoulder.

When Yank reached the bottom of the fire escape, Walker left his post and went down to help him bring the body to the roof. By the time they'd pulled the man over the lip and onto the hot tar, both he and Yank were breathing heavily.

They laid the man out on the roof and examined him. About six feet tall, he wore black dickies, black combat boots, and a black T-shirt beneath an untucked gray button-down shirt. A shock of black hair rested above a youthful face. Partially hidden by the collar were several tattoos, each of them a stylized Z.

Walker and Yank looked at each other.

"Zeta?" Yank asked.

"Yeah, I think so," Walker said. But what was he doing in a building suspected of being a hideout for an Aztec cult believed to be holding the senator's daughter? "You thinking what I'm thinking?"

"Yeah. Where's Ramon?"

"We need to report this. Holmes is going to want to know."

Yank removed a camera from his cargo pocket and took pictures. They couldn't take the body with them, but the tattoos could indicate who the man was and who he worked for. He snapped photos of each of the tattoos; then they removed the man's shirt, where they also catalogued another dozen tattoos, many of which sported a Z of some sort. When Walker was finished, they waited for J.J., who was coming to replace them. It took twenty minutes, but once he arrived, both Walker and Yank bugged out, making their way back to the home of the Knights and prepping Laws over the MBITR as they went.

28

ALAMOS, MEXICO. KNIGHTS' CASTLE. DUSK.

By the time Walker and Yank returned, the shadows of the buildings had already darkened the streets. With the dark came a chill uncharacteristic of the coastal areas. The nature of the high desert allowed for forty-degree temperature swings, and although it was probably only sixty-five degrees, it felt much colder since they'd spent the day in the upper nineties. When they went in the door, they headed straight to a coffee urn they'd seen when they'd left. They had just finished pouring themselves steaming cups of joe when they heard a friendly bark.

Both Walker and Yank turned.

A Belgian Malinois with a short, light tan coat beneath a harness came spilling down the stairs toward them. For a second, it seemed as if the dog might tumble into a mess of broken legs, but she was too much the athlete. She caught herself, skidded a few steps, then plummeted toward them, grinning from ear to ear, tongue flailing.

Both Yank and Walker tossed their cups aside as if they were primed grenades and knelt, where they were momentarily assaulted by the happy welcome of the team dog, Hoover. After a moment, they stood, Hoover wagging her tail furiously and lapping up the coffee they'd spilled.

"Hoover, show some decorum," YaYa said from the landing. Walker noted that his color was a little off, but he seemed otherwise okay. It looked like he might be shaking off whatever bug it was that had him. "Hey, guys." He walked over to them to shake their hands. As he passed Hoover, lapping up the coffee, the dog moved out of his way.

"YaYa, how's it hanging?" Walker asked, extremely pleased to not only see YaYa, but to have the team once again back together. "You go see the docs at Balboa?"

YaYa nodded. "I hear I missed the sea monster."

"Wasn't no sea monster," Yank said. "Some giant salamander is all."

YaYa blinked and gave Yank an odd smile. "You don't think that's a sea monster? Giant Aztec salamanders in the Sea of Cortez are pretty far-fucking-fetched."

"Everyone here?" Walker asked, looking up the stairs.

"If you mean did your girlfriend come on the mission to hold your hand, then yes. She's up there setting up computers with Musso and two others."

Walker both wanted to see her and didn't, and in that moment he knew not only that she was a distraction, but that there'd come a time during the mission that he'd be off his game because of her. His hands made fists of frustration at the thought of it, and when he realized this, he made them relax. He turned to see if anyone was watching him, and of course everyone was. He knew he was turning red.

The question was did he go upstairs or stay downstairs. He was saved from making the decision when Holmes spoke into his earpiece, commanding him and Yank to report. Walker indicated for YaYa to follow, and all three of them passed several Knights lounging in wide leather chairs on the way to a room set up as the command center.

Like the other rooms, this one had fifteen-foot ceilings made of wood. A map of Alamos was up on one wall. On it were strings tacked to different sites; those led to index cards with notations.

On the opposite wall was an even larger map of Mexico, broken down by region. This had more strings, making it look like a giant cat's cradle run amok. Several tables were set against one wall, while a central table dominated the space. On this were arrayed a variety of weapons, ammunition, and clips, including several swords and odd-looking daggers.

Holmes stood next to Laws, both of them chatting with Ramon. Behind them making a notation on an index card sat Vega. As Walker and the other two SEALs entered, the men looked up.

Laws spoke first. "Welcome to the command center. Not exactly NORAD, but it'll do."

"Let's see the pics," Holmes said.

Yank pulled out his camera and began to scroll through the collection, pausing at each one.

"Recognize this one?" Holmes asked Ramon, who was hovering over the team leader's shoulder, trying to see the small screen.

After a moment, Ramon shook his head. "So many kids these days want to be an enforcer. What kind of weapon did he have?"

"A Dragunov," Walker said. "Yank buried it at the scene."

This caused Ramon to think. "Pretty advanced weapon for a low-level thug. I'd have expected an old hunting rifle. The boy could have inherited it, but we'll never know."

"How do you explain that he's even at the asylum?" Yank asked.

Ramon looked as if he'd been slapped, and glanced at Holmes, who returned his gaze. Ramon made a face as he answered, "I can't. Hell, I don't have to. There are places in Mexico you can't swing a dead cat without hitting a member of a cartel, much less the Zetas, who are still one of the largest."

"It's a little bothersome that a member of the Zetas is here and you don't know about it," Laws said, stroking his chin.

Ramon sighed. "I'm on the outside looking in. I learn about things by hearing things. No one actually tells me anything."

"You mean you don't have any friends left in the cartel?" Holmes asked, feigning shock.

"No, I do. But I—"

"Then go find out why the Zetas are partnered with this group we believe kidnapped the senator's daughter."

"Right now?" Ramon asked, a confused look on his face.

"Yes, now. You got something else you have to do that's more important?"

Everyone watched Ramon leave the room, at first stiff-legged with anger, but by the time he was at the door he was cool, as if it was all his idea.

After Ramon had been gone for half a minute, Holmes gestured for everyone to sit around the central table. Once they were in their seats, he asked, "Now what was all that about when you were talking about the comic books and the speed?"

Walker and Yank glanced at each other. Walker had forgotten that anyone could hear their conversation, making the list of those listening a lot longer than he'd planned. If Holmes had the uplink switched on, that list could include even the White House. In the future he needed to remember who could be listening in before he opened his big mouth.

Seeing the grin on Laws's face, Walker realized that he knew what he was thinking.

"Ramon moves too fast," Yank began, staring at his hands. "He runs like a... cartoon. I'm not sure how to explain it without using comic books as a reference, but it's like he was being sped up and everyone else was being slowed down. It was just so out of place."

"Could it be because he's a werewolf?" Laws asked.

"The hell you say," YaYa said, surprised. "You mean that guy is a werewolf? I thought he was the agency contact."

"It appears that he's both," Holmes said.

"Fucking agency," YaYa said under his breath.

"Not unless the other guy was a werewolf, too," Yank said, answering Laws's question.

Laws looked at Holmes, then back at Yank. "What other guy?"

"The Zeta facilitator. Juan Carlos. I saw Ramon chasing him

and they were both moving that crazy fast shit."

Holmes took a moment to digest the information. When it seemed he had it right, he said, "Describe again what you mean as moving too fast."

"Fast," said Yank.

"Crazy," said Walker.

"Shit," added YaYa. "I saw the same thing in the City of Industry. The Zetas cartel hijacked the chupacabra bones and set up some sort of laboratory. Looked like they were working on the bones in some way. We had a firefight and one of the Zetas took off like he was the Flash on crystal meth."

"If this has been going on for some time," Laws said, turning to Holmes, "how come we're now just hearing about it?"

Holmes shook his head. "Do you think they're using the bones to make some sort of, I don't know, super serum?"

Laws had his fist beneath his chin, concentrating on something. "I seem to remember something in the Anasazi history about a ceremony that made them travel extraordinarily fast. I wonder if that had anything to do with the 'cabra?"

"Clearly it's a Zeta thing. We're going to have to have a conversation with Ramon. Meanwhile, get SPG on it and have them work with the techs from the Salton Sea to see if there's any truth to this." Holmes rubbed a hand against the back of his head. "So YaYa, while we're talking about your mission, NCIS is reporting an odd thing."

"What's that, boss?"

"They've misplaced an entire NCIS agent."

YaYa glanced at each of them. "Misplaced an agent? I don't understand."

"They don't know where your contact is. She seems to have disappeared."

"Do you mean Alice Surrey?"

"The very same. Know anything about that?"

Walker jerked his head toward YaYa as he noticed something he'd missed before. He felt a little something. Not a lot, but there was certainly a feeling emanating from the SEAL.

"Nothing at all, sir. She left me at the airport. Dropped me off at LAX."

"There's no record of you being on a flight, Chief Jabouri," Laws said. The use of YaYa's full name and rank made everyone sit up a little straighter.

"It was too long before the next flight, so I ended up taking a rental car and I drove to Coronado."

"Which rental company?" Laws asked.

YaYa shrugged. "One of them. I was still sick. I'm sure I have the receipt back at the Pit. What's the third degree for?"

Laws relaxed. "We're being asked some questions is all. We want to be able to back you up in case there's a witch hunt."

"Witch hunt." YaYa laughed humorlessly. "Last thing I need."

Laws's eyes narrowed; then he addressed the group. "We have about thirty mikes and then we're going to reconvene on the asylum. If the senator's daughter is in there, we need to move fast. In the interim, Vega's reinforced J.J. with several of his own men. They don't want to go in, but they'll make sure no one gets out before we get there."

29

ALAMOS, MEXICO. KNIGHTS' CASTLE. NIGHT.

Walker left the room, but instead of continuing upstairs for a reunion with Jen, he turned left and found a private corner. His proximity to YaYa had brought back a flood of memories he'd rather have cut from his brain with a steak knife.

Little Jackie Walker waiting in the pile of trash. The liquid from banana skins, coffee grounds, and rain-soaked rags seeping through his clothes, making him shiver. His teeth chattering. He feels what could be gravel or hardened chunks of dog shit against the soft skin of his bare chest. A piece of rubber he'd seen thrown away by the Hookers on Llollo Street in Barrio Barretto rests like a deflated sausage two inches from his nose. A wasp crawls inside, causing the rubber to wriggle and jump. He feels rats scurrying along the backs of his legs. When they sniff at his skin, he fights the urge to jerk as their whiskers tickle the soft underskin of his knees.

Feral.

Like a pig.

Like a dog.

He is wild and eager to gnaw on something that screams.

Walker had been possessed for a time and it had almost killed him. Now, the blood-memory of the event was used as a

144

supernatural early-warning radar, and as he'd sat near YaYa it had gone off like NORAD during a Russian multiple-nuclear-launch drill. He'd tried to define the strange energy coming from the SEAL. Walker had been unable to put it into context while he'd been close to YaYa, but now that he was away, he was able to define it. Malice. Pure. Concentrated. Malice. And for a young man whose joie de vivre was contagious, malice was the last thing Walker would have expected coming from him.

But Walker had to be sure before he went to Laws and Holmes. He didn't want to be wrong about this, so he tracked down Yank, who was trying to talk to one of the Knights about food.

"Do you speaky Englisho?" he was saying as Walker jerked him away.

"Follow me," Walker said, without further comment. Hoover fell in beside the two SEALs as they went up the stairs. He saw Jen through a doorway, working, but didn't go inside. She wore jeans and a simple white blouse, and had her red hair pulled into a loose bun. He wanted to kiss her. He wanted to hold her. But that would have to wait.

He checked the rooms on the right side until he found YaYa sitting on a bed, glaring at the floor with barely contained… malice.

Walker and Hoover went into the room first. "Come in and close the door," he said to Yank.

Hoover's ears were laid back. Her tail was between her legs. The hackles along her spine were at attention and her legs were bent, not to leap, but to cower. And if there was one thing Hoover had never done, it was cower.

When the door was closed, Yank joined Walker at the foot of YaYa's bed. The room was little more than a monastic cell. A cross hung on one wall beside a single window. The small twin bed pressed against the other. Beside it was a small table with a bible and several unopened bottles of spring water.

"What's going on?" Yank asked.

"Ask YaYa." Walker felt the buzz like an undercurrent of

electricity. It set him on edge. He brought his upper and lower jaw shut to keep his teeth from chattering.

It was clear that Yank couldn't feel what both the dog and Walker had zinging through their senses. "What's going on, YaYa?" Walker asked.

YaYa had been looking at the floor this entire time. He turned his head slowly and appraised the two SEALs with glowing eyes. He pulled his mouth into an impossible grin, the edges of his lips almost touching his ears. But instead of speaking, he chattered like an insect.

The sound sent shivers up Walker's spine, shivers that were so painful, he wanted to cry out. But he couldn't. Other than YaYa himself, Walker was the only one who knew what was going on and he had to keep his head about him.

Yank's jaw had dropped about as far as humanly possible. "The fuck is going on?"

Walker pulled his headset from where it hung at his waist, and spoke low and quick. "Break. Break. Ghost One and Two, this is Ghost Four. Come to my location now. Bring flexicuffs."

A second passed, then, "Four, this is One. What's your location?"

"YaYa's room. Second floor. Left of stairs. Sixth door on left."

YaYa had returned to normal. "What are you doing?" he asked with unnatural calm.

"Don't worry. It's going to be fine," Walker said. "Be ready, Yank."

"For what?"

No sooner had Yank asked the question than YaYa launched himself not at them, but toward the window. Glass crashed as his arm bashed through. Yank dove and caught YaYa's feet with no time to spare and jerked him back inside. YaYa ended up on the floor, his right arm gushing blood, but that didn't stop him from fighting. He lashed out with a leg and caught Yank downtown central. Yank fell to one knee, which brought his face closer to YaYa. Walker never remembered Jabouri being anything other than average in combatives, but the speed and energy delivered from his fists to Yank's head were incredible.

Feet pounded in the hall and the door swung open.

Holmes and Laws braced in the doorway.

"Possessed!" Walker cried. He grabbed Yank and hauled him backward as Holmes and Laws descended on YaYa. One grabbed his legs, the other his arms. The bed hit the wall and the nightstand overturned. Blood flew everywhere as YaYa barked and hissed, trying to shake loose as his teammates hogtied his ankles and wrists. He wouldn't give up. His limbs rattled on the wooden, impossible drum rolls of *leavemethefuckalone*.

"He's going to break his back!" Laws cried. He turned YaYa onto his stomach and cinched the ankle and wrist cuffs together. Trussed as he was, YaYa's hysterics were reduced, but his convulsions threatened to dislocate every joint in his body.

Three Knights appeared at the door, Vega in the forefront. "What have you brought into our house?" he commanded.

"We need a priest," Holmes shouted at him.

"I *am* a priest."

Holmes paused only briefly. "Of course you are. Get the fuck in here and do something about this."

"Not here. Not now." Vega gestured for one of his men to enter.

A slender guy with a plastic box in his hand stepped into the room. He slid to his knees and opened the box. He pulled free a syringe and plunged it into YaYa's stomach like a pro. The effect wasn't immediate, but about five seconds later YaYa's limbs slowed and his howling dropped to a mere whimper. After half a minute, YaYa was as still as the dead.

"What'd you do to him?" Holmes asked, sitting up and rubbing his jaw from where he'd been hit at least once.

"Put him out. Can't work with them this way. I never understand it either. They know they're going to be found out, so why fight it?" The slender guy stood and left the room.

Vega pointed toward YaYa's still form. "Have your men take him and follow Rodrigo. We have a special cell for him. A place where he won't get hurt until we have time for an exorcism."

"You're not taking him anywhere without my permission." Holmes stood, putting himself between YaYa and the door.

Vega gave as good as he got. "Then you're going to give me that permission. You brought this evil into my house. I cannot with any good intention let it go upon the free world. Now that he's here, we're going to try to get him out of his current state. SEALs or no SEALs, you must not try and stop us."

Holmes's face was implacable when he said, "Fine. Laws, make sure he's in a good place. We have to go out on mission, but once we're done, it's back here to see if we can save YaYa."

Walker and Laws grabbed YaYa and lifted him by his arms and legs. As they passed by, Holmes placed a hand on YaYa's head. "You fight that thing inside you, YaYa. Fight it like you've fought nothing else in your life."

30

ABANDONED ASYLUM. NIGHT.

SEAL Team 666, minus Chief Petty Officer YaYa Jabouri, who was currently confined to a specially designed padded cell in the basement of the building the Knights of Valvanera called their castle, waited in the tree line outside the asylum for a word from J.J., who was atop the same building Walker had used earlier. Instead of Walker performing his duties as team sniper, he was detailed to provide direct support to the close-quarters battle (CQB) that they expected to transpire. Everyone was up-armored, wore MBITRs, had nines strapped to their right thighs, knives strapped to their left thighs, and carried their HK416s sunk deep in their shoulders, barrels low and ready. Outside their armor, they wore Rhodesian military vests because of the multiple pockets for storing extra ammunition. Protec skate helmets painted black did little to protect their heads, but strapped to each of their chins was a curiously alien-looking set of night-vision goggles with four lenses called QuadEye. Four 16mm lenses reduced the need to pan left and right by re-creating peripheral vision and incorporating the multiple feeds into a head-up display (HUD) similar to those used by combat helicopter pilots. The SEALs were uplinked through Special Operations Command to allow external monitoring of each SEAL's feed during the mission. But only Holmes had the ability to receive commands, if and when someone in the cheap seats wanted to weigh in. Such a thing rarely happened, although if it did, it would surprise no one. Because they were moving to recover a serving senator's daughter, there was interest at the highest levels.

The plan was simple. They'd already had an NSW proprietary micro unmanned aerial vehicle (MUAV), the RQ-11B Raven, circling the target building at five hundred feet. Its lookdown radar was integrated into the QuadEye's HUD, and could be monitored to detect movement or to track anyone leaving the area. The Raven was controlled in real time via satellite from SOCPAC headquarters in Hawaii, with local command authority detailed to Lieutenant Commander Holmes.

In addition to the Raven, operators controlled two whisper-mode Draganflyer X6s, each carrying a multispectrum camera. These remotely operated unmanned helicopters had a six-rotor design, giving them the ability to hover in thirty-knot winds. The Draganflyers had spotted and assessed target sets through windows, helping to gather the data needed to most effectively rescue the senator's daughter.

There were a dozen Knights arrayed around the asylum to keep anyone from leaving. Reports from J.J. and the Knights indicated that there was little or no reaction regarding the missing Zeta sniper. If he'd been positioned to provide security, he must have been a singleton, or else they were a lot less organized than commonly believed.

Employing Ramon in the attack would have been a plus, but he was nowhere to be found. Walker doubted he was out looking for a Zeta connection. More likely he'd decided to bail after they asked him about the Zeta presence. His inconsistency was one reason they wouldn't make him part of the plan.

Now that it was night, Triple Six would bring more technology to bear. The combined efforts of the Raven, Draganflyers, and J.J. combined with Walker's observation through the IR function of his Stoner allowed them an almost complete understanding of the beegee positions. So far they'd counted fourteen warm bodies moving about and five lying prone. They could be sleeping, reading a book, jerking off, or prisoners. The IR resolution from this distance wasn't exact enough to do any better than that. But four of the five were located on the third floor in the same wing, so that would be their first target. Holmes figured they had thirty seconds tops before all hell broke loose after they went in.

The Knights of Valvanera had orders to shoot Los Desollados on sight. They didn't have issue with that. Although they rarely crossed paths with the neo-pagan Aztec cult, the reality of them competing for the souls of the people of Mexico, the very idea that the Virgin could lose followers to a leprosotic Old World god drove them to accept murder as their divine right.

Walker felt the familiar dryness in his mouth. He mentally inventoried his equipment. His weapons were ready. He wore ballistic forearm pads and gloves. His armor plates protected his kidneys, back, chest, and abdomen, and fit snug into the carrier. Other than the weight, he barely knew they were there. He also had three fragmentation grenades, resting in quick-release pouches.

The team's only odd uniform concession had been to wear hockey masks which covered their faces but left holes for the eyes and slits for the mouth and nose. The masks gave the SEALs the look of a group of tactical Jason Voorheeses. The SEALs normally wore the masks if they were concerned with video surveillance and for ballistic protection, but that wasn't the case here. They wanted every edge they could get, and if that edge came from scaring the lepers, then so be it.

Holmes's mask was black with a white slash across it.

Laws wore a mask with a green camouflage pattern.

Walker's mask was bloodred, to honor their fallen team member, Johnny Ruiz.

And Yank's mask, from the tried and true tradition to fuck with the new guy, was fuchsia.

No telling what the beegees were going to think when they saw Triple Six enter the room. And they would see them, because

Triple Six had decided to leave the power on so as not to give away their advantage of surprise.

"Be ready in ten, nine, eight, seven, six…" Holmes went silent as each of the team counted down themselves. Silence was their ally, and all their rifles and pistols had suppressors.

Their CQB stack included Hoover, who was in the fifth-man position. She wore tactical body armor that protected her sides and chest. Her eyes were protected by specially designed ballistic goggles.

"Move," Holmes ordered.

In the tight bunch they called a stack, Triple Six moved forward in a single file—Yank, Laws, Walker, Holmes, and Hoover. They moved in a combat crouch, weapons alternating sides. Even Hoover seemed to creep forward on alligator legs. And they were fast. Like a single beast they moved to the front door, opened it, and stacked into the well-lit room.

Yank buttonhooked to the left, searching for targets through his QuadEye. He found two, double-tapping each before they could even notice he was there.

Laws entered next, buttonhooking right. A pair of beegees stood in the center of the room, uncertain of what was going on. These belonged to Walker, who did his own double-tapping.

Holmes followed, checking the quadrants. "Clear," he said.

At first Walker thought the beegees were all wearing gilly suits—apparel worn by snipers with hanging pieces of material used to resemble foliage to help the sniper to blend in with his surroundings. But on closer inspection, he saw that it was skin… long lengths of skin. The skin appeared to be stitched into shirts and pants, draping the wearer in multiple layers. When Walker had learned about Los Desollados, or the *leprosos* as Juan Carlos had called them, and their penchant for wearing skin in honor of their god, Xipe Totec, he didn't at all think it would be something like this. Not only were they terrible to look at, with some of the skin rotting and flaking, but the stench was unbelievable. Even the zombies they'd fought days earlier hadn't smelled as bad.

Triple Six had a choice to go up to the top floor and work down, or take the left or right wing. All but one of the prone figures were on the top floor, so they stacked up the stairs, moving against the walls and ignoring any targets in the hallways.

When they hit the top floor, they moved right. They'd wanted doors to close behind them, but there were no doors to the hallway. So Holmes knelt and aimed down the hallway to the left while the rest of Triple Six stacked to the first door. Yank opened the door, then let Laws take up position one, buttonhooking into the room and taking out the beegee lying in bed. This one had removed his skin suit, which was draped across the back of a chair. He was just a man, thin, balding, old, and now very dead.

They repeated the entry into three more rooms before someone decided to put up a fight. Just as Yank and Laws entered a room, a beegee exited a room two doors down. He wore very little skin and carried an MP5. He brought it up just as Walker was turning. Walker fired first and moved toward the man as he continued to fire. He kept moving and kept firing until he was standing over a dead man. He kicked the weapon away, then checked the room he'd come from.

As he looked into the room, Hoover ran past him. Walker jerked his head back out and watched as Hoover leaped into the air, coming down on the face of another man. The dog buried her head in the man's neck and ripped upward, coming away with a meaty length of throat, showering the wall and herself in a curtain of blood.

But Walker should have been paying attention to his own piece of the mission, rather than watching Hoover. A *leproso* stepped from behind the door and stabbed at his face with a knife. The point of the blade hit his ballistic mask and slid sideways onto the buckle of his vest, across the side of a hand grenade, then down his chest, cutting through the material holding his chest plate.

Walker jerked back and as he did, he felt the plate shift, then fall free, leaving his chest unprotected. His opponent kept coming and Walker swung the butt of his weapon up, catching him in the chin. The man's eyes lost focus as he began to sag to the floor. Walker followed him down, took the knife from his loose fingers, and plunged it into the middle of his forehead. Then he reached down and grabbed his armor plate, using it to hammer the blade into the skull, once, twice, and just as it seemed he was done, he turned and hammered one last time, driving the knife to the hilt so that the blade pierced the wood floor behind his attacker's skull.

"Nice one, Ghost Four," Laws said. "But you're supposed to be wearing that armor, not using it like a hammer."

"Stuff it, Ghost Two. Ghost Four, clear the rest of the wing with Hoover, then on me. Two and Three, on me," Holmes commanded.

Holmes stood from where he'd been kneeling and made his way down the other wing, with Laws and Yank behind him. The Draganflyer operators gave Holmes guidance and the three SEALs moved down the hall until they were at the fifth door on the left. Walker reminded himself that he had his own mission and turned away just as the other three SEALs moved into the room and fired.

"Hoover," Walker said in a low voice.

The dog padded over, wearing a rakish smile and half a gallon of blood. Together they cleared the remaining rooms, finding them empty.

The entire team met back at the stairs just as all hell broke loose on their coms.

"Ramon—he's back," J.J. screamed. "And there are others! They're changing... they're—"

"What the *fuck?*" came the Draganflyer operator, now witness to something that would require a nondisclosure agreement and a week of debriefing.

Holmes linked the team into the surveillance feed. They watched from the vantage of a hovering Draganflyer as the bodies of Ramon and two other men in front of the asylum remolded, bones snapping, hair shooting across skin, mouths lengthening and fangs descending. But what came next surprised the SEALs.

Instead of turning and converging on the asylum together,

the three skinwalkers launched themselves at each other. Then Walker saw it. Not each against the others, but two on one. The two slightly smaller and lighter-haired skinwalkers were attacking Ramon, who rose on his hind legs, much like a human, and slashed one of his assailants across the face.

"What do I do?" J.J. asked breathlessly.

"Nothing," Holmes said.

Walker agreed. Ramon wasn't one of them. It might be because he was a born traitor and an assassin, either of which shared qualities with the lowest examples of humanity. How could the SEALs trust someone whose loyalty came from being a traitor to someone else? It just didn't feel right. And even as he thought it, Walker added to himself that it was more than the feelings generated by the man's supernatural ability to walk in the skin of a Mexican gray wolf.

One of the smaller skinwalkers circled around behind Ramon and leaped on the back of his neck, trying to bite down and crush the spine with his massive human-wolf-beast jaws. But Ramon, who already had one talon-tipped fist around the neck of the other skinwalker, grabbed the creature on his back and flung him bodily over his head and onto the ground.

The skinwalker landed, stunned. Ramon brought both hands to bear on the skinwalker in front of him. He adjusted his grip from the neck and placed both hands on the side of the beast's head. Even from the top down vantage of the remote-controlled helicopter, Walker saw the talons pierce the skin and skull of the smaller skinwalker. They all then watched as Ramon's muscles bunched impressively and in one quick move, he snapped the neck of the beast. But it didn't stop there. Ramon roared into the sky, the sound carrying both through the feed from the Draganflyer as well as in real time, echoing up the stairs. Then he twisted harder, ripping the head from the body. Blood exploded from the force of the manual decapitation.

The second smaller skinwalker had made it to his feet, but instead of fighting, he fled, hunched over and afraid.

Ramon roared after it, shaking the head of the first skinwalker, then hurling it after the creature who wouldn't dare face him.

Yank shifted nervously.

"Steady," Laws said.

"What if it comes up the stairs?" Yank asked.

"Then we kill it," Holmes said.

Yank nodded. "Good."

Ramon turned toward the asylum. His arms hung at his sides, each talon seemingly longer as it dripped blood. His head was down and his eyes and mouth were hidden. Walker remembered a cover of a Golden Age *Batman* that had a similar creature in a similar position, shrouded in shadow, but somehow darker than the darkness.

Then someone from inside opened fire. The camera on the Draganflyer caught several muzzle flashes coming from the open door to the asylum. Los Desollados had finally decided they were tired of all the noise coming from outside.

The rounds caught Ramon in the chest but had little effect other than to knock him backwards.

"On me, Triple Six," Holmes commanded.

He moved downstairs and the others followed, stacking down. They surprised three beegees wearing other people's skin who were converging on the stairs, looking down as if trying to figure out what someone could be firing on. The beegees should have been looking up, because the stack of SEALs didn't even pause as they put rounds into the men, sending them crashing to the floor before they knew what hit them.

As they approached the first floor landing, they saw four beegees, two barely wearing any skin, alternating fire at Ramon. Holmes ignored them and moved down the left hall. The others followed suit.

"J.J., take them out," Holmes said.

"Do I have to? I'm having fun watching them try and figure out why their rounds aren't working."

"Just do it."

The sounds of the automatic weapons' fire faltered as Walker's Stoner opened up from where J.J. was situated on the roof.

Triple Six stopped at the door to the room that held the remaining prone form. On the count of three, Laws kicked it in and the SEALs charged inside. The thing on the floor was a man, his own leprosotic flesh revealing muscle, bone, and in one place on his arm, tendon. He didn't need a suit to be a leper. He *was* a leper.

He sat up and growled and Holmes put a single round through his head. The beegee fell back on his pillow.

"What now?" Laws asked.

"We search the whole fucking place until we find something," Holmes said.

They moved out of the room and were confronted by an immense skinwalker. Walker remembered now—*Batman #255. Moon of the Wolf.*

The SEALs snapped their weapons up and aimed them into the face of the great beast. Hoover stood her ground and growled. The beast was easily a full head and shoulders taller than Holmes, the largest member of Triple Six. J.J.'s words echoed through Walker's head. *Having fun watching them try and figure out why their rounds aren't working.* Yeah, the rounds wouldn't work. They were made of lead, not silver. It seemed that some of the legends were true. He thought of his grenades and his knife and began devising a plan to slice and stuff, hoping that silver or not, an internal explosion of the TNT sort might do enough damage.

Thankfully he didn't have to get that desperate.

Unfazed by their weapons pointing at his head, the skinwalker pointed toward the floor. "Down," it said in a voice that came from the roots of the earth.

Holmes stared at the floor. "Damn. The basement."

31

ASYLUM BASEMENT.

Yank gaped into the darkness at the bottom of the stairs. His throat was dry enough so that he had to repeatedly swallow to keep his airway open, but the skin beneath his body armor was soaked with sweat. Room clearing a building full of hajjis was one thing, but the continual aromatic and visual affront of the men in other people's skins was something else entirely. He'd seen bodies blown apart, shot, knifed, gutted, hit with cars, trucks, trains, and even a tank. He'd become used to the multiple sensories of death. He'd reached the point where it was funny, in that gallows humor way only those in the military can appreciate. But there was nothing funny about someone walking around in another person's skin. Laws had tried to explain to him that it was an homage to being reborn, like a snake shedding its skin, but the difference remained that a snake shed its own skin and not some other snake's.

Of course, what was completely strange was that he was more concerned about the propriety of skin ownership than he was about the presence of a werewolf among them. A werewolf. Teeth. Hair. Tail. Howling at the moon. He felt himself coming to terms with the idea that such things were ordinary for Triple Six. Still, he was happy the wolf hadn't joined them.

"Let's go. And remember, we're live," Holmes said, meaning

viewers from Dam Neck to Coronado to the White House could be tuning into this episode of *SEAL Team 666 Kills Monsters*.

Yank was first, followed by Laws, Holmes, and Walker. The sniper was last because of the loss of his body armor. Holmes had initially ordered him to remain upstairs, then changed his mind and placed him at the back of the stack. So in the back of Yank's mind was the reality that if there was danger, he had to put himself between whatever it was and his team member if it came down to it.

Halfway down, he paused. "Switching to infrared." Yank's vision suddenly flipped to a world of contrasting grays. The bottom of the stairs was still cloaked in darkness, but as he switched on his helmet IR light, it added texture and depth to the image so the different levels of black were discernible.

He continued moving, stepping with his toe and letting the heel of the same foot down before taking another step, reducing the potential for creaks and groans from the aged wood of the stairs. Three steps from the bottom he stopped, holding up his left fist. Almost to the landing, he could see that the stairs opened to the right. To the left was a wall.

Yank let his HK hang on its sling and dug into his right cargo pocket. He brought forth a rolled metal tube. He screwed one end into his QuadEye, and held the other end in front of him. He depressed a switch on the night vision device and his vision changed from the ninety-five-degree image of the landing to a much more limited fish-eye view of the same. He stepped down and fed the metal tube around the corner, bending it to allow it to see around the angle. An image crystallized through his QuadEye, broadcast to all members of Triple Six and their external viewers, of a room with no furniture. He swept the camera back and forth to allow him to take in the entire area. For all intents and purposes it appeared to be empty... except that every now and then he'd catch a hint of movement. On each occasion, he tried to find it again, but it was as if whatever he was seeing knew he was looking and was ducking just out of sight.

"Do you see it?" Laws asked.

"Something, but I can't make it out," Yank whispered, aware of his closeness to the source of their concern.

He moved the device in a star-shaped pattern and was able to make out a figure far across the room, facing him. Once he caught the image, he stopped, pinning it through the darkness. The image didn't seem to be moving at all now, and was just standing there with impossibly long arms, twice the length of its legs and an angular monkey-like face with fangs. Yank wondered if the creature could see him. Then the image across the room did something unexpected. It reached out, grabbed the device, and tugged it. How could it reach all the way across the room? Yank didn't understand, unless it wasn't across the room, and instead right in front of the—

His head slammed against the wall as the creature grabbed the mechanism and pulled. Yank let go and wrapped his hands around his head to keep the QuadEye from being torn free, or worse, his head going with it.

"The *fuck!*" he yelled.

"Dude!" Laws shouted.

"Homunculus!" Walker cried.

Once, twice, three times Yank's head hammered against the wall before he was able to twist the device free from his QuadEye. The image of the creature disappeared with the feed and the SEALs keyed back true-life IR.

"Here's what we're going to do," Holmes commanded. "Walker and Yank take high. Laws and I will take low. Hoover will attack from the ground. And for God's sake, no one shoot the dog."

"But there's just one," Yank said, trying to shake the butterflies free from his noggin.

"There's never just one," Walker said.

"Then what are they?" Yank asked.

"Fucking Freddy-Krueger-Chucky-Stretch-Armstrong serial killers, Yank," Laws whispered. "Watch your field of fire and shoot them. Shoot them all."

Yank's already bad feelings crescendoed as he felt the others' anxiety. They hadn't been worried about the *leprosos*, nor had they been worried about the werewolf, but these homo-whatever-they-were-called creatures unnerved the hell out of them. He didn't have time to ask and he figured he wouldn't have to. After all, he was about to be in the shit.

Holmes counted to three then ordered, "Ready... move!"

Yank and Laws spun around the corner, one high and one low, sighting through their QuadEyes into an IR-lit darkness. The stark outlines of basement walls shot into geometric patterns. A table rested against one wall. But the homunculi were nowhere in sight. A shadow detailed a turn of the basement, promising the possibility of something farther in.

"Clear," Walker said.

"Moving." Laws stepped with him as they moved in a hurried crouch to the next corner.

Laws ducked his head around the corner for a split second, then reared back. "Seven."

"Of them?" Holmes asked.

"Roger. All at floor level."

Walker could feel his breath come quicker behind his mask. He became acutely aware of his missing armor plate and remembered how the homunculi had chowed down on the FBI agent in a similar basement beneath a certain Chinese restaurant in Imperial Beach.

"Ready..." Holmes said. *"Go!"*

All four SEALs spun around the corner, ready to fire—only to find an empty room. They adjusted their fields of fire, barrels traversing, trying to find a target. But there was nothing. It was as if there had never been anything there at all.

Walker felt a tingling sensation.

Hoover growled and crept with them.

The rectangular room ran about ten meters, then doglegged to the right. There was no evidence of a way out until the wall to their left suddenly jerked aside. Little homunculi poured out of the opening with Olympic speed.

Hoover leaped and caught one in midair, jaws around its throat. But even as they fell to the ground, the diminutive creature with the impossibly long arms wrapped its own hands around Hoover's throat. They rolled, locked in a battle of who could kill who first.

The SEALs opened fire on the others, their HKs double-tapping and missing as often as they found a target.

Walker felt one wrap around his leg. He brought the butt of the rifle down hard on its head and crushed it. He was barely able to get the barrel back up in time to fire and hit another attacker point blank in the forehead, sending it tumbling backwards.

Soon the SEALs were back-to-back.

Hoover joined them, limping, but as badass as ever.

Walker became aware of a sound as he searched for and fired upon the creatures that moved into his line of sight. He was finally able to tune it in about the same time Holmes ordered Yank to be quiet. The FNG had been chanting in a barely audible way, *Fuck me, fuck me, fuck me,* over and over. Walker grinned beneath his mask, remembering when he too had felt the same way.

Laws screamed from beside him. Twisted his barrel toward his own leg and fired. Luckily he missed his leg. If he hit anything else, he didn't know.

Then there was nothing.

No movement.

No sound.

Nothing except the heavy breathing of four SEALs and a Belgian Malinois. Hoover began sniffing at the bodies.

"Team, ready," Holmes commanded.

Walker eyed the room that had been revealed by the moving wall. Try as he might, he couldn't plumb its depths. He didn't like it. Although they couldn't see in, it was entirely possible that whoever or whatever was in the room could see them.

Laws pulled two flash bangs and tossed them into the room.

"Eyes," he said.

Walker dialed his QuadEye blind until the concussive bangs ate the silence. He returned his sight as the light died and in that moment he saw several figures with weapons, raising them. He grabbed Laws and tumbled to his left.

"Beegees! Weapons!"

The men in the room suddenly opened fire.

Holmes took three rounds in the chest and one in the thigh before he was able to dive clear. Yank had already cleared himself and pulled the team leader the rest of the way, where the SEALs crouched to the left of the opening. Hoover leaped away just as a dozen rounds chewed the pavement where she'd stood.

Walker pulled two fragmentation grenades from his vest, freed the pins, cooked them off, then tossed them into the room. The detonation was immediate. Two grenades going off at eye level eviscerated sight and sound. The concussion was fifty times greater than the flashbang, the 3.5 ounces of explosive in the M67 sending the composite pieces of the grenade into the faces and bodies of all who were arrayed before them.

Walker counted to three, then peeked around the corner. The room dripped with pieces of what used to be the men who'd planned on doing them harm. Chalky smoke and almost-evaporated concrete and wallboard filled the room in a haze, making it almost impossible to see.

"Light," Holmes commanded.

Every SEAL flipped their QuadEye up and locked it in position atop their helmet. Then each switched on the Maglite attached to his helmet and the light attached to his rifle. Eight high-intensity beams pierced the grenade-created gloom, dipping and moving as each SEAL turned to examine the carnage. Red, pink, and even orange pieces of meat dripped from the ceiling and slid down the walls. Torsos and AK-47s from four men lay absolutely demolished in the center of the room. Random boots and hands were scattered around and barely recognizable amidst piles of even more unrecognizable steak-sized pieces.

No one was hurt except Holmes. The body armor had absorbed the rounds, but one had also wounded his thigh, just missing his armored thigh pad. He bandaged the wound by wrapping gauze directly over it.

Hoover entered the room and began to sniff at the remains. She moved to a particular pile that had a few fingers, and squatted, leaving a thin trail of urine. When she was finished, she looked back at the team, but before she could receive any direction, she snapped her head forward, planted her feet and growled, low and deep.

A man stood slowly. He'd been sitting in the back of the room the whole time. Covered in white plaster dust, he appeared to be unscathed, which Walker found incomprehensible. The room had been a damnation alley of shrapnel and supersonic death, and no one could have remained uninjured. Yet here this man stood. Or was it a man? Perhaps he had been hurt. His skin hung in putrid lengths. And it was *his* skin. Unlike the others who'd clearly been wearing suits, this man, this being, had skin which was as rotten as the skin of the suits.

He shook himself, the pieces of skin moving like fringe. Clouds of dust billowed outward, revealing the unhealthy colors of purple, black, and green skin.

"Hold it right there," Laws commanded.

The man's face turned toward them. His head was bald and misshapen. His eyes, which at first appeared almond-shaped, were like that because of the rotten skin sloughing from his face. He simply pointed at Laws and in that motion, caused the SEAL to fall to the floor writhing.

Walker felt it like a lightning bolt. Power. Sickening, terrible power.

Laws dropped his weapon and ripped his face mask free. Black and green lines were invading the purity of his skin as if it were rotting it from the inside out.

"Make it stop," Holmes commanded, raising his HK.

The man gestured at Holmes. The SEAL team leader fired simultaneous to the man's unleashing of power. Holmes fell to his hands and knees and retched violently. But the man remained unharmed. The bullets simply pierced the skin like they would a hillside of mud. Gouts of vomit seeped from the sides of Holmes's mask. He barely managed to rip it free before he fell onto his back, gasping.

"Why have you desecrated my temple?" the man asked, his voice equally tinged with a Spanish accent and another element that made his voice echo.

Walker ignored his question.

Hoover was dancing along on the fringe of the room, not knowing what to do.

Yank began to fire and was the man's next target as the SEAL's rounds entered the man's skin with nothing to show for their firepower. Yank joined Holmes on his knees, retching and pushing his insides out.

Walker had an idea and let his rifle dangle from its sling. He snatched the long knife from his thigh sheath, leaped forward and brought it down on the creature's outstretched arm. It sliced neatly through, sending the man's hand and half of his forearm falling to the basement floor.

The result was instantaneous as the man reared his head back and roared in equal parts agony and disbelief before turning to his attacker. Walker felt slammed by a sickening power. He fought bile down in his throat as he tried to launch himself for another attack. But he was tossed aside by an even greater force coming from behind him. As he fell, he saw Ramon, still in werewolf form, grab the leprosotic creature's head and rip it from its torso. Pressing his claws together until his muscles bulged, he smashed the sides of the head, the remains splattering like a gigantic egg. The body fell lifeless to the floor, but that didn't stop Ramon. He followed it, tearing into the pieces with his claws until there was no piece larger than a man's hand.

Then he stood again, turning to survey the SEALs around him. He reared back as if he were about to attack, then chuckled, dropped to all fours, and ran back up the stairs.

Walker heard shots from above, probably J.J. trying to hit a moving target. Then nothing. Nothing except for his own heartbeat and Laws cursing on his hands and knees.

"Tastes like when my prom date threw up in my mouth," Laws said.

32

KNIGHTS' CASTLE. NIGHT.

It took a while for Triple Six to make it back to the castle. The streets were jammed with worshippers following the statue of the Virgin. J.J. had given the team robes, which covered their armor and weapons. But Holmes was limping badly. Not only had he taken impact on the armor on his thighs, causing deep bone bruises, but one of the rounds had penetrated his leg. How bad they didn't know, but they needed to get him back to the castle right away.

Whatever the sorcerer had done was temporary. The rotting skin had gone with his death.

Jen met them at the front door, along with a pair of Knights dressed in scrubs. She insisted that all of them get checked out and hovered over them.

After a cursory triage, Walker and Yank were released. Walker had Yank secure the weapons and prepare them for mission. If Yank could find J.J., he would get his help as well. Laws was declared fit for duty, but he looked the worst for wear of them all. It turned out that Holmes had a through and through wound. It needed treatment and might hurt like hell, but it would let him RTD (return to duty).

Walker readied to leave. He wanted to check and see how YaYa was doing. He gestured at Hoover and the dog slunk behind him, as if she knew she was going to see the crazed man who was once her number one pal. They were almost at the door to the medical suite when Jen approached.

"We've barely had a chance to say hi." She smiled, her face less than a foot from his own. "Hi."

In another time, another place, Walker might have acted like John Wayne and snatched her around the waist, kissing her deeply. But this wasn't that time, nor was it that place. So he smiled and squeezed her hand. That would have to be it for now. He needed to keep the act of killing and the act of loving separate. For how long, he didn't know.

"Hi back," he said. He saw hurt in her eyes, but didn't know what to do about it. He went to a corner sink, stripped down to bare skin, and began washing away the stink of the kill.

She came up behind him and watched, her arms crossed in front of her in such a way that she gripped both elbows. "You didn't find her," she said rather than asked.

Walker shook his head. "She wasn't there. As far as we can tell, there was no sign of her ever being there to begin with. When it was all done, we sent Hoover through the rooms but there was nothing."

"So we don't have any leads?"

"It's as if she evaporated."

"No one evaporates. Everyone leaves a trail."

He grinned. "Tell that to the evaporated."

"Seriously." She stepped forward and pointed to a spot on the side of his head. "Missed a spot. What is that?"

"Probably skin. Not mine, from those lepers." He hesitated as he considered. "Or it could be a piece of one of the men we blew up."

She made a face.

Walker wondered what she was thinking. "Sorry, Jen. I'm still in the mode. Takes a while to turn it off."

She was silent as he finished washing. He was about to apologize when Ramon burst into the room. Gone was his fur and back was the man in the white linen suit, clean as the day it came off the rack. He was making a beeline for Holmes, whom they were finishing up with on the table. Walker leaped in front of Ramon and grabbed him by his shoulders.

Hoover crouched by the door, growling.

"What the hell did you kill him for?"

"Get out of my way, kid," Ramon said.

He tried to shove Walker, but Walker stood his ground. Then Ramon jerked backwards. Walker let himself go toward Ramon, allowing for the weight to create the momentum which took them both to the ground. Walker ended up on top and straddling Ramon, his left hand gripping the man's collar, his right hand reared back for a punch.

Ramon growled, "Get off me, boy, or I'll turn."

Suddenly Jen was there, leaning down, pressing a shiny, thin blade against Ramon's temple. Where it touched, Ramon's skin sizzled. "This is silver, Mr. Ramon. You so much as harm that SEAL and I'll plow it into your head."

Ramon stared wild-eyed at the knife.

"Understand?" Jen asked.

Ramon nodded.

Walker lowered his fist and grabbed Ramon's collar with two hands. "Why'd you kill him? He was our only lead."

"He's not our only lead."

"Then what?"

"The other skinwalkers. They were in league with them."

"But you killed them."

"One got away. If we can find him, then we know where the girl is."

"You know what I think? I think that you're—"

"Walker," came Holmes's voice. "Enough."

Walker turned and as he did, he released Ramon.

Holmes had a fresh bandage on his thigh. He stood in nothing but UDT shorts. Scars and muscles rippled across his body. "Let the man up."

Walker allowed Ramon to push him off. He stood and

reluctantly helped Ramon to his feet. The other man swiped at the wrinkles in his suit.

"Are you going to apologize?"

"No. Are you?"

"Walker?" came Holmes's stern voice.

"What?" Walker gritted his teeth and turned toward his boss.

"Enough."

Jen still held the knife in front of her, ready to use it if needed.

Ramon regarded it with a baleful eye, but turned nonchalantly to Holmes. "I guess you are glad I was there, no?"

"You're right. I was glad you were there no."

Ramon's eyes narrowed as he made out the gibe. "You didn't need my help?"

Holmes leaned back on the bed. "You have this way of killing people we want to talk to."

"That thing never would have spoken. He had the spirit of Xipe Totec in him."

"Nevertheless, we're the sort of people who like to try. You'd be amazed at how many people and things we can make talk."

Walker watched with increasing appreciation as Holmes began to effortlessly dominate the other man.

Ramon seemed about to remark, then held his words. He spread his hands. "Now I know. I thought I was helping."

"I'm sure you did." Holmes stood straight and for the first time gave Ramon a look much like he'd given Walker the first time they'd met. "But this is a military unit and to function as such we need order and command. I command. Everyone else works to execute my orders."

"Orders?" Ramon wasn't quite sure what Holmes meant. Either that or he was being intentionally obtuse.

"Yeah. Orders. As in if you ever kill a prisoner again you'll have to answer directly to me."

Ramon stood taller as well. "And you think you can take me?"

Walker watched Holmes with concentration. He knew his boss well enough to gauge the look, which said to all the world *get the fuck out of here,* but he also watched as it softened. Then Holmes did something uncharacteristic. He chuckled. He stared at his open hands. "I have a feeling we're going to find out sooner or later, Ramon. Until then *I* am in charge. Understood?"

"Oh, yeah. Understood loud and clear." Ramon turned to go, then paused. "Can I go?"

"Not yet. Tell me about the skinwalkers."

Ramon paused uncomfortably, a far cry from the king of cool he'd been back in Cabo. He glanced at Walker, then moved to recover some of his lost attitude.

"They're Zeta hit men like I used to be."

"What were they doing with the lepers?"

"Protecting them. They were assigned to bring in the girl."

"Wait." Holmes eyes had narrowed to slits. "Do you mean the Zetas are directly involved?"

Ramon nodded.

"So then we *do* have a lead. You point out the local Zeta headquarters and we go there. If the girl isn't there, we take the leader hostage until they deliver the girl."

"Won't work that way. This feels different. It could be a power grab. I wouldn't be surprised if the Zeta leadership wasn't even aware of it."

"Why do you say that?"

"Usually the Zetas take care of their own problems."

"Can you be sure?"

"Not yet. If I can get my hands on the other skinwalker, I can get the information."

Holmes nodded. "What about the girl?"

"I'm betting Mexico City."

"Just like that," Walker said, surprising himself. "Mexico City."

"Yes. It's the only other place I know where the *leprosos* are."

"So it's a WAG?"

Ramon frowned. "I don't know this. What is this WAG?"

"Stands for Wild Ass Guess," Jen said. "We've been tracking communications from the asylum for the last twenty hours and have had limited success. Most of our resources are on the other side of the world. But we did track a communication between someone in the building and someone due south by fifty kilometers."

"What'd they say?"

"Didn't say anything. It was a beeper."

"So someone in the asylum called to alert someone south of here," Holmes said, working it out out loud.

She nodded.

Laws interrupted. "Let's get someone to go back to the scene and see if they can find the phone that made the call. Is there any way to track it?"

"Only if we call it."

"Then call it."

"Now?"

"No time like the present."

Ramon started to leave.

"Where are you going?" Holmes asked.

"To track down the other skinwalker. Timing is critical. It's already been too long."

Holmes nodded, letting the man leave. Once Ramon was gone, he turned to Walker. "What do you think?"

"I think he's hiding something."

"Me, too. The question is, is it a big something or a small something?"

"My guess is it's something big."

"Me, too."

Laws suddenly burst into the room. "You're not going to believe this."

"What?" Holmes, Jen, and Walker said simultaneously.

"YaYa—they did it! While we were gone they performed an exorcism."

"They *what*?" Holmes's face turned red and creased with anger. "Is YaYa all right?"

"He's good. He's great. He's back to normal."

33

EXORCISM CHAMBER. NIGHT.

Walker, Laws, Holmes, and Jen crowded through the doorway of the monk's cell in the basement of the castle. The walls were off-white plaster, bare except for a simple wooden cross centered above the twin bed. YaYa sat with his back against the headboard, Hoover in his lap, upside down and enjoying a belly rub. Vega and another priest stood at the head of the bed.

Holmes strode into the room. He'd put on one of the Knights' robes and had a look of a beardless Gandalf about him.

"You okay, son?" He put his hand on YaYa's shoulder.

"Never felt better. It's like I've been sleeping for a long time." He looked around. "If I did anything stupid, please forgive me."

"If you mean barking and licking yourself, then we already have that up on Facebook. Don't worry," Laws said.

YaYa's face paled. "Seriously? I did that?"

"What do you think?" Holmes said. Then he turned to Vega. "Why didn't you wait?"

"It was a simple thing." He shrugged. "No reason to wait."

"But it was my man."

"If it was one of my men, I'd have wanted you to do the same in my position. No reason to make someone suffer out of convenience, no?"

Holmes seemed to think about this for a moment. "I suppose not," he said. "Still, I'd have liked to be consulted."

"If you'd been here, I'd have consulted you."

Laws stepped into the conversation. "You said it was a little thing. What do you mean?"

"It was a small demon that had entered his soul. It was no match for the power of the Lord," the priest said.

"But YaYa is Muslim," Walker pointed out.

Everyone in the room seemed to pause as they looked first at the cross on the wall and then at YaYa. Finally it was Vega who spoke.

"His belief is not what's important. It is the belief of the demon. The demon recognized the strength of Christ and was compelled to leave."

Holmes scratched his head. "So the demon was Christian?"

Both the priest and Vega crossed themselves.

"No, never. It was an abomination. It was a piece of something greater once, but by itself it was nothing."

"Where'd it go?" Jen asked.

"Wherever such things go." The priest shrugged. "All I can say now is that it is gone."

Walker felt awkward listening to the priest's response. He could hardly believe that YaYa's personal beliefs mattered so little. And the idea that a random demon would automatically recognize the power of a religious symbol just seemed so... far-fetched.

Laws saw the look of mental distress on Walker's face. "It's a conundrum. Have you ever heard of the Jewish vampire?"

Walker shook his head. Was this a joke?

"So a vampire walks into a room and a man pulls out a cross. The vampire says that he's Jewish. The man doesn't care and pulls the cross on the vampire anyway. The vampire can't get near the man because of the power of the cross. Do you know why?"

Walker shook his head again.

"It's not what the vampire believes, it's what the wielder of the icon believes. In this case the man believed in the cross, carrying with him the beliefs of millions that added to his own powerful belief. It's as the priest said. *He* needs to believe, not the victim."

Walker shook his head. He understood conceptually, but something didn't sit well with him. He turned toward YaYa and walked over to him. He shook the other's hand. "How do you really feel?"

"I feel good. Seriously, I do. I want to get out of here. I want to contribute."

"Can he work?" Holmes asked.

"He has a clean bill of health," Vega replied.

Holmes pointed to a new bandage that had been wrapped around the young man's left forearm. "What about that?"

"We changed the bandage and applied our magical elixir."

All eyes went to him.

"An-ti-bi-otic," he said, sounding the syllables out as if they were the words to a spell.

Laws and Jen chuckled.

Holmes squeezed YaYa's shoulder. "Get off your ass and get in gear. We have work to do."

"Aye, aye." YaYa started to get up, then realized he had nothing on under the thin cover. He yanked it back over him and glanced at Jen.

"I'll be leaving now," she said, turning.

"We'll all leave," Holmes said. "Let's go to the command center. I need to speak with Billings and we have some searches we need to commence."

Everyone left except for Walker, who lingered.

"Are you sure you're okay?" he asked. "You were pretty far gone. Frankly, I didn't know if you'd make it."

YaYa nodded thoughtfully. "We now share something. Were you ever afraid it would come back?"

"Every day."

"Even now?"

"Even now. And you? Are you afraid?"

"Terribly." YaYa sat up straight and kneaded the sheet in his hands. "I can remember bits and pieces. There was a part where I remember barking and I wanted to stop but I had no control over my body. I can still feel the other being pushing me down. It was like it cut the strings of my ability to command my own body and then sat on me."

"You're never going to forget."

"How do you deal with it?"

Walker laughed. "For a long time I blocked it out. I forced myself to forget it had ever happened."

YaYa reached around and grabbed the cross from the wall behind him. "I don't think I can ever forget." He stared worriedly at the wooden symbol. "And this bothers me."

"Was it what I said?"

"Yeah. You voiced something I didn't know how to put into words. And you know what? It bothers me that my own belief has so little to do with it."

"Well, there's hardly any empirical data to support what Laws and Vega said. They may be right. They may also be partially right. Ever seen a man walk on hot coals?"

"At a luau in Hawaii once."

"Do you remember how he did it?"

"Big guy. Talked about believing in his inability to get burned while firewalking."

Walker nodded. "I think I saw the same guy. It wasn't like he skipped across the coals either. He stepped pretty firmly and didn't get burned."

"And it was because of his belief," YaYa added.

"Exactly," Walker said. "So there *is* something to the idea that what we believe makes a difference. Remember that."

"So it's not just about what's in our blood?"

"I don't think so," Walker said, poking an index finger at his head. "It's what's in our mind. In our soul. Even skinwalkers like Ramon can decide when to change and when not to."

YaYa took it in. "Thanks, Walk."

"Don't mention it." Walker stood, feeling the aches and pains of the mission. "I'll see you and Hoover upstairs when you feel up to it."

As Walker turned to leave, he saw YaYa rubbing at his left arm. Whatever it was, it was a stubborn healer.

He left, walked down the hall, and paused. Two weeks earlier he'd returned to Quezon City. He'd returned to the Philippines to try and lessen its hold on him. Walker had thought about going back for years, but had always been afraid that his presence might bring back the things that had happened to him. But after the mission to Myanmar, he believed that there was little left of the grave demon which had once inhabited him except for an exceptional ability to detect the presence of something supernatural in others. They'd tried his powers on the two-hundred-plus years of trophies that adorned the walls of the Pit only to discover that they were copies, the real ones removed to the Salton Sea Research Center, where he eventually spent a week moving among the artifacts, fine-tuning an ability that had once merely been a nuisance.

So standing on Flores de Mayo Street on a warm, misty Manila afternoon, he was at once struck by how different everything was and yet how similar it all seemed to him. For so long he'd been that terrified child of eleven who'd found himself living on the streets, his father dead, his brother far away, his mind enthralled by the vicissitudes of a demon laid upon him because of his father's greed. Now the U.S. Navy had pulled out. No longer were there colorfully dressed hookers and garish signs, neon innuendos promising happy endings for all. The stench of garbage was slight on the wind, nothing like the terrible rot that had anchored his memories. Gone were the piles of trash. Gone was the gnarled old man he'd chased down the street. All that was left was a stain on the concrete where he and a million others had peed, slept, lived, wept, and prayed, a way station atop an impermeable concrete surface.

He'd stayed at the Crown Plaza on Ortigas Avenue for two nights before he'd gathered the courage to seek out the orphanage. The Franciscan monks there had been fierce in their determination to mold him into something other than a Caucasian mutt with no future. Had he the wherewithal, he might have succumbed. But those years were so filled with a feeling of helplessness, he doubted he could have changed even if he'd wanted.

Finally he'd dared to go. He'd taken a jeepney across the city, wedged in between a woman with a live chicken stuffed into an admirably realistic Coach bag and a young man playing a first-person shooter on his iPhone. Several times Walker had closed his eyes to try and bring back the child he used to be, but try as he might, that boy had been exorcised along with his demon. The child who'd dreamed of his father coming back and saving him was gone forever. Where before he fit into Filipino culture like a native, he now felt foreign, only understanding every other word, whether out of mental spite or because he'd purged the necessary knowledge to translate.

Then he was there.

St. Francis School for Boys.

The orphanage was smaller than he'd imagined, but then again, he'd been smaller too. The world had been smaller. But as small as it was, it had seemed immensely imposing. With a steepled center, two wings flowed from right to left. Three stories, each window had white painted wooden shutters that he remembered chattering during the many storms like his own teeth when the monks set their eyes upon him.

Then a memory hit and almost drove him to his knees. The Filipino monks had tried to insist he speak Tagalog, withholding anything other than old rice and water for weeks until he was able to learn enough rudimentary words to please them. He could still picture himself hammering his little fists against the stout wooden door of his closet-sized room, begging for food, milk, his father, his brother, television, comic books... anything to sustain him and keep him from realizing that his parents were dead and he'd been ripped from everything he knew.

Walker felt faint as the heat of the past filled him. He knew his face was red. A pair of Filipinas scooted away, avoiding him as if he were a common drunk. They hurried down the street, much as they would have had they known him when he was younger, wrapped in entrails and feces.

His first year in the orphanage had been perhaps his worst. He was forbidden to speak English. The Franciscan monks were constantly watching to see if he'd lapse. They seemed eager for him to speak his native tongue. Punishment was delivered immediately whenever they even suspected that he'd slipped into the language of the colonialists, as Brother Sindep referred to any American or European dialect. The inability to communicate was one of the most torturous punishments he'd ever received. Not being able to explain that something hurt, not being able to relate his fears, not being able to socialize with the other kids, all of it left a hollowness in his chest as wide and deep as the hole created by the death of his father. So when Yevgeny Marcos arrived at the orphanage, Jack saw in the white-skinned, half-Russian, half-Filipino the possible antidote to his agony.

At first they were kept separate. Jack would only get fleeting glances of the other from across the schoolyard, or in the hall between classes. There were 950 boys at the orphanage and they were but two specks of white in a great yellow melting pot of childish anguish.

Yevgeny was a walking target. Small and frail, he had the frame of a girl rather than a boy. Jack would discover later that it was because of a year spent in bed from meningitis, but when he first saw the other boy, he'd been curled beneath the kicking feet of a dozen *Pinoy* boys. The second time was when they'd both hidden in the coal cellar. They'd rubbed the dust over their skin and pretended to be *Pinoy*, each of them speaking in broken Tagalog, pretending to be anyone other than who they were.

They became fast friends after that. Although they weren't allowed to spend time together, they'd exchange glances and hand signals from across crowded rooms. They'd find reasons to sneak away, often returning to the same coal cellar that had brought them together.

But ultimately they were found out. The *Pinoy* boys began to call them *bakla,* shouting it whenever the monks were out of ear shot. They made sexual gestures, often pulling down their pants and waving their childish peckers suggestively.

Jack had already learned to fight. He had gotten better each time he was beaten and now was at the point where he could defend himself.

But Yevgeny wasn't so lucky. He was too small. He was too sickly. He just didn't have the heart. It wasn't long before he climbed to the fourth floor of the dormitory, the floor where the monks lived, found an open window and stepped out. He hit the ground face-first.

Jack had seen it happen. In fact he'd called after the boy when he'd gone inside, but Yevgeny had ignored him. To this day Jack wondered if he had said something different, maybe gotten his attention, Yevgeny might not have killed himself.

The monks had said that the boy had died because he couldn't come to terms with his sexuality. It was a load of bullshit, of course, but they tried to make it a teaching point for the other kids. As if the death meant anything other than that the poor boy was dead.

Walker had to be careful. He knew what he was doing and it wasn't healthy. Jen had counseled him on his idea that he had to fight to repay the dead. The dead weren't owed anything, she'd told him in so many words. The living was who he should be fighting for. He should be fighting to make them safe. He should be fighting to return to them. To fight for something other than that was a rabbit hole from which he'd never return.

34

EXORCISM CHAMBER. LATER.

Walker was gone thirty seconds before YaYa let out his breath. He hoped he'd put on a good enough show. What had happened was so terrifying that his toes were still curled and the muscles along the base of his spine were still clenched. If this had been anywhere near what Walker had gone through, then YaYa's appreciation of his fellow SEAL skyrocketed. Flashes of the priests screaming at him and him screaming back were interspersed with rapid-fire images of torment, him in different poses as if seen by a third person—coiled and ready to strike, curled in a ball, standing empty-eyed, frothing at the mouth, barking at shadows, laughing uncontrollably. It was as if he'd become a mere passenger in his own mind. Whatever had taken him over had shoved him aside and taken control, and if it hadn't been for the priest and the Knights of Valvanera, he'd still be in the thing's grip. What had the priest called it? A little demon? YaYa couldn't imagine the full power of a big demon.

YaYa rubbed absentmindedly at his left arm as he thought about what his father would have done if he'd seen him possessed. The fact that he was a Navy SEAL was bad enough. To think that part of him had joined to impress his father, even though he knew the man would never be impressed, expressed the folly

180

of his attempt. The formula for his father's love was comprised of an equation he'd never been able to learn, which is why he'd continually done more extravagant and dangerous things. It had started with cross-country running in high school. Then he'd gone to half marathons, then iron man competitions, then full marathons. He'd won his first iron man at age nineteen and his first marathon at age twenty. Even after he'd joined the navy, he'd continued, finally discovering the glory of ultramarathons and thematic road races such as the one held in honor of Bataan Death March. He'd gone on leave after one such race, his feet bloody and his toes black with bruises. His father had seen them and merely commented that it was "the price you pay for doing the things you do." If his father saw his arm or knew how bruised YaYa's soul was from the possession, he imagined the old man would say the same thing.

He frowned and shook his head. As he did, Hoover's demeanor changed. The dog stared worriedly at YaYa, then slid off the bed. She found a place near the door and lay down, never once taking her eyes off him.

Running had given YaYa a long time to think. Somewhere between the Bighorn 100 in Wyoming and the Zane Grey Highline in Arizona, he'd ascertained a truth about his father: The man would never forgive YaYa for joining the forces that had aligned themselves against the cause of the Koran. He'd heard his father drinking tea with the other men and talking about the state of Islam. He'd heard him yelling and them agreeing, at a table in their suburban American backyard, but he'd never allowed that information to become part of his own analogue.

His father believed that the U.S. government had begun a pogrom against the Muslims and that it wouldn't end until the last Muslim had been rounded up and sent to a camp or killed. The justice system, the Department of Homeland Security, and the U.S. military were in the process of fulfilling this pogrom. The term came from Russian, to destroy, to wreak havoc, and was used to describe the Russian attacks against the Jews in the nineteenth and twentieth centuries. How ironic that his father would use it to describe a supposed American design to attack the Muslims. And if the U.S. military was the tip of the spear used to conduct these attacks, U.S. Navy SEALs were the shiny blade of that same weapon.

Yeah, if his father had seen him, the old man would have said the possession was something YaYa deserved. Just then, that piece of his heart he'd reserved for his father hardened. A son had an obligation to love his father, but he had no obligation past that. He'd spent what had seemed like an eternity trying to be something he wasn't.

35

COMMAND CENTER, KNIGHTS' CASTLE. MIDNIGHT.

Laws and Holmes were already engaged in a heated conversation when Walker entered the twenty-by-twenty room. Pete Musso and two other techs Walker didn't know were working furiously on a bank of computers. Jen held a pair of tablets, and she passed one to Walker as he came in and the other to Laws, who grabbed it without looking.

"We should cut him loose right now," Laws said. Although he was sitting, his body was coiled like a spring.

"I shouldn't have to tell you about old Chinese proverbs," Holmes said. He was standing by a window, occasionally looking out at the throngs filling the streets. Even after midnight, the celebration of the Virgin was in full swing.

"*Ji Xi Nan Gai*," Laws said dramatically. "You want a Chinese proverb, try that one on for size."

Holmes sighed. "What's it mean?"

"*Ji Xi Nan Gai*. A leopard can't change its spots."

Holmes turned from the window and nodded. "I agree. Wholeheartedly. But I'm thinking of another Chinese proverb. Keep your friends close and your enemies closer."

Laws shook his head.

"What? You don't agree?" Holmes's eyes were wide with surprise.

"I agree with the sentiment, but there's no evidence that it's a Chinese proverb. It's often attributed to Sun-Tzu, who said, 'Know your enemy and know yourself and you will always be victorious.' But it was Michael Corleone in *The Godfather* who said, 'My father taught me many things here.'" Laws switched into an admirable imitation of Al Pacino. "'He taught me in this room. He taught me—keep your friends close but your enemies closer.' The character in the movie attributed it to Machiavelli, but there's no evidence of that either. If one wanted to attribute it at all, then I'd either choose Mario Puzo, the writer, or Francis Ford Coppola, the director."

"I can always tell you're pissed off when you begin spewing Hollywood trivia," Holmes said. "Keep that. Stay pissed. And if there comes a time we need to take care of Ramon, then let it fly. But until then..."

Laws frowned but nodded. "I know, I know."

Holmes noticed Walker. "Good. You're here. How's YaYa?"

"Good as can be expected. He seems like himself again."

"Excellent. We'll give him some rest, then see if he can join us for the rest of the mission." He turned to Jen. "The floor is yours."

She stepped forward. "Walker, if you can share your tablet with Yank, and Laws, yours with Holmes, we can begin. I've synced them to mine so that you can follow during the brief. Let's start with the BLUF—Bottom Line Up Front. Emily Withers is still missing. We don't have a solid lead on her. We do have a tenuous connection with the Zetas. We also have a connection with Los Desollados, which we can trace back to her abduction. Regarding that, there's been a development." She toggled an image they all knew well. A still from Emily's capture showing the sea monster grasping her in its mouth.

"Don't tell me," Holmes said.

"Sorry, but I have to. The picture and video are fakes."

Everyone sat forward and stared at their tablets as if they could discern this with the naked eye.

"The whole thing?" Yank asked. "Even the girl? Does that mean she wasn't taken?"

"No, Emily Withers was taken. This we know. Given the time, we were able to pierce the sophisticated masking algorithm and the result was this." Jen toggled a picture into view that showed two men in full scuba gear aboard a DSRV, one with his hands around her waist, the other driving the machine at high speed.

"What the hell?" Laws sat forward. "And we're just now breaking through?"

"Couldn't be helped. We pierced the algorithm as fast as we could. Thank Musso for even seeing that there was an issue."

As if on cue, Musso, a thin, geeky young man with a *Star Trek* emblem on the collar of his jacket, left his workstation and joined them. He took the tablet from Jen and began to scroll, which made the other two tablets do the same.

"As you can see, looking at the raw view of the image, I noticed a slightly larger size of the image than should have been noted. Now, normally the size will be dramatically larger if an image had been superimposed. I've become used to looking for such things. In fact, I almost disregarded this except for my gut feeling."

"Hooray for Musso's gut," Laws said dryly.

Musso didn't respond. "What they did here was create an algorithm that reassigned quadrants of color. The increase in file size was due to the algorithm. The creation of the monster to replace the two divers was free of charge and apparently took no additional size value. Basically, they used colors already present in the original picture to create the creature. This is about as sophisticated as they come."

"Who could do such a thing?" Holmes asked.

"Pretty much anyone with algorithmic capabilities and a laptop. These days, this kind of thing is being taught in community colleges."

"I thought you said it was sophisticated?" Holmes asked.

"I should have probably used the term 'elegant.' Although there are a lot of folks out there who could do it, doing it *this* way, with almost no footprint, was elegant. And to answer your question, no, I don't know who made this." Musso handed the tablet back to Jen. She nodded at him and he returned to his computer.

"Comments?" she asked.

The room was silent for a moment. Then Laws spoke. "Remember the mission to Myanmar? Remember how it was all a lure? I'm getting that same feeling."

"I am, too," Holmes said. "People are giving us a reason to press forward, but I don't know to what end."

"It doesn't have to be complicated," Walker said. "It could be as straightforward as 'let's get rid of the world's toughest group of men so we can have open season on the United States.' Ramon might be full of shit on some levels, but when he briefed us about the cartels, I got a lot out of it. Nothing more important than each of them has a reason to be pissed off at America and would do pretty much anything they could to make our lives miserable. What if several of them have banded together?"

"What if *all* of them banded together?" Yank added.

Everyone turned to the new SEAL.

Holmes let out a slow whistle. "I don't even want to think about such a thing, but it could be possible. Perhaps the cartels held a Star Chamber meeting and decided to work together just this once." He turned to Jen. "Okay, let's try this. Have your techs get with counterparts at the Drug Enforcement Agency and Central Intelligence Agency and see if we can do link analysis on calls. I want to know who's talking to whom outside the cartels. My guess is we already have such a capability; we just need to be included in the conversation."

"Done. What next?"

"Any results from the beeper?"

"It's on Highway 150, heading south at high speed."

"What's south on 150?"

"A hundred small towns and villages."

"Is Mexico City one of them?" he asked.

"It eventually leads there," she said.

"Can we get eyes on? I can have GAFE standing by."

Jen shook her head. "It's not like a smart phone that constantly communicates with nearby cell towers as it changes position. This is a dead device that only comes alive when called."

"What if we plot the route of travel and try and predict the location, then have someone in the air call and coordinate contact?" Walker asked.

"Nice. Let's do that," Holmes said. "But if we call the beeper too much it might get destroyed by whoever's carrying it. That they still have it supports the idea that it's still going to be used, so we need to be careful. They could have the senator's daughter with them."

"Done. What next?" Jen asked.

"What do we have on Mexico City?" Holmes asked.

"I can tell you what's *not* in Mexico City, and that's a lot of Zetas," Jen told them. "We've been trying to make a connection with the Zetas and it just isn't working. I understand what Ramon said, but it doesn't jibe with what we have thus far."

"So what's in Mexico City?" Laws asked.

"What's *under* Mexico City is the newly excavated capital of Aztec civilization, Tenochtitlán."

Yank and Walker exchanged a look. "Now we're back to the lepers."

Jen offered Walker a professional smile. "Among many other buildings, a temple created for the worship of Xipe Totec was uncovered as part of the excavation. Archeologists have found more than eighteen hundred bones and fifty skulls at the site, all dating back to the fifteen hundreds."

"So that's it, then. We're off to Mexico City."

"Even if they want us going there? Even if it might be a trap?" Laws noted.

"Even so," Holmes said. "Knowing in advance that it might be a trap puts us at a significant advantage, unlike in Myanmar. Everyone be ready to go by seven. I'm arranging transportation. Stay inside, please, and watch where you step." Seeing the questioning looks on the faces of the others, he added, "These Knights have their own secrets. We can leave them alone. Let's respect their privacy. So that means no going into the catacombs. Got that, Laws?"

"Yes. Got it."

"Okay. Dismissed. I'll be down shortly."

Laws gave Yank and Walker a perplexed look, then headed out. Walker and Yank followed, knowing that the rest of their time would probably be spent recovering the equipment from the last mission.

36

KNIGHTS' CASTLE. WITCHING HOUR.

Instead, Laws had taken Walker away to do something mysterious, leaving the youngest and newest of the SEALs to recover the equipment, which was just fine with him. He found the task relaxing and enjoyed the mechanical movements of breaking weapons down and putting them back together. But while his hands were busy, his mind was free to go where it wanted. Yank had never had the discipline to just turn things off. Normally, when his mind began to work or remember something, he just let it go. Like now, when the day his mother died replayed itself for the thousandth time in his mind's eye.

It was the crash of breaking glass that brought him awake. At first he thought it was from across the street, but then the sound of a car's tires biting into the street before they peeled off brought him to a sitting position. Then he heard a whoompf *and shot to his feet. He wobbled unsteadily for a second. He'd been dreaming of something with that girl from school, Shawna, a talking pumpkin, and an Italian restaurant. And then he saw the telltale orange glow of fire, like what might have come from a living room fireplace if they'd had one. He rushed to his door and stuck his head out just in time to see the couch turn into a gush of living fire. He stood transfixed as it sent long fingers creeping* up the walls to the ceiling. Wherever the fingers painted a line of flame was created, until the front wall was covered with what could only be the art of an invisible pyromaniacal monster, intent on eating his house alive.

Then he remembered his mother. He forced himself to turn away from the fire and rushed down the hallway. He shoved the door open with his shoulder, cracking the fake wood.

"Mom, wake up—fire!" he cried, each word capturing his desperation and fear.

But she lay unmoving. He scanned the bedside table and saw her glass of gin, half full, where she'd left it before passing out, just as she had every night for as long as he could remember. She claimed it was for the leg pains she got from cleaning floors on her hands and knees.

He rushed over and shook her shoulder. She moaned something unintelligible but didn't wake. He shook her again, this time hard enough to dislodge the wig that made her look sort of like Whitney Houston.

"Mom, wake up! Fire!" He was beginning to feel the heat from the front room blasting through the doorway. He glanced at the windows. Like all of them, this one was barred to protect them from the outside. Their only way to get out was through the front or the back doors.

He shook her again, hard this time, and in his fear, pushed her hard in the shoulder, a half push that was as much a punch. He felt scared to hit her. He felt scared not to. She wasn't reacting. He grabbed the side of her head and shook it. Her eyes fluttered open.

"Uhnn. Shonn."

"Mom, please wake up! The apartment's on fire!"

Her head lolled and she sighed, expelling a cloud of noxious gin fumes that snapped him into action. He grabbed her by her shoulders and heaved. Her wig fell askew and he fought the urge to fix it. His back was beginning to sting. He wished he was big and strong like his cousin or the other boys, especially Lebron. He'd been left back two years and was the strongest of them all.

Yank managed to jerk her off the bed. Even when she hit the floor, she didn't wake up. He fought back a sob. He glared through tear-prismed eyes at the half-full glass of gin and juice, and in that moment knew that it had killed her.

He was pulling her through the door when a piece of the ceiling fell on him.

He screamed as his face and hair caught fire and his entire existence was consumed by a pure, crystal moment of pain. Then he was pulled and grabbed. He heard people yelling as he was screaming. Then he was outside, red lights strobing the world as white men pointed at the orange glow behind him.

His screams became sobs as he was rushed to an ambulance and a white woman with a ring in her nose and a tattoo of a hummingbird on her neck began to work on his face. She laid him down. He sobbed and let her turn his head. Then he realized he'd somehow held on to his mother's wig. The edges were singed and slightly smoking. As his face was caressed by what felt like razor blades, he tried to let go of the fake hair but his fingers wouldn't follow his commands. So he held it as the sirens screamed and his mother was cremated along with any chance of him living a normal life.

37

KNIGHTS' CASTLE. EARLY MORNING.

Walker and Jen lay in her single bed, blankets twisted around them. Jen's head lay in the pocket of Walker's shoulder. Their breathing was still quick. Sweat shone on their skin from the light coming through the window.

"I wish I could stay like this forever," Walker said.

Her barely audible words were spoken directly into his ear. "Then why don't you?"

"Because we'd get hungry eventually," he offered.

She punched him in the chest. "Seriously."

"Because I'm a SEAL," he said simply.

Jen didn't need any more explanation than that. She got it. She knew. Just like every other woman who'd dated a SEAL, she'd hoped she could change him. Part of Walker wished she could. But another part—the part of him that needed to be at the center of everything—demanded that he be a free ship in the patriotic storm.

"Still, I'll take that as a compliment."

"Will you, now?"

She was quiet for a while, then asked, "What took you so long?"

He looked at her in surprise.

"Not that, silly." She punched him again. "I meant getting up here. Where were you?"

"Laws wanted me to help him with something down in the catacombs," he said. "I hurried as fast as I could."

"I thought Commander Holmes said not to..." She looked at him. "Oh. It was one of those."

"One of those?"

"You know, the 'I'm telling you not to do something in order to make it clear I want you to do that.'"

"I don't know what you're talking about," he said. He smoothed her hair and kissed her forehead.

"Sure you don't." She snuggled closer and pulled the sheet tighter.

"Part of me wishes you weren't even here," he said.

"Thanks a lot."

"You know what I mean."

She pretended to have a deep voice. "'I'm not a big tough Navy SEAL so I might be in danger.' Is that sort of what you mean?"

He chuckled. "That's exactly what I mean."

"But I'm safe now."

"We don't know what's gonna go down in Mexico City. We might even be hijacked on the way. There are things going on with the cartels we don't understand."

"I'll make sure I stay behind and out of trouble."

Walker knew better. He understood the vicissitudes of combat much better than she did and knew that there'd be at least a moment during the next few days when this woman he loved was in the crosshairs. He just had to hope that when that happened he would be there to keep her safe.

They both lay still, staring at the play of light across the ceiling and listening to the celebrations from the streets.

"Do you think YaYa is going to be okay?" she asked.

"He seems fine."

"But is he really?" Her voice was on the edge of sleep.

"There's no medical procedure I know of that can tell if a person is possessed. The priest says he's okay and so does YaYa. My own little fucked-up radar hasn't been going off. I suppose we'll just have to keep an eye on him."

Her breathing became regular. He looked down and saw that she was asleep. He should be so lucky. He was worried about YaYa more than he was willing to let on. He knew how a demon could lurk inside a person, then creep forward to assert control. For all his comments about the power of mind over blood, part of him was worried it still might happen again, even after all these years.

As he fell asleep to the gentle breathing of his girlfriend, he thought about dancing naked and peeing on the old Filipino man. It was always the Filipino man. It was as if his repayment for his mistreatment was to haunt Walker's dreams. So it was that Walker fell asleep with the gnarled old man grinning at him, possessing the knowledge of what had been done, his look carrying condemnation through eternity.

38

KNIGHTS' CASTLE. MORNING.

Walker woke when someone burst into his room. He scrambled to a sitting position, the sheets like pythons trying to hold him down. Startled, he looked around for Jen, but she'd left sometime in the night. Sunlight shot through the windows.

"Get dressed and downstairs," Holmes commanded. "We have a problem."

Walker stared bleary-eyed for only a moment, then surged into his gear. He slipped on his shorts and shirt, pulled on socks and boots, then ran downstairs. As he hit the bottom of the staircase, one of the Knights pointed down the hall. Walker ran until he saw a room filled with people. They parted as he entered to let him get a view of what they'd placed on the table. A naked body. Headfirst toward him.

Black skin. Jagged cut at the neck. Bloodless because it had been done hours ago. So deep he could see the spine and the suppurated edges of the esophagus. Above this stood a diamond-shaped soul patch, obstinate in death. And above the face's rictus grin and the hollow, milky eyes sprung a head of yellow Afro.

J.J.

Walker became aware that people all around him were talking at once.

"I knew we couldn't trust him. Fucking bastard, Ramon!" Laws said, spittle flying from his mouth. Walker had never seen him so furious.

"We don't know that it was Ramon." Holmes turned to Vega. "Tell us again how he was found."

Vega gestured to a slight man, dressed in the robes of the Knights. His face was weasel-slender but his eyes remained intelligent and focused as he retold what he'd seen.

"He headed south out of town in a car he'd taken," the man began.

"You followed him?" Laws asked.

The man glanced at Vega.

"I ordered it," Vega said with a shrug. "We like to know what's going on in our town. Now can my man continue?" Holmes nodded.

"At Piedra Blanca, he pulled into a cantina. The man, Ramon, was already inside. They sat with each other and spoke."

"How did they interact?" Laws asked. "Was it like an interrogation? Was J.J. angry?"

"Not at all. They seemed to be friends. They smiled several times. They even laughed."

Walker exchanged a worried look with Yank, YaYa, and Laws, while Holmes stared hard at the body. The meaning seemed obvious, but Walker would wait until someone else said it. To do otherwise seemed a desecration of the former SEAL's friendship, even if it was for another purpose.

"They laughed?" Holmes asked.

"Yes. Several times." The slight man watched Holmes warily, as if he might explode.

"Go on," Holmes finally said.

"They spoke for about half an hour. Then Ramon went to the back. I figured he was going to use the water closet. I waited, knowing that it was your man I was concerned with. Fifteen minutes later, your man also went to the back. I knew then that I'd been made. I hurried around and that's where I found him."

"And Ramon?"

"No sign of him."

"He gave you the slip," Holmes stated.

"Completely."

"You're telling me that you were able to track them to this place and then you completely lost Ramon?"

"Sí."

Holmes launched himself at the slight man, grabbing him by the fabric covering his chest, and slammed him onto the body on the table. Everyone began shouting as Laws tried to stop Holmes and protect him from the others at the same time. The remaining SEALs pushed and punched their way through the crowd of Knights until they had their backs to the table, protecting their own as hands came forth to punch and grab.

Hoover leaped atop the body and snarled ferociously, snapping at anyone who was stupid enough to get their hands near.

Walker was hit twice, once in the eye and once in the jaw, but he held his ground, punching one Knight square in the face and sending him back into the crowd, then catching another in the groin so hard his target's eyes crossed.

Beside him, Yank was a one-man pain delivery mechanism, his hands and feet firing outward in precise movements that were almost faster than the eye could track, catching Knights in knees, hips, kidneys, and the pressure points beneath the armpit and on the sides of their necks.

More Knights came from the hall and poured into the room. For a moment Walker flashed to a vision of the Three Musketeers hopelessly outnumbered by the men of Cardinal Richelieu. The press of men became such that he couldn't even get a punch off with any power. He was in danger of his arms being pinned to his chest by the weight of the man in front of him. He felt his breathing begin to constrict as the mass of Knights pushed into him, pressing him against the table behind him. Just as it seemed as if no more bodies could fit into the room. Holmes fired a pistol into the ceiling. The yelling, the screaming, and all the movement suddenly stopped.

In the immediate silence that followed, plaster dust rained down on Holmes and Colonel Inquisidor Juan Francisco de la Vega, whom he held in front of him, his left forearm cutting off the air supply of the Knights' leader.

"Stop!" Holmes shouted. Blood trickled from the right side of his nose and he had a black eye swelling above it. A small skirmish broke out by Yank and he fired again, this time sending plaster dust on top of the fighters. "I said fucking *stop!*"

All eyes focused on him.

Walker felt the pressure of bodies increase as those in the hall tried to push their way into the room to see what was going on.

"Vega, I think we need to call this a draw. No good can come of this if we continue."

Like a switch, all gazes shifted from Holmes to Vega.

Vega swallowed and nodded.

Holmes released him but kept his pistol at shoulder level, the barrel pointing into the air. "Please tell your men to disperse. If you will allow, I'll have my people organize their withdrawal and we'll try and be out of your place within the hour."

Vega nodded. "I think that is best." He spoke in rapid-fire Spanish and all but four of his men left the room. They did so grudgingly and it took almost five minutes for them all to back out. When the room was finally clear, it was Vega who looked upon Holmes with something worse than contempt. "Why did you do this?"

Holmes wiped away the blood dripping from his nose with his gun hand. "I have no excuse. Please apologize to your man for me." He turned to Laws, who had a fat lip and blood seeping from a gash above one eye. "See to it that SPG is ready to go in an hour." To Walker and Yank, he ordered, "Secure all weapons and equipment and have them staged by the front door. I'm going to arrange transportation."

"This is not the way I expected you to behave when I allowed you into our home," Vega said, scolding him like a disappointed father.

Holmes, who had seemed willing to take a bit of it, wasn't

willing to accept this. He nodded to Laws, who pushed his way out of the room and down the hall. Walker heard him yelling for Musso and Jen.

"I find it hard to believe that your man lost Ramon so easily," Holmes said in a barely controlled voice. "There was probably a vantage point that allowed a view of both the front and the rear. Why didn't he choose the rear?"

Vega lowered his eyes and shook his head.

"What I've found in your country is a complete duality of loyalty, Colonel. I am sure that the men are loyal to you and the Knighthood. But I am also sure they are loyal to cartels. After all, if they can't be home to protect their own, it is the cartels with whom their loved ones must deal."

"It is time for you to leave now," Vega said.

"Your cartels are worse than our mafia ever was. Our mafia had a rule that civilians were not meant to be harmed. When it was broken, the mafia made their own pay. In your country, it seems that life has very little worth. Your cartels kill at will and the Mexican people still support them."

Vega gave Holmes a pained look. "I don't need you to come to my country and tell me how bad it is when you have armed men going into your schools and shooting children."

Holmes held up a finger on a hand that shook with anger. "The difference, Colonel Vega, is that the American people rise up against such things. We fight to make it not happen again. When are the Mexican people going to rise up against the cartels? When are the Knights of Valvanera going to do something for the people of Mexico other than protecting an icon?"

Vega stepped back as if he were struck. He glared at Holmes for a long moment, then resurrected his pride. He straightened his shoulders and his shirt. "My people fight in their own way as they always have. My Knights fight things you can't imagine. As for you, I expect you gone within the hour." He bowed slightly. "Thank you for removing the foul cult of Los Desollados." Then he spun and strode away.

Holmes watched him depart, staring at the empty doorway for a moment. Then he realized Yank and Walker were still there, watching him. "What? You didn't hear me earlier?"

Both Walker and Yank hurried from the room, intent on being away from the ire of their leader. But not fast enough that they weren't able to hear Holmes ask quietly, "Why'd you do it, J.J.? Why did you do it?"

39

ALAMOS PRIVATE AIRFIELD. MORNING.

Seventy-two minutes later they had a couple of Vietnam War-era two-and-a-half-ton trucks with canvas tops, provided by the local militia, waiting for them out front. Triple Six loaded their gear while several Knights watched. They all had bruises from the fracas and were eager for the SEALs to go.

Walker noted the presence of several men across the street. Although they were leaning casually against the side of a building and smoking cigarettes, their attention was resoundingly on the events in front of the old factory the Knights called their castle.

Once loaded, the trucks carried them from the castle and along Las Auroras Boulevard to the private airport that served the greater metropolitan area of Alamos. Used mostly by Mexicans and the rare vacationing American, there wasn't so much as a terminal. Yet as desolate as it was, the airport boasted a five-thousand-foot runway. Overkill for private airplanes, but something necessary for the billionaires and jets hauling cargo from sketchy South American countries.

Laws sat in the front seat of the first truck, with Walker, Yank, Jen, and two techs in back. Holmes was in the front of the other truck with YaYa and Musso in the back. They brought J.J. with them, his corpse wrapped in a body bag and resting on top of the gear in the second truck.

The airport was surrounded by a ten-foot-high chain-link fence, but the entrance was nothing more than a guard shack with a piece of wood that could be raised and lowered at the doorway. A laconic guard pulled himself away from a black and white television set and approached the driver's door of the first truck. He wore military fatigues, a New York Yankees baseball cap, and flip-flops. He carried an AK-47.

After a few moments of conversation, including the donation of two hundred American dollars, the guard let them through. Walker watched the man return to his seat, then pick up the telephone.

The trucks roared to the far end of the tarmac. The distance to the fence was across fifty meters of dead grass. Yank and YaYa climbed out first. Holmes had decided to up-armor everyone and put them on alert. Not that he was worried about the Knights retaliating, but he needed to keep his men and the SPG personnel safe at all times. Everyone else stayed inside. A GAFE C-130 was inbound, but it would take the better part of an hour to arrive.

It was ten o'clock in the morning and the temperature was beginning to rise. The insides of the trucks were stuffy, but at least it kept them out of the sun. Jen got Holmes's attention and beckoned for him to join them in the back of their truck.

As Holmes passed Walker, he squeezed his SEAL's shoulder, then found a seat along one of the benches. "What gives?"

"We have some information about our mystery beeper." Holmes raised his eyebrows expectantly. "SPG-JSOC took the task while we were down," she continued. "They found a choke point a hundred and fifty klicks north of Mexico City. Construction has routed everyone along a frontage road that then siphons traffic through a tunnel. We have a platform on task to provide overhead visual." She paused, seeing the surprise on his face. "Yeah. Suddenly we get a satellite. I wonder how that happened?"

Walker and the rest of them knew the answer to this hypothetical. Senator Withers had happened. He'd probably been saving up markers for quite some time.

"Go on," Holmes said.

"We have the vehicles narrowed to a line of ten. Six cars, three trucks, and a motorcycle. We've discounted the motorcycle, but have left the other nine vehicles open as possibilities, although we're thinking one of the trucks might be the best bet."

"Can't we just call and narrow it down further?" Holmes asked.

Jen nodded. "The number of the caller appears on the beeper. We did it once, but don't want to do it again. They can explain away one wrong number, but more would compromise the device."

"What's the plan, then?"

"We're going to take a few snaps and run the faces through databases. It's a long shot, but if one of the nine men driving has been affiliated with a cartel, we'll know."

"What if all of them are affiliated with a cartel?" Holmes asked, the same question Walker had.

"Then we'll stop all of them. My agency has been in contact with SEDENA, the Mexican Secreteria de la Defensa Nacional, which governs our counterpart. They're more than pleased to cooperate. Moving closer to Mexico City is to our benefit, really. The U.S. can call in some favors on multiple levels, unlike out here in the country."

"I don't want this to become some huge party. Remember, Ms. Costello, we don't exist."

"Coronado Pest Control," she said, referring to the sign out front of their headquarters back on the island. She winked. "Gotcha. Musso is tracking the movement of the vehicles via his tablet."

"Were you able to get a data pack about Tenochtitlán?"

"It's downloaded and ready."

Static erupted from the MBITR Holmes had draped around his neck. "Ghost One, this is Ghost Five. We have beegees at nine o'clock."

Holmes stuck his head out of the back of the truck and looked. On the other side of the fence, two pickup trucks filled with men had already unloaded and another two pickups were at the main gate where no guard currently stood.

"What the fuck is this, the Wild West?" Laws said over his MBITR. "SEALs, get your game on. Walker, get the cannon ready."

Holmes leaped down and assessed the situation.

Walker opened the case and assembled the SR-25 within moments. He heard Holmes shout and saw their two drivers running away in the direction of the tree line, which meant at least part of the local militia was involved. Had the Knights of Valvanera set them up?

He also became aware that the canvas would offer no cover if there was a firefight. And judging by the arsenal the men in the pickups were unloading, it appeared that there was going to be one hell of a war. Walker ordered all four members of SPG out of the vehicle and made sure the vehicle was between them and the attackers.

Holmes assigned YaYa and Hoover to keep the civilians safe, ensuring that no threats would come from the tree line opposite the attacking forces. As YaYa moved into place, he sent Hoover racing to the tree line to find out whether or not hostile forces were lying in wait.

Walker snapped the tripod into place and shimmied beneath the truck. The M35 two-and-a-half-ton truck, or deuce and a half, as it was better known, had ten wheels, two in front and four on each of two axles in the rear. The fuel pod was on the passenger side, which was the side away from the attackers. Whatever dumb luck had made that happen, Walker hoped for some more. He set up the barrel of the rifle midway beneath the cargo carriage, with his lower body jutting out from under the passenger side of the vehicle. He had a clear field of fire, and was in defilade. The closer their attackers moved toward the vehicle, the more impossible it would be for them to hit him. And with their AK-47s, at their current distance, he felt as safe as a nun during communion.

The two pickups at the gate were coming through. They were old Toyotas with two men in each of the front seats and a pile of angry men in the back of each one.

Walker sighted in on the driver's-side wheel of the lead truck, breathed easy, then fired. The tire exploded. Sparks began to fly as the metal tore into the asphalt. The driver did exactly what he wasn't supposed to do. He turned the opposite way of the blown tire and flipped the truck. Several men were flung free, but most ended up underneath the truck as it tumbled.

But Walker had no time to count. He sighted on the driver of the second vehicle, whose mouth was wide open as he watched his compadres become ground meat. Walker fired, sending a 7.62mm round across thirty meters to pierce the glass and enter the man's mouth, exploding the back of the man's head onto the rear window. The driver's reflex sent him turning the wheel to the right in a tight turn, which had he been going faster, would have caused the truck to flip. But when he died, so did the pressure on the accelerator, and the truck rolled to a stop.

Yank and Laws opened fire with controlled three-round bursts from their HK416s. Without the suppressors, the sound of each bullet leaving the barrel was an assault on the very idea of peace, smashing it with the same sound little boys had once imagined when they'd fired finger pistols against aliens and commies in their backyards and on playgrounds.

Only this was no playground.

Nor was it supposed to be a battlefield.

This was a civilian tarmac on the edge of a town in the center of Mexico, where the thin veneer of civilization was being ruined by the realities of the ruling cartels. These criminal soldiers had probably intimidated everyone with whom they'd come in contact. With murderous diplomacy, they'd bullied and killed until they'd gotten what they wanted. But they'd never come in contact with SEALs, much less the men of SEAL Team 666.

Yank and Laws stood two meters apart in tactical crouches. Each of their rounds found a home inside the soft meat of a cartel soldier. Whether they were trying to bring their own weapons to bear, were trying to stand, or just trying to hide, they never made it. They fell, shocked and gut-shot, under the controlled, professional violence the SEALs were unleashing. Had they lived, they might have realized that what they'd thought was the art of modern warfare was a far cry from the reality.

Holmes shouted, "Fall back!" and he opened fire on the survivors so that Yank and Laws could move to safety, check their weapons, and replenish their ammunition.

Walker shifted his aim to the men outside the fence just in time to see the explosive cloud behind a man holding a small tube.

"LAW rocket!" he shouted.

He heard everyone hit the deck as the 66mm antitank missile susurrated through the air. The rocket moved slowly enough for the eye to track it, but Walker didn't try to look at it. Instead, he had his arms covering his head, well aware of the several tons of steel above him that was about to become an explosive shrapnel factory. But instead of exploding, the missile continued past. He heard the Doppler sound of it receding, then an explosion as it hit a tree somewhere in the tree line. The explosion was followed by brush crashing to the earth, then nothing more.

"Fuck me," Laws said in amazement. "It went right through the canvas."

Everyone knew how lucky they were. If the missile launcher had been fresh off the assembly line, a mosquito fart would have set off the detonator, but now it was forty years past its sell-by date, and no telling how many times the case had been rattled, shaken, and dropped. The detonator had completely ignored the fabric. Had it hit one of the three crossbeams, or had it hit the side of the truck, they might all be dead.

Walker wasn't about to give them a chance to fix their mistake. The M72 Light Anti-Armor Weapon rocket system was a point-and-shoot one-time-use system, but that didn't mean they didn't have more. And as he sighted in on the previous location, he saw that they did indeed have another. A man was bringing it out of a box now. Walker waited as the guy depressed two buttons and extended it to full length, then charged the weapon, making it firable. He continued to wait until the man brought it to his shoulder and took aim.

Walker fired. His round met the missile just as it was coming free of the firing tube, forcing the crystal in the nose section backwards into the warhead, bypassing safeguards, and sending an electric charge into a detonator designed to pierce up to eight inches of steel plate or two feet of reinforced concrete. It detonated at eye level with the shooter and, with nothing to stop the force of the blast, killed everyone within ten feet.

"Nicely done," Laws said.

"Plane. Incoming." Holmes's voice was low and steady. "We need to clear the area of beegees or they won't sit down."

They knew what needed to be done.

Yank pulled two hand grenades and tossed them toward the two disabled trucks. They cooked down in midair and exploded as they hit. If there'd been anyone hiding, they weren't any longer.

Walker, Laws, and Holmes began a systematic takedown of the men near the fence. Like a game of Mexican cartel whack-a-mole, as soon as one showed his head, a round found it. Walker was quicker on the trigger than the other two, but after sixty seconds, they'd cleared the area of anyone alive.

Walker heard two things next. The deep drone of a C-130 coming in to land and the sound of sirens from somewhere near town. One thing was for sure, they didn't have time to get rolled up by the authorities. No telling what diplomatic hurdles they'd have to jump through just to get a phone call if they all ended up in a Mexican jail. The impulse would be to shoot their way free, but as protectors of freedom and the idea of law, it wasn't something they'd ever really do.

Walker pulled himself from under the deuce and a half. As he turned, he spied the ugly bug shape of the airplane coming in fast and hot. C-130s didn't need a lot of space to land. This pilot ignored the first two thirds of the runway and came down on their end with a thump, followed by a squealing of brakes.

"Everyone grab something," Holmes shouted. "We need to be airborne before the sirens get here."

Walker glanced over and saw Jen, fear etched across her

features as she grabbed a bag and a pelican case full of computer hardware. Her gaze was pinned to the ground in front of her. She was in shock. He'd seen it before. The brain pretty much shuts down until it can figure out a way to process what it has just seen and heard.

The plane swung past and nosed back up the runway. The rear ramp was already down. Everyone ran toward it and threw their gear inside. Two more trips, and they had everything they came with. Holmes urged everyone inside and the plane began to gather speed.

"Wait," shouted YaYa. "We don't have Hoover!"

Everyone spun to stare out the back, when suddenly the dog broke from the edge of the brush. She ran as fast as she could, but the plane was already going too fast.

Holmes grabbed the crew chief. "We're not leaving without the dog. Either slow down or park this fucker."

The crew chief, a thirty-something Mexican who looked like he didn't take shit from anyone, immediately began to yell through his communications gear for the pilot to slow down. He had to repeat the word *"perro"* three times, but eventually the pilot got it. The plane slowed to crawl long enough for Hoover to close the distance, leap aboard the ramp, and collapse in a pile at the feet of YaYa. The dog's fur was matted with blood and brush. Her tactical harness was also bloodstained. A piece of uniform was caught in her teeth.

"Looks like she took care of the drivers," YaYa said.

The ramp snapped shut about the same time the pilot took the C-130 Hercules straight up into the air. Everyone held on, praying the engines wouldn't stall before the pilot had a chance to level out.

40

MEXICAN SPECIAL FORCES C-130 HERCULES. 22,000 FEET.

Ten minutes later they leveled off.

Laws and Yank were recovering and organizing equipment.

YaYa was cleaning Hoover's fur as best he could.

Holmes had produced a Thuraya satellite phone and was speaking animatedly to Billings.

Which left Walker, who took some time to check each of the SPG civilians, leaving Jen for last. For the most part they'd held up. As firefights went, it had been pretty one-sided. Still, as one of the techs mentioned, it was much louder than the first-person shooters he liked to play in his mother's basement.

When Walker finally sat down beside Jen, he placed a hand on hers. She jumped, then gave him a quick look.

"Sorry," she said. "I was just..."

"I know. Let's talk through it," he said. "Tell me what you saw."

"I saw them come after us and I saw your bullets go into them." She stared at him with a look halfway between awe and fear. He hoped she'd never look at him like that again. She licked her lips and lowered her eyes. "You're very good at what you do."

"And the man with the LAW? Did you see him too?"

She nodded. "He just… disappeared."

"He was trying to do that to us, Jen."

She looked at him sharply. "Don't you think I know that?" She pulled her hand away and covered it with her own. Try as she might, she couldn't stop it from shaking.

"What is it you thought we do, Jen?! We're SEAL Team 666. We fuck up those things no one else is capable of fucking up."

She stared at him in shock.

Looking around, he realized that everyone was looking at him now, too. Even Holmes.

He turned to her. "Jen, I'm sorry. Listen…" She turned away from him. He put his hand on her shoulder, but she shrugged it off.

Laws came over and pointed to where he was sitting. "This seat taken?"

Hell yes, it was taken. Walker was sitting in it. But then he saw Laws raise his eyes and make a serious command face. Walker reluctantly stood and traded places, going over to help Yank with the equipment.

"Looks like you handled that pretty well," Yank said after a few moments.

"Fuck you," Walker said. He lowered his head and began the mechanical work of breaking down the SR-25 and cleaning its separate parts.

"Although maybe yelling at her and dropping F-bombs wasn't the most sensitive choice," Yank added.

Walker felt the heat rise in his face as he glared at Yank.

"Easy now," Yank said, not even bothering to look in his direction. "There's a lot of stress bouncing around this here Mexican airplane. No reason to let it affect you. Why don't you recite some poetry or something."

"Poetry?"

"Yeah. Poetry. Shit like, *I think that I shall never see a poem as lovely as a tree.* That sort of poetry. I'm told it calms you down."

Walker couldn't help laughing. "You were told that, were you?"

"Sure was."

"And who told you that?"

Yank glanced at Walker before he answered. "Oprah."

"As in the talk show woman?"

"The same."

Walker laughed again. "You watch Oprah?"

"Don't go hating on the big black successful woman. She got more money than Trump."

"I'm not hating on her. I just thought it was funny, you watching Oprah."

"Got shot in Afghanistan last trip. Had to remove my spleen. It was either that or watch Maury do DNA tests for people who shouldn't even be having kids."

"I didn't know you were shot in the Stan. What happened?"

"Playing rodeo with the MARSOC boys in their motorcycle gang."

"What?"

"SOCOM created a long-range reconnaissance unit with motorcycles as our primary delivery mechanism. We moved in and out fast and we could go where other vehicles couldn't. This one group, AMC 120—stands for Afghanistan Motorcycle Club—was mostly Marine Special Forces with me as the token SEAL. We were doing village stabilization operations, trying to win hearts and minds, when this truck took off like a bat out of hell. Me and a jarhead followed it into an ambush. My buddy got his head crushed by a boulder. Can you believe it? They set an avalanche on us. Talk about fucking old-school. Anyway, they shot me and my bike up pretty good, but I managed to escape. My armor took all the damage except for the round that took my spleen."

"Motorcycles and combat," Walker said, shaking his head. "Where'd you learn to ride?"

"My adopted father used to take us out on the sand dunes and let us go crazy on little 250s. Riding is cool."

"Even when there's an avalanche coming down on you?"

"Maybe not then."

Walker looked over at Jen for a moment before he spoke again.

211

"I was always worried she'd find out about the blood and violence. I used to come home and she'd claim to know what I did, but she only knew what she saw on video or read in a report. Being there is *so* different."

Yank grunted. "I'd never let my girlfriend go out on a mission. Well, if I had a girlfriend."

"Like I had a choice."

"You had a choice who your girlfriend was. There are plenty of girls outside the fence who are screaming to get into SEAL UDT shorts."

"But they aren't Jen."

"But they aren't Jen," Yank repeated. "She got you good, brother."

"Yeah. She got me real good."

"So what about that poem. Do you know one?"

"I know a couple. There was this guy on the USS *Tennessee* who used to recite it at all hours. It made me want to find a girl just like the one in the poem."

"What is it, *There was a girl from Venus?*"

Walker kicked Yank good-naturedly. "No. Nothing like that."

"Okay, Mr. Poet Master, give."

"Let me see if I can remember." Walker put down the pistol he'd been cleaning and stared into space. Then, when he was ready, he said, "'She walks in beauty, like the night, Of cloudless climes and starry skies, And all that's best of dark and bright, Meet in her aspect and her eyes.'"

When he finished, Walker looked over at Yank, whose jaw hung open. His eyes shined wistfully. "Man, that was beautiful." He reached out toward Walker.

Walker pushed him away. "Very funny."

Yank laughed. "Seriously. Where'd that come from?"

"I wanted the woman from the poem and I found her." He stared over at Jen with a longing he usually kept a tight hold on.

"Then you'd better figure out a way to get back over there. If your woman is all that, then she's completely out of your league."

"Oh, I knew that from the beginning. Completely."

"You ever tell her about the poem?"

"No. Never."

"Why not?"

Walker gave him a look that meant to convey *Do you know how embarrassed I'd be?*

Yank shook his head. "Fuck that. A poem like that is like a nuclear weapon or a silver bullet. You use it and that's all you'll need."

"You think?"

"Am I black?"

"Wait? You're black? With a name like Yankowski I never knew."

Yank chuckled as he cranked up a middle finger. When he was done, he asked, "So who wrote that poem?"

"Lord Byron."

Yank nodded. "Of course he did. The original lady-killer strikes again."

41

SOMEWHERE DARK.

She felt every bump, turn, and stop. With her wrists and ankles tied, she'd been unable to control herself as she rolled around in the back of what she'd come to call the *pain box*. She sensed it was probably a truck, but without the benefit of sight, her mind had begun playing tricks on her. Once she'd slammed into a side so hard she'd blacked out. Didn't they know she was rolling around back there? Weren't they smart enough to know that she wasn't supposed to die? After all, how could they get the ransom from her father without proof of life?

She'd seen all the movies. She'd even been to a Secret Service class, preparing her on the possibility of being kidnapped. The instructor, an old agent who'd taken a bullet for President Reagan, had gone into great detail about what to do and what not to do. Antagonizing her captors was one of the things she wasn't supposed to do.

But for the last God-knows-how-many miles she'd been doing her best to do just that. She realized that her gag kept them from actually hearing her through the metal of the damn box she was in, but that didn't stop her one bit. She began with an evolutionary postulate regarding their mothers and specific animals from the order of primates, and the probability of offspring occurring as a result of the unlikely mingling. Then she moved on to the idea that being able to fornicate oneself was possibly a good thing, encouraging them over and over to do this, and to enjoy it, and to do it some more. Finally, she succumbed to the tried and true measure of anger, which was to combine both ideas into one, encouraging and hypothesizing what a creature might look like if it was the result of man on beast copulation, with said procreation coming out their collective asses.

And then finally the pain stopped.

The truck slowed, then pulled over to the side of the road.

And for several heavenly minutes, she was still, unmoving, unrolling, basking in her full body bruises, breathing heavily through her gag.

She felt the truck shift as someone got out of the cab. The scrabble of a key in a lock, then the rattle of a handle, then light so blinding that it felt like her eyes were pierced by spikes full of sun. She fought to see past the pain. First there were two figures, then one seemed to remove the head of the other; she heard it bounce wetly past her and rebound off the far wall. The body was placed inside, next to her. She willed herself not to scream behind her gag as the man's neck, still gushing blood, rested inches from the edge of her peripheral vision.

Then the remaining man pulled her to the door.

"I am here to rescue you," he said, his English well-spoken but with a Mexican accent. He removed the ties about her ankles and untied her wrists. Then he put his hands on her shoulders. "Tell them thank you for their help."

She tried to speak, but her voice was dry and cracked. Finally, she managed, "What?"

"You heard me, girl. Tell them the man in the white suit thanks them."

"Who... who are you?"

"*Adios.*"

He turned and walked away into the painful light. He was speaking into a cell phone.

"Wait!" she cried. "Where are you going?"

"I have a meeting with your father."

"Stop—help me. At least tell me where I am."

He turned back and said, "Do not worry, little *burra*. Help will soon be here. Rest. Stay. Your heroes will come for you."

There was a certain finality to his words. But as he started to leave once more, she couldn't help herself. "What about my father? Will you tell him where I am?"

The man stopped once more. "I most certainly will," he said with a smile. "Now rest. Help will come soon."

He took three steps and merged with the light. She tried to see where he was going, but the light was too bright. Still she stared and eventually the brightness dimmed and her vision started to adjust. She was on the side of a road somewhere. Cars and trucks were roaring by. Occasionally a large truck would pass so close that her smaller truck would rock back and forth.

She didn't know how long she'd been sitting or how many times the truck had rocked, but eventually she felt something roll into her lower back. It stayed there. She knew what it was without looking. She couldn't move. If the head resting against her back moved, she might just scream.

Then came another truck.

Then came the rocking from side to side.

The head rolled to her left and touched the hand she'd put out to steady herself. She stared at the face of the dead man and it stared back at her. And finally she did scream.

42

MEXICAN SPECIAL FORCES C-130 HERCULES.

Twenty minutes away from landing and it looked like Walker might have made up for being an ass with his girl. Laws watched as they sat together, uber-aware that they were the center of attention, their hands resting beside them on the bench, barely touching. Where she wouldn't even look at him before, Jen was now at least giving him the time of day. Not being able to hear what they were saying, Laws created his own dialogue:

I'm sorry.

You're an idiot.

I'm sorry.

You're an idiot.

Over and over and over.

He could almost make the words fit as he read their lips. The idea that they might be saying what he was thinking made him smile.

Holmes scooted down and relaxed beside him. "We got a problem."

"Jesus Christ on a Big Wheel, what now?"

"Do you want the good news first or the bad news?"

"Fuck it. It's been a long day already. Between a fake sea monster, a cult of people who wear other people's skin, a Mexican Monty Python Revival Tour featuring *We are the Knights who say Virgin,* fucking homunculi, a sorcerer who can make my skin rot, and a fucking attack by some misguided Mexican cartel, I feel like a combat Alice way the fuck down the rabbit hole."

Holmes stared at him. "Are you done?"

But Laws was just getting started. "And it *is* a rabbit hole. We're on a one-way trip down a Mexican slip-and-slide, following a fucking Zeta assassin werewolf who looks so much more like Ricardo Montalbán every time I see him that I want to start yelling, 'De plane! De plane!' just like Hervé Villechaize did every fucking episode of *Fantasy Island.*"

"Now are you done?"

"Hardly, Sam. I'm just getting started. I—"

"We found the girl."

All heads turned to Holmes.

"You what?" Laws used a hand to close his jaw, which had dropped open.

"We identified the truck. Emily Withers is inside."

"Hot damn!" Walker cried.

Yank and YaYa high-fived.

"Please tell me she's alive. Please tell me that's not the bad news you're going to give."

Holmes nodded. "She's alive."

Laws held up a hand. "Wait, do we have any other proof of life?"

"Only that their confidential source provided the information."

"Confidential source?" Laws laughed. "I'll give you two guesses who that is. I'm telling you, I don't trust him."

"Me neither. But we have to trust this until we have other information."

Laws shook his head. "Then what's the bad news?"

"Ms. Billings and Senator Withers are inbound on a private jet. They're scheduled to land forty-two minutes after we land. Our orders are to wait and escort him to the embassy, where he'll be reunited with his daughter."

"What about the girl?" Jen asked. "Who's going to secure the girl?"

Laws nodded. "Costello is right, Sam. We need to make sure the girl is secure."

"She should reach the embassy about the same time we do. She's under guard and has a police escort."

"It seems too easy," YaYa said.

"Yeah, and if it seems too easy," Walker added, "then it *is* too easy. Something's not right here."

"Do you feel it too?" Holmes said, voicing his own worry.

Everyone nodded. Hoover growled as if she were answering, too.

"Then what do we do, boss?" Walker looked at Holmes.

"Have any great ideas?" Laws asked.

Holmes gritted his teeth, his mouth a thin, worried seam. "Not as long as we're locked aboard the plane." Then a light brightened his eyes. He stood and walked over to where the crew chief was dozing. Holmes woke him and they had a quick conversation. The Mexican sergeant seemed to be arguing, then acquiesced. He immediately moved to a locker and began pulling out parachutes.

Everyone stood, watching as he stacked four huge packs in the middle of the floor. Laws recognized them: T-11s. State-of-the-art if you wanted a nonmaneuverable parachute, but pretty fucking crappy if you wanted to actually plan on where to land. They were even slower than their predecessors, the T-10C. The T-11s allowed for a descent of nineteen feet per second, while the T-10Cs allowed for a descent of twenty-four feet per second. Not something he wanted to strap on unless the plane was burning, and even then... "Uh, boss? If you have a plan, sharing is caring."

"Musso, go up in the pilot's cabin and help vector them in to the senator's daughter."

Just as Musso stood, the plane hit a pocket of air and shook with the turbulence. He looked a little green as he caught his balance. One of the other techs handed him a tablet, and he made his way to the front.

"Sam?" Laws asked. He hated when his boss got this way. The mission plan was obviously fully formed in Holmes's mind, all five paragraphs of the operations order were already written, and if it were business as usual, he wasn't going to share until right before he absolutely positively needed to.

The C-130 powered into a right-hand turn, sending Laws ass over head until he came up against one of the parachutes. The engine whined as it was suddenly powered for ascent.

Scrambling to his feet, Laws was about to unleash a torrent of vernacular when Holmes noticed him standing beside the chutes.

"Good idea. Everyone except YaYa armor up and strap on."

Jen and the other techs stood uncertainly, looking around for something to strap on to.

"SEALs," Holmes said. "Every SEAL except YaYa. Ms. Costello, you and the techs will meet the senator. YaYa, you're in charge."

The Arab American SEAL made an act of looking relieved. "Thank Allah. I thought he was going to put the dog in charge."

"At ease that shit. I could still change my mind."

Hoover looked at YaYa, and if a dog could grin, she was doing it. Finally Laws couldn't take it anymore. "Boss, your plan. Please."

Holmes joined them, putting on his body armor. When Yank began packing HK416 rounds into his vest, Holmes placed a hand on the young SEAL.

"No HK rounds. We're going into civilian-heavy Mexico. Mexico City has nine million at last count. We don't need them thinking they're being invaded by an American armed force. Knives and pistols only."

Walker held out his helmet. "What about nods?"

"No nods. No Pro-Tecs. No vests. T-shirts and combat pants and baseball caps. Armor beneath the shirts. And let's break out the bone-conducting commo gear. I want something no one can really see."

Developed by the Defense Advanced Research Projects Agency specifically for SOCOM, the BCCGs didn't cover the ears, nor did they cover the mouths, freeing them of communications wires. Using Bluetooth technology, they came in three pieces. One transmitter, a quarter-sized listening device that fit behind the ear, and a piezoelectric vocalization square that fit beneath the lower jaw.

Yank was the first with his gear on. "Please don't tell me we're going to parachute onto a police-protected moving vehicle using these cargo chutes."

"I thought the Marines used these," Walker said, snapping down his legs.

"Like I said," Laws said, "cargo chutes."

"Dude," Yank said, shaking his head and trying not to smile.

Laws was getting pissed. He was supposed to be second-in-command. How could he provide input to a plan that was already in effect? But there was nothing to be done at this point. "So is that the plan?" he asked in the most even voice he could muster.

The crew chief shouted, "Five minutes!"

Holmes pointed at YaYa and the techs. "Tie everything down that's not attached to the plane. That includes Hoover. I don't want her jumping after us without a parachute."

The inside of the aircraft buzzed with activity.

Holmes gestured for everyone to gather around. When they did, he produced his own tablet with a map of an area north of Mexico City. "Here's the plan. Costello, contact your people and get the stop lights changed at this intersection and this intersection." He pointed. "I'll be in contact with you and give you a ten-second countdown."

She looked shocked. "You want me to arrange to have one of our government agencies break into a sovereign country's transportation system and figure out the wire diagram for more than a million stoplights just so we can make it go from green to red at the appointed time?"

"Yep. Can you do it?"

She laughed suddenly. "I'll see what I can do."

"Good." He smiled for the first time. "Hopefully it'll come off without a hitch."

Laws laughed, too. When did it ever work out like it was supposed to?

They checked each other's rigs and attached their static lines to a ring in the floor at the base of the ramp. They were two minutes out. They'd be jumping from four thousand feet. The wind was ten knots, and the pilot corrected based on their selected landing zone, which was a soccer field.

Holmes had given Laws the map, while he and the other SEALs inspected each other's chutes. The light near the ramp switched to amber. The crew chief pressed a button and the ramp descended. The rush of air overtook all sound as the ramp dropped level. Laws stepped out with one hand on the ceiling of the Hercules. He checked the ground for comparison to the map on the tablet in front of him, searching for landmarks. The plane was heading downwind and he didn't want to overshoot the field. He seemed ready to give up when he saw a factory and a pond that matched exactly what was on the map. They had six klicks left. Doing the math, he realized they had less than twenty seconds before they had to jump.

"Ready, SEALs."

One last check to ensure the static lines were secure. He stashed the tablet in his cargo pocket.

"Steady." He nodded to the crew chief, who turned the light from amber to green.

"Go, go, go!"

And as one, four SEALs embraced the Mexican air and were sucked free, letting their static lines deploy their chutes and jerk the meters of fabric from each pack.

Almost at once, all the SEALs were jerked sideways; then they swung beneath their deployed canopies. Laws spied their drop zone far ahead. By his measure, they weren't going to make it. He was used to much faster chutes and was worried he might have misjudged. Instead, it looked like they were headed straight for a sewage plant.

His heart sank as he realized that the circular ponds beneath him were pools of Mexican nastiness and the last place he wanted to begin swimming. He pulled on his risers and began to bicycle madly with his feet.

43

They cleared the sewage-treatment plant with a combination of skill and a heaven-sent updraft that tossed them past the ponds, over a school building, and onto their designated landing zone— the soccer field. They were thankful not to have been drenched in other people's feces, but realized one small problem that the map had caused. The LZ was flat, it was wide, and it offered them plenty of space to land... had there not been a soccer match and several thousand spectators watching what was an obvious rivalry game between two equally matched teams.

Holmes flared and landed first. No stand-up landings in these chutes. It was a parachute landing fall (PLF), used to absorb the sudden impact on the ground—feet, knees, hip, then shoulder. The chute came down on a young man in a yellow and red soccer shirt doing a bicycle kick. The fabric completely covered him and several other players.

Next came Yank, who tried to flare enough to stand and almost made it, going to one knee instead. He quickly unhooked the chute from the harness so he wouldn't get dragged, then shucked the harness.

Walker and Laws hit at the same time. By the time they were standing and removing their chutes, the crowd was in an uproar.

A referee and several players were running toward them, shouting and cursing. Walker grabbed his hat from his pocket and slung it onto his head, pulling the brim low so it rested on his sunglasses. The other SEALs did the same.

Holmes searched for a way out, then headed toward a goal. The others followed, and soon all four SEALs were running Indian style, one behind the other, passing the stunned goalie, crossing a parking lot, then diving into a concrete culvert meant to catch water during monsoon season. They left the shouts and cries of the soccer game behind, and also left their chutes as souvenirs of the day four men rained from the sky. The culvert took them down below street level. Open at the top, the left was bounded by a wall and a railing to keep the cars on the road. The right side had another sloping wall. The floor was littered with trash, dead animals, discarded clothes, empty bottles and cans, and other detritus of one of the world's largest cities.

Holmes slowed to a jog and the others followed suit. As he ran, he checked the tablet and the moving map and noted they were less than two kilometers from their target. They could travel perhaps another five hundred meters in the culvert; then they'd have to leave it and join the rest of the world. Walker had to admit that running as if they were in a concrete half-tube made Mexico seem a lot less crowded. For those brief moments before they'd landed, it had felt like they were all alone in the universe. Then they'd landed and in the space of a moment, several thousand people were upon them. And now—back to this. Walker decided that he definitely preferred the wide-open spaces.

"This way, SEALs." Holmes ran up the side of the cement wall at an angle, followed by Yank, Laws, and Walker. When they reached ground level they slowed to a walk. They had to find a way to appear inconspicuous. As it was, three physically fit white men and one black man all wearing tight black T-shirts, khaki pants, baseball hats, and glasses stood out in a nation of men where blue jeans and plaid shirts were the norm.

They split up. Yank and Holmes stayed on one side of the

street, while Walker and Laws slid between honking cars and a mule pulling a no-shit apple cart to get to the other side.

The road ran almost to the buildings on either side of the street, leaving a thin sidewalk where people had to push past each other and the occasional vendor selling fruit, vegetables, or churros. Advertisements for Corona, Chiclets, and Bubbaloo leaped off brightly colored signs on the side of a Super Dulceria La Nueva. Pink-and-yellow signs advertising bullfights were plastered on telephone poles beside announcements for the political elections that were to be held in a few weeks. The blue sky was crisscrossed with hundreds of telephone and electrical wires running from roofs, windows, even straight into walls. As Walker moved past a woman walking a little boy to school, he was pleased they'd found an open space on which to land. Trying to navigate the chaos of the lines would have surely led to a hangup and possibly an electrocution. He doubted if the wires this deep in Mexico were coated with enough insulation to pass an electrical inspection.

They passed a pizza place, then a loan shark, then a taxi stand before they reached the corner of Alfredo del Mazo Oriente and Gregorio Montiel and turned right. A police stand was on the right side of the road. Walker and Laws paused to buy a Coke from a kiosk on their side of the street while they watched what would happen. If the police moved even a twitch to detain the other two, Walker and Laws would have to get involved. He wasn't sure what *getting involved* would end up meaning, but they couldn't have a local *federale* arrest a SEAL during an operation. It just wasn't done.

Luckily, the policeman continued reading his newspaper and chain-smoking filterless cigarettes. Walker and Holmes dropped their Cokes in a trash can halfway down the block. They were about to cross the street when Holmes pulled up and faced the building. He stood beneath a butcher shop with several suspect carcasses hanging in the window.

Suddenly Walker heard Jen's voice in his ear as Holmes added the rest of the SEALs to the feed.

"—unable to coordinate the stoplights, but that's no longer an issue. The suspect vehicle has stopped moving."

"What's the location?"

"You're less than a kilometer west of the vehicle. It's a white panel van parked in the dirt on the west side of Via Jorge Jiménez Cantú. What looks to be a truck mechanic with yellow awning and signs is right beside it."

Holmes began to move, as did the other SEALs.

Walker couldn't help feeling worried and he saw his own feelings mirrored in the expression of the team's deputy commander. Why had it stopped moving?

"Any sign of a driver?"

"None." Even in that simple word, Walker knew her well enough to detect her anxiety. "One more thing."

"What is it?"

"The rear door is open."

All four SEALs sped up to the point of running. They tried to act as cool as they could as they moved by men sitting on stools, women hawking food, and children playing with little *lucha libre* dolls, but they still couldn't move fast enough. They finally gave up all pretenses, dodged into the middle of the street, and ran as fast as they could, cars and trucks honking. Yank got there first, with Holmes and Walker second. Yank skidded to a stop by the rear door. Only he could see inside and his face blanched.

"Damn." He pulled his pistol from where it was hidden in his left pouch and trained it on the inside of the van. He glanced toward the other SEALs, his face a mask of concern.

Walker planted his feet and slid into place beside Yank. Flies swooped drunkenly into a massive pool of blood inside the truck. Some had become stuck in the viscous, blackening substance. A head rested against the right wall, a body right behind it.

Laws reached over to the head and grasped the hair. He held the head up and to everyone's surprise, it wasn't the girl. Instead it was a Mexican man who looked surprisingly familiar. Walker thought for a moment, and then it came to him—the other

226

werewolf. This had been the man Ramon had been fighting out in front of the asylum. The one who had supposedly gotten away.

"Madre de Dios," came a voice from behind them.

They turned to see an older man, dressed in mechanic's overalls. He must have come out from the garage to see what they were doing.

Laws glanced at the head, and dropped it.

Walker felt his hand going toward his pistol, wondering what Holmes was going to require them to do. He didn't want to shoot the old man.

Then they heard a whimper. It came again, louder.

The man started to back away, his gaze pinned on the pistol in Yank's hand. Even though Yank held it pressed against his leg, it was still visible.

"Please," came a woman's thin voice.

Walker gripped the side of the truck and leaped inside. He stayed to the left and saw her, huddled in the back left corner, her knees drawn up, her arms clenched around them, her face buried. He stepped over the blood and hurried over to her.

"Emily Withers, we're United States Navy SEALs. We are here to help."

She managed to get to her feet as he approached. Her wide eyes took him in as if she couldn't believe what she was seeing. Then she threw her arms around him and hugged him fiercely.

Behind him, Walker heard Holmes giving commands. Then Walker felt someone get in the back and close the doors. He heard two bodies slam the cab's doors as they got in the front seat.

He pulled her carefully down to the floor and held her with one hand, while searching for a handhold inside. He found a tie-down pinion just as the truck lurched forward.

A light snapped on. Holmes had a mini-Maglite in his teeth. He unspooled a length of the 550 cord each SEAL kept in their cargo pockets and tied it down to the pinion next to him, then crawled over and cinched it down to the pinion Walker was holding, creating a taut nylon line capable of keeping all of them from sliding into the blood. What it didn't do was keep the body or the head from rolling into them, so Holmes sat with his back in the rear right corner, his legs extended. Every time the van slowed or took a turn, he and Walker kept the body parts at a leg's length.

Walker began to check Emily. "Are you okay? Did they hurt you?"

"Bruised," she said.

"And the man? Do you know who he was?"

"The driver? Killed right in front of me."

"We're sorry, Emily. But now you're safe."

"We've got a problem," Yank said through the coms.

"Detail," Holmes clipped.

"We have traffic in front of us and a *federale* hot on our tail."

Walker paused to listen. "I don't hear any sirens," he said.

"Lights flashing. They're five cars behind us."

"Man must have called it in," Laws said. "Can you lose them?"

"This isn't exactly a Porsche 911," Yank said. "But I'll give it a shot."

Centrifugal force threw Walker into the left wall. He cushioned Emily as best as he could, but she still grunted with pain. Holmes lost the light and it rolled into the blood, soaking the lens and turning the inside into a red-tinted hell. Just as Walker seemed to get his balance, he was flung the other way. The light spun madly and the head hit his leg and flew over it, impacting the wall. He held on to Emily, keeping her from flying loose. Holmes cursed as the head landed in his lap. He grabbed it by the hair to keep it from rolling.

"What the fuck, Yank," Walker growled.

They heard sirens now, several of them.

They were knocked around for thirty more seconds when Laws came on the line.

"Prepare to dismount."

"What's the 411?" Holmes asked.

"Vehicle change."

The truck slammed to a stop, sending the body chest-first into the wall between Holmes and Laws. Then Yank began a series of turns, finally pointing them 180 degrees in the other direction. After that, he backed up and shut off the vehicle. The sound of booted feet running across the top of the van was followed by the sounds of two men leaping to the street before the rear doors opened.

Light streamed into the interior. The blood was now everywhere. Emily and Holmes were covered with it. Walker had missed most of the flying blood because he'd been holding Emily, but the bottom of his pants were drenched in the stuff.

Laws waved. "Come on. *Hurry.*"

Holmes scrambled out first. Walker pushed Emily toward him, then ducked under the 550 cord that was threatening to clothesline him. Holmes pulled Emily into his arms and carried her like a child. She put her arms around his neck and sank her face into his shoulder.

Walker pulled his pistol from his cargo pocket just as the sirens came upon them, skidding to a stop on the other side of the vehicle. Taking in the entirety of the scene, Walker admired how Yank had set them up. The truck had essentially plugged an alley that ran between two three-story brick buildings. The rear of the truck opened into a long alley which had another alley coming in perpendicular and forming a T. Holmes ducked around the corner into this one just as the police began to shout commands through their loudspeaker from the other side of the truck.

Peeking around the corner, Walker saw that there was less than a foot and a half between the sides of the van and the walls. If the police were going to come and get them, they'd have to either go over or under.

He took off after Holmes. As he turned into the cross alley, he saw Laws using some of his own 550 cord to tie the hands of a man in a delivery uniform. He was pressed against the hood of a yellow van with a picture of an ecstatic chicken on the side below the words POLLO FELIZ. After Laws finished, he spun the driver around. The man's eyes danced wildly above his gag. Laws pulled out a bag and placed it over the man's head. Then he picked him up, carried him over to a dumpster, and tossed him in.

Meanwhile, Yank started the vehicle and pulled forward. Holmes got in the back with Emily. Walker joined them, happy that the back of the truck was filled with cooked chicken instead of a decapitated body. Benches lined one wall and he sat by the rear door. His vantage was perfect. It wasn't until after they pulled out that a rotund policeman ran around the corner. He glanced once at the truck, then dismissed it. Instead, he had his pistol trained on the back of the restaurant where the truck had just made a delivery.

They turned the corner and pulled into traffic.

"Shit, shit, shit." Holmes tapped his ear. "I can't get through to the others."

"Hey, Yank, want some chicken?" Walker yelled, checking on the trays of cooked meat.

"You asking me because I'm black?"

"I'm asking you because I'm hungry and you stole a chicken truck." Walker reached under a piece of tinfoil and pulled a leg free. It had been slow roasted. The smell was succulent. The meat begged to fall off the bone. He was bringing the leg to his mouth when he noticed Laws frowning. "What?"

"You're *hungry?*"

Walker grinned and cleaned the chicken from the bone in three fast bites. "I'm always hungry during an op."

"I think I'm going to be sick," Emily said, her face turning the color of a turtle's underbelly.

"Walker, try and establish coms," Holmes ordered.

Walker dropped the bone onto the counter and wiped his hands on his pants. "Roger."

"So no news on the senator?" Laws asked.

The girl perked up. "My father? Is he coming here?"

Holmes nodded. "He was coming down to meet you."

She smiled. "So that's what the man meant—the man who killed the driver. He said he was there to save me and that he had a meeting with my father."

"Who was the man who killed the driver?" Laws asked. "What did he look like?"

"Tall. Light-skinned. He was Mexican but more Spanish. He was wearing a white suit."

"Know who that sounds like?" Laws said to Holmes, who nodded in return.

She squeezed shut her eyes. "It was really strange. I don't know how he cut off that man's head. I never even saw a weapon."

"Didn't you say that he had a meeting with your father?"

She nodded.

"How'd he even know the senator was coming? What sort of meeting is he going to have?"

"The sort of meeting where the senator leaves in the custody of someone else." Holmes punched his leg. "You think Ramon had this planned the entire time?"

Walker suddenly got a weak signal. "—are in trouble... senator is gone." He could barely understand Jen's voice. There was a problem with the reception. "YaYa—oh my god, YaYa!" Then she began to sob, and the sound was so terrible and miserable that if he could've, Walker would have reached through the headset to make it stop.

Yank banged on the steering wheel. "What the fuck is going on?"

"Airport. Laws will give directions. *Go now,*" Holmes commanded.

Yank's face showed stone-cold rage. "What the hell is going on?"

"Shut up and drive," Laws barked.

"This isn't like any mission I've been on. We were always briefed. We always knew. We—"

Laws cut him off. "This isn't like any other mission because we aren't like any other SEALs." Then he added, "Take a left at the next light."

Yank complied, but couldn't help but cry, "Bullshit."

"We've been over this. This is what being a member of Triple

Six is about." Laws shook his head and slapped Yank on the shoulder. "It's not all crazy monsters and supernatural mumbo jumbo. It's being able to make the best decision you possibly can without any thought whatsoever."

Walker knew that there had always been speculation about selection to Triple Six. Every SEAL had three days of screening and selection consisting of interviews, role playing, and test taking. They compared their answers when they were drunk, but most of the questions had been individually purposed. No one could figure it out. If there were any common denominators, it was the ability of a Triple Six member to react on their feet and not be dedicated to the exact replication of a preplanned or prepracticed ideal.

Holmes once again proved to the universe why he was the leader. "Everyone calm the fuck down and stop jumping to conclusions," he said in an emotionless, even-keel voice. "We'll find out what's going on once we get there. If this is all a misunderstanding, we'll all have a beer and laugh about it. If this really is what Ms. Costello says it is, then we'll have to postpone the beer and laughter until after we rescue the senator and save the day. Understand?"

Nicely done, thought Walker.

Yank nodded, then said, "Yes, sir. Sorry, sir. This is just fucking with my head."

Laws began to laugh. "This is nothing, SEAL. If you think this is fucking with your head, just wait. It gets better." He laughed again. "It gets so *much* better!"

44

MEXICO CITY, MEXICO. AFTERNOON.

Walker stood at the Hotel Majestic's floor-to-ceiling window staring out at the Zócalo, or Plaza de la Constitución. The immense plaza had been a gathering place since Aztec times. Surrounding the Zócalo were government buildings and modern museums. Beneath the Zócalo were temples from the time of the Aztecs, most of them still unexcavated. The Zócalo was a place where kings and queens were received, where military parades celebrated Mexico's liberation from Spain, where speeches by everyone of influence occurred. Even now there were a thousand people chatting, eating lunch, reading, playing chess, kicking soccer balls, and flying kites. If this was the population in microcosm, then it didn't seem so bad, these thousand people standing in a historic concrete field, the Mexican flag rising from the center on a hundred-meter-high flagpole.

But like anywhere, if you looked closer, you could see the stain of sin, like watching the universe through a flyspecked screen, and Walker was beginning to wonder if the stain in Mexico, like it was in so many other places, wasn't something permanent. From the moment conquistador Hernán Cortés de Monroy y Pizarro rode into what was now modern-day Mexico, perhaps he'd brought with him the seven deadly sins: lust, gluttony, greed, sloth, wrath, envy, and pride. The country's entire bloody history was carved by these sins, as a conquering army came and took everything. The only problem was that they never really went home. The conquerors stayed and in the staying realized the only people they had now to conquer were themselves. YaYa had been right.

The other SEAL had said something once, when they were talking about going on a weekend vacation to a Mexican resort. They hadn't gone because cartel violence had put it off limits to the American military, but YaYa had been against it from the start.

"Sounds like a bad idea to me. You've seen the way people are down there. Greed is in their blood. They'll do anything to get more of everything. I bet if I took down a bucket of sand they'd steal that, too."

"Kind of harsh, don't you think?" Walker had said. *"People get like that when times are hard."*

And YaYa had shaken his head viciously. *"No. Not at all. Mexico is different. They've been living in an Age of Blood ever since the first Aztec rolled the head of a farmer down a temple stairs. Never in the history of the world has there been one place with so much violence, so much self-hate, so much revulsion at the reality of how great they were and how far they've fallen. It's like the conquerors came, never left, and became their own victims."*

Walker thought that much the same could be said for America. Although there was no great Aztec nation present when the first Europeans began to plunder the bounty of the nation, the indigenous peoples had their own way of doing things. Early American Indians were called savages because of how they acted. But wouldn't anyone act in the same manner if everything they knew was being taken from them? In the end, who were the savages? The conquerors or the conquered?

And now SEAL Team 666 was living in their own personal Age of Blood. Walker turned from the window and sat on the edge of the bed. He reached down to pet Hoover. Yank was already snoozing in the bed next to his. He could hear Laws, Billings, Jen, and the two techs talking in the other room. Musso had been taken to the hospital. He'd been shot. Correct that. YaYa had shot him in the stomach.

Everything was so fucked up.

Holmes had decided to put them in a hotel because there were issues. He didn't want to return to the embassy or else he knew he'd lose command and control. As it was, he'd gone radio-silent from all support so he wouldn't have to answer the messages from NSW Command that unequivocally stated the FBI had current jurisdiction on the missing senator and his aide, and that Triple Six was to stand down, despite having successfully saved the senator's daughter.

They'd tried to drop her off, but she refused to leave. She'd said she was tired of being part of the problem and wanted to be part of the solution. Holmes had decided to keep her, just in case she could shed some light on her captors.

Because Holmes was furious.

SEAL Team 666 *would* get the senator back.

Period.

But Walker realized how hard it would be. They were off the grid, which meant no help from anyone back in the States and no help from anyone connected to the embassy. They were all alone, except for Holmes's and Laws's contacts inside the Mexican military.

They had none of their equipment, except that which had been on their persons. Everything on their plane had been confiscated because the FBI considered it a crime scene. The FBI had also confiscated the plane the senator came down in, which held much of their additional ammo and equipment requests. Gone were their other weapons, ammo, computers, and surveillance devices. Unless there was a local Spy-Mart or SEAL-Mart, they'd be hard pressed to figure out how to MacGyver their way to figure out where the senator was and save him.

According to the official statement, immediately after Senator Withers's plane had set down, YaYa had received a phone call. He then began acting strangely, barking and laughing much like he had prior to his exorcism. Then when the senator's plane had pulled next to the open ramp of the C-130 Hercules, and right after he got out to meet the fine young Americans aboard the plane, YaYa had opened fire. He shot the commo box in the rear of the C-130, then leaped atop two Secret Service agents, knocking them both unconscious. Musso had tried to be a hero and was gut-shot for his daring. Everyone had screamed for YaYa to stop, but as Jen had described him, he was less a man and more animal. After coldcocking the Mexican crew chief who tried sneaking up behind him, YaYa had dragged the senator away.

No one followed. Instead Billings, who'd stayed in the jet and had seen it all, radioed their emergency. They managed to shut down the airport, but not soon enough. YaYa and the senator were gone. They had no leads. They had no evidence. All they had was a member of SEAL Team 666 who'd gone batshit crazy and taken the senior serving senator on the Sissy.

The door opened and Holmes came in, his face a cartographic merging of worry lines. He went straight into the other room. Walker woke Yank, and they joined him.

Jen, Billings, and Laws sat on one of the beds, while the other two techs, whose names turned out to be Goran and Patrick, fussed with two tablets, trying to maneuver through the local wireless using their own shadow IPs. Holmes sat heavily on the other bed. Out of habit, Yank went to the window to check outside. Walker remained where he was in the doorway, hoping their commander had a plan.

"So here's the deal," Holmes said. "I had some friends in Dam Neck contact USSOCOM to check our status and it's not good. We've been put on the blacklist, which means any contact has to be reported and they're not going to stop until they find us."

"They don't think we did anything, do they?" Yank looked from one SEAL to the other.

Holmes shook his head. "They don't know. The operators have probably figured it out, but the bureaucrats learned all their strategy from Hollywood, therefore we *have* to be involved somehow." He laughed hollowly. "So we're not going to be getting help from our own anytime soon."

"But we knew that already," Laws pointed out.

"We did," Holmes said, nodding, "but I wanted to check out how far they went with it."

"All the way to blacklist, looks like." Laws put his head in his hands.

"So what now?" Walker asked. He hated being cooped up in the hotel room. There had to be something they could do.

"We can do two things. Waiting for someone to contact us is a possibility. The problem with that is they have no way to do that. Cell phones are dumped so we can't be tracked. If YaYa wanted to reach out and contact us, say in the event he came to his senses, he couldn't even do that."

"I'm hoping it wasn't something he planned," Walker said, encouraging the others to come to his friend's rescue. "I mean, we all know it wasn't YaYa who did this, right?"

Yank looked at Walker and shook his head. "Sure looked like the same crazy motherfucker."

"But that must mean that thing must still be inside him."

"Then why didn't you feel it, Mr. Radar?" Laws asked, his voice angry.

"It must have hid from me. It must have—"

"Stow it." Holmes stood and went to the window. "We'll worry about guilt or innocence when we have the senator back safe and sound. Until then, let God sort it out." He turned back to the men and women in the room and folded his hands behind his back. He stared at them for a long moment.

It was Laws who spoke first. "You have a plan."

Holmes nodded and allowed himself a small smile.

"And you have an ace in the hole," Laws added.

Holmes nodded again, ever so slightly. His smile remained in place.

Laws high-fived Walker, who wasn't sure what he was high-fiving. Then he turned back. "So give. What's the plan?"

Holmes checked his watch; then he raised his chin. "Hey, Rosencrantz and Guildenstern, you able to hack into the police database?"

Goran and Patrick both grinned. "If it's a Linux system it'll be easy enough."

"Wait, do you speak Spanish?" Jen looked from one to the other. "I didn't know you spoke Spanish."

Goran explained, "We don't have to know Spanish. Linux is written in English for all intents and purposes. If we can get in, then we vector the information through Google Translate or another third-party program."

Jen wasn't convinced. "I still think we should have someone who speaks Spanish. Do we have anyone?"

Laws raised his hand.

"What don't you speak?" she asked. "Swahili. It's all those pops and clicks that confuse me," he said.

Jen addressed Holmes. "So if they get inside, what do you want them to find?"

"Any reports of vehicles stolen from the airport during a two-hour period starting an hour before the senator's plane landed and ending an hour after he was taken. I need to know if he was working alone or with help. If he had help, then we're probably lost because whoever met him brought the vehicle with them."

"They could have stolen it from the airport," Walker offered.

Holmes shook his head. "We're not going to be that lucky, but we'll check. Of course, if YaYa was working alone or if he had to obtain his own transportation, then there should be a record of the missing vehicle."

"What if it was taken from the long-term lot?" Guildenstern asked. "You might never find it then."

"I doubt YaYa would be able to get that far carrying the senator. My guess is that he found the nearest vehicle he could get his hands on. Based on the layout of the airport, something nearer the private terminal."

"And once we find the vehicle, we can insert an all-points

bulletin for the car into the system," Jen said. Her eyes were wide as she stood and began consulting with her two techs.

"What about us?" Yank asked. "What if we find him? All we have are P229s. As much as I like them, I think we need bigger guns."

As if on cue, someone knocked on the door.

Yank and Walker pulled their weapons free and aimed at the door while Holmes moved to check it. Seeing what he wanted to see through the peephole, he waved for the two SEALs to put down their weapons and he opened the door.

Navarre walked inside. When the door was closed, he and Holmes embraced.

"Tough day, amigo," Navarre said. "This is not a good situation."

"An understatement," Holmes said flatly. "I've been told to report to headquarters. They want a full account of my assistance to you and your team about... how do you say it, boon dangle?"

"Boondoggle, sure. Our government wants plausible deniability." Holmes punched his left palm with his right fist. "But I understand. You need to take care of you and your own."

"I've taken care of you first, old friend. That shit on the border with the 'cabras has been bothering me. I want to make it up." He reached into his pocket and pulled out a keycard from the same hotel. "Room 333. It's a suite. Your gear is in there."

Yank, Laws, and Walker all began talking at once, but Holmes made a chopping motion with his left arm that shut them up. He embraced Navarre once more, then closed the door behind the Mexican after he left. Holmes didn't say anything. Walker wanted nothing more than to hear in detail what was happening, but he had to wait for Holmes. Finally their leader spoke.

"It turns out the C-130 can't be a crime scene and that the State Department had no right to impound it."

"How's that?" Jen asked.

"It was a Mexican military craft on Mexican soil. No way were they going to turn it over to the Americans. The crew chief ordered it airborne. They landed it at a military base nearby and unloaded all of our gear, which is now sitting in Room 303."

"No shit?" Walker asked, more than a little stunned.

"No shit," Holmes answered. Then he pointed at Walker and Yank. "You two get cleaned up and get down to 303. Yank, I want a complete inventory list in thirty mikes. Walker, find out what Rosencrantz and Guildenstern want from their stuff and bring it to them. Now that they have access to their high-speed techie magic crap, I expect they'll be very happy." He glanced at the techs, who were all smiles.

"Finally," Laws said with more than a little joy in his voice. "We got a fucking plan."

Holmes smiled tightly. "The world works better with one. Now get over here and let's talk courses of action."

Walker went into the other room to clean up, leaving the two senior members of Triple Six to plan. He had to admit that knowing they had their stuff back made more difference than he'd thought it would. It gave him back the confidence he hadn't realized he'd lost.

45

HOTEL MAJESTIC, MEXICO CITY. DUSK.

Jen spent the next ten minutes in the bathroom, staring into the mirror, her hands trembling as she splashed cold water on her face. She couldn't get out of her mind the insanity in YaYa's eyes as he'd fired his pistol point blank into Pete Musso's stomach. Why had Pete tried to save them? He'd never showed any sense of valor before. Not that in suburban San Diego he'd had the chance, but Pete was an analyst. Her eyes filled with tears again as she relived the moment over and over, the worst part being the agony and fear on Pete's face as he'd fallen to the deck of the plane, his hands clutching at his stomach as blood pulsed out of him.

She shook her head to get rid of the image. Dwelling on this wasn't helping. Maybe Walker had been right. Maybe she should never have come. Maybe analysts weren't needed on the scene.

She gave herself five minutes, then wiped her face, washed her hands, and left the bathroom. She passed Goran and Patrick, who had set up their systems and settled on the sofa by the window. Alexis Billings was already sitting there, too, leaning on her left side, her hand supporting her head. She stared off into space.

After a few moments, Alexis spoke. "It's not your fault."

"I know," Jen said a little too hastily. "I mean, I understand what you're saying, but I'm the one who brought him down here."

"You had no control over what happened," Alexis said in a monotone.

"It doesn't mean I'm not responsible," Jen said.

Billings sighed.

Jen looked at the other woman, who was now staring at the floor.

"Do you want to know who's responsible?" Alexis asked, her voice rough with emotion and barely above a whisper. "I'm responsible. This whole mess. Me. *I'm* the one."

"Don't you think you're being a little hard on yourself?" Jen asked.

Alexis chuckled hoarsely. "If only. The bottom line is that I chose them."

"Who'd you choose?"

"The SEALs. YaYa, Holmes, Walker—all of them. I knew what we were getting into. The senator told me more than once I was playing with fire and I didn't listen to him."

Jen didn't know where Alexis was going with this, but her curiosity was piqued. "What did you do?"

Alexis shrugged. She reached up and released her long hair, shaking it out. "I did what I was supposed to do. I chose these SEALs for a reason, you know. I knew we had to have someone special. I knew we had to develop a more modern mechanism to recruit SEALs into our unit." She turned to Jen and held her with wide eyes. "Do you know how they used to do it before? They held séances. They read Tarot. They even threw bones, for God's sake. They'd have entire rooms full of these 'magic' people doing juju over files and pictures of our best U.S. Navy SEALs." She laughed again, this time tilting on the edge of her own craziness. "When I took over I changed all that. I turned the magic into a science. We now have PhDs in game science, neurology, and statistics at the core of our team. Psychologists interact with each recruit prior to attending SEAL training, so we can establish a database of supernumerological scores for each and every recruit. We rack and stack these based on their statistically manifested abilities and keep them ready, like they're weapons in an arms room."

Jen shook her head. "I don't get it. What do you mean?"

Alexis gave her a stern look. "Do you think for one minute that Navarre coming at the last minute with our equipment was by chance?"

Jen thought it was odd that Alexis would have used that particular phrase—"by chance." She didn't know where this was going, but she wanted to find out. "I thought it was lucky, if that's what you mean."

"Exactly!" Alexis snapped her fingers. "Luck. Holmes was tested and he was found to be extraordinarily lucky through our game-design tests. In fact, did you know that he's not allowed to set foot on the gaming floors of Vegas casinos? The word was out on him long before he became a SEAL. He was raised in Vegas and can't even go into a casino. They think it's because he counts cards."

"Are you saying Holmes was chosen because of his *luck?*"

"That's exactly what I'm saying. During game play, whether it was cards, board games, video role-playing games, first-person shooters, or even MMORPGs, he showed an unexplainable ability to not only not die, but to win in the end. On a consistent basis he accomplished the statistically impossible. Which is one reason he's been in charge of Triple Six for so long."

"Then I shouldn't worry—they won't die?" Jen asked, still trying to get a handle on what Alexis was saying. While the information was beyond interesting, its relevance to the present seemed tenuous at best.

"You'd better worry. His luck is *his* luck. He has a better chance of surviving alone than he does on a team. His luck might extend to the others, but it is *his* talent." She got up and grabbed a soda from the counter and popped the top. "Of course, he could run into a null. We had one of those before, during the Roosevelt presidency." She sat back down, then added, "The first Roosevelt, that is." She drank deeply.

"When you say a null, you mean—"

"Someone who takes away luck. Like a cooler. Casinos

employ them. There are those who can make people unlucky. Say someone's having a run at a table, then the casino will have this cooler touch or bump the person and watch how much they lose after that."

"Alexis," Jen said, "this all sounds a little far-fetched."

"You'd think so, right? And just in case you don't know, but this is strictly a special access program, so you can't share it with anyone."

Jen leaned back and crossed her arms. "Great, thanks. But what does this have to do with blame?"

Alexis crossed her arms, holding the soda in her right hand. "I chose YaYa, too. I chose him because he's a font." Seeing the look on Jen's face, she explained. "Some people call them polymaths, although that's not the right term either. Ever meet someone who seems to fit in perfectly wherever they go? If you watch them closely, they'll take on the speech and demeanor of the group they're trying to fit in with. They don't do it consciously. It comes naturally. What we've discovered is that the same is true for the supernatural. They are *drawn* to *it* and it is drawn to them. So we call them fonts. But instead of providing something, fonts provide a space for something, like holy water fonts at the entrance to Catholic churches."

"So you knew this was going to happen?"

"Of course not. How could I have—"

Jen shook her head, cutting Alexis off. "I mean that he could be inhabited."

"The term is possessed," Alexis said without any sense of humor.

"Possessed then. Did you know?"

"We knew. We counted on it."

Jen's mouth dropped open.

"Now do you see what I mean? This is absolutely my fault. The idea about a font is that we could capture an entity, then use it somehow, study it perhaps."

"And did YaYa sign on for this? Does he know that this is his special talent, to go out and unwittingly capture spirits?"

Alexis stared hard at Jen for a moment; then her face softened.

"No. He doesn't know. And neither does Yank. He doesn't know his talent either."

"Are you going to tell them?"

"No. And neither are you."

Jen heard the unspoken addition *if you want to keep your job* loud and clear. She should shut up now, but she had one more question for which she needed an answer. "Was he going to get any training in his font ability?"

"Eventually. We were assessing him. He wasn't ready yet."

Now it was Jen's turn to give a bitter smile. "What you mean is that you didn't know how he'd react once he found out. Does that about sum it up?"

"It does."

Jen stood and smoothed out the wrinkles in her slacks. She took a moment, then faced Alexis. "Listen, I don't know how much of the blame you should really take. These are U.S. Navy SEALs who happened to have some talents which made them suitable for Triple Six. If YaYa is so wide open, it could have happened any time. It might have even happened before and we don't know it." She could see Alexis begin to appreciate her comments. Now it was time to bring her back down. "But you should let them know their talents. Otherwise it's like giving a pistol to a three-year-old." She shook her head. "If you want to blame yourself for something, blame yourself for that, because I know if you saw a three-year-old reaching for a pistol, you'd run into the room and do whatever you could to stop the inevitable." Then she turned and walked out. She stepped into the other room in time to see Walker and Yank returning with two Pelican cases.

· "Hey, gal. What's up?" Walker asked.

Even with all the bullshit, she was glad to see him here and it made her heart warm.

46

HOTEL MAJESTIC, MEXICO CITY. LATER.

Yank was thrilled to get his equipment back. Going into battle with only a pistol and a knife made him feel like a samurai attacking Godzilla, especially in light of recent events. Without their weapons and equipment, defeating the homunculi wouldn't have been so easy. Likewise, the QuadEye and the HKs had contributed significantly to their complete domination of the crazy leper people. Their ability to communicate and attack in a synchronized fashion was integral to their success. He'd always believed that if the Crips, Bloods, or MS-13 of his hometown Los Angeles had even a modicum of SEAL training, they would have taken over L.A. long ago, instead of firing from car windows like overgrown Shriners in spoke-wheeled clown cars.

Downstairs they'd found all of their gear, plus some appreciated ammunition and pyrotechnics courtesy of GAFE. The Pelican cases of computer gear were brought up first so the techies could begin their search for the mystery vehicle Holmes believed YaYa had taken. Personally, Yank felt it was an incredible leap in reason to assume that YaYa had stolen a car. He just as easily could have had an accomplice. Didn't they say there'd been a phone call right before YaYa had begun acting strangely?

Yank felt a surge of goose flesh flow over his arms. If the

call had "activated" YaYa then they had a chance of targeting whoever was controlling him. Even money was on Ramon, but Yank wasn't so sure. Ramon was a werewolf or skinwalker. Did he really have the power to control someone over the phone? It just didn't feel right.

So then who?

They'd been back and forth from Room 333 to their own on the seventh floor three times. On the way back down, the elevator stopped on the fifth floor. A white family with a little boy and a little girl stepped into the car. Behind them came two Hispanic men, both dressed in suits. Yank looked for it and saw the bulge of a weapon underneath the left arm of each of them. They stepped aboard but didn't make eye contact. Yank let his gaze slide to the floor, and searched for a bulge at the ankle. The taller of the two had one, but the other man didn't.

Yank exchanged a quick glance with Walker. He'd seen the same thing.

Yank and Walker were back against the rear of the car. The family was probably getting off in the lobby, starting a day with coffee, juice, and cinnamon churros in the plaza. Yank had already depressed the button for three. Now he wished he hadn't. Whatever was going on, they didn't want to show these people the location of their weapons cache.

So when the car stopped, the control panel dinged, and the door opened, he and Walker remained motionless. For a few uncomfortable moments, no one moved. Then the blond-haired little boy turned around and stared at Yank. The kid seemed about to say something, when his father turned him around and hugged him to his side.

The door closed. Yank glanced up and saw that the taller of the two men was looking at him. Yank gave him a gentle smile, even though he felt anything but gentle on the inside, then resumed staring into space, all the while keeping everyone within his peripheral vision.

The car began to descend. When it reached the lobby, one of

two things would happen. Everyone would get out or the two men would keep Yank and Walker from leaving. Yank's fingers itched to pull the knife from his right cargo pocket. In close quarters, it was the perfect weapon.

Yank let his gaze stray toward the shorter of the two men. The haircut didn't have the spit and polish of an American agent. For that matter, neither did the suit. On closer inspection, it was ill-fitting and looked more like what an insurance agent would wear rather than a businessman.

The ding of the elevator was followed by the door opening onto a bustling lobby. First the family got out, then the two men, then Yank and Walker. To stay would bring more attention to them than they needed. The men went straight to the counter. Yank made for the restaurant. Walker followed close behind.

As Yank moved through the crowd, he became aware of how unlike everyone else he and Walker were dressed. Had they paid attention, they wouldn't have left the room looking like road-worn military contractors, the modern mercenary, or tactical Mormon missionaries. With their military haircuts, boots, tactical cargo pants, and sweat-stained T-shirts tight over well-muscled chests, they looked like anything but tourists. What they needed to blend in were shorts and flip-flops. Realizing that they were being noticed by several people of unknown origin, Yank opened the door to the stairs and they ran up the three flights.

Thirty seconds later they were in Room 333.

"Who were they?" Walker asked.

"Don't know." Yank put the privacy chain on the door, then ran over to check the lock on the sliding glass door that led to the balcony. "One thing *is* for sure, though. We shouldn't be seen out in public unless we have a change of clothes."

Walker looked at the equipment spread over the two beds in the small room. "And we shouldn't leave this room unguarded. The last thing we need is a maid coming in, or worse. I'll take the first shift. Why don't you go up and tell Holmes."

"I'm sure he'll concur."

"Maybe see if someone can't go out and buy us some clothes."

"Good idea, but that might depend on the plan."

"You mean Holmes's plan?"

"None other."

"A little light on details, though, wasn't it?"

Yank grinned. "It'll come together. I'm pretty damn sure of it."

47

BENEATH MEXICO CITY.

The barking wouldn't stop.

Loud, then soft.

Savage, then timid.

Rapid-fire, then monotonous.

A growl came now and then, but it was always the barking. No matter which bark, it rang hollowly in the darkness, the immense space magnifying the sound and smashing it against the stone walls, where instead of being shattered, it bounced back even more powerful.

They'd chained him to the steps. The chain was thick, tasted cold, and bit into the skin of his ankle. Where it touched, he was already bloody. He didn't know why the chain was there. He was their dog. He'd been their dog for a while, the thing inside him recognizing the thing inside the master. Both of them were from the same family. Both had been old when man first broke wood to make fire.

They'd told him to stay.

They'd told him to guard.

They'd told him he was a good boy for bringing them the senator.

He stopped barking for a moment and ran on all fours to a bowl of water. He lapped both furiously and happily, vaguely aware how strange it was for those two emotions to be so intertwined. He snapped at the water and watched it splash on the stone beside the bowl, darkening the stone, making it almost black. Then he saw himself in the water. He recognized everything and nothing. For a moment he remembered a time when he'd stood upright and he'd been called by a different name.

Then he struck the water with his hand, destroying his image.

He turned and ran the other way to the length of the chain and began to bark once more.

Barking. Always barking. It felt so joyous to do so.

48

HOTEL MAJESTIC. LOBBY. NIGHT.

Three hours later Walker was wearing flip-flops and shorts. What had started out as a joke had become reality, except that he now had a knockoff Hard Rock Mexico City shirt and pink sunglasses, and was sitting in the lobby with Jen, pretending to study a tourist map, but really watching the frenetic population of the hotel lobby. American, Canadian, and French families wore garish clothes and dragged along tired children and small, ratlike dogs. Men in stylish suits commanded small groups of thugs in cheap suits who stood around glaring at each other. A small army of staff wearing charcoal-gray clothes and red-and-white name tags moved to the gravitational pull of everyone's needs, most happy when they were crossing the lobby, their eyes on problems yet to be reported.

Rosencrantz and Guildenstern had discovered something very interesting when they'd slipped into the police database looking for a possible missing vehicle. Evidently, the hotel they were staying at had a special notification that put it off limits to the police. This raised a red flag the size of the Goodyear blimp and necessitated Laws making several calls, which resulted in a disturbing, if not interesting, revelation. Of all the hotels in Mexico, more than five thousand, they'd chosen the single one that seemed to be having a government-sanctioned reunion of the Los Zetas cartel. As it turned out, it wasn't a reunion. Several of Laws's criminal contacts had reported that all of Los Zetas' middle management along the Mexican-U.S. border had headed south to Mexico City. No one seemed to know why.

And they also discovered a vehicle that they believed was YaYa's getaway car. A 2003 Corolla had been stolen from passenger drop-off within minutes of the senator's plane landing. The car was then traced through traffic cameras to a location a mere hundred meters from the hotel.

The convergence of events was too coincidental. It was no secret that Holmes disbelieved in such coincidences. So they'd gone from searching for the senator to figuring out the mystery of the presence of Los Zetas, with the presumed promise that once they solved one, they'd solve the other. That created the unprecedented situation now, as Jen and Jack played little missus and mister American tourist right in the middle of what was supposed to be a personnel recovery mission of the most desperate kind.

All of which necessitated getting back on the grid.

Laws was upstairs continuing to work on a series of throwaway phones, using criminal contacts he'd established over the years. Not only was he trying to ascertain the exact names of the Zetas in the hotel, but he was also establishing ratlines, calling assets they had on file to use in the event they needed a quick and secret way to leave the city. As it was, they were in such a hive of activity that leaving might prove impossible.

Holmes and Billings were also working the phones, using voice-over-Internet protocol (VOIP). Paired with a roaming shadow IP, it allowed them to each use a computer system without fear of being discovered. Holmes was busy coordinating support from Navarre and his GAFE forces. He also unofficially contacted several friends at Naval Special Warfare Command in both PACOM and Coronado. Some of the things he desired they weren't willing to provide. But others, especially those which could be hand-carried, were more than a possibility.

While Holmes was working to get help for the team, Billings tried one last time to get their own government assets on board. She and Holmes had discussed it and they'd decided to try and coordinate official assistance, while he was coordinating unofficial assistance. So she'd contacted the embassy and after a ten-minute argument with the chief of station, the head of the FBI legate team, and the Secret Service agent in charge who'd come down from the States, she switched to Plan B. Now that it was clear they'd get no official help from their own, she put across the notion that they were traveling south and out of the city and wanted to have assistance waiting for them should Triple Six make it to Veracruz, where they'd had substantial leads. The bureaucrats had, of course, not been willing to comply and were keeping her on the line attempting to track down her location via NSA traces. She could hear the frustration in their voices as they worked to keep her from hanging up. In reality, it didn't matter how long she stayed on. There was no way they could track her as long as her IP kept roaming, but she didn't want them to know that. So in the end she cut them off and hung up, hopefully leaving them to believe they had the superior technological upper hand.

"Walker, we're looking for this man," Laws said into his ear through the BCCG. "He works Nogales and runs the border operations for the Zetas."

Walker glanced down at his tablet, which had been ripped by the techs so that it could no longer broadcast its own location with a static IP. They'd also disabled satellite uplink, allowing only for the use of wireless, in this case, thanks to the hotel. A police photo of a middle-aged Mexican man was on the screen. Jen saw it too and snuggled closer, as if they were both looking at a picture that could have been a sunset, a kitten, or a dolphin, and not a bloodthirsty Zeta leader.

Walker stared briefly across the lobby and saw the man talking with several subordinates. "Got this one, too," he said into the BCCG, as he switched his gaze to Jen, as if they loved each other and wanted to lose themselves in each other's eyes. That part wasn't hard at all.

"That makes six Zeta lieutenants. My sources were right on. Whatever's going on is big."

"Jen thinks it has something to do with Xray," he said, using the code they'd defined for Senator Withers. They could explain a lot away if overheard or if someone read their lips, but the title and name of the man they were searching for was so unique, they'd decided they'd refrain from even mentioning him from here on.

"We're open to that possibility."

"Think about it. We're in one of the three hotels overlooking the plaza, under which are the archeological digs of Tenochtitlán. Xray could be beneath us even now." He winked at Jen as a couple of tough guys stalked by. "Any plans on getting us down there?"

"R and G are working it. They've found several ways, but they think they have something even better."

"Oh, joy," Walker said feeling anything but. "God bless the good-idea fairy."

"I know." Laws laughed hollowly. "What would we do without the feckless bitch."

Walker noted that several of the cartel men had begun staring at them with a little more than minor concern. He leaned over and kissed Jen on the neck and as he did, said, "We might have just been made. Moving back upstairs."

"Roger. Go to three first, then we'll bring you up."

Walker and Jen got to their feet and headed toward the elevators. A pair of Zetas detached themselves from the Nogales lieutenant's group and followed. Walker and Jen concentrated on being eager lovers. As it turned out, it wasn't so difficult. They were joined on their elevator by the two Zetas and another young couple, even more eager to demonstrate their love by the way their hands moved over each other's bodies.

Walker and Jen got off on three. So did one of the Zetas, tall with large hands and wide shoulders. They moved toward Room 333 with the Zeta several steps behind.

Their room was on the left. Jen fumbled with the keycard on the door, while Walker pretended to be an overamorous suitor, urging her to hurry. He stood behind her, which necessitated the Zeta either stopping, or pushing his way past. As he pushed past, Walker moved into action. He spun to his left to get behind the man. Simultaneously, he grabbed the man's left wrist with his own left hand, and brought his right hand up to rake across the man's face.

The Zeta tried to turn to the right, but Walker's grip on his left wrist wouldn't allow it. By then it was too late. The Zeta tried to turn to the left, which allowed Walker to snake his hand inside the Zeta's arm and around the back of his neck, gripping his left arm, which now pushed against the back of the man's head. Walker stepped back and sank in the choke nice and deep. An experienced fighter would try and remove Walker's balance. An inexperienced fighter would try and remove the arms. The Zeta was inexperienced and desperately tried to pry Walker's arms away, losing precious time, and eventually, his consciousness.

Jen had the door open and they pulled him inside.

Walker checked the hall, then closed the door behind them.

After communicating with the rest of the team, Laws and Holmes joined them moments later.

When the Zeta awoke, he wore only his underwear and was tied and gagged on one of the mattresses. The other mattress was against the door to muffle any sounds that might be made. Jen and Walker stood with Holmes to one side, while Laws sat in a chair, cowboy style, grinning at what he was about to do.

Ten minutes later, Triple Six discovered the missing link. In two hours, the Zetas were to attend a special ceremony in one of the excavated areas of Tenochtitlán not open to the public. The Zetas didn't know what the reason was for the ceremony, but they were all promised it would provide the cartel with unlimited power, which flowed into what Billings had been told of the cartel's desire to bring back the old gods. He also mentioned that they were to be rewarded with a special hostage.

Over the next sixty minutes, Triple Six planned the mission and shut down operations. Rosencrantz, Guildenstern, and Billings, along with moral support from Emily Withers, would monitor operations as best they could from the room, while Laws and Holmes would form one group, and Yank, Jen, and Walker would form the other group.

When they were ready, everyone dispersed to their areas. Walker and Jen headed downstairs. "We're going out into the plaza," he said through his BCCG. "See if you can watch our back."

The Los Zetas security would be heightened with their missing man. They'd left him tied in the room. He'd be found eventually, if only by the maids the next morning. But that didn't help them. Since he was last seen following them, their presence would definitely generate interest. Which is why they made a beeline to the crowds outside.

Guildenstern responded. "We have a Raven in the air. We'll have your back."

As they exited the elevator, they turned and strolled toward the revolving door, with Walker well aware he was giving up his back. He counted the steps to the exit, figuring there were twelve to make it to the door, then another four to completely exit. He made it to five when he heard someone shouting behind him. He didn't turn. He felt Jen's shoulders tighten and her hand grip his a little more insistently.

He heard someone running.

Then he was at the door. He and Jen stepped inside. As the door began to revolve, moving them outward, he had a look at a man running through the lobby toward the concierge stand. He threw his arms around another man and they both hugged furiously. It looked like they were old friends, rather than out to get them.

Walker kept his smile, but let the tension bleed away as best he could. Then they were outside, the sounds and smells of the street slapping them in the face. The smell of cinnamon churros fought with the smell of too many people, which in turn fought with the overwhelming undercurrent of exhaust, which was at constant odds with the flowers carried by dark-brown-skinned women who could trace their lineage back to Montezuma.

They ducked into the crowd, becoming part of the shifting mass of humanity. There had to be a thousand people mingling, moving through, standing, playing music, conversing, selling, and every other thing one could do in a plaza. But like any such place, it had a pulse and once Walker found it, he made themselves a part of it.

"Raven on station," came a clipped comment from Guildenstern.

Walker reached into a blue boutique bag that completed their tourist disguise, removed the tablet, then searched through the wireless settings until he found the Raven's broadcast. After typing in the password, an image began to resolve on the screen. At first it was too confusing to make out; then he let his mind attune to the idea that it was a bird's-eye view from a MUAV patrolling overhead. He and Jen strolled arm in arm, the tablet close to their chests. It was Jen who found them first, and pointed. Her red hair beside his blond hair was a colorful island in a sea of dark brown and black hair. Walker nodded and watched the pattern of movement until he understood it; then he and Jen turned and they cut across the pattern. It didn't take long, but he saw three people cutting across the pattern after them, each one at different intervals beside and behind them. It was a classic move, designed to bracket them and to keep the surveillants from losing the surveilled.

They moved around the plaza several times, taking nearly half an hour to do so. To anyone watching, they were a young Caucasian couple, probably American or Canadian or European, in love and walking together while watching something on their tablet that could be anything from a music video to a love story. But Walker was watching those who were tracking them, wondering why they'd been selected, and hoping that they'd leave him and Jen alone.

But the longer they moved around the plaza, the closer the

three came. It wasn't until their fourth circuit that he realized they were being herded, which meant that there was also someone in front of them. He wanted to search the screen, but instead he tore his gaze away from the overhead scene, closed the feed, and switched to a movie.

A man bumped them hard enough to make him stumble.

"Lo siento, amigo," the man said, close enough for Walker to see the wide pores on his face, and note his bad teeth and breath that smelled of old meat and spices.

Walker allowed the tablet to fall forward, which the man grabbed with ease. As he glanced at it, Walker observed him and noted that he was of the same cloth as many of those he'd been watching inside the hotel—middle-level muscle of the Zetas.

"Hey, that's ours!" Jen cried.

Bad Breath held up the tablet and smiled. "You walk with tablet? You watch this movie?"

"Give that back," Walker said, holding out his hand. "That's mine, eh."

"Who are you?"

Walker nodded and tried to grab the tablet from the man, but Bad Breath was playing keep-away. "Hey, come on."

"I'm getting scared," Jen said, her voice perfectly plaintive.

Walker plastered a mean look on his face. "You don't give that back to me I'm calling the local mounties, eh." Walker sadly realized he could never be an actor, but just hoped his ruse was enough so they'd lose interest.

Bad Breath met someone's eyes over Walker's shoulder. The movement was minuscule, but Walker had been watching for it. A slight north-south-north tilt of the head. He handed the tablet back.

"My apologies," he said.

Walker took it and hugged Jen closer to him as the man melted back into the crowd. He thought about turning around, but knew he wouldn't see anyone there either.

They started walking again. When he was certain no one next

259

to him was paying attention, he dialed up the feed once more. He watched for a time and was pleased to see they were being left alone.

Now for Part Two of the plan.

49

MUSEO DE HISTORIA NATURAL. NIGHT.

Yank and Hoover were waiting for them at the side entrance to the Museo de Historia Natural. Across the plaza, an earthquake siren began to blast its banshee wail. Earthquakes were common in Mexico City and the government continually practiced evacuation drills. The locals fled first, followed by everyone else as the bone-vibrating sound filled the square. The only problem was that no one wanted to run into any of the buildings, so everyone milled around like frantic refugees, waiting for the ground itself to move beneath them.

All this meant no one was watching the two pretend-Canadians running toward the side of the Museum of Natural History, nor were they seen as they slipped inside. Yank shut the door behind them and chained it shut.

Yank's sweat-sheened face reflected his nervousness. He pulled a duffel bag from where it lay against the wall behind him, then pulled out another duffel bag and passed one to each of them.

"What's that?" Walker straightened and pointed to the second duffle.

"Holmes wants her to gear up."

"She's a civilian." Walker reached for the bag, but Yank jerked it away. "She's not wearing it."

Yank shook his head as he held fast to the bag. "He wants her to have some armor in case something happens."

"That's bullshit."

Jen and Yank stared at Walker, waiting to see what he was going to do.

The problem was Walker didn't know *what* he wanted to do. Worse, he knew that Holmes was listening in over their bone-conducting communications gear. He had to be. Walker didn't like it, but the inevitable conclusion that if Jen was to follow them into combat she had to have armor was an inescapably correct idea.

"Want to talk to him?" Yank asked.

Walker shook his head, furious, but he understood. "No. That's fine."

He stripped and put on black camo fatigues. He traded his flip-flops for socks and boots. He checked the leads and attachments for his BCCG, then slipped on his level-six armor. After adding the Rhodesian vest and his ballistic gloves, he put on his mask. Yank gave him a HK416 with a suppressor, which Walker cleared and then loaded. Finally Yank tossed him a holster containing a P229; this Walker strapped to his right thigh.

Meanwhile, Jen had on her own boots and fatigues, but was struggling with the body armor. It wasn't exactly made for a woman's figure. Walker moved to help her as Yank watched their perimeter.

"Listen," Walker instructed her. "You stay behind us unless we're running, then I want you in front." His voice was calm but firm. "Follow our lead. Keep your eyes on what *we* do, not what the enemy does."

"How can I tell who the enemy is?"

"We're normally shooting at them. Now, this armor will stop pretty much everything they can fire at you with a handgun. Not that you should be brave, just don't be so scared you put yourself in a position where you can get hurt." He patted her rib cage. "This area isn't so protected because we need to have freedom of movement."

He came to the last two things in the bag, which were a ballistics mask, orange with a white diagonal stripe, and a P229 in a holster. He handed the mask to her, which she put on. But he held on to the pistol, staring at it.

"We don't have comms for you, so you'll have to stick close to one of us. This is for defense. Period. I don't want you to... you don't need to be charging into anything. This pistol holds fifteen nine-millimeter parabellum rounds. It fires quick. Keep your grip tight and steady if you have to fire it." He handed it to her as if it were a live grenade. "Understand?"

"Jack, I—"

"I asked if you understood."

She nodded, then added, "Yes."

She began to attach it to her thigh in a drop-down holster as Walker had done, but her hands were shaking. He took it from her and attached the two straps, adjusted them to her leg, then slid the 9mm into place.

Damn it all to hell, Holmes, he wanted to shout. *Wasn't there any other way? Why couldn't she be topside with Rosencrantz and Guildenstern?* But Walker knew the answer. She'd made herself a known quantity by going operational with him. She'd already been part of their distraction. It wouldn't be long before the Zetas investigated the operation of the seismic alarm to see if a drill had been scheduled. If the Zetas decided to roll everyone up, she'd be in danger. She'd been necessary to help them identify some of the players and now because she'd been seen, she'd be sought out, interrogated if she was caught, and probably even killed. No, her coming with them was the best choice. Perhaps even the only one.

So instead of shouting at the moon, he squeezed her shoulders gently and stared into her eyes. Behind the mask his own eyes were twisted into pools of emotion. "Keep low. Keep cool. Everything will be okay."

She nodded, the look in her eyes trying to work itself into something he'd find reassuring but failing miserably.

He placed her Pro-Tec helmet on her head, then slid into his own. He pulled out the QuadEye and slid it into a pouch in his vest. The night lights inside the building were functioning well enough so that he wasn't going to need it.

"Ready," Walker said as Yank was finishing gearing up Hoover.

Yank and the dog had originally traversed the area as a blind man with his guide dog. The ruse no longer needed, they were the epitome of combat-ready. Yank was dressed much like Walker, except that he wore a fuchsia-colored mask, as opposed to Walker's bloodred-colored mask. Hoover, on the other hand, had undergone a makeover. Gone was her usual tactical harness, replaced by a K9 Storm Intruder. Custom fitted, the Intruder was a high-tech multi-functional body-armor harness that protected the dog's sternum, as well as her central body. An integrated camera periscope rose from the dog's back, providing night vision and IR up to a thousand meters, which could be remotely fed. An antenna allowed for communications to the dog in the event that she became separated from the team. Hoover wore green-lensed IR goggles, giving her a bug-eyed appearance. Storage pockets held grenades and a first aid kit, as well as several vials of holy water, a cross from the Second Temple of Solomon, and two blue blankets.

Walker leaned down and scratched Hoover behind one ear.

The dog stepped backwards and stared at him as if to say, *How dare you touch me!*

Walker whispered, "Don't be a prima donna."

Hoover gave him a long blank look, then shook his hand away.

Walker laughed on the inside. He supposed it was a good thing that the dog thought of herself as a badass.

Yank nodded and began to pad down the side of a maintenance hallway. Walker and Jen followed after him. Walker and Yank held their HKs at tactical ready. Jen's hands were free, held out beside her as if they could give her some balance in this new combat universe. They arrived at a door.

"Team One, ready," Yank said.

"Team One, proceed," came Holmes's voice.

Yank placed an electronic surreptitious entry device (ESED) over the security pad, depressed the red button on the side, and let the device do its business. Ten seconds later they heard a click; that was followed by the red light on the slide flipping to green.

After placing the device back inside a vest pocket, Yank opened the door and nudged the barrel of the HK through. He followed it, checking left and right. "Clear."

Walker and Jen joined Yank as they began to edge down the left hallway. They passed several rooms on the left. On the right were dioramas showing Mexico City in stark relief, Aztec pyramids rising from a bloodred floor with the Popocatépetl volcano commanding the background.

They came to a bend in the hallway and Yank pointed to a camera, a green LED signaling it was on.

"Team Two, first checkpoint reached," Walker asked.

"Roger, One. Remain in place," said Guildenstern, which meant Laws and Holmes had already moved out and were heading to their mission start point.

They'd patched into the museum security system and were tracking the guards. Additional signals had gone out, running an interval deletion loop that would ensure that no recordings were made of their time inside the museum.

Walker glanced back at Jen, whose gaze was on the floor. When she caught him looking, she met his eyes. He couldn't read her. He couldn't even smile reassuringly. But she nodded. She was doing okay.

After twenty seconds, they heard, "Team One, advance to Checkpoint Two."

The three of them moved down the left side of the hall at a half jog. They passed a gift shop, then came to a foyer that boasted a large staircase made from marble and polished silver. They moved to a door that had a black silhouette of a woman on the front and slipped through it.

"Team One at Checkpoint Two."

"Hold."

Another thirty seconds passed; then came the words they hadn't anticipated. "Oh, shit."

"Report," Walker said, wondering about the depth of trouble they were in now.

"Guard is coming your way."

"Female?"

"No, male."

Yank motioned for Walker, Jen, and Hoover to find a stall.

While they did so, Yank used the knob and the transom to climb to the ceiling, where he wedged himself between the edge of the transom and the corner of the room.

The sound of a man whistling grew louder and louder.

Guildenstern counted down from ten, leaving the last three numbers for the team to count beneath their breaths. Walker did so, and as he got to zero, the door opened and a museum security guard strolled in, whistling. He carried a thirty-eight in a holster on his waist. Keys and a flashlight dragged down the other side, leaving his stomach pressing precariously at the beltline. He was about the same height as Jen, but twice the weight. He entered the room oblivious to Yank hovering in the corner above him. The guard selected the stall at the end and spent several minutes doing his business. All the while he whistled, the sound reverberating off the tiles in the bathroom. No one dared say anything, much less shift their stance.

The whistling stopped for a moment. By the jangling of the keys, they knew he was tucking his shirt in and cinching his belt. As he exited the stall, he began to whistle again.

The man washed his hands, then went to the door. This was the moment that made Walker the most nervous. Heading straight to the door, all the guard had to do was look up and he'd see Yank. The problem was, what would they do if he saw him? The guard was a noncombatant and none of them wanted to see him harmed. Thankfully he opened the door and went back into the foyer.

Everyone breathed a sigh of relief… until the whistling suddenly stopped.

Yank leaped from his perch, landing on the bathroom floor. He hurried to the stall the man had used. Jen and Walker were already there. Walker hissed for Hoover, who tore around the corner and joined them. They closed the door. Walker got up on the porcelain and squatted. Yank and Jen climbed up on either side of him, counterbalancing with their weight. Yank and Jen lifted Hoover off the floor by grasping either end of the dog's vest.

The bathroom door swung open.

"Qué aquí?" the guard asked.

He shuffled around the entry for a moment, then opened the first three stall doors. Each time the slam of the door against metal made Jen jump. When he was at the final door, he stopped. They heard him laughing to himself. Then he turned, his keys jingling in his wake as he resumed whistling.

50

MUSEUM SUBBASEMENT.

They'd reached the subbasement and were poised before a bright and shiny steel door. Once more the ESED gained them entrance.

"Bet I could sell this puppy in Compton," Yank said with a twinkle in his eye.

Walker and Yank attached QuadEyes to the front mounts of their helmets and set them in place. He told Jen to hold on to his rear vest. Then all three of them stepped through the door. Walker closed it behind them, plunging them into a completely new environment. Gone was the antiseptic cleanliness and stark smell of the museum, replaced by the heady scent of old earth and animal musk.

The darkness was absolute. Both Walker and Yank keyed their AN/PEQ-2s on their HK416s to the fifth setting, sending high-power illumination with the targeting laser, and their universe turned bright green in their QuadEyes. Jen placed her own AN/PNS-7s on her helmet and turned it on, just as she'd been shown. All four stared into the green.

They'd passed through the Museum of Natural History and into its subbasement. Part of it was situated over the underground complex, but the rest was directly beneath the Templo Mayor Museum, which was situated over much of the underground complex, and included many original icons as well as some of the monoliths that had been unearthed beneath the Zócalo. The museum was adjacent to the surface excavations, but through vicissitudes of five hundred years of earthquakes, cave-ins, and poor construction, much of the temple area still remained buried. Several hundred meters beneath the museum was a different story. Although the excavations were continuing, these weren't visible to the public, nor would they be. Rumor from Laws's sources was that the Catholic Church had become involved and was unwilling to provide the old iconography for possible worship. Whatever the reason, much of the excavation was carried out in secret, and in secret was where archeologists made some of their greatest discoveries.

Rosencrantz had revealed that in 2008 the funding for the excavation had changed from public sources to private, the largest of which was a charity that, after being traced back through several shell corporations, led to Lee Treviño Morales, aka Z-1, the leader of the Los Zetas. The team could only figure out one reason why a narco-criminal drug cartel was funding a public undertaking: Whatever had been discovered beneath the city was of such importance and such power that the Zetas were willing to pour billions of pesos into the endeavor.

Twenty minutes earlier, according to the reports from Rosencrantz, the Zetas who'd been gathered in the hotel had marched across the plaza, and had entered the Templo Mayor Museum, probably taking the archeologists' route into the main excavation site nearly a hundred meters beneath the surface. The earth above was supported by metal beams and wire mesh and the area was lit by phalanxes of halogen lights. Triple Six wouldn't know what was down there until they saw it for themselves, but if it was something worth keeping secret, it was something worth their time.

Their chosen route was through the subbasement in the Museum of Natural History. Early in the excavation there had been a second entry-exit point in the event something happened to the other. By all reports, this avenue of egress hadn't been used since 2008. The newness of the lock on the door said otherwise.

Walker took point. They tried to check in with Rosencrantz and Guildenstern, but their location beneath the surface wouldn't allow it. Neither would it let them contact the other team, which meant they must still be in the sewers. The path, about five meters wide and ten meters high, wound down and past foundations and pipes. The walls were hand-cut from stone and dirt. Lights dangled from wires running the length of it, but they weren't activated.

They moved inexorably down for about five minutes before Walker began to experience an odd feeling. The exhilaration of the mission was being replaced by something else, something he had felt on a mission only once or twice. Butterflies began to crash-land in his stomach. The feeling worked its way outward until tingly fingers had grabbed hold of his torso, his legs, and his arms. He found himself not moving and looked down at his own arms.

"What's wrong?" Jen asked.

He wanted to say that he couldn't feel his own body anymore, but he found that he couldn't speak.

Hoover growled low.

Jen whispered, "Is that—"

Yank moved up beside Walker.

Walker fought to look up. It was as if his head were traveling a hundred miles and the effort it took was like trying to shrug free from the gravity of irrational fear. When his gaze came level, he saw what the others saw—an apparition.

Ice water showered his nerves. A ghostly woman stood on the path. Her body was turned away, but her head was facing in their direction as she looked back at them. She wore a single piece of fabric that could have once been a dress. Her hair hung long and had beads at different intervals. Her feet were bare and the toes were implausibly long. But it was her hands that were the most disturbing. They were wrong, nothing like a woman should have. Instead of five fingers, she had talons like those on the feet of a crow; instead of arms, she had black-ridged bones, like the legs of a crow.

Walker was finally able to look upon her and felt his skin burn with her gaze. Her nose was twice the length of a human's and curved like a beak. Even in the green universe of IR, her eyes were twin black balls of greedy hate that dug into him and urged him to step forward so she could feed.

He wasn't alone.

Both he and Yank began to step drunkenly toward her.

Behind them Hoover growled louder.

"Oh no, you don't," he heard Jen say. But Walker paid no attention. His body was locked into the apparition's vise of black hatred and his entire being vibrated with the need to touch her, to be with her, to give himself to her.

It blinked at him with its black eyes, the motion undeniably avian.

Jen pushed her way past Yank and Walker and stepped in front of them. She held a cloth in front of her, much as a toreador would to a charging bull.

The apparition turned fully toward them. The cloth she had been wearing was ripped down the middle and her stomach had been opened, revealing a wet, black mess where her womb should have been. She reached out with bird-claw hands and snapped her talons together.

Jen began to speak in a powerful voice. "Remember, O most gracious Virgin Mary of Guadalupe, that in thy celestial apparitions on the mount of Tepeyac, thou didst promise to show thy compassion and pity toward all who, loving and trusting thee, seek thy help and call upon thee in their necessities and afflictions. Protect us, La Morenita. Protect us from this demon. Protect us from this thing that would take men's souls."

The apparition made a sound for the first time, halfway between a hiss and a whine.

Jen repeated the prayer twice more, advancing step by step toward the thing as she did so. The apparition turned away, brought its arms to its body, and hugged itself, the long taloned fingers stark against the light of its dress.

By the end of her third recitation, Jen was close enough to throw the cloth on top of the apparition. When it hit, the cloth caught fire and as it burned it fell, until there was nothing left of the apparition.

When the last spark of cloth disappeared, Walker felt a release. He staggered back and fell against the side wall.

Yank did the same. They stared at each other for a long moment.

"What the hell was that?" Yank asked in a trembling voice.

"It was a Cihuateteo, I think. The data pack said that they are spirits of women who died in childbirth and turned into vampires," Jen said. "As a follower of Cihuacoatl and related to Itzpapalotl, she seeks men to establish her revenge."

"Jesus," Yank gasped.

"No," Jen corrected. "Mary."

"That was one of the cloths we got from the catacombs?" Walker asked, remembering the side mission he and Laws had taken. "They didn't look like much."

Jen nodded. "Sometimes it's the simplest things." She rubbed her hands together.

Walker put an arm around her. "So she's gone?"

"Yes."

"And the blanket?" Yank asked.

"It was consumed in the process," Walker said.

"Do we have any more?" Yank asked.

"One more. Want one?" When Yank held out his hand, Walker took it from Hoover's pouch and passed it to the other SEAL.

While Yank stuffed it into a side pocket, Walker breathed for a few moments as he once again regained control of his body. He could take zombies and chupacabra and *qilin* and any number of creatures that could be destroyed through the liberal use of firepower, but he hated things that couldn't. Things like the grave demon that had once inhabited him. Like this apparition that had taken control of them. If Jen hadn't been there, he and Yank would be dead. Like the *thing* that inhabited YaYa and refused to release him.

"Weren't you scared?" Yank asked, inspecting the place where the apparition had been.

Jen smiled tightly. "Not really. According to the research, a Cihuateteo won't harm a woman. Still, it was the first time I'd seen one." She shook visibly for a moment, then seemed to pull herself together. "Now that's just stupid, to be scared after it happened."

"Nerves," Walker said, grinning as he pushed himself away from the wall. "Happens to me all the time."

"So when you shake, you're not afraid?" she asked, laughter on the edge of her question.

"Exactly. Just bleeding off adrenaline."

"Well, you were sure bleeding off a lot of adrenaline there, Mr. U.S. Navy SEAL."

He nodded. "I sure was. Glad that's fucking over."

51

TUNNEL UNDER ZÓCALO.

They reached a point where there'd been a cave-in. It looked like the ceiling had reached down to hug the floor. For several long minutes they thought they might have to retreat and find a different way. But Hoover began to dig about halfway up the fall, her claws moving aside the dirt. Soon she had made a hole the size of her head.

Yank joined her and found a spot where the dirt was soft, between two metal beams about three feet apart. They managed to clear enough debris for Hoover to clamber through.

Walker dialed in the feed from Hoover's Intruder harness. He saw a clear space on the other side of the cave-in, followed by a long hallway. Light sprung from an unknown source at the end of it. By his judgment, they were almost to their target set. Could that be it?

He explained what he was doing to Jen and Yank, then ordered Hoover forward. The feed came from the periscope on the dog's back, so the view swayed back and forth as the dog moved. The crown of her head and her ears were visible in the bottom fourth of the feed. She padded down the hall until she was bathed in enough light to wash out the feed. Walker toggled the view to ambient light rather than IR, and the view instantly darkened.

He ordered the dog to crouch and she did.

He ordered the dog to move forward and she did.

As the dog's head and shoulders moved around the corner, so did the feed, and it revealed a large open area sixty feet below the level of the doorway. Walker didn't take the time to examine the area. Instead, he snapped a picture from the feed and ordered Hoover to return.

Once the dog was back on their side of the cave-in, they hastily re-covered the hole; then Walker ported the picture to Yank and to the tablet that Jen had brought from her cargo pocket.

"Jen, what is it we're looking at?" Walker asked as he took in the image of a great cavern. On the left side, a man-sized pipe dripped brown water from a hundred feet up as if it had been broken during the excavation. On the right, a long staircase had been cut into the wall and reinforced. A rail ran its length. At the rear of the cavern was a great Aztec pyramid rising in the distance. Several dozen men in gold-and-red-brocade, floor-length robes stood on different intervals, looking toward the top, where five Los Desollados stood. Human skin hung from their bodies like lunatic fringe. Before and beside it were several smaller buildings, no greater than the mausoleums they'd seen in the New Orleans cemetery before the start of the mission. On each of these was a stone figure, reclining. Several oval areas had been bored into the basalt. Within these, snakes were captured, intertwining with each other. To the right, beneath the staircase, was the roof of a long rectangular building. The aspect of the picture didn't allow for them to determine its purpose.

"So the temple area that makes up the Templo Mayor on the surface was the primary temple of Tenochtitlán," Jen told them. "The pyramid that all the tourists see is the remains of the Grand Temple of Huitzilopochtli. He was the god of sun, war, and human sacrifice and was the patron god of Tenochtitlán. But his wasn't the only temple. The Aztecs worshipped many gods, goddesses, and beings, many of whom have made it into popular culture, much like Our Lady of Guadalupe, who is also the mother goddess Tonantzin.

"The stone statues on top of these smaller buildings are chacmools. They're actually Toltec icons, pre-Columbian, and date back to around 500 AD. They are heavily prevalent at Toltec sites such as Chichén Itzá. Their appearance here indicates the worship of some lesser god which transcended and survived as one Mesoamerican belief system imposed itself over another."

"Do we know what or who they represent?" Walker asked.

"Could be a corn god. Could be Santa Claus. I have no idea."

"What about the temple?" Yank asked. "Looks like some of our friends are camped out on top."

Jen shook her head. "It's of classic construction but not overly large. Without looking at the iconography on the sides, I don't know. See there at the base of the pyramid?"

Walker saw a rectangular area standing about the height and width of a man, with round objects lined up next to each other and stacked atop each other.

"That's a skull rack. Those who have been sacrificed have their heads placed there to remind everyone of their gift to the goddess."

"Oh, joy," Walker said, grimacing.

"You said 'goddess,'" Yank pointed out. "Does that mean you know?"

"I don't... maybe I do. I only just recently became an 'expert,'" she said, laughing awkwardly. "I'm just trying to make sense of what I studied. Hold on a minute." She dialed up some information on the tablet, read for a moment, then returned to their shared view. "With the snakes and the smallish pyramid, it could be the temple of Cihuacoatl. It would make a certain sense. The Cihuateteo are her followers. Cihuacoatl is a mother goddess. She's a fertility goddess too. It's believed that along with Quetzalcoatl, she ground up the bones of the previous peoples to create the current human peoples."

"What would Los Desollados be doing on her temple?" Walker asked.

"Good question," Yank added. "Xipe Totec, was it?"

"Right. Los Desollados are worshippers of Xipe Totec." She

checked the information on the tablet once more, then snapped her fingers. "See the shadows in front of the rectangular building on the right?"

Walker and Yank nodded. "Xipe Totec's temple is underground. I believe those are entrances. They called it Yopico, or the place of Yopi, the Zapotec name for the god. The Zapotecs date back to six centuries before Christ, so like many of the gods, it's the same god with a different name."

"You mentioned Itzpapalotl. What does *that* mean?" Walker asked.

"It translates to 'obsidian butterfly,' or maybe 'clawed butterfly.' Why?" she asked.

"See the reclining figures, those chacmools," Walker said, indicating the figures on the mausoleums. "Doesn't it look like they have protrusions coming from their backs? As if they might be folded wings?"

"Something like a butterfly's wings?" Yank asked. "Yeah, maybe. What's the background on Itzpapalotl?"

"She ruled over a realm which is the resting place of dead infants and the crucible for humanity."

"Seems to fit a theme." Walker wanted to get a better look at the area. The men arrayed around the main temple couldn't be distinguished in the picture.

"She's also a vampire," Jen said.

"Seriously?" Yank asked, looking up. "Seriously? We got a werewolf and a vampire? What's next, Creature from the Black Lagoon?"

"Be careful what you wish for," Walker said, without a trace of humor.

"But I don't think the temple of Itzpapalotl is here. Even if the chacmools look like them, she'd have something greater than even this pyramid."

An idea crept into Walker's mind. "They could be like bishops."

"What do you mean?" Yank asked.

"In the Catholic Church, if a bishop dies, he gets buried in the cathedral's crypt with a sarcophagus, usually with a relief of the one who was buried there. I wonder if this might be the same."

"Like a priest or priestess of Itzpapalotl? Something like that?" Jen asked.

"Yeah, something like that."

Yank straightened and removed the image from his QuadEye. "Somehow this whole place has the look and feel of a crypt." He checked his watch. "Let's get in there. I have enough background to ace a test, but not enough to get out of this alive. Let's see if we can get some good information from a little reconnaissance."

"We need to get set before the others arrive, anyway," Walker said. "I need to make a hide site."

52

AQUEDUCT ENTRANCE. MEXICO CITY. NIGHT.

One kilometer south of the plaza stood a man-high gate secured with an old, thick lock. Brown water gushed through it, just above their boots, falling into a trash-laden aqueduct below and behind them. A drunk called out to them, his words too slurred to understand. If he was ever to report them, he'd remember two black-clad men in shiny helmets—aliens—entering the sewers. If the Mexican authorities believed him, and if they decided to climb into the aqueduct, it would be long after the events that were about to unfold, because right now the police were responding to bank alarms signaling from all over town. More than three hundred alarms were being triggered at alternating times, causing every local and federal policeman to rush back and forth, leaving the area around the plaza even more free of police than it had been.

Laws snapped the lock. He and Holmes entered, and then he secured it with a bicycle lock. He tossed the keys up the aqueduct, where they sank. Then they began to move forward, carefully, but quickly. They had a lot of ground to cover.

Without knowing the extent of their underwater travel, they'd opted for the worst scenario, which is why they were wearing a closed-system scuba, with full-body neoprene and a full face mask that also covered their ears. The DARPA-provided mask was constructed from Gorilla Glass and featured an internal head-up display (HUD), which gave them full-spectrum views from the two forward cameras. They wore ballistic gloves on their hands and Vibram Spyridon toe shoes with carbon-polymer-reinforced soles. The latter provided them a much surer grip in the slippery wash on the bottom of the old pipe than anything else they could have chosen.

Pure oxygen was being pumped into the mask, courtesy of the LAR V Draeger rebreather system. Worn with a modified horse collar and a low profile that reduced the bulk as well as the amount of oxygen it provided, it still wouldn't get in the way of OTB operations with the DARPA mask.

No skin or hair was in danger of touching the vile liquid that was coursing around their ankles. With levels of lead, Diazinon, carbofuran, chlorpyrifos, and malathion more than thirty times that of the most polluted American river, the tests didn't even take into consideration the molecular biological threats present in the sewer. Although they'd entered into the unknown, they knew that even a drop of the substance would probably kill them, whether it was today, tomorrow, or ten years from now when their bodies were so full of tumors they wouldn't even have enough space for body fat. The full-body suits were a nod to more than convenience. They were an acknowledgment that they could be killed by something their HK machine guns couldn't protect them from.

They'd chosen to leave the HK416s behind. Even with their OTB capacity, they were concerned with space and the longer weapon might be impossible to bring to bear, especially with the suppressor they'd decided to use. So instead of the 416, they returned to the HK MP5, with rail adaptor system, suppressor, and the AN/PEQ-2 infrared targeting laser. The MP5s had the same OTB capability, but also had the benefit of being 311 millimeters shorter.

They moved in a tactical crouch as quickly as they could

through the five-foot diameter aqueduct, their lasers aiming down the tube, dancing as they ran, lines of light in the green universe produced by the IR view of their HUDs. They encountered several smaller tubes connecting to the tube they were in but they kept to the larger one, following it around several corners, over heaps of trash and what appeared to be an empty safe, and finally around a dam made from three shopping carts wedged together.

Suddenly Holmes stopped.

"What is it?" Laws asked.

"Didn't you see it?" Holmes's breathing was rapid from running in the close confines.

"I didn't see anything."

Holmes flipped the selector on the AN/PEQ-2 from 2 to 5, which sent high power illumination along with the targeting laser. The interior of the aqueduct filled with green light. Far at the end something seemed to be moving. Something with glowing eyes.

"There. See it now?"

Laws wished he could get a closer look. They wanted to keep their firing to a minimum, so the usual way of finding out what it was by shooting it wasn't going to work. If he'd been back in the States, he'd say it might be a raccoon or a possum. Certainly a varmint larger than a rat. Then again, if they were in New York City it could've been any number of things, including one of the immense crocodiles purported to be living deep beneath the city.

"Fuck it." Holmes took aim and squeezed off a controlled four-round burst. The eyes winked out.

Laws peered over the weapon's iron sights. Using the HUD instead of his actual eyes wasn't the easiest thing to do, but they'd practiced using the mask with all of their weapons and were prepared for the awkwardness. They weren't going to win any marksmanship contests, but they could hit what they were aiming at.

None better than Holmes, who rushed forward, hugging the HK to his shoulder, wary of any creature that might try and breach his suit.

Laws followed and when they were about halfway there, the small body was pulled backwards from sight.

Both SEALs came to a halt.

"Did you see that?" Laws asked.

Holmes breathed into the microphone. "It had to be some sort of predator."

"Or it could have been its mother." Laws chuckled as the stress bled from him. "Great going, boss. You just pissed off the Great Underground Possum of Mexico City."

"Very funny."

They continued forward. The pipe turned about forty-five degrees. Holmes popped his head and shoulder around the corner for a brief second, then brought it back.

"Get back," he whispered.

Laws began to back up, but had to ask, "What is it?"

Holmes popped around the corner one more time, then turned toward Laws. "Fucking. *Run!*"

They hurtled down the pipe as fast as their feet and balance would allow. Twice Holmes pointed his MP5 behind him and let it cough blindly.

When they finally reached the place where the carts had come together, Holmes called for them to halt, with the carts in between them and their pursuer.

Laws twisted and laid the barrel through a square of metal. He dialed his own AN/PEQ-2 up to five and added his light to that of Holmes's.

"Remember the tunnels in Arizona?" Holmes asked.

"Fucking 'cabra." Laws felt his stomach tighten. "How many?"

"Looked like a pack."

"And you killed a little one."

"That I did."

They peered down the pipe and there, on the farthest edge of their vision, were sets of chupacabra eyes. But where the aiming laser touched them, they moved, as if they could see them. But that was impossible, unless they had their own version of infrared vision.

There were a lot worse things out there than chupacabra. They didn't require any special ammunition. Chupacabra could be killed using regular ammo, as long as they were shot through the head or the side and there was a lot of it. Their sternums and skulls were too dense to penetrate with anything other than a high-explosive round.

The biggest problem was their intelligence. A chupacabra alone could take out a pack of hunting dogs, one by one, luring them, separating them, killing them silently. A pack of 'cabra could take down a platoon of soldiers. Laws had seen it happen in Indonesia, during a low-light condition exercise that went wrong. The 'cabra had gone through the men like a mower through grass, leaving them screaming and shouting. Then it had stood back and waited until those who hadn't been injured came to the aid of their fellow soldiers. Then it attacked again. Two minutes later, it trotted free and easy into the forest and not a single Indonesian had remained alive. If Laws hadn't been in a hide site high in a tree, he could have been next. As it was, Laws remembered the 'cabra glancing at him, as if it had known where he was the entire time, which was impossible since Laws was so high in the air. Then again, with 'cabra, nothing was impossible.

"What are they waiting on?" Laws asked.

Holmes shook his head. Then he turned and shined his light down the pipe behind them. Just in time, a 'cabra was revealed, as large as any Great Dane and with front legs twice the size of its rear legs. Its face resembled that of a baboon and it had jaws full of too many sharklike teeth. It had a whip tail with a ragged ball of wiry hair at the end. Its bark was more like a cough from someone who'd croaked out the words *"Sorry, fella, but it's time to fucking die."* The beast stood looking at them, its green eyes appraising them and perhaps a little disappointed that it couldn't finish sneaking up on its two would-be victims.

Then the 'cabra launched itself into the air just as Holmes let loose with the rest of his magazine, riddling the beast with lead.

Its jump switched to a tumble as it crashed into the water,

sending a miniature tsunami splashing him and Laws. Laws turned to the beasts coming from the opposite end and opened fire with more control than Holmes had shown. Laws could afford to do so; they weren't right on top of him like the one that had been behind them. Which begged the question... *Why not?* What were they waiting for? Then it hit him.

"Fucking guard dogs?"

"I was thinking the same thing," Holmes said as he finished loading a new magazine.

"Or they're just your random pack of inner city sewer chupacabra. No, these beasties are here to keep us out. And since they're not coming to us..." He let the words die.

"We'll have to go to them."

Laws checked his magazine. "Which is just fucking great. Fucking great. I can't wait to write home about this when I'm all fucking done. Dear Mom and Dad. It's so much fun to be a SEAL. I'm up to my asshole in shit and about to be eaten by real live land sharks."

"Are you ready?" Holmes asked. "Or do you need another minute?"

"Naw. I'm ready. Just shooting a bird at the divine windmill Mr. Hilarious placed in front of us."

"Good," Holmes said, cocking the receiver and setting the first round. "Because we're on a timeline. Let's get this over with."

And they began to move forward.

They heard about a dozen coughs welcoming them.

Cough cough. Sorry, fellas, but you're both about to die.

53

TEMPLE CHAMBER.

Yank slipped over the side and lowered himself sixty feet down the rope. He slid to the ground in less than a moment. The rope was retrieved almost as fast and pulled into the hide site Walker had created in the mouth of the tunnel. To anyone looking it would appear as nothing more than a raised section of floor. It enabled Walker to provide overwatch, but limited his ability to fire directly beneath his position. Luckily, the only thing beneath his position was a pile of broken metal which looked as if it had once been a scaffold or a staircase to the tunnel above.

Hiding inside the stack of metal, Yank had a ground view of the excavated temple area, or as Yank was referring to it in his mind, the Secret Evil Temple of the Zetas. The ground was comprised of concrete and rock substrate. It looked as if it had been compacted, but here and there were rock protrusions that would trip someone not paying attention.

Yank low-crawled to the left edge of the metal. To his immediate front was one of the depressions with snakes in it. He hated snakes. But looking at the wide, flat area between the depression and the nearest building, an obsidian butterfly mausoleum, there was no way he'd make it any other way without being seen by the leper magicians preparing things atop the pyramid.

"Oh look, it's a SEAL trying to infiltrate our Secret Evil Temple." Then they all shoot magic necrotizing lasers from their fingers and he puffs into dust. He realized his version of things had a comic book quality to them, but it was his way of dealing with the irrational fact that he was about to attack monsters, magic, and the supernatural. The ghost had totally freaked him out. If he encountered one of those now, he might not be able to make it. That he had a blue Mary blanket helped, but not much. So the idea of getting into a pit with a bunch of scrawny snakes didn't seem like a big deal at all to him.

After ensuring that no one was looking in his direction, he leaped to his feet and sprinted the fifty meters to the depression. His HK416 was strapped to his back. He had a knife in each hand, so when he reached the pit and slid into it, he'd be ready. But it didn't happen that way. When he reached the lip and began to slide down, he saw that there weren't a bunch of scrawny little snakes inside. There was one impossibly large snake in it. It was white and yellow, and he could tell it was albino. He hit it and bounced across its back. He stabbed it with the knife in his right hand, sending six inches of steel into the snake's flesh.

The snake's head whipped around and clamped down on his left hand, completely engulfing it, the knife in his hand, and his arm up to his elbow. The snake's coils moved beneath him and one came up and wrapped itself around his stomach and began to squeeze.

"Ghost Three, you okay?"

"Yep. Okay. Just fine," Yank whispered.

He was thankful he didn't have to talk out loud. He didn't have enough oxygen. He needed to extract himself. If Walker had to save his sorry ass, the report of the shot, even with the suppressor, would most likely be noticed. Yank needed to take care of this without Walker coming to his rescue.

He tried to grab the knife that had become embedded in the snake. As the coils of the snake danced around him and squeezed, the blade came within his reach several times. One time his fingers slid across the grip, but he wasn't close enough to snag it.

Then the snake took another bite. His entire arm was now inside the snake's mouth up to his shoulder. Not that it was chewing on him. Snakes ate things whole, letting their digestive juices kill and decompose the unlucky meal inside. They ate things like rats, and squirrels, and mice, and, apparently, U.S. Navy SEALs.

Yank turned his head and found himself staring into the face of the creature now mere inches away. The next gulp would take his head. He had very little time.

Not only was he almost out of air, but the stench of the creature was getting to him. It had a foul odor, a combination of mulch and urine. It wasn't coming from its mouth, but rather its whole body.

In a desperate move, Yank reached into the front of his vest with his right hand, rifled in the central pouch until he found what he wanted, then brought it to bear—his weapon's cleaning kit. He held a long nylon pouch and tried one-handed to get it open.

A single great green eye watched him, its oval north-south iris making it as alien as anything he'd come in contact with.

"You sure you're okay?" Walker asked.

Yank wasn't sure of anything except for the fact that if he didn't get this fucking pouch open in the next few seconds, SEAL Team 666 would be hosting open auditions for the next great SEAL to do something stupid and die. At last the pouch opened, and as it did everything fell out. He squeezed it, hoping he wasn't too late. He felt a length of metal inside and let it drop into his hand.

Just then the snake opened its mouth. The coils helped push Yank's head and shoulder inside and the jaw snapped shut. He couldn't count the levels of fucked up he now found himself in. He felt his vision dimming. He felt his head beginning to grow fuzzy. At the last moment he realized that the arm with the length of metal, part of a cleaning rod for his rifle, was still outside the mouth of the snake. He also realized that his left hand still held a knife inside the mouth of the snake. He simultaneously tried to stab the snake with both hands, but his left hand refused to move. Either the arm was broken or the hand had gone numb. His right hand moved rapidly, however, stabbing the snake's face over and over, searching blindly for the great green eye, which when—

He felt his hand stab something that gave.

The snake began to writhe violently. It opened its mouth.

He brought his right hand to his left, transferred the knife, then brought it upward where he felt the snake's brain should be. He jabbed it three times. Each time the blade ate up to the hilt.

The snake shuddered and went limp. Its head came down on Yank's chest. The coils loosened. He stopped jabbing. He was fucking exhausted, but he was alive.

He lay like that for several moments before he asked, "Why didn't you shoot?"

"Looked like you had everything under control."

"Under control, my ass."

"Whatever you do with your ass is not my business."

Yank thought about laughing, but as he moved, he realized he might have a broken rib. "What about the others?"

"They looked toward the pit, but I don't think they can see into it from their position."

Yank pulled one leg free, then the other. He realized that somehow his HK had come free from the sling. He reached down and yanked it out from under the snake. What he saw made his heart sink. The sighting device was twisted fifty degrees and the magazine was bent. Without a screwdriver, he couldn't remove the rail system and the sight. Even if he could, the injection mechanism might be completely fucked. To try and fire the weapon now would be suicide.

He tossed the rifle aside and pulled his P229 free from its holster. Although the holster had twisted on his leg, the SIG Sauer still functioned. At least he had his knives and a pistol. He also had two M18 colored-smoke grenades, two M84 stun grenades, and two M67 fragmentation grenades. Given a choice, he'd much rather use a knife than a grenade. Things that exploded were too messy.

"Am I clear?" he asked.

It took a moment for Walker to respond. When he did, it wasn't what he expected. "Fuck me. YaYa is a *dog.*"

Yank closed his eyes briefly. "What do you see?"

He heard the barking before Walker answered. It sounded almost like a human, but with something more, something that resonated.

"Coming from the underground temple is another leper. He's holding a leash attached to a collar around YaYa's neck."

"Oh, shit. Where are they going?"

"The temple." Walker paused a moment. "He's moving like a dog. His legs... they're *reversed*. Fuck!"

Yank tried to imagine what Walker was describing, giving YaYa a dog's legs that had knees that bent backward instead of the forward-bending knees of a human. It was a hard thing, but the image was ugly.

"He's staking YaYa to the base of the temple. Now's the time to go, if you're going to do it. Keep low."

Yank turned and got his hands and feet under him. He felt the twinge in his lower left side. Probably his floating rib. Then he was up and running. He saw the activity at the temple pyramid. He also saw YaYa, and as if the SEAL-turned-dog knew what was happening, it turned and barked at him.

Twenty meters.

Ten meters.

Yank slammed into the side of the left-most obsidian butterfly mausoleum, out of breath and afraid he'd been seen.

"Clear?"

"Clear."

From his vantage point, Yank could see into the Yopico. Beneath an overhanging roof was a wall with images in relief carved upon it. He couldn't make out all the details, but it had images of men cowering beneath giant winged beings. A door on the left side was lit from behind. Shadows cast themselves back and forth, promising that there were more things in the interior of the underground temple. What those things were was another matter.

Yank turned and examined the mausoleum. Made of stone, it was cut with smooth sides and sharp corners that rose about seven feet high. He could reach up and grasp the top. He was able to check three sides but still couldn't find an opening, which meant that the opening had to be on the front.

His gaze was drawn to the left, where the water fell from the pipe. The foul liquid caught in a wide pool that flowed toward the rear of the chamber and seemed to disappear. Besides the way they came and the stairs, it might prove to be another way for them to escape.

"Ghost Four, any news about One and Two?" The others were due to come in contact anytime now.

"Nothing, Three. Should be hearing something real soon."

Yank hoped that Laws and Holmes were okay. They should have been on-site by now. He was sure they'd run into something. It could have been an apparition like he and Walker had seen, or it could have been something worse. The longer he survived SEAL Team 666, the more Yank realized it wasn't what you knew, or what you'd practiced, but how well you reacted when the supernatural shit hit the fan.

Suddenly he heard a great grinding of stone. He ducked and put his back against the rear of the mausoleum. Pieces of rock rained down on him.

"Do not. Fucking. Move," Walker said in his ear.

Rock broke and crumbled, then there was a beating of wings.

"Seriously. *Don't move.*"

"What is it?"

"Remember the chacmools?"

"Yeah."

"They're not there anymore."

"Where are they?"

"In the air. Now they are scary-as-fuck skull-faced obsidian butterflies."

Against his better judgment, Yank looked upward. Out of the corner of his eye he saw just a hint of movement. An eye, blazing white. The feet and legs of a giant bird beneath a woman's iron torso. A wing cut like a giant Damascus blade, layers and layers of metal, swirling to create an almost beautiful pattern.

Beautiful if it wasn't so damned terrible.

54

SNIPER HIDE. TEMPLE CHAMBER.

Walker remembered his first mission in the Chinese sweatshop with the women whose lips had been sewn together so they couldn't tell anyone the secret of their craft—that they were creating suits from the many-tattooed skins of dead people. Then came the creatures. Too many and too different to count. Back when he was still green, he'd had a lot of thoughts working in his mind, not the least of which had been the introduction of not only the idea, but the *reality* that there were creatures and forces out there that had an intent to harm his great Red, White, and Blue. The U.S. Navy and SEAL training had prepared him to fight other men, only to have him discover that he was now fighting creatures whose existence could only be foretold in mythology of the *Dungeons & Dragons Monster Manual*. As a kid in the orphanage he'd dabbled in the game, creating a Paladin to fight the evil hordes. He'd learned about orcs and dwarves long before the *Lord of the Rings* movies made them popular. He'd chosen a Paladin because of the armor and the sword, but also because if he fought hard and did well, he'd have a chance to have a Pegasus as a steed. The idea of a flying horse had captivated his eleven-year-old mind and kept him playing long into the nights when he should have been sleeping. But the monsters and their evil had only been as powerful as his young mind could create, and no matter how inventive an eleven-year-old might be, he couldn't conceive—nor would he want to—the absolute malignancy of a being whose only design was to see the human form be broken.

But the Aztec gods were different. They didn't care about good or evil. Such ideas were human creations. Aztec mythology was based on rules of absolutes. If one wanted a good harvest, this is what you did. If one wanted to defeat an enemy, then this is what you did. There was no negotiation. Period. So it came as no shock to him to see the assembled Los Zetas middle managers being escorted one after the other from the Yopico toward the top of the pyramid. In the hotel they'd been big cheese, flaunting their power, ordering their minions around and flashing gold-toothed smiles, each and every one kings of their own particular trash heap. But they could be replaced. In the upwardly mobile world of narcotrafficking, any enterprising soldier could get promoted as long as he didn't steal from his boss or sleep with his boss's wife/sister /daughter/mother.

The Zetas in the hotel had ordered men to their deaths, women into their beds, and families to work harvesting the spoils of their war against the American anti-drug machine. Now they were sacrifices. Stripped of their clothes, they wore only underwear and socks, the sight as clownish as it was awful. Many of them were overweight. Some were hairy from head to toe. Others were in shape, their bodies not yet having the opportunity to become attuned to success. They came with scars, tattoos, and burns, all reminders of what it had taken them to get where they'd been. The only unifying trait they shared was the walleyed look of shock mixed with a stultifying knowledge of their inexorable death. Of the fifty Zetas, only one turned and ran.

The gold-and-red-robed men watched placidly as the obsidian butterfly that had been resting halfway up the pyramid rose into the air. It flapped its Damascus wings and soared after the pathetic man, even as he screamed and wailed, his lone voice speaking for them all. Then the butterfly was upon him. With a few beats of its flint-hard wings, it sliced him into several pieces, his torso hitting the floor before his head.

The others watched this, then turned to their own demise. They were either too stoned or too resolute to care.

Atop the pyramid, the priests of Xipe Totec began their terrible work. One after the other, they shouted toward the unseen sky then lopped the head off a Zeta. As blood began to coat the temple steps, the heads rolled to the bottom, were caught by two men, and placed in the skull racks.

The last man in line queued up. This one was escorted by a figure that was as instantly familiar as the man whom he was escorting. Senator Withers was naked from the chest up. He still wore ragged suit pants and shoes, but his belly hung over his belt. His face was a visual narration in misery. Both eyes were black and swollen almost shut. His face was yellow with bruising. More deep purple bruises dotted his chest and arms and back. Blood had dried at his nostrils.

The man escorting him was the immaculate opposite. Ramon wore his usual white linen suit. Walker couldn't imagine him wearing anything else. It was as much a uniform as what Walker was wearing now, as was the look of calm contentment on Ramon's face as he stopped the senator and motioned for him to wait.

The two men who had been recovering the heads wore similar clothing. Now that Walker saw Ramon, it was an easy guess that they were together with him, which also meant that they were most probably werewolves. Walker had something for them. Either his silver-tipped, 173-grain M118 match ammunition or the T101E armor-piercing incendiary rounds would do the trick. He had ten of the former and five of the latter. He also had ten SLAP rounds, which used a tungsten penetrator to punch through armor or stone to deliver the polymer sabot contained within the round. Walker had barely used the M948 round, but was looking forward to seeing what he could explode with it.

Walker glanced to the side to make sure Jen was okay. She was busy trying to get communication with the home base as well as the other team. Walker's orders were to wait for the command to attack unless it looked like the senator's life was in danger.

Then came the biggest surprise.

A tall African American with dyed-blond hair and a goatee walked stiffly from the Yopico toward the pyramid. As he began to ascend, Walker recognized him in a moment of shock—Jingo Jones, alive! Walker sighted through the scope and the image leaped forward. Correction. The former SEAL was dead. Dead as the zombies in Madam Laboy's cemetery. What made him alive was anyone's guess. But what they were going to use him for was obvious to Walker and any other of the SEALs of Triple Six. He'd found the missing tattooed skin suit: Jingo Jones was wearing it. Pieced from the skins of a hundred tattooed people and stitched together by seamstress slaves owned by the Chinese Snakehead mafia, the suits were designed to allow the wearer to not be affected by whatever supernatural entity it channeled. The businessman who had become a demon god during their mission to Myanmar had been proof of the suit's magic.

The others moved aside as Jones climbed up the pyramid. When he reached the top, the Los Desollados gathered around him. They raised their arms and began chanting.

Whatever god or goddess they were about to resurrect, it wasn't going to be good. Walker might be the only one available to stop them. He laid out his rounds on a cloth by his right side. He'd have to load and fire quickly. He loaded the SLAP rounds in their own twenty round magazine, then did the same with the armor piercing rounds. A SLAP round was like no other and could easily be recognized. The incendiary round had a yellow tip. The silver-tipped rounds he placed in a third twenty round magazine, which could easily be distinguished by the gleam of the precious metal. Finally, he prepared two magazines of regular 178-grain match rounds.

Gunfire suddenly erupted from somewhere near the other side of the pyramid—the pipe. Everyone turned their gazes toward the sound. The men at the base of the pyramid snapped up weapons and aimed. MP5s appeared from beneath the robed-men's red and gold. Whoever was fighting up there would be surprised when they reached the opening. Which is where Walker came in.

He and the Stoner were going to even the odds.

He doped the scope to 10+2 and sighted on the most obvious target atop the pyramid. Jingo's eyes were bone white. His face was slack. But there was no doubt that there was some sort of undead life within him. Walker counted to three and squeezed the trigger. At 2,571 feet per second, the round was there so fast it was as if Walker had reached out and split the man's head asunder. Zombie or not, the threat in the tattooed skin suit was dead—for good now. Jones fell to the ground, his body nothing more than a cage for bones.

As Walker fired again, he began to hum the chorus to Jingo's unasked-for namesake, *Jingo was his name-o*. Walker shot the Los Desollados to the right and to the left of Jingo. He fired again and killed another. His next shot failed to find a home. He fired again with the same result. He couldn't tell at this distance, but his gut told him they'd thrown up a force field.

The last two Desollados stared in his direction and pointed. That caught the attention of everyone else in the temple area. It didn't really matter. There were enough targets.

Walker shifted his aim to Ramon's men at the base of the pyramid. He slipped in the magazine with the silver-tipped M118 rounds, doped the scope down, and shot each of them through the chest. They turned toward him as their bodies began to shudder and bend into a wolfine form. He put a round through each of their heads and watched with satisfaction how they fell in midchange, never to complete the transformation.

Ramon howled, pulled free a pistol and fired in his direction. He might as well have been throwing rocks. Walker was too far for the weapon to have any effect. From his vantage point he might as well be invincible.

But he spoke too fast.

A squad of Zetas ran from the lower temple. Seven of them

carried FX-05 Xiuhcoatls, which translated into classic Nahuatl meant "Fire Serpent." The weapon was the Mexican military's homegrown assault rifle and fired the same rounds as his SR-25. Not as grand a weapon, but the rifle was very capable of putting the rounds on target—in this case, him.

Walker shifted fire and took out two of them before they were able to get their weapons to bear. Then came an eighth squad member carrying an Ultimax 100 machine gun with an ammo drum capable of holding a hundred of the same rounds as the Fire Serpents, and capable of delivering the rounds in less than ten seconds.

Walker pulled back and covered his head just as 5.56×45 rounds chewed savagely at the ceiling above him. Behind him he heard Jen scream. He couldn't move to look and could only hope that she wasn't hurt too badly.

55

AQUEDUCT PIPE. SURROUNDED.

Their MP5s hung empty and useless. Blood and gore covered their masks. They were as blind as they'd been back in the New Orleans cemetery. Now, instead of being in impervious armor, they wore torn and tattered neoprene suits that had been so destroyed, they couldn't even protect them from the cold of the water and the heat of the 'cabra blood that coated every crease and private place.

Laws figured they'd killed a dozen of the creatures, putting them down with the sheer weight of 9mm rounds poured from their MP5s. Now that they were out of ammo, it was going to get a lot harder. They could hear the other 'cabras breathing heavily, snarling, sniffing at their dead and plodding toward them.

Chupacabra were far from stupid animals. They certainly had enough brains to trick a pair of SEALs into exposing themselves. Both Laws and Holmes had found good positions. But when it had looked as if they were going to be flanked, they'd run deeper from the aqueduct system until they found a six-way junction. The moment they'd arrived, the 'cabra had been ready and waiting for them in each of the tunnels, including the one they'd just left.

They'd dealt with 'cabra before. It was a known fact that Los Zetas used them in most aspects of their business, including narcotrafficking, as they'd done in Arizona on what seemed like a thousand missions ago. In fact, chupacabra were a Zetas signature, as powerful a symbol and as prolific as the ace-of-spades cards that the 101st Airborne Division had laid all over Vietnam.

How the creatures were trained was another thing altogether. Laws had been trying to work through the problem. A man trying to be firm with a 'cabra would get his arm chewed off. But not if that man was the alpha male of a pack, a man such as Ramon—who was really only half a man. If Laws managed somehow to survive, he might run the idea past Rosencrantz and Guildenstern to see if it had any legs.

That is, if he survived. For now, all he cared about was getting through the next few minutes. He and Holmes were back-to-back, their bodies touching. They had to stay tight. They didn't want to be separated. Together they had a chance. Apart, they were dead. If there was one thing 'cabra just loved, it was to attack from behind.

"Stay close," he whispered.

"Like conjoined twins," Holmes replied, his voice tight with pain.

They each held a 9mm pistol and a knife. They were not only back-to-back, but they were also elbow-to-elbow, so when one elbow went forward the other went backwards. They were a single machine, four arms, four weapons, two SEALs.

They didn't have long to wait for the attack. First one 'cabra feinted, then another, then another. Neither Walker nor Holmes took the bait. Instead, the SEALs rotated slowly in a clockwise direction, their hands always moving, creating an impassable barrier. So when the first 'cabra leaped, it met not one but two knives, because they were moving in a circle. Laws couldn't be sure which part of the 'cabra his knife sliced, but it was soft and blood gushed over his hand, almost making his grip too slick to hold on to the knife. He kicked out with his right foot, sending the 'cabra flying.

Then one attacked from the other side.

They had no vision, but they had hearing and they had touch. He felt a jolt from where his elbow touched Holmes, as if he'd jabbed the 'cabra through an eye.

They kept rotating.

Two attacked this time.

Each Seal brought up a knife and a gun. One stabbed, the other fired. Then one fired and the other stabbed. Both the 'cabras fell.

They kept rotating.

This time the growls around them grew louder. Too loud, as if there were more than a dozen.

"Switch," Holmes said, the single word said with force, command, and confidence. Enough of all three that Laws felt a little more hope as they began rotating in the opposite direction.

Then it was as if all the 'cabra attacked at once.

Like a multiarmed unconventional-warfare interpretation of the Hindu goddess Kali, they moved as one being, rotating, slashing, firing. The barks from their pistols lit up the space, but the SEALs never saw it. Their eyes were slammed shut, every ounce of concentration on their other senses. But as successful as they were, the 'cabra began to connect. A scratch here. A slice there. Holmes was bit, but killed the damned beast that did it. Laws was bit as well, missed his chance, rotated, then felt Holmes connect. They fought faster and faster and faster, until each of the SEALs was screaming, drowning the cries, whines and growls of the chupacabra.

Laws felt his arms grow tired. He felt his legs turn leaden. He felt his lungs burn. He felt his body abdicate the possibility of winning and prepare to give up. But Holmes fought on, and it was Holmes's desire to continue that made Laws continue fighting for one more chance, one more strike. So instead of quitting, Timothy Laws went back to his California roots, drawing up every Hollywood hero he'd ever watched, channeling John Wayne, Charlton Heston, Bruce Willis, Steven Seagal, Sylvester Stallone, and a hundred more.

And they fought.

And they shouted.

And the 'cabra screamed in outrage as they died beneath the SEALs' onslaught.

56

BASE OF TEMPLE. CHAINED.

YaYa had seen a 'cabra run to the edge of the pipe and slip free, falling to the pool below. It hit the water with a great splash, moved to try and get up, then sagged back into the water. Soon, it trembled and shuddered as its head fell beneath the surface. Its body spasmed as it choked and drowned.

YaYa had barked at the scene. Even when one of the men on the temple came down and kicked him, he still barked. All he could do was bark. It was his sole voice. As he did so, pieces of who he once was returned to him.

Scenes from a mall.

A run on the beach.

The cherry-flavored kisses of a woman called Kelly Manfredi. The camaraderie of friends.

The gloriously acrid bite of an ice cold Coke first thing in the morning.

The smell of hot shawarma on a cool day.

Standing at attention saluting the Red, White, and Blue.

As the images came, he grabbed them and tried to hold fast. He knew he had to. His body had been remade. His mind was that of a dog. His left arm was twice its size, black and orange pus evidence of the foreign invasion making everything happen.

But his soul was still his own. He was still Chief Petty Officer Ali Jabouri and a United States Navy SEAL. He didn't know what any of that meant, but he knew that it had once filled him with pride. He wanted a return of that pride. He wanted to find out what a Petty Officer was. He wanted to relearn what it was to be a SEAL. More importantly, he no longer wanted to be a dog, soul-chained to a creature that lived in his arm and controlled him at the cellular level.

He'd been jerking at the chain holding him and it was loose. He knew he only needed a few more hard pulls, and he'd be free. But then what? With every passing second he was becoming more and more human.

Then came the gunfire and he knew who it was. He knew the type of gun. He could envision breaking it down. The image of a tall blond man came to him—Walker. He remembered when the other man had saved him from the warehouse in Myanmar. He remembered when they'd ridden the old Ural motorcycle and played chicken with the supernatural Chinese creature known as a *qilin*. He remembered being pulled into the woods and barely saving himself. And of course he remembered driving a blade into the back of the ancient demon Chi Long.

Where had that person gone? He wanted to be that person again. He wanted to re-become Chief Petty Officer Ali Jabouri, aka YaYa, aka U.S. Navy SEAL assigned to Special Mission Unit SEAL Team 666. He screamed at the universe but it came out as a bark.

Someone kicked him.

He whimpered.

He fell to the ground and curled into a ball. He covered his head with his hands and thought about who he really was. And with each passing moment, more and more came back to him, more and more of who he'd been and who he'd be again. Like a dog that sat on a porch watching a truck go by day after day, year after year, he promised himself that one day he'd leap from the porch and catch the truck, the moment he'd wrap his strong jaws around the bumper as rapturous as the invention of the universe.

57

AQUEDUCT PIPE.

Laws staggered to his feet. He took inventory. His breather was gone, as was much of his suit. His body armor remained in place over bare skin, probably the only thing that had saved him. His right arm dangled uselessly. Sometime during the fury of the last few moments it had dislocated. He could pop it back in given the correct surface, but right now he needed to be sure he wasn't going to die. Besides his shoulder, he had a chunk torn out of his right thigh and his left side. These gushed blood. Exposed to the bacteria of sewage, there were probably enough microorganisms in the wounds to kill him. He was halfway ready to sit down and let it take him.

God, was he fucking tired.

He noticed Holmes in the gloom of the pipe, face first on the ground, water pouring around him, heading downhill toward where they believed the underground temple complex to be. Laws staggered over, reached down with his left hand and grabbed one of the shoulder straps holding on to the body armor. Using only one arm, he somehow managed to lift his team leader to a sitting position and lean him against a wall.

"Sam, you alive?" Although the light was low, there was enough of it coming from the pipe opening for Laws to check pupil dilation. They reacted, but barely.

Laws searched around. He needed to get moving, but he couldn't do it with one arm. He stood and approached the side of the pipe wall. He reached around with his good arm and grabbed the wrist of his right hand. Then he gritted his teeth as he slammed his shoulder into the wall. The pain was exquisite, like a shiv through the spine. But the shoulder hadn't snapped back into place.

He staggered back. He knew he had to do it again, but he wanted to do anything else except that. He pulled hard with his left hand on his right wrist, stretching the arm as far as he could. Then he ran into the wall.

A second of pain, then the ultimate relief of a pop, as the shoulder went back home.

He gasped as he brought his right hand in front of his face. It trembled a moment, then stilled. Now to find some ammunition.

He found pieces of someone's vest. He grabbed it and pulled out a red smoke grenade and a 9mm magazine. He felt on his thigh, but he'd lost the weapon—probably eaten by one of the 'cabra. Feeling around Holmes's thigh, he found a pistol. Laws pulled the slide back, cleared it, checked its function, then shoved it into the waistband of his UDTs. He found two more 9mm magazines and a broken HK MP5. Weighing them in his hands, it took three seconds for him to figure out that they weren't worth it. He tossed them to the side and kept searching.

He was looking for the butt pouch Holmes had been carrying. In it were two D rings, two Palmer rigs, and 150 feet of nylon rope and some 550 cord. Without them the next step was going to be difficult. But try as he might, he couldn't find anything even remotely like a length of rope, a ladder, or a portable escalator. A flash of childhood memory invaded his nasty reality—Donald Duck going camping drops a box on the floor, presses a button, and out pops a mansion, complete with swimming pool. Laws would be happy with a simple ladder. Hold the Jacuzzi.

Laws realized he was a little loopy. Some of his thoughts

weren't making sense. All he knew was he needed to figure out a way to get them from up in the pipe to down in the battle. Then he had a great idea.

He counted seven dead 'cabra nearby. Each chupacabra weighed more than two hundred pounds. It was hard to move them, but he was finally able to get them near the pipe opening.

He got down on his hands and knees and peered out.

A pyramid. Thugs with weapons aimed at him.

Laws jerked back just as the roof of the pipe above him was scored with a dozen rounds. He ducked, feeling chunks of concrete bite and sizzle into the exposed place on his back. He was lucky that he was in defilade. They could fire all day and couldn't hit him. Their angle was all wrong.

He pulled the first 'cabra toward him. Adjusting his position, he got behind it and pushed it toward the opening with his legs. Five seconds later it was falling through the air. He heard it impact with a splash. The sound of water gave him hope. After he pushed the next one over, he snuck a look over the edge, hoping that everyone's attention was on the dead 'cabra. He was right. No one fired at him and he spied the dead 'cabra floating below in what looked to be a least ten feet of water.

This time when he pushed out a 'cabra, they opened fire right away, hoping to catch him. A round sizzled past his foot, almost ripping through it.

But then he heard a different sound. A suppressed SR-25. Walker! The gunfire shifted toward the new source. But if Walker was where he should be, it was on the high ground. The suppressed rifle chatted with the cracks and pops of pistols of several different calibers. Walker was a crack shot and Laws had no doubt that every one found a home.

Laws used the time to push out four more 'cabras. But he was getting tired, too tired to push any more monsters out of the pipe. He had just about enough energy to get Holmes to where he needed to be. Boy was he going to be pissed. It was a good thing he was unconscious or he'd fight to not get dropped onto a pile of dead 'cabras. He shouldn't worry, though. If he missed the dead monsters, he'd hit the water.

A voice rose out of the red mist in Laws's mind, suggested he sit down and wait until help arrived. Like any decent SEAL, Laws shook it away. He got his arm underneath Holmes's shoulder and pulled him to the edge. The extra weight made Laws's wounds scream. His right leg threatened to give out on him. Still, he made it.

He didn't have long. He glanced down long enough to make himself dizzy. He almost fell. Instead, he adjusted his grip on Holmes, aimed as best he could, and let go.

The leader of SEAL Team 666 fell like a dead weight. Had he been awake, he might have struggled and caused himself to spin. As it was, he fell flat, his left side impacting the uppermost 'cabra in the pile. But then he did something unexpected. He bounced and as he bounced his eyes opened. He reached the apex of the bounce, was about to scream something at Laws, then fell and hit the water.

A round chewed at the pipe between Laws's feet. Instead of moving, he pulled his pistol out and fired. His third round took out the thug far below. How the hell had he hit the man? Laws stared at his gun as if it were magic and grinned.

Laws was about to begin firing on everyone with his magic gun when a life-sized butterfly came up from below.

58

TEMPLE FLOOR.

Yank saw it all happen, including the moment when Laws dropped Holmes from the pipe. The way the team leader fell, he had to be dead. Yank was at once sad and angry. He didn't even remember drawing the knife in his other hand. He didn't know what he was going to do with it, but he had it ready nonetheless. Then the obsidian butterfly—God what a crazy misnomer—took to the air and flew toward the pipe to investigate. Butterflies were supposed to be something little children played with. This hellish creature looked like it *ate* children. Its movements weren't quick but languid, its great wings catching the air and pulling it free from the Earth's gravity.

Then Laws did something completely unexpected. He leaped from the relative safety of his perch and embraced the butterfly in midair. And Laws looked *horrible*. All he had on were UDT shorts, Vibram toe shoes, and blood. He grabbed the obsidian butterfly around its neck. The butterfly brought up birdlike feet and tried to claw him away, but Laws twisted around until his legs were wrapped around the creature's midsection.

The butterfly madly beat its wings, buffeting Laws in the face with nothing more than wind.

Laws brought the pistol up and fired point-blank into the creature's mouth.

All that happened was the butterfly fell a few feet, then caught itself.

Laws almost lost his grip. He had to let his pistol fall or else join it in a similar fate.

But it was clear that the butterfly couldn't carry both of them. It was inexorably sinking toward the earth, the extra weight pulling it down.

All the while, Walker had been systematically taking out those Zetas arrayed around the pyramid, as well as the men in robes. They'd almost ceased firing back in favor of trying to find places to hide. Several had stacked up the bodies of the dead to form a barrier. Then came an explosive round that tore a head-sized hole through the meat, bone, and muscle of a dead Zeta middleman, revealing more of the same, huddling behind the body.

On the very top stood two of the leper sorcerers, along with Ramon and the senator. They were protected by some sort of force field.

Now that he had the lay of the land, it was time to move to help Laws. While no one was watching him, Yank launched himself, running as fast as he could with his rib biting into his body with every jolting step. He was right there as the obsidian butterfly fell heavily to the earth, its legs buckling beneath it.

Yank took a wide stance, took aim at the creature's back, and fired. Five parabellum rounds hit and ricocheted off. He fired three at the Damascus-curved wings and the same thing happened. Fuck! How was he going to make the creature stop?

It twirled drunkenly. Laws was refusing to let go, his weight keeping it off-balance.

Yank almost laughed at the image of Laws hanging on to the monster's chest like a baby in a harness. But the evil reality of the obsidian butterfly stilled any hilarity. It glared at him with white glowing eyes. Yank felt the gaze like a weight and wanted to run, jump away, do anything to be free from it. But he forced himself to hold fast.

Beneath the eyes was a proboscis. Even as he watched, a spiked tongue unrolled and found the back of Laws's neck. The tongue rose as if it were its own creature, then dove, its spiked end embedding itself into Laws. The SEAL in turn flung out both of his arms, releasing the creature. Laws fell to his knees. His head tilted forward and rested against the abdomen of the creature as it sucked greedily from his spine.

Yank pulled a colored smoke grenade and tossed it toward the creature. Then he opened fire, aiming for the tongue. By some miracle he hit it. The obsidian butterfly screamed, pushed aside Laws, who still had a piece of tongue undulating from his neck like a giant leech, and stormed toward Yank.

The SEAL emptied his pistol, then turned and fled. He felt rather than heard the beating of its wings as it flung itself into the air after him. He threw himself to the earth and turned over. The creature passed above him, and as it did, a wing came down, the edge slicing his shoulder and leaving an inch-deep furrow.

As the creature landed a few feet away, Yank rolled to his feet and ran into the now billowing smoke. He loaded his 9mm as he ran, then skidded to a stop. He turned just in time to get the butterfly's taloned feet in the chest. Instead of knocking him over, it grabbed him and pulled him up into the air.

The words *OH MY GOD* became the only ones he knew as he rose and rose toward the ceiling. He had no doubt that the creature would let him go, so he did the only thing he could think of. He shoved his pistol into his armor and grabbed one of its legs with his left hand. It felt like a chicken foot, only a hundred times the size. With his right hand, he reached down and pulled free his belt. He wrapped it several times around the leg, and made a simple knot.

Then he had an idea.

In the universe of ideas there are good ideas, bad ideas, insane ideas, wondrous ideas, ideas that can change the way people do things and think, and ideas that fall flat, their potential forever unknown. This was none of those. This was the singular sort of idea known as an *IF YOU DO THIS YOU WILL FUCKING*

DIE, WHAT THE HELL ARE YOU THINKING? idea.

Yank pulled an M67 fragmentation grenade from his pouch. He glanced below him and saw that he was now about a hundred feet in the air. He wedged the grenade into the belt, then tugged a length of 550 cord from his cargo pocket and tied it around the bottom of the butterfly's foot. Finally, he wrapped it several times around his right hand. As he reached up to pull the pin on the grenade, he felt the bird let him go. But he was still holding on. So with a moment to spare, he pulled the pin, then dropped.

The ground began to rush up to meet him. He reached the end if the cord and held on as it tightened; then his shoulder jerked free from its socket. He screamed, but the sound was obliterated by the grenade's explosion. A wave of pressure shoved him to the cavern floor and all breath left him. Pain blossomed into a nuclear firestorm, and then all went black.

...someone was screaming.

Blackness.

...he recognized his own voice.

Blackness.

...he staggered to his feet.

Blackness.

...his back was afire with pain.

Blackness.

...the obsidian butterfly crashed to the cavern floor.

Blackness

...someone was rifling through his vest. They pulled something free. Laws fell on top of him. Then came another explosion. Then more blackness.

59

CHUPACABRA PILE.

Holmes watched it happen but thought it was all a dream. It had to be. No one would be so stupid as to leap onto a flying monster. But the idea must have been contagious, because another SEAL did it, too. Then the second SEAL, a young, scarred black kid whose name he knew he should remember, exploded a grenade in midair. Then, after the guy who dropped him onto the dead doggies threw himself onto the black kid, Holmes knew he needed to get involved.

SEALs were fucking up everywhere.

Holmes tried to stand, then staggered a little to his left. His left hand was mangled. The last two fingers so broken and twisted he couldn't make a fist. He wondered how it had happened. He was in the water beside the dead beasts. They smelled of musk and offal. It made him gag as he pushed himself back to his feet. He wore body armor and UDTs. A scrap of neoprene was on each calf, as if he'd been wearing something else before he'd woken up a bruised and battered, semi-naked GI Joe.

Then a memory slammed into him like a sabot fired from the main gun of an M1 Abrams tank. Two SEALs, back-to-back, blind, bodies touching, four arms whirling with knives and pistols, inventing death in the face of unmatched odds. Pain. Glory. Screams. Growls.

He lurched forward and everything snapped into place. Glancing to his left, he spied the Aztec pyramid, men on top of it and men at the base, their attentions competing with what Yank and Laws were doing, as well as Walker, sniping at targets from his hide. Ramon using Senator Withers as a shield on top with two of the *leprosos*. Men were dead or dying all over the place, indicating that his SEALs had been busy while he'd been drooling in the Land of the Lotus Eaters.

Holmes snatched a length of rebar and staggered toward Laws, whose back was a mass of torn red meat. Getting down on one knee, he checked the two for breathing. Their pulses were strong. He spied the pistol stuck in Yank's armor and dropped his metal club in exchange for a real weapon. He held it as steady as he could, sighting down the rail as he moved stiff-legged toward the once-terrible creature.

Where it had been tall and lean with beautiful slate-like wings, it was now a broken mass of sculpture. Its legs were completely gone, as was its left wing, which instead of shattering, had broken off and was stuck in the floor like a giant knife in frozen butter.

Automatic fire opened up from across the chamber. Holmes ducked behind the dead creature, waiting for the impacts, but they never came. He searched and saw hundreds of rounds chewing away the lip of the tunnel where Walker had his sniper site. There had to be a machine gun out there somewhere firing at Walker.

Two grenades arced free from Walker's hide site and fell toward the source of the gunfire. Although Holmes couldn't see them from his vantage, he could tell from both explosions that serious damage was done. Even men on the front of the pyramid went down. Holmes opened and closed his mouth, trying to clear his ears from the change in air pressure.

But then he saw another grenade arcing out... this one straight toward him. Holmes opened his mouth to scream, then saw the shape of the grenade. Still, he ducked. The canister grenade fell and rolled.

Good SEAL, Holmes thought. Walker was giving him some

concealment to do something rather than stand stupidly in the middle of a battlefield. Holmes spun and moved. His vision swam with the movement.

The grenade began billowing red smoke.

He grabbed Laws and pulled the SEAL to his feet. He was alive and ambulatory, just barely conscious. Yank was moderately better. He was awake, but in incredible pain. That he still had his pouch meant that they might be able to make things better. Holmes dragged Yank upright. Holding on to the both of them, like a clumsy six-legged man, they tripped and fell toward the water. Just as they made it to the pile of dead 'cabra, the gunfire resumed, rounds sizzling into the water right next to them.

With one last heroic push, Holmes got his two SEALs behind the wall of monster flesh and began to check them for wounds. Both had backs made of ground meat. Laws had a strange wound on the back of his neck. Holmes pulled at a piece of what looked like tongue and felt rubbery resistance, like it was a leech or a worm. He jerked it and Laws snapped completely awake.

"What the hell?"

"Keep calm. Daddy's back."

"Holmes—you're alive!"

"No thanks to you." Holmes reached into Yank's pouch and was relieved to find the med kit still wrapped. He opened it and grabbed two Fentanyl lollipops. He stuck one in each of the SEALs' mouths. The pops would deliver opiate pain relief immediately to their systems. They'd replaced morphine syringes, were much more powerful than their predecessor, and were the drug of last resort.

"What'd I do?" Laws asked, sucking greedily on the pain reliever.

"I have this memory of falling. Do you know anything about that?"

"I have no idea what you're talking about," Laws said with a straight face. "Yank, you alive?"

Yank nodded as he grabbed two packs of QuickClot, which contained microscopic zeolite crystals as the hemostatic agent. When introduced to blood, it soaked up all the liquid, leaving only platelets and hastening clotting to an almost miraculous effect. The only downfall was that it produced heat as a by-product, sometimes in excess of 170 degrees Fahrenheit.

"Let's put these on your backs, then you seal it," Yank said.

Holmes looked at him and the packs, then nodded. "It's going to hurt, though."

"We always have the lollies," Laws said.

Holmes opened one pack and sprinkled it on Laws's back. Then he did the same for Yank. He could almost see it taking effect. He could also see the two SEALs biting down on their medicine, their faces turning white as the heat of the absorption began to burn along their backs.

Holmes then pulled out a pair of cyanoacrylate tubes, which were nothing more than medical superglue. He spread a tube each across the back of each SEAL. It would keep whatever blood the zeolite couldn't get from leaving the SEALs' bodies. The wounds on their back weren't bad enough to stop mission, but if they continued losing blood, it would cause hypovolemia, or shock from loss of blood volume. If untreated, that could kill them as efficiently as a bullet to the head.

Then he pulled out a packet of smelling salts and waved it under each of their noses. The reaction was immediate. Both their heads snapped back. He did the same to himself, then found a bag containing six pills. He emptied them into his hand and smashed them with the butt of the pistol. He licked a third, then let Yank, then Laws do the same until the powder was gone. Specially made for 666, these Adderall-like tablets contained elements of zolpidem, dextroamphetamine, and amphetamine, and snapped each of them immediately awake to the point of hyperawareness. Finally, Holmes made them put away their Fentanyl lollipops.

Now, through the magic of modern medicine, the SEALs were once again ready to fight. Two were almost completely naked and one had lost half of his uniform, and they only had one pistol between them, but they were still U.S. Navy SEALs. Holmes's only problem was... what were they going to do now?

60

SNIPER HIDE.

Walker was glad to see the others recover behind the dead chupacabra barrier. For a while he'd wondered if he'd end up being the only survivor. The option was a terrible one and beyond comprehension. That his teammates were safe meant that they could treat each other and hopefully get back to work.

During the events that had begun when Laws had shoved the first 'cabra out of the pipe, Walker had done his best to take out as many of the beegees as possible. He'd started with those on top of the pyramid, but they'd been able to erect some sort of force field to protect themselves. When the squad with the machine guns and the Ultimax decided to try and excavate the wall he was hiding inside, he'd thought he might be in serious trouble.

Jen had been struck in the foot by a stray bullet. It was a through-and-through, with the bullet fragment ricocheting from the ceiling and tearing through the center of her foot. Stopping the bleeding wasn't an issue, neither was taking care of her pain. He'd given her a Fentanyl lollipop that had put her in a better mood, even with her foot injury and the dozens of micro-lacerations to her face and arms caused by flying chips of stone. Walker reminded himself that when they got out of there he'd make sure she was awarded a Purple Heart, or the equivalent. If her agency

315

hesitated even in the least, he'd give her one of his. God knew he had enough of them.

He was uninjured, as was Hoover. Hoover neither liked the smells, the sounds, nor the gunfire. She was constantly nudging him for release. But it wasn't as if she could leap down. It was too far. Any descent would require Walker's help and at this point, he held the high ground. He'd be stupid to give it up, especially considering that he was the only member of the team not in danger.

That the others were in dire straits wasn't lost on him. He'd wanted to leap to their aid several times. Hell, if this had been his first mission, he would have done just that. He still remembered the stern conversations Holmes had had with him, especially the Ring Speech on a Starlifter high above the Pacific Ocean. The single thing that had been drilled into his head was to keep to his own mission. He sighted toward the mass of dead 'cabra and spied Yank, Holmes, and Laws, looking like they were about to attack.

He swung the scope toward the temple and back. Then he lifted his sight and looked in real time, trying to discover what it was the other three SEALs were about to attack.

Then Hoover began to growl.

Walker's vision blurred and his hands began to tingle.

Oh, hell.

He shifted the scope to the other chacmool and realized it was gone. Where it had been atop the other mausoleum, the roof was now bare except for pieces of broken stone.

"Jen, honey?"

"Mmm, yeah." She sounded high.

"You need to get back."

"I'm okay."

"No, really, Jen." He spared a glance in her direction. She sucked on the lollipop with the same grin of satisfaction he'd seen on the faces of the low men sitting in the back alleys of Manila after a night smoking on the opium beds the old Chinese provided. He should have taken it away from her, but she'd been in such pain and he hadn't had time to play medic. "You need to get back."

He grabbed the rifle and stood. It was a good thing he did. His legs began to vibrate with the knowledge that there was a supernatural power around. Had he been prone much longer, he doubted he would have been able to stand.

Hoover's hackles spiked along her neck. She backed toward Jen, her head low as she stared expectantly past Walker.

Scanning the rounds laid out on the ground, Walker knew immediately that he had the wrong ones in the weapon. He leaped forward on unsteady legs and grabbed the magazine with SLAP rounds. Seeing how hard it was for Yank and Laws to take down the other obsidian butterfly—and he was pretty sure that's what was coming—Walker knew he needed something better than a regular powder-filled 5.56 round. The tungsten penetrator was the equivalent of a miniature SABOT round, using tungsten to get through the target, in this case stone, then delivering the explosive charge once inside. Of all the rounds he had, this was the only one he felt gave him the possibility.

Walker snatched it with his left hand and at the same time ejected the other magazine with his right. But that's as far as he got.

The creature rose like a Soviet HIND-D helicopter and Walker was all out of antiaircraft missiles. His entire body trembled with the proximity of the creature. He thought back to the time of the Grave Demon and time-shifted forward through every creature he'd ever noticed, some rendering him a weeping shell of a human being.

But those times were long gone.

He'd been practicing.

He brought the magazine filled with SLAP rounds to the Stoner, jammed it upward, and missed. The magazine's edge caught on the lip of the receiver and slipped from his fingers. He reached out as it began to fall, the universe sinking in his stomach, and watched helplessly as it hit the tip of his fingers and fell to the floor of the tunnel.

Bent over with no ammo, he looked up and saw the terrible visage of the obsidian butterfly. He'd always had a sneaking suspicion that butterflies were up to no good, always holding on to his hand like it was a drummet and they were hungry. Now, confronted with a seven-foot-tall version with Damascus wings, taloned feet, and an alien face, that feeling was reaffirmed. This beast meant him incredible harm and if it got the chance, Walker absolutely knew it would treat his entire body like it was the last drummet at an all-you-can-eat SEAL fest.

He reached for the magazine and almost had it in his hand when the butterfly landed on the lip of the tunnel and brought its wings in tight. Walker had little choice but to dodge away from their deadly edges. He'd seen what they could do.

He straightened a little too quickly and fought for his balance. He stepped back automatically, and that's what saved him. The obsidian butterfly shoved its left wing toward him as it edged closer. It sliced the air mere inches from his face.

Walker was forced to backpedal. He needed to put distance between him and the creature, whose glowing white eyes appraised him with an unnatural clarity of focus. It dipped its head as it stepped, moving its six-clawed foot forward, then easing the rest of its behind inside the mouth of the tunnel. He was thankful it couldn't operate freely in the space. Then again, neither could he, and he had nowhere to run.

Then the back of his legs hit something... someone.

Jen!

He grabbed at her and pushed backward, but Hoover stood in his way, the hackles on her neck like a mohawk. Her growl turned into a snarl of warning.

Walker had no choice but to launch both himself and Jen into the air as they dove backwards over Hoover. The ground came up and smacked him and Jen right in their faces. She went limp and he felt his own vision grow dangerously dark. He fought to overcome it.

Hoover was barking madly now.

The obsidian butterfly hissed in response.

Walker found himself alive and awake, and turned to see Hoover make a suicidal dive through the creature's legs, until she ended up on the other side. Hoover had gotten the creature's attention, but it might mean her death. There was only ten feet between the creature and the edge of the tunnel. With a sixty-foot drop behind her and the creature in front of her, death awaited the dog from both directions.

Walker made a wild decision. He'd have loved to push Jen through the cave-in where she might be safe, but she was deadweight right now and it would be like trying to shove a wet spaghetti noodle through the eye of a needle. And that wouldn't do anything to protect Hoover, who was as much a member of the team as any of them. No—he had an idea. What mattered most was staying away from the edges of the creature's wings and from the vamphyric tongue.

Walker spoke low into his bone-conducting communications device, trying to get the dog's attention. "Hoover. Hoover, listen. Get rope. Bite rope."

In the grand tradition of all dogs barking at a giant winged monster, Hoover continued to bark.

"Hoover, *get rope.*"

The dog actually glanced at the rope curled against the wall by the lip of the tunnel, the same rope Yank had used to descend. But that's as far as she got. She began barking again, this time even more furiously.

"Jesus Christ on a Big Wheel." Walker pulled out his SIG Sauer and aimed at the junction where the wing met the torso. He fired four times. The sound was more devastating than the impact and resulted in nothing more than chips flying free.

The obsidian butterfly turned its head. Sideways as it was, it could fend off both Hoover and Walker, but it could only give attention to one of them. It hissed and lurched toward him with its left wing.

Walker dodged its edge, then hammered at it with the butt of his SR-25 Stoner. "Hoover!" he shouted. "Get the fucking rope! *Bite the rope!*"

This time Hoover obeyed.

Walker lunged backward as the obsidian butterfly swung its wing at him again. As it did, he stuffed the working end of the Stoner into the strawlike protuberance. Without any rounds, it was as worthless as a spear, so that's what he'd use it for. The creature gave a muffled squeal and batted its wings, trying to get it out, but the tunnel was too narrow. Walker took the moment to dive beneath the creature. He scraped against the legs, but managed to come up into a standing position on the other side of it.

He hustled Hoover to the edge. They both glanced down to gauge the distance. Hoover seemed to give him an *I don't think this is a good idea* look, but Walker ignored it.

"Hold," he commanded, knowing the dog was trained to follow that command and not let go... or at least hoping the dog would know better than to let go.

Then he grabbed the remainder of the rope and commanded, "Jump."

Hoover hesitated for only a second, then leaped into the air.

Although they'd tied off the rope to a pinion on the floor of the tunnel, Walker leaned back and held on.

The rope tightened and Hoover slammed into the wall. She held on though, her eyes on Walker, her gleaming white teeth bared in a dog's wince.

Walker quickly lowered the dog. When Hoover was about ten tunnel, from the floor, Walker began taking fire. He pulled his 9mm free and returned it as best he could, then grabbed the rope and started climbing down after Hoover.

Suddenly the obsidian butterfly dove for him. Walker had no choice but to let go and push off the cliff face, knowing that the mess of metal beneath him would break him into a thousand pieces. Still, it was better than being torn to pieces by the talons of the butterfly.

Just as he started to fall, Walker realized that the obsidian butterfly was hovering in mid air to watch his demise. The proximity was close enough that Walker was able to reach out and snag one of the roughly ridged, birdlike ankles. He dropped another five feet, but the creature arrested his descent by flapping its wings.

The butterfly flapped its wings as hard as it could and gained a few more feet. It spun several times, trying to dislodge him. Then it climbed even higher.

Walker saw his chance. He swung out and on the forward swing let go at the apex, landing back on the lip of the tunnel.

Hoover regarded him from down below with a *What the hell are you doing up there?* look.

The butterfly creature spun, not knowing where Walker had gone. Without thinking about it, Walker took two steps back, then ran forward and leaped. As the creature spun, it lost altitude, so Walker fell farther than he'd planned. When he landed on its back, the air was knocked out of his lungs. Even so, somehow he hung on.

The butterfly didn't like being ridden, didn't like that Walker's weight was forcing it inexorably down. It began to buck and shudder, flapping its immense wings as hard as it could. Walker closed his eyes and pressed his face against the cold blackness of the creature's back. He remembered when he'd fantasized about riding a Pegasus and just pretended he was breaking one in.

He was slammed into the wall, but held on.

Fucking Pegasus.

It slammed him again.

Fucking Obsidian Butterfly Pegasus.

It slammed him again and this time he couldn't stop himself from letting go.

He fell hard.

61

MAIN TEMPLE.

The bad guys had regrouped. Three robed men with MP5s hid behind a pile of headless Zetas. At the far side of the pyramid near the base, several men were frantically trying to load their rifles. Several of the Zetas who'd escaped beheading stood aimlessly on the pyramid steps. One or two of them held weapons. Two of the Los Desollados magicians were alive and well, trying to recover themselves atop the pyramid. Halfway up, Ramon stood with a struggling Senator Withers, using him as much as a shield as he was savaging him with wolfen claws. Holmes had to hand it to the old man. Held by a bloodthirsty double-dealing werewolf or not, he wasn't going down without a fight, even with claws finger-deep inside his shoulders. Withers stomped on Ramon's feet and tried to knee him in the groin, but his captor backhanded him, the power in his arms ultimately knocking the senator out cold. Then Ramon tossed the man over his shoulder and loped up the rest of the stairs. It appeared that he still had use for the senator, even if there were only two magicians left.

Holmes didn't have time to sit and contemplate the problem. He had to get his SEALs moving before Withers lost his life.

He spied YaYa, curled into a ball at the base of the pyramid. He'd occasionally scratch himself with his hind leg. That it had reversed like an animal's made Holmes's head hurt. The sight made him accept the fact that he'd lost this SEAL to whatever had been haunting him. The admission carried tremendous weight. Not only had he lost one of the five members of the most special team on the planet, but he'd been in a position to stop it from happening had he taken a few moments to contemplate YaYa's symptoms.

Walker had fallen, but not so far he should be badly hurt. He'd send Laws in his direction and keep Yank with him. Holmes's targets were the two men dressed like Ramon that lay dead at the base of the pyramid stairs. Both had shoulder holsters and they were the closest to him. Plus, their bodies lay next to YaYa, who Holmes wanted to check. Whatever he'd become, he'd once been a SEAL and one of his men.

He told the other SEALs the plan. They weren't a hundred percent. They weren't even fifty percent. But it was all he had. It was all they had. Hell, if they wanted to live, they'd make it work. He was contemplating how he was going to create a diversion when the oddest thing happened. Even though all five members of SEAL Team 666 were on the floor of the temple, someone began firing at the Zetas from the tunnel where Walker had most recently had a hide site. Correction, they weren't firing on the Zetas. Instead, they seemed to be firing randomly wherever they could.

Then it came to him.

Jen!

Every bad guy turned toward the tunnel, worried that they might be the next target. They probably remembered how accurately Walker had so recently dealt death. They didn't have to know that it was some CIA analyst brandishing a weapon for which she probably had only a passing knowledge as to which end was the bad end and which was the good.

Holmes sent Laws toward the downed obsidian butterfly, using that as a way station to connect with Walker. Once they connected, it made sense for them to combine their maneuvers.

Laws surveyed the field. He stood ready and took off toward his first target, weaving as he ran in case he drew fire. But all eyes were still on the tunnel where Jen was indiscriminately firing. Holmes watched as the SEAL made his point and skidded to a stop.

Holmes checked the status of the enemy and saw that not one of them was paying attention to him or the 'cabra pile. He quickly adjusted his strategy. They were going to make a move. He told Yank as much and on the count of three, they ran like madmen toward the skull rack. The distance was fifty meters. An NFL-prospect line-backer could make it in six seconds. Holmes was itchy with the potential of bullets to the head as he ran.

Yank made it first and slid to a stop. Each of the downed men carried 9mm pistols in their holsters. He grabbed one, then got in close to the skull rack, ready to lay covering fire for Holmes.

Holmes got there and dropped to the ground. He pulled the 9mm from the other downed man. It turned out to be a Glock 19 with a fifteen-round magazine. He checked the holster for spare magazines and found two. The dead men also carried backup pistols in ankle holsters, Taurus PT740s capable of holding five rounds in the magazine and one in the chamber. He passed Yank a pistol and spare mags for the Glock, then shoved his own mags inside the tight back pocket of his UDTs. He shoved both pistols in the back of his shorts and told Yank to cover him.

Holmes low-crawled the few feet to where YaYa had curled up. The SEAL was naked, and so filth-encrusted it was almost impossible to tell where the dirt stopped and his skin started. His legs had definitely transformed to those of an animal and were pulled under him. His left arm below the elbow was triple the size of the right and infected with something terrible. It held all the shades of blues, oranges, greens, and black. Pus had burst through the skin in several places. Whatever the priest back at the Knights' Castle had done clearly hadn't worked. Holmes couldn't help feeling sorry for the young man. He didn't know how he could possibly recover from this. Still, he was one of his men and he was a SEAL. Dog or no dog, possessed or not, he didn't deserve to be chained up.

"YaYa," he whispered.

The SEAL glanced toward him, then turned his head away. He whined like a beaten dog.

"YaYa. Come on, SEAL," Holmes said as loud as he dared. Out of the corner of his eye he saw one of the surviving Zetas on the pyramid turn toward the sound. "Come on. We have got to go *now*."

YaYa turned and looked at him with suddenly clear eyes. "Boss? Is that you?"

Holmes kept his words SEAL-themed, recognizing that it had worked. "Get your ass in gear, SEAL. We have to move."

Yank suddenly opened fire on the man who'd been drawing a bead on Holmes. The man fell and tumbled down the narrow stairs, slipping in the stream of blood made from the earlier sacrifices.

The others noticed them for the first time.

"Boss, get back here!" Yank shouted.

Holmes pulled his 9mm from his waist and laid down covering fire as he knelt, then worked free the cuff on YaYa's leg. Holmes managed to clip two guys before he hauled YaYa back with him into the cover of the skull rack.

Yank had kept firing, every few seconds getting off a shot to remind their attackers of the danger they'd be in if they tried an assault.

Holmes turned to YaYa, who had tears running down his already tear-striped face. "I can't—" he began, his eyes searching for words that could only be found inside. "I want—"

Holmes reached out, but his touch made YaYa jump. "We'll figure this out when it's all over," he said with as much authority as he could muster.

YaYa stared at his arm. "It's here. I can feel it inside. I can feel it talking to me." He looked up at Holmes. "Can you hear it, too?"

Holmes shook his head, sad beyond reason for the boy.

"I want it out. I want it gone." Then YaYa's eyes changed shape. The irises went from human to animal in a split second. He growled.

Holmes backed away, but resisted aiming his weapon at the young man.

YaYa barked once, then twice, sounds impossible for a human to make.

Holmes reached out a shaky hand, hoping that a human touch might bring YaYa back.

But YaYa would have none of it. He took off like a shot toward the back of the chamber, running on four legs toward the 'cabra pile. Gunshots peppered the ground around him as he ran, but YaYa was a constantly moving target.

Then he reached the fallen obsidian butterfly and skidded to a stop. He howled once, the sound of a tortured animal turning into a horribly human scream. He held out his left arm and approached the wing. He held it high, then suddenly slammed it down, letting the viciously sharp edge of the wing of the obsidian butterfly sever his arm from his body.

Blood spurted as YaYa screamed.

He toppled to the ground, his life flowing from his body.

Holmes started to run to his aid, when something landed next to him, a shadow covering everything around him.

The other obsidian butterfly.

62

BACK SIDE OF THE TEMPLE.

Laws was close enough to Walker and Hoover to call out to them, but when he heard YaYa's scream, he turned and watched the other SEAL fall, saw his blood pumping out of his arm stump like something from an Akira Kurosawa picture. He had no choice but to jump to YaYa's aid. He turned and ran, calling for Hoover over his shoulder.

The dog followed and they arrived at about the same time. She paced nervously as she saw her one-time handler lying in a growing pool of blood. She started to sniff at the severed arm, then backed away and growled instead.

YaYa had already lost a prodigious amount of blood. Laws put a knee and all of his weight on the soft spot of YaYa's shoulder. With his left hand, he shoved two fingers into the remarkably clean wound, applying pressure to the median cubital vein. The amount of blood immediately decreased. With his right hand, he reached into the cargo pouch on Hoover's vest and pulled out a med kit. He grabbed a pouch of QuikClot gauze and ripped it open with his mouth. Then, as best he could, he unrolled one end and began to pack it into the wound, inch by bloody inch. The gauze contained kaolin, which promoted clotting like no one's business. He'd seen a training video where they'd cut the femoral artery of a pig and using just one packet of gauze, had completely stopped the bleeding within minutes.

After he packed the first one, he packed a second one.

The bleeding had stopped, but was it going to be enough to save him?

YaYa came to. "Laws, is that you?" he asked groggily.

"Just leave it, kid. Save your strength." With the loss of blood, YaYa was bound to become hypovolemic, which meant Laws also had to treat him for shock. He needed to find something he could use as a cover. Glancing back at the pile of dead 'cabra, he knew what to do.

But then he saw the obsidian butterfly. It had Holmes pinned against the side of the pyramid. While Laws needed to treat YaYa, he also needed to help the boss.

He fed YaYa the remainder of his own Fentanyl lollipop, then made his move.

63

BENEATH THE SNIPER HIDE.

Walker needed a weapon. Jen was still firing from above, but it had become clear that although she was slaughtering the hell out of the ceiling, there really wasn't much danger of her hitting anything else. Yank had begun firing somewhere near the pyramid, but Walker needed to be careful because the obsidian butterfly had flown in that direction. By the sudden maddeningly increased rate of fire from them, they must have just seen the thing.

Walker had hit hard enough to stun himself when he'd fallen, but he hadn't broken anything. Still, as he stood and his thigh engaged around the deep bruising of the quad, it was pure pain to take the first couple steps. He ignored it. He had to get a weapon.

He picked his way free from the mess of metal and hauled himself to clear ground. He limped as best he could toward where the squad of Zetas had held their stand against him, until he'd overcome them with fragmentation grenades. He hoped that at least one of their weapons might be in working order.

As Walker got near, he noticed one of the Zetas from the pyramid area had a similar great idea. They both reached the dead soldiers at the same time. Each grabbed a Fire Serpent assault rifle, and while Walker did a combat roll to his right, the other did a combat roll to his left. They both brought their weapons

329

to bear at the same time and were both surprised to hear clicks instead of bangs.

They both stared for a stunned moment at their weapons. Then, they dropped what they held, picked up new ones, and combat-rolled in the other direction with the same results.

Click.

Click.

Somewhere in the great sky above Mexico City a god was laughing at them. Walker grabbed another weapon, but saw right away that it was broken. He tossed it aside, then picked up yet another.

The Zeta had beaten him to it and brought a Fire Serpent to bear. He fired once, the round impacting on Walker's chest plate. Walker grunted and staggered backward, then fired his rifle.

Click.

The Zeta grinned and squeezed his trigger again.

Click.

Walker snatched up the Ultimax from the ground and held it in both hands. It was a big heavy weapon, but it wasn't anything anyone could stand against. He was prepared to squeeze the trigger when he saw that the drum magazine was empty. Then he looked up. The other man held a weapon and stepped forward. His weapon looked anything but empty.

"Your mother sucks donkey cocks," Walker said. He couldn't believe that after all this, after all the creatures he'd encountered, it was a piece-of-shit narcotrafficker who would be his end.

The Zeta sneered. "It's *your* mother fucking sucks donkey cocks."

"Really?" Walker asked. "Is that the best you can do?"

The Mexican's eyes narrowed and he adjusted the rifle in his hands. "What you say, dead gringo?"

"If you're going to be the hero of the Mexican people for killing a U.S. Navy SEAL, you need to have a saying which inspires. Can you even imagine young kids at school learning how to say *sucks donkey cocks* every year on the holiday of my death?" Walker gritted his teeth and waited for the man to squeeze the trigger.

The man's eyes widened. Instead of simply firing, he adjusted his stance so he could bring the rifle to bear. That's when Hoover came in low and fast. The Zeta fired but Walker had already dropped.

Hoover twisted instinctively at the gunfire; then she regathered herself, shot forward again, and sank her teeth jaw deep into the Mexican's crotch. The man's screams were overshadowed by the staccato of automatic fire as the rifle rattled bullets against the ceiling, draining the clip at the same time his face drained of blood.

As Walker ran toward him, he pulled a knife clear from his left leg sheath. While Hoover worked the man's crotch like a favorite bone, Walker raked the working edge of the six-inch blade across the man's neck. The Mexican's arms shot out still holding the gun. Walker snatched it, freeing the man's hands, which went to his own neck, trying to pull it back together. His horrified eyes captured Walker's gaze for a moment, begging to get a second chance. But Walker didn't have the power to take the man back to when he'd been a boy and decided to make a life from the sale of drugs to those who really couldn't afford it. So much water had passed under that bridge that Walker had no feeling for the man when he stood. Instead, he loosened his mask and twisted it so that it rested against the back of his neck. Then he reached his index finger into the blood bubbling from the man's neck and made streaks across his own cheeks.

He took the dead man's weapon, then found several working magazines in his cargo pockets. He jammed one into the base of the weapon, charged the handle, and let the bolt carriage snap forward. He put the others into his own pockets.

"Hoover, come," he said.

One round had skimmed the dog across the side of her body armor. She'd be tender, but nothing more.

"Come on, girl. Let's you and me hunt us some beegees."

Hoover growled, the dog's approximation of a high five.

64

TEMPLE FLOOR.

All but two of the Zetas had joined the many dead along the temple floor. The survivors stood beside the Desollados on top of the pyramid. Ramon still held Senator Withers like a shield several steps down. Yank and Holmes had both been cut by the obsidian butterfly. They'd managed to shoot away an edge of a wing and one leg, but it was still mobile. And it was even more dangerous now that it was wounded.

Ramon held a pistol in his hand. He kept it leveled at the senator's side. The senator's eyelids were all but shut. The beating had taken its toll.

Hoover ran low and fast to the base of the pyramid, capturing Ramon's attention. The dog dodged to the right and out of Ramon's line of sight and began to move upward, careful to keep something between not only her and Ramon, but the men atop the pyramid.

Walker raised the Fire Serpent and unloaded an entire clip at the place where the right wing connected to the obsidian butterfly's torso. Chips and sparks flew, but nothing more. Still, it got the creature's attention.

As it turned toward Walker, he shouted, "Remember me? We're not done yet."

He didn't know what reaction to expect. The thing's face seemed incapable of an expression. But by the way it unrolled its insectile tongue then rolled it back into its proboscis, it was definitely a comment thrown back at him that needed little translation.

Still aiming at the creature, he dropped the empty magazine, reloaded a full one, then rained thirty rounds into the front of the spot he'd so recently peppered.

"Come on you wannabe fucking Mothra!"

He dropped this magazine and inserted another. As soon as it was in place, he let loose. The rounds were on target, but the last ten never found a home. The weapon jammed. Instead of clearing it, Walker dropped it and ran.

He heard the swoop of the creature's wings. He ran six more paces, then threw himself to the ground.

It came in close, the edge of a wing just missed slicing him from hip to sternum.

When it passed, he jumped to his feet and ran back the opposite way. Barely pausing to grab the Ultimax, he also scooped a drum from the belt of the dead gunner. Then he was diving into the entrance to the lower temple, the place of Xipe Totec. It was nothing more than an unearthed pit, the ground stained with blood and littered with skeletons of hundreds of women. He remembered the stories of all the missing women in the border towns and wondered if they hadn't died in a similar fashion, maybe in support of some arcane power grab, maybe to fuel the excavation of this unholy place, or maybe both. The ceiling was seven feet high and pressed down upon him. It was made of new wooden beams that held up the dirt and rock. Small mounds of dribbled earth showed how tenuous the support structures were.

A wave of nausea struck Walker like the backhand of a giant fist. He let go of the weapon and magazine as he dropped to his knees. His hands went to his helmet, which he unsnapped and ripped off. Then they went to his head.

A man suddenly stepped in front of him from the shadows in the back, dressed in the ragged skins of dead women. "It spoke to me, your demon. We talked." He reached out and stroked Walker's cheek, and where the man touched, Walker felt his skin curl and crack. "It wants to come back, you know? It wants to be with you again." The man in front of Walker chuckled, the sound of marbles inside a baby's skull. "It wants to do the things you used to do. Remember the old man? Remember how you tormented him? Do you know that he took his own life because of you? Do you know that his last thought before he resigned his soul to hell was of you? Imagine a man who'd rather spend an eternity in hell than spend one more moment with a child. Much like your father."

Walker felt his skin begin to necrotize, but the man's words were like a salve, feeding him just enough so that he could reach out, grab the magician's neck with one hand and *squeeze.* "How do you know it's entirely gone from me?" He let the crazy spill into his eyes. "How do you know he doesn't want you to join what's left of him inside me?"

The magician grabbed at Walker's hand, but it was still covered in a ballistic glove. He could let go to get to a piece of skin, but then Walker would be free to throttle him. So instead, he tried to break the grip of the SEAL. But he might as well have been trying to bend an iron pipe.

Walker brought his other hand up to finish the job. For a moment, he had two killing hands around the man's neck. Then he changed his mind. In one blurred movement, one hand grabbed the magician's forehead and the other grabbed his chin, and then he snapped the man's neck.

Parts of the ceiling started to fall.

Walker spun and saw the obsidian butterfly, bent and moving awkwardly across the dead bodies toward him. Occasionally, the point of its wing would break through the ceiling, causing rock and dirt to rain down upon it. He scanned the area around him and saw nowhere to go. The Ultimax was unreachable behind the creature, so Walker did the only thing he could think of. He led the creature on, making it take a tortuous route over the bodies of the dead women. Walker fell, his feet slipping between the bones. Each time he managed to stand and keep away from the creature as it tried to hurry more and more, wing tips ripping through the ceiling.

Walker had managed to maneuver it so that it was at the back of the chamber. Then, in a final rush, he ran in a crouch toward the entrance. He made it and fell upon the weapon, clearing it and inserting and charging the drum in a blur. He didn't wait for the obsidian butterfly to get to him. Instead, Walker staggered to his feet and began to rake the ceiling with gunfire, concentrating on the beams. He cut one in two and a great gush of soil began to fill the chamber. He backed into the entrance and trained the Ultimax on another beam, with the same result. Just as the drum began to whine and spin emptily, the entire ceiling collapsed.

He turned and ran, trying to keep from being buried himself. He barely made it out of the Yopico, diving into the main chamber as a gout of dirt billowed out and up. When he got to his feet, he saw that Holmes and Yank had killed the remaining men, while Hoover was savaging the Desollados. Hoover had the neck of the one in his mouth, arterial blood pulsing into the air atop the pyramid, much as it had five hundred years before.

Senator Withers lay gasping halfway up the pyramid. Blood poured from a gory wound in his shoulder. Walker ran to him, shouting to the others, "Where's Ramon?" Then he heard the sound of running feet. His gaze went to the stairs that climbed up the side of one wall. He saw the man pause, throw a mocking salute, then run the rest of the way up the stairs. Walker was a thousand miles past exhaustion, but he knew what needed to be done. If they didn't get Ramon now, he'd be stalking them until they were all dead. Walker gritted his teeth and started to follow.

Holmes came to the senator's aid. "Go," he said. "Get the son of a bitch."

"Wait," came a voice he hadn't heard in a while.

Walker spun. "YaYa—you're alive!"

Laws had his arm wrapped around the gray-skinned SEAL's

shoulder. YaYa had lost the arm, but the stump had been tourniqueted and bandaged.

"What happened?" Walker asked breathlessly.

He stepped closer but YaYa shook his head and pointed at the bodies of Ramon's accomplices. "Necklaces. Get them." His voice was little more than a whisper.

Walker looked down at the two linen-suited men, then knelt. He ripped open their bloody shirts. Each of them wore gold necklaces with a small vial containing a milky substance. He grabbed them.

"'Cabra. Drink," YaYa said, pointing weakly toward the steps. "Chase. Kill."

"Drink this?" Walker asked, holding up the vial. But YaYa was out. He glanced at Laws, who looked at him with widened eyes and shrugged.

YaYa had said "'cabra." Would the substance turn him into one of the creatures? Walker found it hard to believe. "Fuck it." Walker rotated his red mask from where it rested on his back, placed it over his face, and tightened the straps. Then he opened the vial. "Drink me," he said, invoking the craziness of *Alice in Wonderland* and laughing a little too maniacally. He tilted his head back and let the liquid flow into his mouth. As the substance hit his system, the entire aspect of the universe changed right in front of his eyes.

65

MEXICO CITY. DAY.

Walker shot up the stairs and through a door like a heat-seeking missile fired from a rabbit hole. The world was bled of color, replaced by a blur of blacks, whites, and grays. Everywhere he looked, the focus was precise and perfect, his vision capable of telescoping several hundred feet in front of him. But his peripheral vision was a blur, the world to his left and right reduced to a state of fuzzy resolution. Gone was his exhaustion, left behind in the alternate universe where SEALs couldn't travel Mach 1.

Through the door, he found himself inside the basement of an ancient building. Dust coated the floors. Webs held the corners together like silken flying buttresses. The walls were carved and it took tremendous focus for Walker to be able to figure out what they were. Religious motifs—but that was as much as he could make out.

He knew what a drunk felt like, if that drunk was also stoned out of his mind on a Mexican cocktail of uppers with a chupacabra speedball chaser. Each turn of his head sent a blur spinning across his vision. He brought his right hand to his head to still the images, but then he spied Ramon walking ahead, smoothing his rumpled pants and running long fingers through his hair, acting as if he were Mr. Cool in a land of ancient filth.

"Ramon!"

He turned at Walker's call and his eyes gave away his surprise. He yanked his own vial out and drained it dry. Then he turned and ran impossibly fast.

Walker followed drunkenly.

When they hit another set of stairs, he tumbled up them, ending in a somersault, then popping to his feet. He'd lost ground. Ramon was already through another door and gone.

Walker raced after him and became aware of the sound of his heartbeat in his ears. The sound took over everything and was his universe. He opened the door and spied Ramon at the end of the central aisle of a cathedral. Mass was in session and the priest was standing with both arms out toward the congregation. When Walker ran into their midst, they screamed at the red-faced devil in camo among them.

He was out the door and into the plaza before he saw Ramon again. They were in the Zócalo once more. This time it was daytime. Ramon was running southeast. Walker chased after him, zooming past people, between groups and around those who were sitting. He was becoming used to the speed. The trick was to plan ahead. Just as he thought he was doing fine, a man pushing a cart with the words LA ROSA prominently on the side moved into his path. Walker couldn't swerve. All he could do was leap it, or else they'd tumble in a crash. Walker jumped early, or at least he thought he did, but his speed carried him over the cart. His leg buckled when he landed and he rolled several yards before he was able to regain control and stand.

But he'd gained ground on Ramon.

The former hit man glanced behind and tried to speed up.

But Walker could still run faster. The potion, if that's what it was, seemed to work on his inherent athleticism.

They left the square and rocketed down the center of Avenida de José María Pino Suárez. It was a one-way road toward the Zócalo, with a bike path on the left and lined with brightly blooming trees and old-fashioned streetlights. A trio of buses lumbered along it side by side and both the chased and the chaser moved to the bicycle lane.

Traffic was moving in the next cross street and the crosswalk in front of them teemed with people. Ramon slowed and Walker did as well. Those who saw them pointed and made space, afraid of the white blur of a man being chased by the red-faced demon. They slid through the crowd and into traffic. A beat-to-hell Toyota pickup truck swerved, lost control, and crashed through the window of a clothing store on the southwest corner of the intersection.

They turned down Calle Venustiano Carranza, heading east.

Walker's heartbeat was growing louder.

The road cleared momentarily in front of them and they both poured on speed. They turned south, then east, then south for three blocks, moving so fast that he couldn't keep track of the street signs. Now they were on the Regna heading east. To their front was the Mercado Central. Barely two lanes, the walls closed in on them. They had no choice but to slow down.

A bus backed out of a park, forcing Ramon to come almost to a stop. Walker caught up to him and plastered him against the side of the bus so hard windows popped and the bus rocked. Walker punched Ramon in the jaw, the increased speed of his arm translating into increased power.

Ramon's head swung on his neck.

But then the man got his balance under him and shoved Walker away.

Walker held his ground and kicked Ramon on the top of the knee with a Kuai Lua kick, sending him to the ground.

Ramon roared and his body began to change. He ripped through his once fine linen suit, his body growing and bulging with muscle. Within moments, gone was the gentle patrician, replaced by a werewolf whose arms and shoulders bunched with a mountain of muscles.

Walker punched the werewolf in the face.

The werewolf shrugged it off and grinned with too many teeth.

Walker felt a sudden sense of his own mortality. He feinted left then leaped. Using the werewolf's head as a step, he was up and over the bus, running toward Mercado Central.

The roaring behind him told him that he was being followed.

Walker ran as fast as he could, the universe a blur with a pin-hole to move through.

If he was going to defeat the werewolf, he needed silver. He'd left the magazine with the silver-tipped rounds back in the temple. His hope was that the central market would provide the necessary tools. Of course, he also hoped that he'd keep the wolf so busy it wouldn't eat all the patrons.

He was forced to slow to enter the open-air market and the werewolf took him in the back. They tumbled like two trains derailing at three hundred miles an hour, taking out tables and goods, leaving people scattered in their wake.

Walker stood first, feeling his speed wane. The blur of the world was becoming less and things were beginning to come into focus. He didn't want to be human. He knew no mere human could defeat a werewolf hand-to-hand, not even a SEAL.

But he had one more vial. He pulled it out and brought it up to uncap it and drink, when he was struck on the side of the face by a dump truck.

He flew through the air, realizing that the dump truck was actually a werewolf fist.

"You should have left it alone," came the guttural lupine voice.

Walker landed on a table of children's clothes, which scattered like confetti. He managed to get to a standing position. Somehow he'd kept his fist around the vial and it was protected. But when he opened his fist, the vial was broken and the liquid ran down his arm.

"I could have owned a god," Ramon roared.

Walker stared stupidly at the liquid, wondering if he'd get the same result if he licked it. Then he turned toward the sound of an avalanche, except it was the werewolf tearing through tables as it came for him.

Fuck it. No time.

Walker wiped his hands on his pants, turned and caught the wolf in midleap, one hand on its groin, one hand on its neck, and he helped it fly. The werewolf landed hard on the ground, rolling and rolling, until it came to rest in a pile of dust at the base of one of the central poles that held up the roof fifty feet above them.

Walker turned and ran. Merely human now, he could see what was to his left and right. He knew what he was looking for. He'd seen them in Tijuana a thousand times, resting on blankets in front of hooker bars. But were they really made of silver? And if they weren't, would silver plated work?

He finally spied a table stacked with religious icons wedged between a table selling used books and a knife sharpener.

He grabbed one of the crosses, but it was too light to be anything but silver painted on wood. He grabbed another and another, all the while ignoring the seller's screams. Then it wasn't the seller who was screaming.

Walker ducked as the wolf raked the air above him with its claws.

He turned and punched upward into the werewolf's groin. Supernatural or not, even werewolves had nuts. The wolf howled and bent over double holding his little wolf cubs in his clawed hands.

Walker backed away, his eyes searching for an advantage. All manner of edged weapons were arrayed on the knife sharpener's table. The sharpener himself was huddled several feet back. Walker gave him a wave, then selected two machetes, both with edges that looked like they could cut through Excalibur.

He turned just in time to swing at the wolf. Both blades dug in. The wolf shrieked. Walker backed away and watched as the wounds closed.

The wolf came for him again.

Walker swung again, this time applying Filipino stick fighting techniques, using the machetes in a Heaven Six pattern, to worry the wolf into striking. The interweaving of the blades did just that. Although they couldn't kill the wolf, they could cause it great pain.

One, two, three. One, two, three. The blades leaped out in a complicated rhythm, daring the wolf to come at him.

Walker backed away as his arms moved.

He saw it in the wolf's eyes before he made a move.

The wolf charged, his arms out in front of him.

Walker fell to the ground, rolled under the outreached arms, and popped to his feet. As the wolf passed, he swung both machetes so that they came together in the middle, then crossed his body. They bit cleanly through the wolf's neck. Its body continued several feet farther, then fell.

They say silver is the only thing that can kill a werewolf. Walker doubted much of anything could survive losing its head.

He found the head and speared it with one of his machetes.

He also became aware of sirens.

The people of the market were becoming brave. They began yelling at him, probably wondering who was going to pay for all of the broken merchandise. They formed a circle around him and the dead werewolf, who'd already resumed human form.

The sirens increased and vehicles skidded to a stop about the time he became aware of some activity above him. His body was suddenly impaled by a great halo of light as part of the roof slid aside.

Police poured into the Mercado, but stopped as they saw two men slide down a rope and land next to Walker. They wore the uniform of the GAFE and were unquestionably Mexican military.

Navarre greeted Walker. "You've made quite the mess."

"I can stay and clean up, if you want. How do you say *does anyone have a broom* in Spanish?"

Navarre chuckled. "We got that covered. Here," he said, handing Walker a Palmer rig.

Walker stepped into it and quickly adjusted the straps. He accepted the rope Navarre offered and wove it through the D rings. The next thing he knew, all three of them were rising into the air. The other two carried the body and the head. Soon they were in the bright sunlight of day, dangling on taut ropes from a GAFE helicopter.

Walker loosened his mask and let it fall free of his face. He inhaled deeply of the morning air. *God, but it was good to be alive.*

EPILOGUE

SIX WEEKS LATER.

Walker and Jen were about as off duty as they were going to get, sitting in the second floor banquet room of The Wharf restaurant on the east end of King Street in Alexandria, Virginia. He leaned over and kissed her, something they'd done a lot more of since he'd finally popped the question in front of the Welcome Home statue in San Diego. She still had some scars from the pebbling during the temple battle, but the dermatologist said that they'd disappear in time. He pushed a lock of hair back from her forehead just as Laws returned to the table with some drinks, a white zinfandel for her and Smithwicks for the two of them.

"You two are going to make me want to settle down and have little Christmas SEALs," Laws said as he sat back and admired the pair.

"You're never going to settle down," Walker said. "You're the eternal bachelor."

"Me and Steve McQueen." Laws patted his heart. "Eternal bachelors."

Jen exchanged a glance with Walker. "Live fast, die young is for the movies. I want you all staying with us for a while."

"I haven't been called young in ages. Thank you, dear."

"Okay, grandpa," Walker said. "Next time you need help

crossing the street, I'll see if I can't get a platoon of boy scouts to help you across."

Yank came up the steps. He looked as fresh as he had as a new recruit, but he stood somehow straighter. "The rest are on their way up." He pointed at the drinks. "Where'd you get those?"

"See Brian downstairs. We're running a tab under the senator's name."

Yank hurried back down.

"Did you deliver the arm to Madame Laboy?" Walker asked. When Laws nodded, he added, "I'm curious to learn what the hell it was."

Laws put his glass down on the table. "She's not sure. It's old. She's seen them before. She called it an *obour* for lack of a better term. No one knows what it is exactly. It's a piece of something older than humankind. It lives in the forests. Some animals recognize it. Birds will flock toward it. She said she saw one once. She knew to look for it because all the birds in the same tree were acting exactly the same way, as if they were one creature."

"Any reason why it only stayed in YaYa's arm?"

"None, except maybe it's hard for one to get a hold of a person. Animals are far easier."

"Seemed pretty easy for it to get YaYa, if you ask me," Jen said. Walker nodded. "Where's the arm now?"

"Usual place," Laws said, meaning the Salton Sea facility.

"I heard they took one of the Los Desollados corpses there to study, too?" Yank said with a shudder. "That was some sick shit."

Walker took a long slow drink of his beer. "At least they gave Jingo a proper military funeral. Hard to believe he ended up that way after we met him on his boat."

Yank turned to Jen. "You guys figure out what they had in mind for him?"

Jen shrugged. "All supposition, but we think they were going to use him to channel a god, while Ramon had made a deal with the Leprosos to be a high priest in exchange for delivering the Zetas sacrifices. According to what we've learned about Aztec theology, the high priests were the ones with the most power. They ran the cults, the people deferred to them, and they communicated directly with the gods."

"I guess we fucked that plan up." Yank slugged Walker on the shoulder hard enough for the SEAL to spill some beer. "Ain't that right, Walker?"

Before Walker could respond in kind, Holmes came up the stairs with YaYa behind him.

"Speak of the devil," Laws said, standing.

They all stood. Walker grinned from ear to ear when he saw YaYa, who now sported a brand new forearm thanks to DARPA researchers. It was a sweet combination of metallic artistry that looked like it could just as easily fit on the arm of a twenty-second-century robot.

"I knew you all were talking about me," YaYa said.

"Some people will do anything to get attention," Walker said, leaning over to slap the other SEAL on the back. "Glad you're back, brother."

"Glad to be back."

"So what's the word, boss?" Laws asked Holmes.

Holmes looked from one to the other. "They want me to move into the Sissy and work with Billings. It means a promotion."

The other SEALs glanced at each other, wondering what to say. Everyone wanted to be promoted, but there were times when you could promote yourself right out of the field and behind a desk. For those who were field capable, this was akin to exile.

"You all don't have to look like someone died. I told them to ask me in another year. You kids need adult supervision and this old snake can't even supervise himself," he said, squeezing Laws's shoulder.

Everyone released their breath just as Yank returned with a new round for everyone, including a tall strawberry drink with whipped cream and a straw. This he passed to YaYa, who nodded and smiled.

They all sat at the table. A Secret Service agent popped up at the top of the stairs. "Everything prepared for the senator?"

"All clear," Laws said.

"Do we have to do this?" Walker asked.

"Cost of doing business," Holmes said. "He wants to thank all of you and since he controls our budget, we'd better be nice to him."

Walker and Laws gave each other a look. Holmes saw it.

"What'd you do?"

"Can you call the strippers off?" Walker asked.

"Not sure. I think they're en route." Laws pulled out a cell phone. "Oh shit—they're downstairs."

"What the hell?" Holmes ran to the window.

Everyone began laughing.

Holmes spun. For the first time in a long time his face turned red. But behind his glower, they could see laughter trying to come out.

Then Senator Withers crested the stairs, holding the hand of Emily. Billings stood prim and proper behind him. Senator Withers took in the scene. "Am I interrupting something?" Although he was in a blue power suit, everyone remembered him half naked and on his knees.

Walker couldn't help it. Neither could the rest of them. They busted out laughing. Eventually, the senator and his daughter joined them. Then they sat and talked, just them, no reporters, no witnesses, just the people who'd been in the shit, bonded together forever by the events that had so recently made them.

ACKNOWLEDGMENTS

Many people helped to make the book you're holding (or viewing or listening to) and I owe them all a sincere thanks. Thanks again to Brendan Deneen, Peter Joseph, Pete Wolverton, and the whole Thomas Dunne team. Thanks of course to my agent, Robert Fleck, for being on the frontlines of publishing so that I don't have to. Shout out to the bands the Eagles of Death Metal, 009 Sound System, Mumford and Sons, QOTSA, and Everlast for rocking me through the writing process for this novel. And thanks most of all to Yvonne, without whose support, wisdom, and love, none of this would be possible.

Special shout-out to Jon Carte for being there at the real beginning of things. Thanks also to Dave Lake, Brian Wallenius, Barb and Dirk Foster, Hal and Gene, and Eunice and Gregg Magill. Thanks to Comic King Walt Flannigan and Keith Giffen (I Heart Lobo) for your props. Thanks also to Brian Keene, Drew Williams, Bob Ford, Geoff Cooper, and Stephen Lukac for a boys' weekend to send me off to Afghanistan. And thanks to Brian K and Tommy H for introducing me to Herb and Diane Harmon (Hi Herb and Diane) and the serenity of Cedar Lodge.

And thanks to all the readers and bookstore workers for making *SEAL Team 666* such a huge success. I had emails from fans from Vicenza, Italy, where the book was in a military base library, to Hawaii, where tourists were buying copies to take out to the beach.

Lots of fan letters. Lots of new friends. I thank each and every one of you for taking the time to write, email, Facebook, tweet, or simply high-five me during a book signing. If you want to reach out to me about this book or anything else, I can be found on Facebook and Twitter under my name and you can always find me at www.westonochse.com.

—Weston Ochse
Kabul, Afghanistan June 2013

ABOUT THE AUTHOR

Weston Ochse is the author of nine novels. His first novel, *Scarecrow Gods,* won the Bram Stoker Award for Superior Achievement in First Novel. He's also had published more than a hundred short stories, many of which appeared in anthologies, magazines, peered journals and comic books. His short fiction has been nominated for the Pushcart Prize.

Weston holds Bachelor's Degrees in American Literature and Chinese Studies from Excelsior College. He holds a Master of Fine Arts in Creative Writing from National University. He has been to more than fifty countries and speaks Chinese with questionable authority. Weston has studied martial arts for more than 30 years, including Tae Kwon Do, Ryu Kempo Jujitsu, Kali, and Kuai Lua.

His last name is pronounced "oaks." Together with his first name, it sounds like a stately trailer park. He lives in the Arizona desert within rock throwing distance of Mexico. For fun he races tarantula wasps and watches the black helicopters dance along the horizon.

SEAL TEAM 666
WESTON OCHSE

One man down after they lost a sniper on a certain mission in Abbottabad, Pakistan, Navy SEAL Cadet Jack Walker is chosen to join the US's only supernatural unconventional-warfare special-mission unit—SEAL Team 666.
Battling demons, possessed humans, and mass-murdering cults, SEAL Team 666 has their work cut out for them. And when they discover that the threat isn't just directed against the US, Walker finds himself at the centre of a supernatural conflict with the entire world at stake.

"A wild blend of nail-biting thriller action and out-of-the shadows horror. This is the supernatural thriller at its most dynamic. Perfect!"
JONATHAN MABERRY
New York Times bestselling author of *Dead of Night*

"Every storyline is as taut as a gunfighter's nerves, and individual scenes pop like firecrackers. I raced through this novel and when it ended, I wanted more."
PETER STRAUB
New York Times bestselling author of *In the Night Room*

"Ochse's background in military intelligence packs this hybrid of military SF and horror (already optioned by MGM) with insider detail and verisimilitude." ***PUBLISHERS WEEKLY***

TITANBOOKS.COM